A Most Curious Destiny

Patricia Snow Ferris

Acknowledgements

The author would like to thank Lindsay Ribar for her excellent editing advice, Jeanie Snow for her constant support, the numerous friends who comprised my first critique circle and most of all Grandpa Boyd. Gramps, your words have carried me through life and can be felt on every page of this book.

Thank you.

ISBN: 1-453-78476-4

CHAPTER ONE

THE FEATHER AND THE BOX

The end.

Well, perhaps not quite yet, but very soon. You see this story opens where most stories come to a close; for this ending is actually a beginning and the subject of our tale has yet to live her greatest adventure even though her life is just moments from the end. Even now, as dusty beams of morning light begin to filter into her room, Lucille Margaret O'Sullivan unknowingly is about to open her eyes on her last day on earth.

****

"You're certain about this?"

A plump old woman slowly circled the small, round crystal table glowing in the middle of the darkened room. Her hands were clasped in front of her, her thumbs nervously tapping together as she stared into the glassy screen set atop the table.

Like the two men standing by watching, the old woman was dressed in a long golden gown that was shimmering in the light emanating from the tabletop. However there was one slight, but highly significant difference in her attire. Around her middle was draped a ruby red sash.

Leaning over the table, the old woman gave a small shudder as the teenage girl on the screen grunted and rolled over in bed.

"She isn't...well, how should I put this...quite what I was expecting."

"Cassiel's got a point, Samuel," said the tall, dark man who had been watching her from the shadows. Stepping up to the table, he stroked his neatly trimmed beard as he bent over to get a better look. His warm brown eyes sparkled beneath a cascade of dreadlocks and his emerald green sash seemed to glow in the eerie light.

"A bit disorganized wouldn't you say," the man mused, as he examined the heap of clothes on the floor and the half-eaten bologna sandwich on the bedside table.

The second man was of smaller frame and wore a sash of sapphire blue. He was quite handsome with sandy hair that touched his shoulders and shocking blue eyes that right now were carefully surveying his friends.

"Yes, yes, I agree," said Samuel. "And as long as we're at it let's throw in that she's a bit young and rather headstrong." He grinned as the girl rolled over once more, her gray flannel pajamas getting tied up in the sheets.

"I know she isn't exactly what we were expecting," Samuel said, turning to his friends, "but Gadwick, you and Cassiel saw what was written. Rarely have the signs been this clear; I'm afraid that despite what we might think we must all agree…she *is* the one."

"Has she completed her task?" Cassiel asked, still eyeing the girl.

"She is very close, but I'm afraid we will have to pull her by the end of the day even if it's not yet completed."

Gadwick and Cassiel looked at Samuel in surprise.

"My friends, this is out of our hands."

The three robed figures stared silently at the young girl who was now splayed across her bed like a rag doll that had been carelessly tossed on top a pile of blankets.

"Well," said Gadwick, clapping his hands together. "Let it never be said that I shied away from a good adventure. What's the plan?"

Samuel smiled. "Emmett's on the ground; he'll be there when it occurs. And I'm sending Truman for transport of course, but…" He hesitated for a moment before pulling out a tightly wound scroll from his pocket, "I think it would be wise to send Harrison as back-up."

"Back up?" Cassiel's brow arched in surprise. "Do you really think that's necessary?"

"Given the circumstances, I believe it would be foolish to believe we are the only ones who know about our new arrival."

A sudden crash echoed from the screen as the girl fell out of bed, looked around the room in a daze, then rolled over and went back to sleep on the floor.

"Heaven help us," murmured Cassiel.

Amen, thought Samuel.

****

Lucy rolled over, hiding her head under the pillow to drown out the light streaming in through her blinds. Downstairs she could hear her mother emptying the dishwasher; the clanging dishes were rattling her sleepy brain awake.

"Luuuuucy… time for breakfast!" Mrs. O'Sullivan called up the stairs in a tone Lucy felt was far too cheerful for this time of the morning. "We're leaving in half an hour…no excuses!"

Lucy sat up banging her head on the bed frame. "Ouch! What the…?" Opening one eye, she gingerly rubbed the bump forming on her head and looked around. *How did I get down here*, she thought as she staggered to her feet and squinted at the clock on her bedside table. Eight a.m.! On a Saturday! In summer! What was her mother thinking?

"Hurry up kiddo! We're walking out this door in 25 minutes whether you're dressed or not!"

Yeah right, like you would let me step foot out of this house in my pajamas, thought Lucy as she pulled her robe out from underneath a large lump on the end of the bed. The lump gave a loud grunt as a plump bulldog rolled over exposing his fat belly.

"Sorry, Oscar," said Lucy, reaching down to scratch behind his ears. "It's no use trying to sleep in, mom wants us up."

Oscar growled and shook his jowls spraying slobber in every direction, then with a thud he jumped off the bed rattling the floor below. Slipping on her blue Cookie Monster slippers and terry robe, Lucy followed Oscar down the stairs, her long red curls dangling in her face making it difficult to navigate the steps.

"You can stop yelling, I'm up," she declared groggily, as she slumped into the kitchen.

Mrs. O'Sullivan looked up from the orange juice she was pouring and groaned, "Lucy, you're not dressed."

Unlike Lucy whose freckled face and red hair made her look like a poster child for Ireland, Katie O'Sullivan had the fresh scrubbed look expected of someone who had grown up on a farm in Indiana. With a milky, freckle-free complexion that Lucy envied, soft brown eyes and thick, chestnut hair, Mrs. O'Sullivan was what Lucy's father used to call "a natural beauty". Unfortunately the quiet farm girl demeanor was nowhere in sight this morning as Mrs. O'Sullivan surveyed Lucy's crumpled figure with fire in her eyes.

"Do I have to go?" said Lucy, making no attempt to hide her feelings about being pulled out of bed on a Saturday. She plopped down on a stool by the counter and reached for the orange juice.

"There's nothing for me to do at Aunt Aggie's. Besides," Lucy pleaded, "it's summer break. I'm supposed to be relaxing."

Mrs. O'Sullivan grabbed a box of cereal from the pantry and slapped it on the counter in front of her. "Eat!"

"But…"

"No buts," said Mrs. O'Sullivan, pouring out cereal that looked way too healthy to taste good. "I promised Aunt Aggie we would stop by today and she'd be crushed if you didn't come. Besides, didn't you promise Bird you would stop by and bring him that awful feather you've been keeping for him?" She slid the cereal bowl under Lucy's nose.

"Crap! I totally forgot…"

Mrs. O'Sullivan glared at Lucy.

"Sorry, just slipped out," Lucy said, suddenly feeling wide awake. Ignoring the bowl of cereal, Lucy jumped down from the stool and bounded up the stairs.

"What about breakfast?" cried Mrs. O'Sullivan.

"I'm not hungry. Just give it to Digby, he told me he loves that healthy stuff!" She smiled knowing perfectly well her little brother's absolute disgust of anything remotely nutritious.

Lucy couldn't believe she had almost forgotten about the gift she had been waiting for weeks to give Bird. Bird, whose real name was Bailey Jenkins, was a tall, exceptionally skinny sixteen year-old boy who lived next door to Lucy's aunt. He had gotten his nickname when, at six years old, he had tried to fly off the roof of their house. The attempt had failed miserably leaving him with a broken arm, a new nickname and a strange obsession for anything that could fly.

Bird's mother had died shortly after his leap from the roof and Mr. Jenkins had been left to raise him without any help. With his mom gone, Bird had retreated into his own world preferring to work on his flying projects instead of hanging out with friends and pretty soon his friends had all moved on without him. But Lucy knew what he was going through; it had been four years since Jack O'Sullivan had been killed in a car accident, but there wasn't an hour that went by that Lucy didn't think of her dad.

Standing in front of the mirror, Lucy pushed the hair back from her face and stared at her reflection. She had long ago realized that she was a mutt – not in an ugly way, but in the made-up-from-everyone-in-your-family way. Her long, red, unruly curls came from her grandmother, her freckles were an unwanted gift from her aunt – the same one she would be seeing today - and her green eyes were most definitely her father's. Yep, there was no denying it; not a single part of her face belonged solely to her. Even Lucy's ears came from her Uncle Earl, more commonly known as Elf.

Lucy picked up the small make-up kit she had received two weeks ago on her 14th birthday. She stared at the squares of blues, greens, pinks and silvers then looked back in the mirror.

"It's hopeless," she sighed, tossing the make-up kit back on to her dresser and hastily tying her hair back into a long, bouncy ponytail.

"ARE YOU READY?" Mrs. O'Sullivan called from the bottom of the stairs.

"Coming!" Lucy grabbed her jeans and a t-shirt off the pile of clothes on the floor and quickly threw them on. Snatching a large, raggedy yellow feather from her desk and the small brown box by its side, she hurried down the stairs secretly stuffing the box in her pocket. It was this box that was to be Bird's real present and Lucy felt a rush of excitement as she imagined the look on his face when he opened it.

"I don't know why you were making such a fuss," she said, breezing past her mother. "I've been ready for hours!" She turned and gave her mother a devilish grin before darting out the door.

"Shotgun!" yelled Digby, pushing Lucy out of the way as she opened the car door. Even though he was rather small for his age, there was nothing shy about Lucy's little brother. With his thick blond hair, blue eyes and perfect complexion, Digby, at ten years old, was far too cute for his own good and his main mission in life was to make Lucy miserable…something he did with uncanny success.

Not having the energy for a fight, Lucy climbed into the back seat but not before whacking Digby on the head.

"Mom!" cried her little brother, clutching his head and pretending to be in terrible pain. "Lucy hit me!

"I was just admiring your pretty hair," said Lucy in a loving voice. "Wonder where it came from?"

Lucy got great pleasure out of suggesting Digby was adopted, which was easy to imagine since he looked nothing like anyone else in the family.

"Honestly you two!" chastised Mrs. O'Sullivan. "Just once I'd like to go somewhere without having to be a referee."

Lucy spent the next hour staring out the window as they drove through the winding mountain pass to her aunt's house. The sun was warm as it poured into the car and Lucy began to feel her eyelids droop. She hadn't slept well. The voices which had been a part of her sleep for as long as Lucy could remember had been particularly loud last night. But that wasn't all; last night there had been something new. As usual her dream had taken her to the field shrouded by a thick white fog with muffled voices floating around her, but then a chill had crawled up her spine and Lucy was certain that somewhere inside the mist someone was watching her.

As the car bumped over the gravel path, Lucy was jarred awake. A shiver ran up her arms and Lucy felt the familiar prickle of goose bumps that usually came before something important happened. Her mother called it a sixth sense and said it was something all the Donovan women had. (Her mother's sister, Jaimie, claimed to be psychic but as far as Lucy knew the only thing she had ever predicted was the weather and when you live in the mountains of Colorado that's not a terribly hard thing to do.) Lucy rubbed her arms wondering what could possibly happen at Aunt Aggie's today that could cause the bumps to appear.

As the clock on the car dashboard clicked over to 10:00, Mrs. O'Sullivan pulled the car into her aunt's driveway and Lucy instantly forgot about the goose bumps. Aunt Aggie had a reputation for being "unique" which was clearly understood by anyone who had ever visited her home. In the front lawn stood a five-foot stone gnome that Aunt Aggie had painted purple, with a tall pointed red hat. The gnome was feeding a reindeer which was decorated with a garland of Christmas lights. At the edge of the driveway was a tall plastic kangaroo her aunt had bought at a garage sale. The kangaroo's pouch was meant to be a planter, which Lucy thought was hideous enough, but Aunt Aggie had decided it would make a wonderful mailbox. Staring at her aunt's array of decorations, Lucy hoped she had inherited her fashion sense from her mother's side of the family.

"Aunt Aggie! You've got mail!" Digby jumped from the car and began rummaging through the kangaroo's pouch.

"Hellooooooo!" Aunt Aggie scurried out from the house, wiping her hands on the bright pink apron she was wearing. Aggie O'Sullivan was short and plump and always smelled of cinnamon. Her curly bright orange hair framed fat red cheeks, and she bounced as she hurried over to greet them.

"I'm soooo glad you're here!" she said in her usual sing-songy voice. She gave Lucy a smothering hug, dusting her with flour from her apron. "I've just baked cookies and the game is all set up."

Lucy didn't have to ask which game Aunt Aggie was referring to. Her aunt loved playing games, and Life was her favorite. "Just think about it," she had once told Lucy in whispered excitement, "the chance to live life over and over and make different choices each time... never regretting a decision...what a wonderful thing that would be!"

Lucy followed her mother and Digby into the house as Aunt Aggie rattled on about her plans for the day. "First I thought we would munch on some ginger snaps while we played our game, then it will be just about time for lunch – I've baked a chicken pot pie! And you'll need to save room for dessert; Violet Jorgenson gave me the best recipe for lemon meringue pie. Of course you'll stay for supper; I've got a pan of lasagna all ready for the oven." Aunt Aggie went on to describe in detail all the food she had prepared, which made Lucy's stomach growl from lack of breakfast.

Sitting down at the game table which Aunt Aggie had set up in her cluttered living room, Lucy felt herself relax. Something about being around Aunt Aggie always made life seem easier. Reaching for the little red car that she always used when they played Life, Lucy wondered why she had ever wanted to stay home.

"Who's ready for pie?" asked her aunt an hour later, as she cleared away the last of the chicken pot pie and began rattling around in the kitchen pulling out plates.

Lucy leaned back in her chair enjoying the feeling of a full stomach and thinking that a nap would be wonderful right about now.

"Oh Lucy, I forgot to tell you..." said Aunt Aggie, scurrying into the room balancing the pie on one hand and plates on the other.

"Mr. Jenkins stopped by early this morning to say that he and Bird were going on a little vacation this weekend and asked if I would keep an eye on the house. He said Bird was terribly disappointed he wouldn't get to see you, oh…and he left you a note." With both hands full, Aunt Aggie used her head to gesture towards her apron pocket.

Feeling her spirits sink, Lucy reached into Aunt Aggie's apron pocket and pulled out a small folded square of paper. Not wanting to share the note, Lucy slipped into the kitchen and shut the door. Carefully unfolding the lined notebook paper she instantly recognized Bird's scrawled handwriting:

Hey Lucy!

Bad news. Dad is making me go to the lake with him to do some fishing. He says it will help "get our minds off things". (That's his way of saying I need to cheer up.) I'm really sorry I won't get to see you, but I'm hoping I'll find some new feathers on our hike. Pegasus is almost done – can't wait for you to see him!

Have fun with Aggie (word of advice: if you let her win the first game you won't have to play all afternoon). I'll talk to you soon!

YBB,
Bird

"Crap," moaned Lucy, instinctively looking up to make sure her mother wasn't anywhere around. This spoiled her whole plan. Bird promised to show her the new sculpture he was working on and she had been looking forward to seeing the look on his face when she handed him the long, scraggly yellow feather, and – more importantly – the little brown box. But now she would just have to leave her surprises in his mailbox and imagine his reaction. Lucy read Bird's note again before folding it back up and putting it in her pocket.

Rummaging through the cluttered drawers in the kitchen, Lucy finally found some stationery with leprechauns skipping around the border. *Note to self*, she thought, grimacing as she pulled out the paper, *buy Aunt Aggie new stationery for Christmas*. Grabbing a pen from the drawer, Lucy bit her lip – a nervous habit she had whenever she was concentrating – and quickly wrote:

Hi Bird!

I hope you had a great time at the lake. The fishing part sounds kind of gross (worms, fish guts...way too slimy for my taste), but the hiking could be fun. In case you didn't find any new feathers, I brought you one. It looks like it might be some kind of parrot feather, but I'm not sure. Anyway, I thought it would add some color to your wings. Can't wait to see the finished product!

The box is something I got several years ago. The real gift's inside. I'm not going to tell you what it fits until I can see you in person. Have fun guessing!!

Time to go hit the game board. (Moan!) Talk to you soon.

YBB,

Lucy

Lucy read over the note. Something was missing. She screwed up her face and bit her lip trying to think of what she had left out, but nothing else came to her. Deciding the note would have to do, Lucy folded the paper and shoved it along with the pen into her back pocket.

"Be back in a minute," she called to her mother, as she ran out of the house. Before Mrs. O'Sullivan could ask where she was going, Lucy slammed the screen door.

Bird lived in the orderly red brick house next to Aunt Aggie. Compared to Aunt Aggie's bright yellow house with purple shutters, the Jenkins' house seemed quite ordinary but Lucy thought it was beautiful in its simplicity. Neatly trimmed rose bushes lined the walkway and a small birdbath sat in the middle of the front yard.

Lucy took the bright yellow feather from her sock where she had carefully stowed it, and placed it inside the folded note. Opening the Jenkins' mailbox, she placed the note inside, setting the small box on top. As she closed the door to the mailbox a thought suddenly came to her. Quickly opening the mailbox again she retrieved the note and grabbed the pen from her pocket.

P.S. Pegasus might not have his wings yet, but your mom does and I know she is using them to fly down and keep an eye on you and your dad. Trust me…I might cheat at cards but I never lie! L.

Satisfied with the revised note, Lucy slipped it back into the mailbox, put the small brown box back in place and smiled to herself as she imagined the look on Bird's face when he found his special delivery.

Lost in her daydream, Lucy barely noticed the man in the wheelchair crossing the street in front of her. Suddenly a blaring horn shook her back to her senses just in time to see a large truck barreling towards the man. Without thinking, Lucy raced into the street pushing the wheelchair out of the way as the horrible screeching of tires filled the quiet neighborhood.

Lucy turned her head just in time to see the blinding glare of the headlights; then everything went white. It was over.

****

In a far off land the air grew darker as clouds bubbled and lightning tore across the sky. The journey had begun.

CHAPTER TWO

HEAVEN...
OR SOMETHING LIKE THAT

Lucy sat up, pressing her hands over her eyes. Although she didn't feel any pain, her head was spinning madly. Clenching her eyes tighter to slow the dizziness, she shook her head and tried to loosen the cobwebs fogging her brain.

"What happened?" she muttered out loud. The memory of the last few moments of her life whirled around in her mind like a tornado of dreams...the old man in the wheel chair...the truck speeding towards them...the headlights...the flash of white.

Lucy tried to open her eyes but the sun seemed much brighter than usual. Squinting so hard she could barely see, she groped the ground searching for the old man. There was no body, no wheelchair, no cry for help. Silence.

As her eyes began to adjust to the light, the world around her came into focus and panic poured in. The old man was gone. So were the houses, the street, the truck...everything!

With legs that wobbled as though they were made with jelly, Lucy slowly got to her feet. Feeling dazed, she turned and surveyed the endless field stretching out in all directions. Thousands...no, *millions*...of brilliantly colored flowers bobbed in the warm breeze and in the distance an enormous, glistening blue mountain punched through a patch of snowy clouds circling its peak. As she stared dumbstruck at the surreal scene, faint notes of an undistinguishable song reached her ears.

"Bit of a shock, isn't it?"

Lucy screamed at the sound of the strange man's voice. She spun around, nearly falling over, and found a young man of about 18 standing behind her. He was tall and slender with short blond hair and deep brown eyes.

"Sorry 'bout that," he said, giving her a wide smile. "I've tried to figure out a way to do this without scaring the daylights out of newcomers; obviously I haven't quite perfected it. I'm Harrison…" The young man stepped forward and held out his hand.

Lucy ignored his hand. Her eyes were busy taking in the long blue tunic and matching sash he was wearing. Closing her eyes tightly, she clutched her hands over her face. "This is a dream…this is a dream…this is a dream…" Slowly she lowered her hands and opened her eyes.

"Still here," Harrison said, holding his arms wide and shooting her a playful smirk.

"This isn't happening," Lucy muttered to herself. She glanced nervously around the open field as though expecting someone to jump out and yell, "April Fools!" But this wasn't April and the goose bumps on her arm gave her the sinking feeling that this was no joke.

"Where am I?" Lucy demanded. "And who are you? And what the…"

"Whoa! One thing at a time," said Harrison, holding up his hand. "First things first; how are you feeling?"

Lucy stared blankly back at Harrison. How did she feel? She had just been rammed by a speeding truck, sent soaring to God-knows-where and now she was standing in the middle of a field talking to a guy in a dress.

"FABULOUS…I feel absolutely *fabulous*!" she ranted, a little louder than intended.

"Wonderful!" declared Harrison, obviously missing her sarcasm. "The journey affects everyone differently; some new arrivals can't stand for days."

"Journey?"

"Don't worry. It will all make sense after a while, Guardian's honor."

"Guardian's honor?" Lucy began to laugh. "This is good, this is really good. I mean I've had some weird dreams before, but this one wins hands down. Now if you'll excuse me, I don't mean to be rude but I've gotta get out of here – wherever *here* is."

Lucy looked around for some sign of the way to get back to Aunt Aggie's, but in every direction all she saw was open field. Deciding that heading towards the mountain was her best shot, she turned back to Harrison.

"Well, this has been fun and I'm sure when I wake up I'll get a big kick out of it, but I think it's time for me to find a way out of this dream." Lucy took a deep breath, gave Harrison a quick wave and started across the field.

"Lucy…" Harrison called after her, "…*before* was the dream. This is all very real."

Lucy felt as though she had slammed against an invisible wall. "How do you know my name?"

"There's a lot I know about you." Harrison pulled a long silver scroll out of his pocket and unfurled it.

"Lucille Margaret O'Sullivan, age 14 years, 2 weeks, 12 hours, 36 minutes. Daughter of Jack O'Sullivan and Katie Donovan-O'Sullivan. Departure point: Mountain City, Colorado, middle of Elm Street in front of the home of Mike and Bailey Jenkins…"

"Hold on!" Lucy's heart was pounding in her throat. "What do you mean 'departure point'?"

"Truman, do you want to answer that?" Harrison nodded to someone over Lucy's shoulder.

Lucy turned around and let out a sharp shriek. An old man in an emerald green robe was standing behind her smiling.

"Why do you people sneak up like that!"

The old man stepped forward and held out his hand. "Hello Lucy, I'm Truman."

Lucy's heart pounded fiercely as she looked down at his outstretched hand. Something about the old man seemed familiar.

"Do I know you?"

"Yes," grinned Truman, "but not nearly as well as I know you."

Nervously Lucy reached out and shook the old man's hand. As their fingers touched a warm tingle shot up Lucy's arm and through her body. Suddenly a wave of memories rolled over her....She was three and falling out of the boat into the lake. Her father jumped in after her and carried her back to shore....It was her seventh birthday and her friends were all standing around her laughing and pointing at the handmade sweater that Aunt Aggie had given her....She was ten and sitting by Digby in the hospital. She had survived the accident but her father was gone....It was today. She was standing in front of Bird's house watching the truck bear down on the old man in the street. Everything began playing in slow motion. As the truck headed for the old man, Lucy ran into the street. She got to the wheelchair seconds before the truck and shoving with all her might she pushed it out of the way but the truck had been too close for her to escape. Just as it was about to hit her, two men in robes had appeared; they reached out and touched her and suddenly it was as if the world dropped away from under her feet. Streams of color sped past her and she remembered light, everywhere there was bright, colorful light. But she didn't really feel as if she was flying. Instead it was more like the old world had fallen away and a new one was racing towards her. Then everything began to blur. Lucy covered her face trying to remember, but it was gone.

"Would you like to rest a while before we continue?" asked Truman, his kind eyes smiling at her.

Lucy shook her head. She didn't want rest, she didn't want to talk; she just wanted to go home.

"I saw you," she whispered.

Harrison and Truman exchanged looks.

"Right before…" Lucy couldn't bring herself to say the words. "You were both there. You were the ones who brought me here."

Truman gave Lucy a warm smile. "Guilty as charged."

Lucy's head was beginning to swim again. "But I don't understand…if I was about to get run over, and you pulled me away and brought me to…to this place…then I must be…but I can't be…I mean my heart is still beating – I know because it's pounding right now!" Lucy began pacing back and forth through the flowers sending an odd perfume up into the air.

"And LOOK! No wings!" she said, turning her head and pointing at her back. "If this were real, there would be wings!"

Harrison looked curiously at his own back.

"Undoubtedly you have many questions," interrupted Truman, "and I promise to answer them all, but I truly feel you should rest first. It takes a while for your energy to adjust to this place."

"Exactly what *place* is this?" said Lucy, waving her arms at the endless field. She had no intention of resting until she knew what was going on.

Truman looked at Lucy for several long moments before giving a long slow sigh. "Very well. I will answer two questions…but ONLY TWO. After that you must rest."

Two questions? It would be impossible to narrow down her avalanche of questions to just two. Lucy glanced at Harrison for help, but he just shrugged and gave her a *whatareyagoingtodo* look.

"Fine," said Lucy, turning back to Truman. "But here's the deal, you have to promise to tell me the truth – the *whole* truth."

"I could do nothing less."

"AND after this little rest you're making me take, you will answer any other questions I have *and* tell me how to get home."

This time it was Truman who looked over to Harrison for support. But Harrison just laughed. "Sounds to me like you've met your match. I think you better agree before she decides to get really tough."

Lucy stood with her arms folded trying to look braver than she felt. She was sure they could see her hands shaking.

Truman looked her over, his smile somewhat faded but his eyes still twinkling.

"It's a deal," he said finally, and Lucy felt herself breathe again. "But Samuel and I are going to have a long talk when I catch up with him."

Harrison laughed and Lucy was tempted to ask who this Samuel was, but only having two questions she decided it could wait.

"Well, let's get to it," said Truman, plopping down in the grass with amazing ease for someone his age. "Fire away, but remember…two questions only."

Reluctantly, Lucy joined Truman on the ground. As Harrison got comfortable on a nearby boulder, Lucy tried to choose which of the millions of questions running through her mind she should ask first. It didn't take long. It was clear to her what her first question had to be. Gulping back the knot that was climbing up her throat she bit her lip and looked into Truman's calm blue eyes.

"Am I dead?" Lucy felt her body freeze as the words hit the air.

Truman paused and looked deeply into Lucy's eyes. The silence seemed to last forever as she waited for him to confirm what in her heart she already knew.

"Dead," said Truman, finally breaking the tension, "is a word invented by people to describe something they cannot understand." He reached down and gently lifted a ladybug off a cornflower near Lucy's foot. "When souls end one part of their journey, they begin another – rather like moving from one room in a house to another." He turned and carefully placed the ladybug on a large, purple snapdragon growing near the boulder where Harrison sat. "The people in the first room no longer see their friend so they believe he is gone…dead. But their friend is still there; he is simply on the other side of the wall. You are not dead, Lucy. You have merely entered a new room."

Lucy stared at the ladybug that was now happily exploring its new home.

"Then does that mean this is…heaven?" The last word stuck in her throat.

"Yes and no. Once again you have asked a question which has no simple answer. This is the Land of Awakening in a world known simply as The Kingdom. All souls come here before moving on to one of the other provinces. Heaven - as you call it – is not so much a location as a state of being. Some discover that place in themselves while here. For those fortunate few this becomes their heaven. For others it is just another leg of their journey."

Lucy stared at the patch of flowers surrounding her. They were perfect. *Why wouldn't they be,* she thought. Was this her heaven?

"A deal is a deal," said Truman, standing and shaking the grass off his robe. "If I am not mistaken, I have upheld my end of the bargain and now it is time for you to rest."

Lucy didn't have the strength to argue. Her mind was numb; she didn't want to think anymore.

Truman placed his hand on Lucy's shoulder and instantly a warm, wonderful sense of drowsiness overcame her.

"That's my cue," said Harrison, hopping off the boulder. "Lucy, I leave you in very capable hands. I'm off to see what trouble I can cause down below." He gave Lucy a quick wink. "Don't worry; you're not getting rid of me. I'll be back when you're ready to start shaking things up a bit." With a flourish, Harrison gave a deep bow and was gone.

"Someone down there is up for a round of excitement I'd guess," chuckled Truman. He continued to talk, but Lucy couldn't hear him. She had fallen into a deep and perfect sleep.

****

When Lucy awoke she felt great. As a matter of fact she couldn't remember ever feeling better. During her brief – or had it been very long – rest her legs had regained their strength. This was fortunate since she now found herself chasing after Truman who was crossing the field at a brisk trot.

"Where are we going?" panted Lucy, as she hurried to keep up. They had walked so far that the meadow had slowly disappeared and turned into a sea of grassy hills.

"You said you would answer all my questions. Our deal…remember!"

"Our deal stated nothing about standing still," said Truman, reaching the crest of the hill.

"Fine," said Lucy, bending over and clutching the stitch in her side. "But can we at least slow down a bit?"

Truman stopped and looked up into the sky. If she hadn't known better, Lucy would have sworn he was actually reading the clouds.

"Slow down? Heavens no! But I do believe we will have time for a small detour." He nodded as if confirming what he saw in the sky. "Not to worry; it shouldn't take long. We will make it to the Village in plenty of time for the gathering."

Before Lucy could ask what he was talking about, Truman had changed directions and was off again.

For a long time they walked in silence. Lucy was sure they had been going for hours, but glancing up at the sky she was puzzled to find the sun hanging exactly where it had been when they began. Time apparently didn't work the same way here.

The field of wildflowers had gradually turned into a sea of rolling hills which eventually gave way to an open meadow filled with odd looking exotic plants. Sniffing the air Lucy noticed a slight aroma of vanilla drifting up from the luminous green leaves. She squinted against the bright sun and saw a group of lights flickering in the distance.

"Truman," she said, finally breaking the silence, "what are those lights?"

To Lucy's relief, Truman stopped walking. A look of contentment crossed his face as he watched the lights bobbing about. "Those, my dear, are welcoming parties; mostly family and friends waiting to greet a new arrival."

"I don't see any people," said Lucy, squinting harder at the lights.

"That's because you don't recognize their energies. To you only the light of their spirit appears, but to the person being welcomed they appear in the form they wore in life. We train our eyes to see the outside but it's the inside that we recognize."

As Lucy watched the group of lights flicker in and out of sight she felt a sinking feeling in the pit of her stomach. She hadn't let herself think about it when she first arrived, but now the thought weighed heavily on her mind. *Where was* her *family? Why hadn't her father been there when she arrived?* She wanted to ask Truman but the ache in her stomach said she didn't want to know the answer.

Lucy shook the thought from her mind. That was it; she had had enough for now. With a thud Lucy plopped down on a patch of grass.

"Truman, isn't there some other way to get wherever we're going?" She fell back in the grass and looked up at the clear blue sky. "Don't you people fly or something?"

"You people?" Truman's eyebrows rose as he looked at Lucy with amusement.

"Well, yeah. You know…angels."

Truman burst out laughing so hard that Lucy sat up to see what she was missing.

"My dear child," said Truman, still laughing, "I am no more an angel than you are."

"Oh, I just thought…" Lucy suddenly felt very foolish. Obviously there was a lot she still didn't understand.

Truman seemed to read her mind.

"Mind if I join you?" he asked. Without waiting for a response, he made himself comfortable on the ground against a boulder which seemed to magically appear.

"Plainly I have been neglectful in my duties. Forgive me. I sometimes forget how little newcomers remember." Truman glanced up at the sky. "Ah, just as I thought; we're a bit ahead of schedule. I think we can afford a small break. Now, I do believe I agreed to answer all your questions." He leaned against the boulder, folding his hands behind his head. "Fire away!"

Lucy didn't know where to start. She felt like a first grader thrown into graduate school…nothing made sense.

"How about if I start things off?" offered Truman.

"Thanks," said Lucy, with a sense of relief.

"Fine then, let's start with the basics. There is obviously some confusion about who…or what…we are."

Lucy nodded.

"This," said Truman, gesturing at the world around them, "is the Kingdom of Celestial Attendants. The residents of this Kingdom are primarily Guides, Guardians and Messengers. Of course there are others – mostly those attendants living in the Village who weren't assigned to a division and really have nothing to do with Walkers."

"Walkers?" Lucy looked curiously at Truman.

"Humans." Truman grinned playfully. "It's a nickname we use."

Lucy suddenly understood how Alice must have felt when she fell down the rabbit hole.

"So does that mean you're one of these…what did you call them?"

"Attendants. Yes, I am a Guide."

"And Harrison…is he a Guide too?"

"Oh my no," said Truman, with a chuckle. "Harrison is a Guardian and a darn good one at that. But please don't tell him I said so. It's best to keep him on his toes." Truman gave Lucy a wink and again she felt as though she knew him from somewhere.

"You can tell our specialties by our robes; Guides wear green robes such as my own, Guardians are in blue and Messengers are adorned in a lovely shade of ruby red."

"Are there lots of you here?"

"Heavens, yes. I dare say once we get to Drookshire you will be quite amazed by our numbers." Truman picked a small blue leaf off a nearby plant and to Lucy's surprise he plopped it in his mouth as though it was a piece of candy.

"Drookshire, is that where we're going?"

"Eventually," said Truman, swallowing down the leaf and picking another. "But first I have a quick stop to make. After that we'll be meeting up with the others in the Village.

"The others?"

"They prefer all freshman attendants transport together from the Village; keeps them from getting lost."

Lucy shot Truman a nervous look.

"Not to worry," he said, waving off her concern. "It hardly ever happens. Besides, we've found most of them."

Lucy made a mental note to keep up with Truman from now on.

"I know what we need," Truman said, getting suddenly to his feet.

Lucy quickly stood up beside him, afraid he might take off again.

With a sweep of his hand the patch of flowers in front of them vanished and a model of the countryside rose up from the ground.

Lucy's eyes grew wide and her mouth dropped open as she gawked at the three-dimensional map. The model was a perfect replica of the land around them down to the tiny flowers rippling in the breeze. There were even little groups of light wandering throughout the field; and up above the map, hanging over two tiny figures, floated an arrow that read "You are here."

"How did you…"

Truman laughed. "That's nothing, really. By this time tomorrow little conjurations like that won't even make you blink."

Somehow Lucy highly doubted that.

"So what do you think of our fair Kingdom?" said Truman, proudly waving his arm over the map.

Lucy stared at the miniature model of the countryside hovering in front of her. To the right she saw the meadow and hills they had just left. Her eyes followed the path they had taken leading to the west and she was surprised to discover that it led directly to what looked to be a small town.

"That's the Village," said Truman, following Lucy's gaze. He beamed as he looked down on the little town that appeared to be bustling with activity. "Fascinating place; sort of the business center of the Kingdom you might say. Of course, there are many other wonderful things to be found there. The zoo is quite extraordinary and there is a lovely little coffee shop with the most delicious pumpkin scones."

Truman's words floated by Lucy without much notice; her attention had been drawn to a shimmering structure nestled in the side of the mountain on the western edge of the map. Walking around to get a better look, Lucy saw that the glittering object was actually a castle – a *crystal* castle - tucked between the mountains and a beautiful green valley.

"What is that?" Lucy asked, her eyes fixated on the glittering castle.

"Ah, I see you found it! *That* is Drookshire Station…your new home."

New home? Lucy felt like she had just been doused with a bucket of cold water. As beautiful as this place was, she didn't want a new home.

Swallowing back the lump that had appeared in her throat, Lucy's eyes followed the mountains as they circled behind Drookshire until they ran into a large, dense forest that bordered the castle on the north. A beautiful blue lake sat in the middle of the forest fed by a river that ran along the northern edge of the map. Lucy stepped back and surveyed the scene in front of her.

"Where are we going now?" she asked.

"There," said Truman, pointing at an odd shimmering area just beyond their tiny selves on the map. "Our first stop is straight ahead."

"What exactly is that place," asked Lucy, staring at the swirling mist that covered the north end of the map. She poked curiously at the mist with her finger and watched as the whirling haze drifted apart like a puff of smoke then quickly wafted back together.

"That…is a surprise." Truman's eyes twinkled gleefully with the pleasure of his secret. Lucy was about to remind Truman of their deal when something on the map caught her eye.

To the left of the mist, on the western side of the mountain that cradled Drookshire Station, was a smoky darkness that looked like immense storm clouds ready to explode into a violent downpour. Lucy watched as the dark clouds churned and bubbled, never quite crossing the mountain to Drookshire.

Lucy didn't like this area. As she watched, splintered flashes of lightning ripped through the murky, rumbling, mass of clouds and she felt a sadness snake through her body.

"What is that place?" she whispered.

Truman drew a deep breath. He seemed to be deciding exactly how much to tell her.

When he finally spoke, the joy in Truman's voice was gone. "You asked before if this is heaven; well, that land is where spirits go who are not ready to accept that heaven exists. It is called Morpheus and it is a land of denial and fear and endless sleep. Inside Morpheus is a place where souls live unaware that a world of light awaits just outside its border. We call it the Forgotten City, but on earth you would have called it Hell."

A shiver ran down Lucy's back. She had always imagined Hell as buried far below the earth, filled with fire and brimstone. However, this sight of Morpheus seemed far scarier than anything she had ever pictured.

"That's enough for now." Truman clapped his hands and suddenly the map was gone. He placed his hands on Lucy's shoulders and the fear that had filled her disappeared. "Besides, the first leg of our journey is almost over."

Lucy looked up and was surprised to see the same glistening mist that she had seen on the map. However, unlike its miniature version this mist filled the entire northern sky like a multi-colored haze that reached from the ground high into the air beyond her sight.

Tentatively Lucy followed behind Truman as he headed toward the wall of swirling color. As they drew closer, Lucy could feel the air vibrating and thought she heard voices coming from behind the curtain of haze.

"Are you ready?" said Truman, holding out his hand to Lucy.

"Ready?" exclaimed Lucy, staring at him in disbelief. "You expect me to go through that thing?"

"A journey delayed is an adventure missed." Again Truman winked and she knew there was no use arguing.

Lucy stared at the vibrating curtain in front of her. She didn't want an adventure. She longed to be back in her bed with her mother by her side and Oscar at her feet.

Glancing back at the meadow she somehow knew that once she stepped through this curtain her old life would be gone forever.

"It will be okay...I promise." Truman wiggled the fingers of his outstretched hand.

Taking one last look behind her, Lucy took hold of Truman's hand and closed her eyes. Without speaking, she lifted her foot and with a deep breath stepped into the whirling mist. In a blaze of sound Lucy felt her body leave the warm meadow behind.

A strong, cold wind pelted her making it impossible to open her eyes. She clenched her grip on Truman's hand, afraid of losing him in the frantic wind. Lucy realized her feet weren't moving but they seemed to be racing through a tunnel of some sort. The wind bellowed through her ears as she strained to hear Truman's voice. She thought she heard him say something about covering her face, but before she could raise her hands a jolt of cold knocked her off her feet.

As she lay on the ground, Lucy realized the wind and noise had stopped. She was no longer cold and everything had fallen silent except for a faint humming in the distance. Slowly Lucy opened her eyes and found herself staring into the black void of space.

CHAPTER THREE

THE LAND OF DREAMS

Truman reached down and helped Lucy to her feet.

"I should have warned you about that last step. It's quite a kicker."

Lucy stood rooted in place. The brilliance of what lay before her was more than she could wrap her mind around. Surrounding her, in the vast blackness of the universe, were trillions of glittering stars. She didn't know what she expected, but this certainly was not it. Moments ago she had been standing in a field of flowers, and now...Lucy looked down and let out a loud scream. Below her was nothing but the infinite emptiness of space. She seized Truman's arm afraid that the invisible floor beneath her might unexpectedly give away at any second.

"A little disconcerting at first, isn't it? Don't worry, you'll get used to it. You must understand that here, where your body is simply a creation of your mind, the air under your feet can feel as solid as the earth below. Go ahead, take a step. You'll see what I mean."

Truman pried himself from Lucy's grasp and she flapped her arms madly in an attempt to stay upright. To her surprise nothing happened; she didn't plummet into the darkness below or float off into outer space; she simply stood firmly planted on thin air. Lucy drew a shaky breath trying to calm her heart which was beating so thickly it shook her entire body. Biting her lip hard she balanced herself on her left foot and gradually pointed her right toe out as if preparing to step into an icy lake. Before stepping forward, Lucy peeked down at the velvety black void below her feet. Nothing was there except for the stars that were blinking as though they were saying that walking on air was perfectly normal.

"Truman, I…I don't think I can do this," she choked in a panicked whisper.

"Of course you can. It's all a matter of faith, and I have tremendous faith in you," said Truman in a reassuring voice.

Lucy smiled weakly. She didn't have the heart to tell him it wasn't a lack of faith she was worried about, it was a lack of solid footing. *This must be what they mean by a leap of faith*, Lucy thought to herself. She swallowed; then mustering all the courage she could find Lucy closed both eyes, shifted her weight onto her right foot and stepped into the night air. With a rush of excitement she exhaled as her foot landed on solid ground!

"It worked!" Lucy exclaimed, looking down at her feet. Cautiously she bounced up and down on her right foot testing to make sure it was for real.

"Congratulations! Now we must be going," said Truman, as he began to walk away into night.

Lucy was shifting her weight from foot to foot in amazement. "Wait! I want to try something," she said excitedly. Turning back around, she counted to three, closed her eyes and then jumped as far as she could. THUD! Her feet landed with such force that it took her quite by surprise.

"I'm…I'm actually walking on air!" Energized by the fact she was doing something that she knew was quite impossible, Lucy quickened her pace until she was practically jogging with the twinkling of the stars glittering both above and below.

Truman laughed as he watched Lucy try out her new skill. Finally he called out, "Fine, fine! Now that you've mastered the art of walking, how about using it to actually go somewhere?"

Lucy, who now was practicing walking up and down invisible steps, stopped in mid-step. In the midst of her excitement she had forgotten that she still didn't know where they were. With a final great leap she landed at Truman's feet.

"What is this place?" she said, pushing a lock of hair from her face. Her fear had vanished and now she found herself quite excited with their adventure.

"Ah, but don't you recognize it?" said Truman. "I dare say you have visited here many times."

"No way," said Lucy looking at the inky black world around her. True, it did look oddly familiar – rather like the pictures in her old astronomy book - but these stars didn't seem to fit into any of the constellations she had been forced to memorize. These stars seemed to appear randomly, and as Lucy gazed at them she realized that the twinkling wasn't coming from the flickering light of the stars as she first thought – the stars were actually disappearing and new ones were reappearing close by. All around her stars were silently popping on and off creating the effect of a sparkling sky.

"Perhaps this will jog your memory," said Truman, sweeping his arms skyward. With a great whoosh several of the bright stars sped toward Lucy screeching to a halt mere feet away from where they were standing. Lucy's mouth fell open. The bright lights she had seen were not stars at all but spinning spirals of light that resembled small, colorful tornadoes. The columns of light danced in front of Lucy as she gazed from one to another. Inside each spinning funnel Lucy could see faint shadows moving about like misty moving pictures.

As Lucy stared in wonder at the whirling lights, Truman leaned over and whispered in her ear, "This, my dear Lucy, is the Land of Dreams."

Lucy tried to speak, but nothing came out. Her mind was spinning faster than the lights in front of her. *The Land of Dreams?* But then did that mean…Lucy looked from the whirling tornados back to Truman, staring fixedly into his calm blue eyes.

"Truman," she said slowly, the pitch of her voice rising with a note of suspicion, "what exactly are those things?"

"We call them passages," Truman answered with the patient tone of someone explaining an obvious fact to a child. "They connect your earthly self to your higher self and they are filled with the dreams and mental wanderings of people below." Truman chuckled at the astonished look on Lucy's face. "My dear, the best is yet to come."

A sudden thought came to Lucy. "Does that mean that people up here were able to see *my* dreams when I…when I was…you know…alive?"

"First of all, let's be very clear – you are still very much alive. And second of all, yes." Truman held up his hand to stop Lucy's protest before it began. "Please let me explain. As attendants it is our duty to watch over and help the people below not only when they are awake, but also as they sleep. After all, some of the greatest dangers we face are in our dreams are they not?"

Lucy hadn't really thought of it that way. It was true that she sometimes had some truly awful nightmares, but she never really thought they could hurt her. After all, they were just dreams. She turned back to the spinning lights, leaning forward to examine them more closely.

"Be careful," warned Truman. "The energy of a dream is very strong. It's best if you keep a bit of a distance."

Lucy began to step away when something happened that caused her to yelp and leap behind Truman. An unexpected voice called out from the darkness.

"Truman, yeh ol' devil! Fancy seeing you here!"

[35]

Lucy peered from behind Truman's shoulder to find a tall gawky boy of about seventeen strolling over to them. His orange hair hung in his eyes, and below the hem of his robes Lucy caught a glimpse of bright green high-top tennis shoes.

"Well hello!" said Truman with a note of happy surprise. "I didn't know you were assigned to dream duty today."

"I'm not actually. Just helpin' Cassiel out with a spinner up the way. Got a bit of a tough one on her hands, so she called in a few extra folks to see if we can't bring this bloke up a tad." Suddenly the young man noticed Lucy.

"Blast it all! I'm sorry, Truman, I didn't know you was givin' a tour."

"No, no, don't apologize. As a matter of fact, I'm quite glad we ran into you. I was hoping the two of you would get a chance to meet."

Truman stepped aside and gently pushed Lucy forward. "Lucy, I would like you to meet a very good friend of mine, Riley."

Lucy gave a polite nod and held out her hand. "Hello. It's nice to meet you."

"And Riley, *this* is Lucy," said Truman proudly.

"Well, well, well, so it is, so it is. About time!" Ignoring Lucy's outstretched hand Riley stepped up and gave her a crushing hug. "I've been waiting a long time to finally meet you in person. Course I feel like I already know yeh from all o' Truman's stories and such." He gave a nod toward the dream tornadoes.

Lucy smiled and pretended to understand what he was talking about, although she didn't have a clue.

"Riley, I have a few things I need to discuss with Cassiel," said Truman. "Would it be alright if we tagged along? I could speak with Cassiel and Lucy could get a first-hand look at the work your group is doing."

"*Alright*? It would be fantastic! Follow me; we're just up the way a bit."

As Riley led Truman to wherever they were going, Lucy lingered behind them taking time to stop and marvel at the funnels of light that continued to pop on and off all around her. The small tornados were spinning so quickly it was hard to make out the figures inside; however Lucy did notice that some of the dreams swirled with bright colors while others seemed very dark and foreboding. As they continued through the black forest of dreams Lucy saw that some of the passages in the distance were surrounded by attendants dressed in various colored robes. Lucy wanted desperately to stop and ask what they were doing but she didn't dare lose sight of Truman and Riley who, being deep in conversation about something called *bounders*, seemed to have forgotten that she was trailing behind them.

"All I'm sayin' is Dunluvy wasn't worth squat against the Weavles," said Riley, coming to a sudden halt. With a sweep of his hand he declared, "And here we are. Got to say it's a pretty motley group of misfits Cassiel's put to work on this one."

In front of them, huddled around a particularly fat passage, was an odd combination of characters hustling about and taking no notice of the new arrivals. A large man with ebony skin was pacing around the passage peering into it from all angles with deep concentration. On the ground in front of the passage were three men who looked very much like Asian monks. They were seated with their legs crossed and eyes closed as though they were deep in meditation but their hands were outstretched towards the whirling tornado and Lucy saw their lips were moving in a silent chant.

Standing closest to Lucy was a plump older lady with short, curly gray hair dressed in a golden robe. Lucy couldn't see her face, but she was speaking very animatedly to the figure inside the passage. As her voice rose, red sparks shot from the passage like tiny fireworks. Gathered around the old lady were a dozen other attendants who appeared to have no purpose other than to observe the bizarre scene.

"Hey! Look who I found!" Riley's voice startled the crowd. Everyone seemed very happy to see Truman and greetings rang out as one by one the crowd filtered over to say hello. Lucy noticed that they were careful not to leave the passage unattended.

"You're just in time!" called the old woman. "He's having a tough time, this one is. Step up and show these youngsters how it's done." She gave a friendly wink to the group of monks who were staring at her with a look of bruised pride.

"I'm just a spectator today, Cassiel," said Truman regretfully. He turned and ushered Lucy out from behind his robes. "Today I am playing tour guide."

"Oh my, I should have known," said the old woman with a gentle smile.

She hurried over and gave Lucy a warm, grandmotherly hug. Instantly a wave of happiness washed over Lucy as memories of her mother flooded in. Without thinking about what she was doing Lucy returned the hug, wrapping her arms around the woman's thick middle. She didn't want to let go. Something about the old woman felt like family, like home. Finally the woman gently pulled away, cupping Lucy's face in her hands and smiling at her so broadly that her whole face crinkled.

"You are as beautiful as I imagined."

Lucy used her sleeve to wipe away the tears that were clouding her eyes.

"I'm Cassiel," said the woman. "It is a joy and an honor to meet you."

Lucy didn't know what to say. Suddenly she realized that everyone was staring at her. Apparently she was much more interesting now that Cassiel had taken notice of her. Riley was giving her an enthusiastic thumbs-up and the group of monks eyed her curiously.

"Have you enjoyed your stay so far?" asked Cassiel.

Lucy wasn't sure how to describe what she was felt, but *enjoyed* wasn't the first word that came to mind. Not sure what to say, she simply nodded her head.

"Wonderful! Now you must excuse us dear, we have a fellow here who needs some help." Turning back to the gawking crowd, Cassiel clapped her hands sharply. "This isn't a tea party, people – everybody back to your stations!"

"She's a real slave driver, this one," said Riley, jerking his head in Cassiel's direction. "Feel free to stick around if you want to see some real professionals at work." He gave Truman a playful elbow in the stomach, then with a grand gesture he rolled up his sleeves and joined the others.

Upon Cassiel's orders, everyone had quickly gotten back to work. As Lucy watched each of the attendants scurrying into place, she noticed that they all were wearing the colored robes Truman had described. Riley and the monks were dressed in red while the others were in either blue or green. Only Cassiel wore gold.

Suddenly Lucy let out a scream. Two hands had grabbed her shoulders from behind.

"I thought I would find you two here." Lucy spun around to find Harrison standing behind her looking pleased that he had caught her off guard.

"It's about bloody time!" called Riley from the far side of the dream passage. "Make yourself useful and get over here. This fella needs a bit of that special Harrison persuasion."

"Ah, no rest for the weary." Harrison gave Lucy a wink and wandered over to join Riley who was casting silver sparks into the spinning passage.

The passage was now surrounded by attendants chanting unrecognizable words and occasionally raising their hands to the whirling mass sending multi-colored streams of light into its center. Lucy stood on her toes and strained to see above the crowd.

"Would you like a closer look?" asked Truman, with a nod towards the spinning funnel.

Lucy looked at the dark, eerie dream passage and shook her head.

"No thanks. I'll just wait over here," she said, backing up. "It looks a little crowded over there, and I wouldn't want to …"

"LUCY, STOP!" But Truman's cries were too late. Lucy had backed up in to a thin, whip-like dream passage spiraling behind her. As her foot touched the swirling mist Lucy felt a sudden jerk as the tornado grabbed her, pulling her inside. Over and over she spun as she dropped through the raging wind. Voices flew past calling her back but she was powerless against the terrific force of the passage. As dark, distorted shapes whirled around her like horrible faces in a fun-house mirror Lucy clapped her hands over her eyes.

Without warning her knees hit solid ground and Lucy felt the wind knocked from her chest. Slowly she dropped her hands from her eyes. She had landed in some sort of strange, misshapen room. A dim light was casting eerie shadows making the walls and furniture look as though they had melted. Squinting to see through the shadows, Lucy patted the ground in front of her. To her surprise her fingers wiggled deep into what felt like a thick wool carpet.

Slowly the swirling colors began to mold into what looked like a very bizarre living room. Walls of red and white stripes appeared, surrounding her like a prison built of candy canes. An enormous, lopsided lime green sofa emerged in the middle of the room; its cushions covered with bright pink ladybugs and in front of the sofa sat an old card table laden with bowls of different sizes and colors, each overflowing with sweets. But the sight that caught Lucy's eye was the tattered purple recliner in front of her and the great pink stuffed rabbit wearing a black tuxedo that was plopped in the middle of its over-stuffed velvety cushion.

Panic began to creep over her as she realized she had no idea where she was, or worse, how she was going to get out of here.

"Momma!" a small voice cried out.

Without thinking, Lucy leapt behind the chair as small footsteps began thumping towards her. Carefully she peered around the back of the chair and saw a small figure running down a set of stairs which had magically appeared next to the sofa.

"Momma, where are you?"

A young boy of about five was jumping down the stairs two at a time. There was a sense of urgency in his eyes.

"I'm right here sweetie."

Lucy covered her mouth to muffle her scream. To her shock a young woman had appeared on the sofa. She was slender with short brown hair wearing a long red velvet dress covered by a flowered apron. The little boy ran into his mother's arms and buried his head on her shoulder.

"My trick! I want to show you my trick, momma." The boy squeezed out of his mother's arms and scrambled over the back of the enormous sofa. A second later he appeared holding a black top hat.

Lucy quickly ducked back behind the recliner as the boy walked over to the rabbit sitting in the chair.

"Come here!" the boy demanded.

Lucy's heart pounded. Had he seen her? She stayed frozen behind the chair trying not to make a sound.

"Come on bunny – into the hat!"

Lucy began to breathe again. He wasn't talking to her; he was talking to the rabbit. If she hadn't been so scared she would have found the whole thing funny.

"No!" said a deep voice from the other side of the chair.

Lucy let out a small scream and fell backwards on the floor in full sight of the little boy and his mother. To her astonishment, neither of them seemed to notice her. Lucy scrambled to duck back behind the chair, but it had disappeared. Nervously she remained frozen in place, not sure what to do next; but neither the boy nor his mother seemed aware of her presence.

The mother, now dressed in a ballerina's tutu, was dancing around the sofa with the stuffed rabbit.

"Bad bunny! You're ruining my trick." The little boy wagged his finger at the bunny as it waltzed away with his mother.

"Bunny! Come back!" The little boy dashed after the rabbit and in an instant the living room was gone and Lucy found herself standing in a long dark hallway. Candles hung on the walls shooting long shadows across an arched ceiling. A soft sobbing came from ahead in the darkness.

"Momma? Bunny? Where are you? I can't find you!"

Lucy felt an ache of sadness in the pit of her stomach as she listened to the boy calling out for his mother. As one by one the candles on the wall began to flicker out, the boy's sobs grew louder. Feeling like she had to do something before they were lost in total darkness, Lucy felt her way up the hall to the boy. His small shoulders shook as his hands covered his face hiding him from the shadows. Reaching out, a cold chill ran through Lucy's fingers as her hand swept through the boy. It was as if he was made of air.

Lucy drew a sharp breath and jumped back running into something very solid.

"Truman!" She threw her arms around Truman's neck, thankful that he felt real.

Truman gently pulled away from Lucy as he peered down the darkening hallway. "You've had quite an exciting first day, but I think we better head back."

"But what about the boy? He's lost, and…" Lucy suddenly realized the boy was no longer crying.

"He'll be fine. Take a look."

At the end of the darkened hall a light had appeared. As Lucy watched, the light grew brighter until it flooded the hallway with a warm glow. A voice was coming from the light – at first it was faint, but then it gradually grew louder until Lucy could make out the soft melodic words calling to the boy. Through the light Lucy saw the form of a woman appear; she was holding something in one arm and motioning to the boy with the other.

"Nicholas, it's okay. I'm here to help you," the soft voice echoed down the hallway.

The little boy slowly started towards the woman. Drawing closer, a large grin broke across his face as he ran to the woman and grabbed the large stuffed pink rabbit she was holding.

Lucy watched in silence as the boy took the woman's hand and together they disappeared into the light. All around her the walls of the hallway began to melt away into a swirl of color.

"What was that thing?" Lucy asked, staring at the swirling mist where the woman had just stood.

"That *thing* was the boy's Guardian," said Truman, looking rather put out by Lucy's terminology. "And now that he is quite safe, it is time for us to return. You had us all a bit worried you know."

[43]

"I don't get it; how come he could see and hear her but not me? Do Guardians have some kind of special power?"

"That one does," said Truman, gazing at the spot where the woman had stood. "She is what we call a Dream Walker. It's a fairly rare talent but there are a few of them in Drookshire. Dream Walkers are able to enter a person's dream and actually be seen and heard whereas the rest of us have to rely on less impressive means to get our messages across."

Lucy thought about stories she had heard of people being visited in their dreams by ghosts. She had even been angry after her father died when he had not shown up in her dreams even though she had asked him to every night in her prayers. Now Lucy felt guilty for thinking he didn't care. It wasn't that he hadn't wanted to come back, he simply couldn't.

"I'm sorry for causing all this trouble," Lucy whispered feebly. She shuffled her feet on the ground kicking up the painted air.

"Sorry? My dear girl, there is no need to apologize for a lesson learned."

Lucy looked up and was relieved to find a twinkle in Truman's eyes.

"Now, we need to get going. This little adventure has put us behind schedule."

"But how do we get out of here?" asked Lucy, looking around at the water colored world surrounding them.

"It's a simple matter of raising your energy," said Truman.

Lucy stared at him blankly. He might as well have said they needed to turn into birds and fly back. A cold chill washed over her. The swirling colors were growing darker and Lucy had a gnawing feeling that soon they would be lost in total blackness. Truman took her hand and gave it a reassuring pat.

"Rule #1: Never let fear stand in the way of discovery. Changing your energy will be something you will learn soon enough, however until then this will help do the trick."

Truman let go of Lucy's hand and at once a tall golden staff appeared in his grasp. On top of the staff was a large round crystal and inside the crystal Lucy swore she saw millions of tiny, spinning stars.

"Quite something, isn't it?" said Truman, giving a nod to the golden staff. "I borrowed it from a friend; I think it will suit our needs quite nicely."

Holding out the staff to Lucy, Truman said, "I want you to think of someone you love very much. Picture that person in your mind; hold them in your heart, then, when you are ready place your hand on the staff."

Lucy closed her eyes and in a flash her mother appeared in her mind. She was folding clothes and humming along with the music that poured out from the old radio that sat on their kitchen table. As she watched, her mother picked up a sweater and began dancing across the room to the music. Lucy felt a tear creep down her cheek. After a long pause, she took a deep breath, opened her eyes and placed her hand on the staff. Suddenly her body began shaking wildly. It was as if a bolt of lightning was bouncing around inside of her, making her hair stand on end and her eyes rattle so fiercely that it was impossible to make out the shapes speeding past.

Without warning there was a blinding burst of light and the lightning inside of her was gone. Lucy stood with her arms outstretched for balance and her eyes closed tightly against the brilliant light. She felt lighter than air, as if the slightest breeze would send her flying away.

"Rule #2," Lucy heard Truman say, "don't go through life with your eyes closed or you will miss what you came here to see."

Lucy carefully opened one eye. The bright light flooded in, but to her surprise she could look at it without any problem. Opening both eyes, Lucy looked around at the world where they had landed. Her mouth dropped open in amazement as she gazed upon the most incredible scene she had encountered so far on this bizarre journey.

A wide grin spread across Truman's face. "Welcome to the Village!"

CHAPTER FOUR

THE VILLAGE

Lucy had grown up in the mountains of Colorado. She loved the columbine flowers that painted the hillside like water colors of blue and purple and pink and the sound of the river that charged through the mountains, spilling over rock beds and spraying a heavy mist on to the banks. But it was the trees that truly owned the mountain. Her father taught her at a very early age that the forest surrounding their home had a spirit all its own and she had spent endless hours wandering deep into its soul.

Shadowing the banks of the river, an army of quaking aspens fluttered gold and red in the light that broke through their branches. On particularly lousy days – many of which followed the death of her father – Lucy would ride her bike to a large circle of aspens that bordered a clearing not far from the river. Lying on her back, she would stare up at the sea of waving, golden leaves and imagine herself somewhere else…somewhere where people didn't leave.

For Lucy, the trees that covered the mountain were like friends. But now, standing at the entrance to the Village, she realized that the trees that she had admired so much on earth were merely pale shadows of the incredible trees that stood before her.

Rising so high that their branches nearly broke the clouds, a circle of trees unlike any she had ever seen surrounded the Village like a mighty green fortress. Between the trees grew heavy thickets of giant roses making it impossible to pass between the massive trunks. The only opening Lucy could see was directly in front of her between the two largest trees. Although the massive trees appeared to stand nearly a hundred feet apart, their great, outstretched arms intertwined to form a mammoth archway into the Village.

Lucy gawked at the sight. Besides being the most enormous trees she had ever seen, they were also the most colorful. As people from the Village wandered in and out under the giant archway, the translucent leaves fluttered different colors.

"Quite something, isn't it?" Truman whispered in her ear.

"They're brilliant," Lucy murmured breathlessly. "Are all the trees here like those?"

"Heavens no. These trees are quite special," said Truman, gently pushing her towards the entrance. "These are Mayanian trees; they are the guardians of the Village."

"Guardians?" Lucy stopped in her tracks. She looked up at the swaying branches wondering what else these trees could do besides change colors.

"See that man over there?" Truman pointed at an old man in a green robe walking towards the entrance. "Watch what happens when he passes under the arch."

Lucy watched as the old man calmly walked under the boughs; as he did the leaves on the trees transformed into a brilliant shade of royal purple. Then, as the man disappeared into the Village, the leaves quietly slipped back to green.

"Mayanian trees have a special talent for seeing into the hearts of those who pass under their boughs. If they sense you have no purpose in the Village they will not allow you to enter." Truman glanced up at the sun which was beginning to shift towards the west. "Come along now; there's no time to dawdle." With that he swept under the archway sending the leaves into a shock of bright lemon yellow.

Lucy paused; she could feel her heart climb into her throat. What if she had no purpose in the Village? Staring up at the trees she imagined them reaching down, grabbing her by the ankles and tossing her over the hill. As she gave a small shudder something caught Lucy's eye. Tacked to the beefy trunk of the closest tree was a worn wooden sign that looked as if it had been there for a very long time. Keeping an eye on the branches, Lucy carefully inched forward until she was able to read the bold black letters etched into wood:

> All who enter in this place
> We welcome your return,
> But beg you do not linger
> For there's much you've yet to learn!

As Lucy read the words out loud the tree quivered causing her to cry out a word her mother had told her never to use. A very proper looking woman in a red robe looked down her nose at Lucy as she passed by.

From inside the Village Truman waved at Lucy to enter. "There will be plenty of time for horticultural studies later; we've got to get hopping."

Summoning up what little courage she had left, Lucy stole one more glance at the menacing branches overhead before darting across the threshold. Out of the corner of her eye she saw a flicker of white in the trees above, but by the time she crossed into the Village the leaves were once again green. For a moment Lucy thought she saw a look of surprise sweep across Truman's face but catching her eye he quickly composed himself and with a broad smile gestured towards the Village.

"Well," he said proudly, "what do you think?"

If Lucy had been astounded by the sight of the Mayanian trees, it was nothing compared to scene before her.

The first thing that came to mind was that she had stepped into some sort of bizarre circus. Hundreds of robed men, women and children were bustling about the Village which looked like a combination between a country hamlet and Main Street in Disneyland.

A wide cobblestone path wound around the Village encircling a large park filled with a strange array of plants and green crystal columns. The other side of the path was lined with a curious assortment of miniscule shops that appeared barely large enough to hold a handful of shoppers, and yet, to Lucy's surprise dozens of people entered through the shop doors seemingly without a problem.

She saw no cars in the Village, but two young women were circling the park in a contraption that looked like an unusually large wagon with wings. Lucy was watching the two women fly by when a crowd of people in front of a nearby shop suddenly scattered as an old man on a skateboard barreled towards them.

"COMING THROUGH!" hollered the old man as he sped past.

Lucy laughed as the old man flew out of sight. "This is incredible," she said, twisting her neck trying to take in everything. She followed Truman up the street towards a small two-story red brick shop. On the top floor was a large round window through which Lucy could see explosions of bright colors flashing one after another. The bursts of color grew in intensity until finally, with a large belch, the sides of the shop bulged out as if the building had just relieved itself of a giant gas bubble. Lucy gawked in amazement as the sides of the little shop settled back into place. In front of the shop a wooden sign swayed from the explosion. As it came to rest Lucy was able to read the large golden letters: *Inventions Through the Ages.*

"Do you mind if we skip that one?" Lucy asked, wiping away the dust that had settled on her nose.

"Wise choice," said Truman. "Supposedly they sell only items which have already been invented on earth, but…" he looked around before dropping his voice to a whisper, "everyone knows it is the shop to visit if you are looking for something a bit more, shall we say, *unusual.*" Truman gave Lucy a wink as if she understood what he meant. She didn't understand at all, but thought it best not to ask any more questions.

Suddenly a shout of excitement went up from a group of attendants circled together in the park. As they moved apart, Lucy could see they were gathered around a strange glass pedestal that seemed to be glowing. The crowd huddled over the table-like contraption with great interest. Occasionally they would let out a cheer, followed by a moan and then laughter. The scene reminded Lucy of how her uncles behaved when they were watching football.

"Truman, what is that thing they are …." But before she could finish her sentence Lucy's eye caught something that made her forget all about the cheering crowd. Just beyond the glowing table, next to a large stone building was a….no it couldn't be. She shut her eyes tight and shook her head. *I must be dreaming*, she thought. Slowly she opened her eyes and felt her mind begin to spin.

"Truman…." Lucy muttered.

Truman had wandered over to a nearby shop and was busy eyeing a basket of marbles labeled *Rain-Makers - Drizzle to Downpour.* He put down a small purple-swirled marble he was inspecting and looked up at Lucy.

"…is that a…a kangaroo *talking* to that man?" Lucy was sure she was hallucinating.

"Why yes. Fascinating creatures, kangaroos. Actually have quite a lot to say. Although if you really want a jolly conversation, there is a bobcat on the other side of the Kingdom with the most marvelous sense of humor."

Truman continued to retell a story he had just heard about the bobcat and a gaseous frog but Lucy wasn't listening; she was focusing on the sights around her. For the first time she suddenly noticed that the Village was filled with animals – and not just cats and dogs. On the far side of the park there were two chimpanzees lounging on a bench, up the walk there was an ostrich which seemed to be admiring a large yellow hat in the shop window and in the street a camel was playing kickball with a young girl.

Lucy felt dizzy as she tried to wrap her mind around the strange new world in front of her. Burping buildings and trees that changed color were one thing, but talking animals were just too much.

"Would it be okay if we sat for a few moments?" Lucy asked, rubbing her eyes again as she watched the ostrich come out of the shop wearing the hat.

"You read my mind!" said Truman, clapping his hands together. "I know just the place."

Lucy followed Truman up the street feeling quite numb. She was so befuddled that she hardly noticed as they passed the weather shop with its long lightning bolt sign that zapped on and off threatening to strike unsuspecting pedestrians. Nor did she give a second glance to the old man doing handstands on his skateboard to the delight of a group of onlookers in street clothes.

"Here we are," said Truman, motioning to a small outdoor café. Looking up, Lucy saw a large sign over the iron gate leading in to the café. On the sign was a picture of a man seated at a table piled high with delicious looking pastries. Under the picture it read *Café Monet – A Taste of*

Heaven in Every Bite. A beautiful young woman with golden braids welcomed them at the gate.

"Hello Truman!" she said, guiding them to a small table facing the park. "Will it be the usual?"

"Just a couple cups of tea today, Molly and perhaps a plate of your wonderful mango muffins."

The woman disappeared inside returning seconds later carrying two steaming cups of tea and a plate overflowing with hot muffins. The aroma was the most incredible thing Lucy had ever smelled. Choosing a plump, orange muffin off the top, she realized that this was the first time she had eaten since she arrived. The funny thing was, she didn't remember feeling hungry. The muffins were unlike anything she had ever tasted on earth and best of all she discovered she could eat as many as she wanted without feeling full.

"I take it you approve of the food," Truman said, as he watched Lucy pop her third muffin in to her mouth.

"D'ey're amaving," sputtered Lucy through a mouthful of muffin. She took a gulp of tea and cleared her throat before grabbing another helping. "Can we take some with us?"

"That will be quite unnecessary," said Truman, sipping his tea. "I think you will find the food at Drookshire Station quite satisfactory."

Lucy didn't feel like arguing; she was feeling much more relaxed and the smell of the muffins mixed with the warmth of the sun pouring down on them had taken the fight out of her. Finishing off two more cups of tea and several more muffins, Lucy sank back in her chair and looked out over the village.

"Truman," she said, lazily gazing around at the Village, "I know this might sound like a bit of an odd question…"

"Good, those are my favorite kind," Truman replied, popping the last muffin into his mouth.

Lucy weighed her words carefully not wanting to sound disrespectful. "It's just that I always pictured heaven – or whatever this place is – to be, well, shinier." Lucy looked around at the cobblestone street and the tiny, rustic shops. "Is the entire Kingdom this...quaint?"

"Wonderful, isn't it?" said Truman, reviewing the Village with pride. "Of course it didn't always look this way. We tried that golden street thing...grand buildings, jeweled towers, the whole bit...but it was quite a disaster. People kept running into each other blinded by the light reflecting off the streets. And the buildings were so tall you couldn't see the sunset. Imagine having this glorious view and not being able to see a sunset! No, this is much more suitable for our needs. It was changed so long ago that there aren't many of us who still remember the way it was back then. Truman stretched out, leaning back in his seat and locking his fingers behind his head. "Of course they left a little bit of the past for sentimental reasons: the Grand Coliseum is just over there behind the Hall of Review." He nodded towards a large stone building on the other side of the Village Square. "It was tucked out of sight so the Council decided to leave it alone."

In the distance, over the tops of the Mayanian trees, Lucy could see the mountains towering above the horizon. Although the sun was still high in the sky, she knew they would be magnificent in the evening with the sun setting over their peaks.

"Well, we better get going," said Truman, heaving a deep sigh. He stood up and brushed the crumbs from his robes. "There are still several things I want you to see before you leave."

Lucy and Truman said goodbye to Molly and headed toward the far end of the Village. Lucy noticed that they hadn't paid a check. Apparently money wasn't necessary here.

As they wandered through the streets, Truman stopped now and then to greet shop keepers and shake hands with villagers who called his name. Lucy was thankful for these brief pauses because they gave her a chance to take in the sights and listen to the conversations going on around her.

"Did you take a look at Occuscope #7?" said an old man in a green robe to a group of attendants gathered around him. "Gadwick's going to have his hands full if they don't do something quickly."

A group of villagers in white robes and blue sashes walked by talking excitedly. "I heard James got stuck on the clock tower during his teleporting exam! It took them two hours to get him down."

Lucy peeked at the nearby clock tower perched upon an official looking white marble building at the west end of the Village. She half expected to see a frightened boy clinging to the spire. But there was no boy, only a large golden clock face with no numbers and a single hand pointing straight up to the word "Now" which was printed where the number 12 should be.

"What is that thing?" asked Lucy, turning to Truman who had just said good-bye to a young man in a red robe.

"What 'thing' would you be referring to?"

"That one," said Lucy, swinging her arm towards the clock tower. There was an awful thud followed by a dull moan as Lucy felt her arm collide with something solid.

"Oh my gosh! I'm so sorry!" exclaimed Lucy, bending down to the young boy sprawled out on the sidewalk. "I didn't see you!"

"My fault," the boy said, trying to lift head. "I was watching the camel; I didn't see your arm coming."

Lucy and Truman carefully lifted the boy to his feet. He looked to be about ten or eleven with scrawny legs poking out under his baggy denim shorts and mousy brown hair that looked like it hadn't been combed in a very long time.

"Puddles! Are you okay?" A tall, dark, teenage boy was running through the crowd towards them. "What happened?" he said, looking at Lucy sternly.

"It's okay," said the young boy. "It was my fault, Ben. I wasn't looking where I was going."

The teenager's large brown eyes softened. "Sorry, I didn't mean to accuse you of anything," he said to Lucy. "It's just that I told his Guardian I'd watch out for him and when I turned around he was gone. I guess I panicked."

"No harm done," said Truman, smiling and holding out his hand. "I'm Truman."

The young man flashed a large smile and enthusiastically shook Truman's hand. "It's nice to meet you, sir. I'm Ben and this is Puddles."

Ben put his arm around Puddles and pushed him towards Truman. The young boy timidly shook Truman's hand, looking as though he might faint at any time. "Actually, my name is Peter," the boy said sheepishly, "but people have always called me Puddles."

Truman simply nodded as if this wasn't at all strange but Lucy got the distinct feeling there was probably an embarrassing story behind the nickname.

"I didn't even ask if *you* were okay," said Ben, turning towards Lucy.

"Huh? Oh, I'm fine," said Lucy, not realizing she was rubbing her arm.

Ben smiled at her and Lucy felt a tingle shoot up her arms. Like Lucy, Ben was dressed in street clothes. His dark skin, large brown eyes and short curly black hair stood out against his pressed white dress shirt. Lucy thought he looked to be about sixteen, although he acted much older.

"Are the two of you here by yourselves?" asked Truman.

"No sir. Mia, the woman who brought me here, is meeting us at the History Pavilion. That's where we were headed when Puddles, uh, ran into you." Ben gave Lucy a sideways glance and she felt her stomach do a strange flop. "Would you like to join us?"

Truman opened his mouth to answer but Lucy quickly jumped in before he could speak. "Thanks, but we just got here and Truman promised me a tour."

Out of the corner of her eye Lucy saw Truman's raised eyebrow, but to her relief he remained silent.

"No problem. Maybe we'll run into you again" said Ben, looking a bit disappointed.

"I'll try to stay on my feet next time," Puddles said, turning slightly pink.

Waving goodbye, Ben and Puddles headed off towards the south end of the village. Lucy and Truman waved after them, then turned and headed in the opposite direction.

"Hey! I didn't get your name!"

Lucy turned to see Ben running back towards them, nearly knocking over an old lady in a blue robe.

"It's Lucy," said Lucy, trying not to laugh as the old lady gave Ben a withering look.

"Nice to meet you, Lucy." Ben smiled and shook her hand. Then giving a nod to Truman and one last wave he turned and disappeared back into the crowd.

"He seems like a very nice young man," said Truman. "Why didn't you want to join him? The History Pavilion is really quite fascinating. You would be amazed to find out how much your history books got wrong."

"It just didn't sound very interesting," Lucy lied unconvincingly. The truth was up until now she just assumed that all the new people here felt as awkward and out of place as she did. But Ben seemed to fit right in, as if all these strange things were perfectly normal. His confidence solidified Lucy's belief that she had no business being here.

"Well, since you seem determined to be burdened with my company, I might as well give you the grand tour," said Truman. "Where would you like to begin?"

The rest of the afternoon passed in a flurry. Lucy couldn't tell if it had been several hours or just a few minutes since she had said good-bye to Ben and Puddles. Time worked in a funny way here. Truman had been true to his word and had given Lucy a full tour of the Village. As they left the collection of never-before-seen instruments in Barney's Boutique for the Musically Inclined, Lucy felt that she could easily spend an eternity in the Village and not get bored with the endless shopping. She was just about to ask Truman if any of the attendants actually lived in the Village when he waved her into yet another shop.

As had happened with each of the shops they had entered, when they walked through the tiny storefront the shop expanded into a large, and rather normal looking, department store. In many ways this shop appeared no different than the department stores back home except for the fact that each of the many rooms appeared to offer clothing from a different country.

"This place must be packed at Halloween," said Lucy, holding up a particularly colorful tribal headdress.

"This shop has a far more useful purpose than mere dress-up" said Truman, trying on a grass skirt over his robe. "Whenever an attendant has a job on earth, this is where they get their work clothes." He examined himself in the mirror. "Obviously it looks better without the robe."

"Wait a minute. Do you mean that you people are walking around down there?"

"If by 'you people' you mean attendants, then yes, 'we people' are often assigned to earth. Of course, there are far more angels than attendants positioned there, but that's to be expected." Truman wandered over to the room marked

United States and began browsing through the cowboy hats.

"Angels?" Lucy dropped the headdress and followed after Truman. "Are you telling me there are *angels* walking around on earth?"

"Why certainly – what good would they be if they all just stayed up here fluttering about? Surely you had moments back on earth when you were amazed that someone showed up in your life just when you needed them."

"Those were all angels?"

"Not all of them…some were attendants, others were just Walkers who were fulfilling their own destiny."

Suddenly a thought came to her.

"Truman, if you…I mean *we*…can get assigned to earth, then it would be possible for me to go back…maybe not right away, but someday. Right?"

For the first time today Lucy felt a sense of hope; if what Truman said was true, then she hadn't lost her family forever. She could go home.

Truman put down the cowboy hat he had been admiring and looked into Lucy's eyes.

"Let's take a walk," he said softly. Lucy recognized that tone, it was the type of voice you used when you were about to deliver bad news. It was the same voice the doctor had used after the accident.

"I don't want to walk anymore," she said, fighting hard to keep her voice steady. "Look, this place is fine for you but I want to go home. I don't belong here…I don't even really know what this place is!"

From behind her a man's voice replied, "Simply put, it's where you will discover things you never knew about yourself."

Lucy turned with a start to see a handsome young man with shoulder length sandy hair smiling at her. He wore a golden robe similar to Cassiel's, but unlike her red sash his was sapphire blue.

"I'm Samuel," he said, holding out his hand. "It is very nice to finally meet you."

Lucy tried to speak but no words came out. Not knowing what else to do, she shook the man's outstretched hand. Samuel's crystal blue eyes were clear and bright and seemed the picture of wisdom and at that moment they seemed to be searching Lucy's soul.

"I was hoping we would run in to you!" said Truman. "Lucy, this is the friend I mentioned earlier – the one who loaned me that handy little device that got you out of the dream. Samuel, as usual your timing is impeccable. Lucy seems convinced that she has arrived in our fair Kingdom quite by mistake. Perhaps you can explain exactly why she is here."

"There will be plenty of time for explanations later, but right now I believe there is one concern weighing heavily on Lucy's mind. Am I correct?" Samuel gazed in to Lucy's eyes, and suddenly she realized that it was true…there was one question she longed to ask more than any other; a question she hadn't dared to ask because she was afraid the answer might be too painful.

Lucy felt her throat tighten as the words spilled out. "Is she okay? My mom, will she be alright?"

"Follow me," said Samuel. "There's something I'd like to show you."

Samuel led Lucy outside to a small stone bench and motioned for her to sit. For several moments they sat in silence and then Samuel looked up at the sky. "See those clouds over there?"

Lucy looked up at a bank of clouds hanging over the distant hills. She could tell by the sheet of mist that hung below the clouds that it was raining.

"A few weeks ago that rain was water flowing in a stream. But then it evaporated and formed the most spectacular clouds. For the last several days the clouds have been remarkable and the people of the Kingdom have basked in their beauty as they treated us to the most glorious sunsets. Today the rains began over the hills, and the clouds will soon disappear. It will seem like the beauty is gone, washed away. But soon the cycle will begin anew and we will once again have beautiful sunsets to admire."

Samuel paused and looked at Lucy. "You have left your mother and she is feeling like the beauty of her life is gone, but it hasn't really left her. Your love, your memory and your spirit are still alive and still living in her. Slowly the pain will pass and she will feel the beauty again. And when the day arrives that you finally reunite, it will be spectacular."

Lucy didn't want to talk any more; she just wanted to watch the rain falling on the hills. The pain she had kept hidden spilled in to every inch of her body. How could she have left? She should have fought harder to stay.

Please help her, she silently prayed. *Help mom be happy again.*

The hairs on her arms stood up as she heard a voice in her head reply, "She will be."

"It's time to go," said Truman softly.

Lucy was surprised to see the sun had begun to dip over the Mayanian trees reflecting golden beams off their flickering leaves and casting a warm glow over the Village.

"Where are we headed?" asked Lucy in a hoarse voice as she rubbed the goose bumps from her arms.

"To the Drookshire portal. It looks like the line is already forming." Truman nodded towards a group of people lining up outside the clock tower. "We best get a move on."

"Are you coming with us," Lucy asked Samuel, who was still sitting quietly by her side.

"I'm afraid I must say good-bye here but don't worry, I am sure we will see each other again soon." He placed his hand on Lucy's arm and instantly she felt a warmth swim through her veins making her feel peaceful and sleepy. Then Samuel lifted his hand and was gone.

"Where did he go?" asked Lucy, feeling a bit groggy.

"With Samuel, one never really knows," Truman said with a chuckle.

As Lucy and Truman joined the odd mixture of people lining up in front of clock tower, Lucy was relieved to see that most of them looked as nervous as she was. One middle-aged man in a business suit was pacing back and forth looking like he might get sick, and an old woman in a gingham dress was being pulled back into the line by her young attendant who was assuring her everything would be all right.

"LUCY! OVER HERE!"

Lucy looked up and saw Ben waving excitedly from up ahead in the line.

"COME ON UP! WE'VE SAVED YOU A PLACE!"

Lucy looked at Truman, not sure what to do.

"I think we better go before he knocks someone over," said Truman, pushing her forward.

Lucy and Truman slipped into the spot Ben and Puddles had carved out for them.

"Is it okay if my friend steps in here?" Ben asked the young man standing behind him.

"No problemo," said the young man who was dressed in baggy, flowered shorts and a clashing Hawaiian shirt. He brushed his long blond hair out of his eyes and lowered his voice, "I'm like totally freakin' bout this place. I mean it's totally awesome but, dudes, it's totally not what I expected. Yeh know what I mean?"

"Totally," said Ben and Lucy in unison causing all three of them to laugh.

"Really!" huffed a young girl standing in front of Ben.

"Sorry," said Ben, stifling a laugh. "Are we bothering you?"

The young girl turned and glared at them. She was tiny, not even 5 feet tall, but she stood erect as if she was the Queen of England. Her long brown hair hung in a perfect plait down her back and there wasn't a thread out of place on what was obviously a school uniform.

"It just seems to me that one would try to be on one's best behavior here and not be cutting in line and guffawing like baboons." With a flip of her head she turned back around.

Lucy, Ben and Puddles stared at one another with wide eyes trying hard not to laugh.

"Whoa, little dudette, you need to chill," said the young man in the Hawaiian shirt.

Lucy covered her mouth to keep from laughing out loud. Luckily, before the young girl could respond, the line started moving.

In the large marble doorway stood an official looking man in a blue robe checking names off a list. One by one people were saying good-bye to their attendants and entering the building. The line was moving quickly and soon the young girl in front of them stepped up to the doorway.

"Hayden Louise Whitney," she said with an air that suggested the man should be impressed.

The Guardian scoured the list but couldn't seem to find her name. The stern looking attendant who was escorting the girl leaned forward and whispered, "Try Haddie."

"Ah! Here it is!" said the Guardian in a relieved voice.

With a rather cold handshake, Haddie said good-bye to her attendant and marched into the building. Then it was Ben's turn.

"Benjamin Jeremiah Walker, sir," said Ben politely with a broad smile.

The Guardian found his name immediately and waved him into the building. Before entering, Ben turned and hugged his attendant.

"Thanks Mia; you've been great." Then he turned to Puddles. "There's nothing to be scared about. I'll be waiting for you when you get there."

Puddles gave him a brave nod.

"You too," he said, flashing a toothy grin at Lucy. "I'll need you to protect me from the little general." He nodded in the direction where Haddie had just disappeared.

"See you on the other side," said Lucy, feeling relieved that she would know someone when she got wherever it was she was going.

Giving a wave to the crowd, Ben turned and disappeared into the building.

Lucy was sure Puddles was going to faint, but to her surprise he walked right up to the Guardian and held out his hand.

"Peter Smith James…sir," said Puddles with a slightly shaky voice.

"Very nice to meet you, Peter" said the Guardian shaking his hand. "By any chance would you be listed under *Puddles*?" A twitter went up in the crowd but the Guardian silenced it at once with a stern look.

"Yes, sir," Puddles said, his voice sounding less brave.

"Fine," said the Guardian checking off his name. "You may enter…oh, and by the way…" he leaned in so only Puddles and Lucy could hear, "they call me Twinkie."

Puddles smiled and thanked the Guardian. Waving good-bye to Lucy, he followed after Ben.

Lucy took a deep breath and looked at Truman. It was her turn. Suddenly it felt like her legs had turned to lead.

"Go on," said Truman. "Twinkie is waiting." He gave her a wink.

Stepping up to the Guardian, Lucy gave him a small nod. "Hello," she said trying to keep her voice from shaking. "My name is Lucille Margaret O'Sullivan, but you'll probably find it under Lucy."

The Guardian had barely glanced at the page before finding her name.

"Welcome, Lucy," he said. "Just step inside; you'll be given instructions on what to do next."

"Thank you," said Lucy, feeling her legs go from lead to jelly. She turned to say good-bye to Truman but the words wouldn't come out.

"I know," he said, giving her a warm embrace. "But as Samuel said, we will see each other soon."

Lucy nodded, feeling the tears building in her eyes. Wiping them away, she turned and walked through the doorway.

Inside, Lucy was surprised to find the large circular room was empty except for a woman in a red robe standing next to a large, vibrating column of light in the middle of the room. Looking around for some sort of sign that would tell her what to do, Lucy nervously approached the woman.

"Welcome to the Drookshire Portal," said the woman in a monotone voice without looking at Lucy. "Simply step into the light and it will transport you to Drookshire Station. It will *not* be painful, and you *cannot* get lost. However for your comfort during transport, we suggest you keep your arms to your sides. Please step forward and have a nice day." The woman continued to stare straight ahead.

Lucy was tempted to wave a hand in front of the woman's face to see if she was real, but decided she shouldn't risk it.

"Uh, thanks," she said to the woman. As she expected, the woman gave no sign of hearing her. Lucy looked at the vibrating column in front of her. It looked a lot like the curtain of mist that she had stepped through to enter the Land of Dreams - an experience she was not anxious to repeat. Behind her she could hear the footsteps of the next person entering the room. Realizing there was no turning back Lucy took a deep breath, closed her eyes, bit her lip and stepped into the light.

Immediately her body was slammed with the familiar wall of cold air. However, instead of toppling her over like before, the wind encased her in a cool, vibrating cocoon that whisked her along a narrow tunnel.

Before she had time to be scared, Lucy felt her feet hit solid ground and a warm blast of air shot over her. Ready or not, Lucy had arrived at Drookshire Station.

CHAPTER FIVE

BATTLESHIP HADDIE

"Come along! Come along!" A sharp voice cut through the air.

Opening her eyes Lucy found herself standing under a tall, glowing archway that led into a small, brightly lit room. She glanced around and saw a dozen more arches each billowing with a luminescent green mist that cast an eerie pall over the figures appearing inside them.

A little man in a sapphire blue robe was hustling about herding people out of the arches and into the next room. He was rail thin, with a horseshoe of sandy hair circling his head and a long goatee that brought his face to a point.

"Don't delay, people! Quickly now…make room for the others," he said, waving them towards the doorway.

Sure enough, as he spoke more people began popping into the archways amid puffs of green smoke. Lucy stepped out of the way just in time to avoid the gingham clad grandma who had tried to escape back in the Village.

"Oh my!" exclaimed the woman, stepping out of the mist.

Lucy quickly helped the old woman out of the archway before she could get knocked over by the next arrival. "It looks like everyone's headed in there," she said, noticing the frightened look on the old woman's face.

Following the flow of people, Lucy and the old woman entered the enormous meeting hall. Gasps and exclamations of surprise could be heard as people stopped to take in the scene. Lucy craned her neck as her eyes scanned the towering glass walls that climbed skywards until they reached the pinnacle where they were capped by an immense crystal dome. Across the room a giant bay window looked out over the western horizon giving Lucy a panoramic view of the Drookshire grounds. The sun had just begun to slip behind the jagged purple mountains bordering the station to the west and as the last rays skimmed the peak they painted the sky the most spectacular array of colors Lucy had ever seen.

"Far out," said the young man in the Hawaiian shirt.

"Yes, yes. 'Far out' indeed," said the little man in the blue robe as he pushed them forward. "I assure you there will be many more sunsets to admire, but now we have business to attend to, so if you please…" He pointed them towards a set of golden bleachers which faced a raised platform resting against the bay window. Not wanting to cause trouble, Lucy quickly took a seat on the bottom row.

"Pssst! Lucy!" A small voice was quietly calling out to her from above. Lucy's heart leapt as she turned to find Puddles shyly waiving to her from the top row. Seated next to him, flailing both arms in the air, was Ben.

"COME ON UP!" Ben called out, not seeming to care if everyone heard him. "WE'VE SAVED YOU A SPOT!"

The rows behind her were already filled and Lucy couldn't see any easy way of climbing to the top without stepping on people.

"It's quite alright, dear," said an elderly woman in the row above her. "We don't mind if you step through, do we my love?"

"Oh no, not at all," said the old man who was holding her hand. He smiled at Lucy and scooted to the side. "Please, step on through."

The people in the next several rows also happily volunteered to let her through, but on the row just below Ben and Puddles Lucy came to a halt.

"I suppose you are intending to cut in line…*again*," said Haddie sharply. Folding her arms tightly across her chest, she gave Lucy a cold stare.

"Well technically this isn't a line," said Lucy, trying her best to remain polite. "But if you don't mind, I would like to sit with my friends." Lucy tried not to blink as the miniature general stared her down.

"Oh, very well," said Haddie, sliding the tiniest bit to the side. "Go on. But be quick or we're likely all to get in trouble for your scooting about."

Lucy mumbled a thank you and quickly sat down between Ben and Puddles. Without thinking about what she was doing she gave each of them a hug. Ben hugged her back, but Puddles sat quite stiffly, turning several shades of pink.

"Isn't this place amazing?" said Ben, looking up at the enormous crystal dome above their heads. Lucy thought he looked like a kid on Christmas morning.

"Yeah, it's pretty amazing alright," said Lucy, a little less enthusiastically.

Puddles didn't say a word. His eyes were wide and his hands were clenched so tightly that his fingers were turning white.

"Don't worry," Lucy whispered in his ear, "Battleship Haddie will protect us."

The corner of Puddles' mouth twitched up and Lucy noticed a bit of color creep back into his cheeks.

A deliberate loud cough came from below and Lucy looked down to see the man in the blue robe on the platform standing as tall as his small frame would allow. The murmuring that filled the hall immediately stopped and the room fell silent.

"Now that we are all here…" he said eyeing the last few people scurrying to their seats, "…please allow me to introduce myself. I am Tobias, Station Master of

Drookshire." He gave a slight bow of his head. Lucy looked around at the others, not sure whether or not she was supposed to applaud. A loud dog whistle followed by wild applause came from the young man in the Hawaiian shirt, while a few others offered a trickle of clapping.

Tobias continued, undiscouraged by the crowd's mixed response. "Let me be the first to welcome you to your new home."

Lucy felt an icy chill run through her. As spectacular as this place was, it wasn't home.

"While you are here," said Tobias, "I want you to feel comfortable in exploring the Station and its grounds; however, until you have completed your training, there are two restrictions you must obey. First: no Grade One Attendant in Training may leave the grounds without the supervision of a senior attendant. Grade Ones – or GOAT's as you may be referred to for the sake of expediency – are never to venture beyond the boundaries of the river on the north and west, the gardens to the east or the library to the south."

He paused, staring gravely at the crowd to ensure they understood the gravity of his words. When no one questioned this rule he continued, "Secondly: the Dream Chamber in the North Tower is off limits to all attendants who have not yet earned their division sash. We will not speak of the severe consequences that would befall anyone breaking these rules as I am certain that no one in this room would be so foolish."

Lucy looked around the room and could tell by the wide-eyed looks that no one took this warning lightly.

"In the beginning you will follow a strict schedule of training. The skills you learn will be critical in your practical applications, so I suggest that you concentrate fully on your studies. After a period of one earthly year your aptitude will be evaluated and if you are found worthy you will begin your apprenticeship in one of the three celestial divisions on the Day of Declaration, or D Day as it is more commonly known." Tobias paused, letting his eyes scan the crowd.

"I hope you understand what a great honor you have been given. To be chosen as an attendant of the Kingdom is a privilege not to be taken lightly. Whether you go on to serve as a Messenger, a Guide or a Guardian, you have the opportunity to make a profound impact on the future of the Kingdom and direct the destiny of mankind. With your position comes great respect...and even greater responsibility."

A squeak of panic slipped from Puddles. Lucy would have squeaked too but Tobias's speech left her frozen, unable to make any sound at all. This was a horrible mistake. She couldn't possibly be expected to influence mankind...she couldn't even influence her mother to let her go to the mall by herself.

Tobias twisted the tip of his goatee, lowering his voice to barely above a whisper. "I feel it is my duty to warn you that the Great Books have predicted grave times ahead. It will require the dedication of every attendant in the Kingdom if we are to once again triumph over the dark forces which are foretold for the days to come."

Dark forces? The uneasy feeling churning inside Lucy threatened to explode. All around her people were exchanging worried looks. Obviously this news came as a surprise to them as well.

"Excuse me..."

The sound of Ben's voice made Lucy jump. He was standing up, waving his hand high in the air.

"*What are you doing?*" whispered Lucy under her breath.

"Yes," said Tobias, looking rather chafed by the interruption. "May I help you?"

"Thank you…my name is Ben…"

"Yes, I know," said Tobias, with an air that suggested it would be absurd for him not to know every new attendant's name.

"Well, I was just wondering…," continued Ben ignoring Tobias's look of annoyance, "Mia…she was my escort…she told me about some prophecy that claimed someone is going to show up to fight whatever's coming…is that true?"

Lucy stared at Ben in amazement. While she and Truman had been busy sipping tea and chatting about mango muffins, apparently Mia and Ben had been discussing more important things.

Tobias's face tightened making it look even smaller. He seemed to be weighing his words very carefully before speaking.

"It is true that there are some who choose to believe that a mysterious *protector* is going to ride in and save the day." He gave a small snort of disdain. "If others wish to place their faith in this so-called celestial warrior then that is their prerogative. However, it is my belief that it would be foolhardy to depend on the help of someone who may – *or may not* – exist; therefore, since the responsibility of your training rests on my shoulders, we will prepare ourselves fully to be called upon when the moment comes." His look made it clear the subject was closed.

"He's a real bottle of sunshine," muttered Ben under his breath as he took his seat.

"Now, if there are no further questions…" Tobias stared down the silent students. Ben began to stand up again, but Lucy pulled him back down.

"I don't think now is a good time."

"Very well then. As I was saying, there are dark times ahead…"

"Now Tobias, let's not scare them off on their first day."

"Samuel!" The word slipped out before Lucy could clap her hands over her mouth. She felt her face burn red as all eyes turned her way.

"Well, I must say...what an unexpected surprise," exclaimed Tobias, not looking altogether pleased by Samuel's unanticipated arrival. "To what do we owe this honor?"

"Oh, just passing by," said Samuel, climbing the steps to join Tobias on the platform. He turned to survey the group of wide-eyed newcomers who had finally torn their eyes away from Lucy to gawk at this impressive new visitor. Lucy couldn't help but notice that standing tall in his magnificent golden robes, Samuel's presence made Tobias seem even smaller than before.

"Hello, everyone! My name is Samuel, as you have just heard." He winked up at Lucy and her face burned hotter. "I am the Keeper of the Book of Destiny. I trust that you are all totally befuddled by what you have heard so far?"

A twitter of laughter scattered through the bleachers.

"Ah, good. Then you are perfectly normal." Samuel's face broke into a warm smile that managed to breathe life back into the crowd. Lucy felt the boulder in her stomach growing smaller. With Samuel here she somehow felt safer.

"I have just stopped by to welcome you all and assure you that you are all in for a great adventure." There was a twinkle in his eye as he spoke. "But please, don't let me interrupt the festivities. Tobias, I believe you were about to introduce our esteemed Cottage Masters?"

Samuel gave Tobias a look that suggested Tobias had no choice but to proceed with introductions.

"I suppose I could finish my welcome speech at another time..."

"Something we all look forward to," said Samuel, slapping Tobias on the back and making him stumble forward.

Puddles gave a small laugh; even he seemed to relax in Samuel's presence. Without another word Samuel gave a wave of his hand and instantly the lights inside the Meeting Hall dimmed; only the platform remained bathed in light. When Lucy's eyes adjusted to the darkened room she discovered Samuel was gone.

Outside the sun had finally dropped behind the mountains leaving behind a velvety blackness. Looking through the dome overhead, Lucy noticed that the clouds had parted to reveal a sky full of shimmering silver stars. Back on the mountain she used to marvel at how close the stars appeared, but gazing up at the carpet of glistening lights hanging just above the Station she swore that they must be sitting at the very edge of the solar system.

Suddenly everyone jumped and Puddles let out a yelp. A loud BANG had erupted from the back of the hall as two magnificent golden doors swung open and a line of attendants filed into the room smiling and waving at the crowd as they made their way to the platform. The first to climb the steps was a tall, dark man dressed in a sapphire robe. He was followed by a skinny young man with tan skin and dark hair wearing a robe the color of rubies. Next in line were two men both dressed in green; one was pudgy with a gray ponytail, the other a tiny man with shocking orange hair. Bringing up the end of the line was a beautiful woman with long black hair that nearly touched the hem of the red robe that draped gracefully over her willowy figure. They formed a line to the left of Tobias, and waited to be introduced.

Tobias stepped forward, clearing his throat. "These honorable attendants," he announced solemnly, "are your Cottage Masters. During your first year of training you will live in one of our five cottages. It is the responsibility of your Cottage Master to guide you through your training. These are wise and knowledgeable individuals, and it would do you well to listen closely to their counsel. I assure you, their experience will prove invaluable in your training."

"Careful there, Tobias," boomed the deep voice of the first attendant. His throaty laugh rolled through the room. "That's a mighty lofty pedestal you've just put us on. How 'bout we lower that down some?"

The tall man with ebony skin stepped forward dwarfing Tobias. His bald head glowed under the spotlight. "Welcome!" His voice echoed off the walls. "I am Banks, Master of the Cottage on the Hill. This handsome young fellow to my left is Sri; he oversees the Island Cottage."

Sri gave a polite nod.

"Continuing down the row we have two fine fellows: Fortegue and Finnigan. Master Fortegue heads the Forest Cottage while Master Finnigan keeps watch over the Garden Cottage."

Fortegue held up both hands and waved heartily to the crowd while Finnigan did a little jig ending with a deep bow that nearly touched his orange hair to the ground.

As the applause died down Banks cleared his throat to introduce the final Cottage Master but she quickly held up her hand.

"I believe I can handle this on my own," said the tall, willowy woman stepping forward. The chill in her voice matched her cool appearance and Lucy instantly hoped she did not end up in her cottage. Banks, however, did not appear insulted by the interruption and graciously stepped back to allow her to take center stage.

"I am Salina, Head Mistress of the Mayanian Cottage," she said importantly and Lucy had the feeling she was waiting for gasps of awe. When the room remained silent she continued, "As our illustrious Station Master mentioned, it is our responsibility to guide you…and your responsibility to be guided. If we each do our part this will be a productive, and peaceful, year."

Lucy glanced down and noticed Haddie was sitting with her arms crossed eyeing the Cottage Masters with a look of uncertainty, apparently trying to determine if they were as worthy as Tobias claimed.

"Thank you, Salina. You were inspiring as always," said Banks, reclaiming the spotlight. As Salina gracefully swept back into line, Banks continued in a rich, deep voice that reminded Lucy of rolling thunder, "In a moment I will ask each of my fellow Cottage Masters to read off a list of names. As your name is called, please step forward and join your group. Once everyone has been divided into cottages your Cottage Master will give you more information. Are we all ready then?" He clapped his hands together with a look of gleeful anticipation.

People squirmed in their seats and Lucy felt the boulder in her stomach begin to grow again.

Banks turned to the slender young man beside him who looked to be no more than seventeen. "Sri, let's not keep them waiting any longer. Who are the lucky new residents of the Island Cottage?"

The young man stepped forward and unrolled a silver scroll before calling out, "Chen Li!"

An elderly Chinese man in the second row jumped at the sound of his name. He quickly regained his composure and made his way to the floor as applause broke out. Before the clapping had died, "Maude Silverstein!" was called to the floor.

And so it went. After all the names were read from a list, the Cottage Master would lead their group off to a far corner of the room and the next Cottage Master would step forward. Lucy anxiously watched the bleachers empty as one by one the people around her were called forward. When Salina stepped forward Lucy felt her heart begin to pound. *Anyone but her*, she thought as Salina began to read off names. After nine names had been called, and nine frightened looking people had slowly descended to the stage, Salina announced in a voice that sounded as though she was making a proclamation, "And now for the final member of our family..."

Without thinking Lucy reached out and grabbed Ben and Puddles' hands and squeezed tightly. Holding her breath, she closed her eyes and waited for the last name to be called.

"R.J. Carter!"

Lucy exhaled as a wave of relief washed over her. "Thank you," she whispered, looking up at the black sky overhead.

"Uh, you can let go now," said Ben.

"Huh?" Lucy looked down and was horrified to see she was still clinging to his hand. Quickly letting go, she felt her face flush as she said, "Sorry; I didn't mean to...it was just..."

"It's okay," said Puddles shaking his hand. "I didn't like her much either."

Banks was smiling up at the handful of people left in the stands. "Well I guess that means you're mine! Come on down and let's find out who we've got."

Nudging Puddles along, Lucy and Ben followed him down the steps and joined the others who were gathering on the floor. Suddenly Lucy stopped dead in her tracks. In the excitement of realizing she hadn't been separated from her new friends, she hadn't noticed who else was left sitting in the bleachers. There, standing in front of her looking quite cross about being last to be chosen, was Haddie.

"Great," muttered Ben as though he had read Lucy's mind, "looks like we've got the General on our side."

Lucy managed a weak smile, immensely thankful that at least she wouldn't have to put up with Haddie by herself.

Once they were all gathered on the floor, the group nervously glanced around the circle at each other. It was a rather odd mixture of people; besides herself, Ben and Puddles, there was the old couple who had kindly let her through the bleachers, the young man in the Hawaiian shirt, a lovely woman with dark eyes and sandy hair and a small middle-Eastern looking man with a thin black mustache. And, of course, there was Haddie.

"No need to be shy," said Banks descending from the platform to join them on the floor. "I can assure you that before your training is over the people standing next to you will seem no stranger to you than your own family."

"That's not saying much," whispered Puddles. "He's never met my family."

Lucy caught Ben's eye and both dropped their heads to keep from laughing.

"Now, who wants to start the introductions?" said Banks, glancing around the circle.

"I will!" declared Ben and Haddie in unison.

Banks looked from Ben to Haddie as their eyes locked. "Well, well," he said, a touch of amusement in his voice. "It looks like we have two willing volunteers and I'm fresh out of coins to toss."

"It's okay," said Ben, breaking away from Haddie's glare. "She can go first."

Lucy stared at him in disbelief.

"Wonderful!" exclaimed Banks. "Let's start with the basics: name, where you lived on earth, how old you were when you left and how you died."

Haddie stepped forward into the center of the circle and looked smugly around at the others who were sizing up this tiny girl with the air of royalty. Standing unnaturally erect to get the most out of her miniature frame, she gave a falsely sweet smile and cleared her throat. "I am Hayden Louise Whitney, but you may call me Haddie." She paused as if waiting for applause. The group remained silent so she continued. "The Whitney family has resided in London for over six centuries. As my grandfather, Captain Whitney of the Royal Navy, always said, 'If it is good enough for the Queen, then it is good enough for the Whitney's.'"

Lucy's feelings for Haddie were quickly turning from annoyance to dislike and from the looks of the others around the circle, she wasn't the only one. Banks alone seemed unfazed by Haddie's superior attitude.

"Please continue," he said politely.

"I was eleven when, much to everyone's surprise, I died quite unexpectedly from a pesky tumor which had fixed itself in my head. It was a terrible shock for mummy and daddy. I suppose they'll never get over it."

"Undoubtedly tragic," Banks agreed, but Lucy noticed he didn't seem too concerned.

Looking proud to be the center of such a tragedy, Haddie stepped back in line next to Ben giving him a victorious look.

"I believe you are next," said Banks, nodding towards Ben.

"Thanks." Ben straightened up and flashed a smile that made Lucy smile in return. "Hi everyone, I'm Ben. I live...I mean I *used* to live in Washington D.C. and I am...I mean I *was* 16."

"And how did you die?" asked Banks as calmly as if he had just asked Ben his favorite color.

"I was shot," said Ben matter-of-factly. Lucy felt her jaw drop. She hadn't thought to ask him how he had died, but she never would have expected this. Why would anyone shoot Ben? She tried to catch his eye, but he seemed to be deliberately avoiding her gaze.

"Interesting…" said Banks rubbing his chin in a way that made Lucy think he found this information quite important. He thanked Ben who stepped back into the circle looking relieved to be done.

Next in line was the old woman. She smiled sweetly and took her husband's arm guiding him into the circle with her. "Hello everyone, my name is Anna and this is my husband Arthur."

"Greetings!" said Arthur, waving at the group.

"We lived in Salisbury, England, for such a wonderfully long time. Then, several years ago when I was about 70, my heart gave out bringing me to this lovely place. I've been waiting for Arthur ever since."

"That's my girl," said Arthur, giving Anna's hand a loving pat. "I always knew she would be here waiting for me….my own personal angel. When my old body finally gave up at 81 I wasn't a bit surprised to see her standing by my bedside ready to bring me here."

Looking at Anna and Arthur standing together made Lucy think about her mom and dad. She wondered if her father was waiting somewhere for his wife to join him.

As Arthur leaned over and gave his wife a kiss on the cheek, the young woman with deep brown eyes gave a whistle. Her skin was tan and she had the look of someone who had spent their life outdoors.

"G'day!" she said loudly, giving a nod to the group. "The name's Sandy. I'm happy to say I lived 76 marvelous years – most of them in the outback of Australia. It was a lousy joey…that would be a kangaroo to you folks…that got me."

Lucy stared at the young woman in disbelief. "Excuse me; did you say you were 76?"

"You bet your mama's bloomers! And I would have lasted a lot longer if it wasn't for that rotten creature jumping out right in front of my jeep."

Sandy continued to expound on her untimely death, but Lucy wasn't listening. The woman standing in front of her couldn't be more than 35.

"Lucy, is something bothering you," asked Banks.

Sandy, who was in the midst of demonstrating how she had been thrown from her jeep, stopped in mid-sentence looking a bit annoyed for being interrupted right before the climatic ending.

"It's just…I don't get it," said Lucy. "How can she be 76? She's beautiful!"

"I like her," said Sandy, elbowing Puddles in the stomach causing him to grunt.

"I probably should have covered a few of the basic rules of the Kingdom before we began," said Banks. "You might have noticed that an unusual number of the Kingdom's residents appear quite young…"

Lucy looked around the group. It was true; other than Anna and Arthur, almost everyone she had met seemed remarkably young and in good health.

"The reason is simple," said Banks, straightening up to show his own strong physique. "When you leave your body back on earth you will appear as you remember yourself at your best. For some that means wrinkles and gray hair…or no hair at all." He smiled at Arthur who laughed and rubbed his bald head. "But for most of us, we liked the way we looked when we were young and full of energy, so that's the self we show. What's important to remember is that the body is just a shell we use to recognize each other – kind of like a costume; it's not the real you. The real you is ageless."

Puddles was busy feeling his face. "How old do I look to you?" he whispered to Lucy.

"I don't know…maybe thirteen?" Lucy's voice squeaked as she lied. In truth Puddles didn't look much older than ten.

[81]

"Yes!" Puddles said a little louder than he intended. His face flushed red as Haddie shot him a withering look.

"Guess it's my turn to give the ol' bio," said the young man in the Hawaiian shirt as he brushed his long blond hair out of his eyes.

"The name my dear ol' dad gave me is Timothy Isaac Bitterman the Second."

Ben choked back a laugh.

"Like, I know, *way* too dark suit for me, that's why everyone calls me Tibs. I hung in the most righteous spot on the planet – Malibu! The Big Guy called my number when I was a mere 45. Health food did me in."

"Health food, my dear?" exclaimed Anna, clutching her chest.

"Totally….I choked on tofu." Tibs wrapped his hands around his throat in a dramatic reenactment.

As the introductions continued around the circle, Banks wandered behind the group, stopping now and then to glare into the back of someone's head as if reading their thoughts. Next in line was the small man with olive skin.

"Good evening," he said with a slight bow, "I am Babu."

"Hey Boo Boo!" Tibs crooned in his best Yogi Bear voice. "How's it shakin' little buddy?"

"It is *Baaa Bu*, not *Boo Boo*, and I am, as you say, *shakin'* quite well, thank you."

Lucy tried to hold in her laugh, but ended up snorting instead. Ben pretended not to notice, but Lucy could see his sides trembling.

"Sorry…I had a tickle in my throat," she said, feeling her face turn hot.

Babu gave her a polite nod and continued. "Before coming here I lived with my family in a small village in Pakistan."

"Is that where you died?" asked Banks. He was standing behind Puddles who gave a jump at the sound of his voice.

"No, I am sorry to say I was far from my homeland when I died. I was run over by a taxi while visiting my cousin in Chicago."

"Dude! I love Chicago!" Tibs slapped Babu on the back sending him lurching forward. "My buds and I did this cross country thing where we just got in the car and ...like...drove...and when we hit the big Chi town we thought....cool, this is totally awesome! Man, they have like the best pizza on the entire planet. I bet even those Italian dudes couldn't make a pie like that."

Puddles was still staring at Tibs with his mouth hanging open when Banks whispered in his ear, "I think that brings us to you."

Puddles took a small step forward. Slowly he lifted his eyes and looked around the circle. Anna was smiling sweetly at him, giving him an encouraging nod. Sandy gave him a wink and Tibs enthusiastically held two thumbs up.

"Hi," he said in a small voice, "I'm Puddles...well, actually my name's Peter but no one calls me that. I lived in Toronto with my dad and sister until I was twelve. That's when I...well, you know."

"And how exactly did 'you know' happen?" asked Banks.

"I was swimming and I...well, I guess I hit my head on the wall of the pool. I must have passed out and drowned. Pretty stupid, I know."

"Stupid? I was killed by a bloody hopper! Doesn't get much more stupid than that," said Sandy.

Puddles smiled and stepped back. By the relieved look on his face Lucy could tell he felt much better.

"Looks like that leaves you." Banks smiled at Lucy and she felt her heart jump into her throat.

Was it her imagination or had the entire room become extremely quiet? Nervously stepping forward, Lucy looked around at the eyes all focused on her. She hated being in the spotlight. Back home Digby had always gladly been the center of attention, letting her remain comfortably unnoticed. Suddenly Lucy missed her brother more than she ever thought possible.

"What is your name, dear?" asked Arthur.

"Lucy…Lucy O'Sullivan."

"And where did you live?" prompted Anna.

"Colorado." Lucy could feel her face turning the color of her hair. Why were the words sticking in her throat? Out of the corner of her eye she saw Haddie impatiently tapping her foot. *Oh come on,* she told herself. *Just open your mouth and speak!*

"I…I was fourteen when I was killed by…"

Precisely as the words spilled out of her mouth, the blast of a trumpet filled the air drowning out all other sounds. Forgetting about Lucy, everyone turned to see what was happening.

Thankful to no longer be the focus of attention, Lucy quietly slipped back out of the circle.

"It appears that your surprise is ready," said Banks, stepping into the middle of the group, "but before they open the doors and I completely lose your attention, let me say *well done everyone!*" Banks heartedly applauded causing his robes to billow around him. "I dare say you might be my best group yet."

A wide grin lit up Puddles' face. Lucy had a feeling Banks probably said this to every new group, but she didn't say anything; it was nice to see Puddles happy.

Just as Banks had predicted, the giant golden doors swung open and suddenly sharp screams of delight pierced the air. A group of robed individuals had entered the room and her new cottagemates, along with everyone else in the room, scattered towards the crowd.

"Grandma Tess!" Ben ran over to an elderly woman with short curly gray hair and a smile identical to his own.

Anna and Austin were taking turns hugging a young man and woman dressed in red robes, and Babu was excitedly shaking the hand of a man in a green robe who looked to be his twin. Lucy stood alone watching as everyone greeted friends and relatives who had come to see them.

"Hello, Lucy," said a familiar voice by Lucy's side.

Tears sprang to her eyes as Lucy turned to face Samuel. "I'm so glad you're here," she said swallowing down the lump in her throat. "There's been some mistake." But before Lucy could tell Samuel how she didn't belong in this place he interrupted her.

"That can wait," he said. "I believe your guests have arrived." He looked over her shoulder and nodded.

Lucy turned and immediately her heart gave a jump. Truman and Harrison were enthusiastically waving from across the room.

"SURPRISE!" they shouted together.

Lucy ran over and wrapped her arms around them both. "Thank you!"

Harrison laughed as he pried himself out of Lucy's arms. "What are you thanking us for? We wouldn't have missed this for the world."

"He means it," said Truman. "I planned on coming by myself, but this party crasher wouldn't hear of it."

"I think what I said was 'Just try to ditch me old man!'"

Lucy spent the rest of the evening introducing Harrison, Truman and Samuel to her friends and their guests. Everyone seemed to know Samuel and they all appeared quite impressed that he had come to see Lucy. Her favorite moment of the evening came when Haddie pushed her way through the crowd to speak with Samuel. She was accompanied by a tall, stern looking woman whose blue robe matched the color of her hair.

"Excuse me, sir," said Haddie, cutting into the conversation between Samuel and Puddles' uncle, "I would like to introduce my Great Grandmother."

"Isadora! Nice to see you again." Samuel took the old lady's hand and gave a slight bow.

Haddie looked smugly at Lucy and Puddles and Lucy wondered if Tobias had a rule against pushing someone off the North Tower.

"Keeping an eye on Tobias?" asked Isadora Whitney in a tone that mimicked Haddie's.

Samuel laughed. "An impossible task I'm afraid. No, tonight I am here to congratulate a friend. Please, let me introduce you." Samuel took Lucy by the hand and pulled her forward. "Isadora, I would like you to meet Miss Lucy O'Sullivan."

Lucy hardly noticed what the elder Mrs. Whitney said, she was too busy watching the horrified look on Haddie's face.

Exhausted by the day's events, Lucy was glad when Tobias finally announced that it was time to retire to their cottages. Banks led his group out of the Meeting Hall in to the lobby of Drookshire Station. Like the room they had just left, the entrance hall was immense with towering transparent walls that gave a panoramic view of the world outside.

"Amazing," said Ben as he gazed in awe at the stars hanging just above the glass ceiling.

"I agree," said Banks. "Unfortunately nighttime passes quickly here so we need to get you to your rooms. Tomorrow will be very busy and you need your rest."

"Why do we need sleep?" asked Puddles yawning widely.

"Good point!" said Sandy. "What's the good of gettin' rid of your ol' body if you still gotta sleep?"

"Have patience," said Banks, as he led the group through the crowded foyer. "Eventually sleep won't be so important, but you need to give yourself time to adjust. You might not have the same body you had down on earth, but you still need to keep your energy up."

He guided the group to a massive pillar that stood in the middle of the entrance hall. Around the column were five glistening archways similar to the ones they had used to enter Drookshire Station and each was filled with the same glowing mist. Lucy saw that above each arch was pinned a golden plaque engraved with the name of a cottage.

As Bank led them around the pillar, Lucy read out loud the signs, "Garden Cottage...Island Cottage...Forest Cottage...Mayanian Cottage." Finally they stopped in front of the arch that read *Hill Cottage*. Her new cottagemates nervously lined up in front of the opening that was pouring out a lime-green fog, but Lucy's attention was drawn to the right of their arch where a waterfall ran down the column into a large round reflecting pool. The splash of the water mixed with the conversation filling the lobby to form a soothing buzz that caused Lucy to suddenly feel very sleepy. As she stood hypnotized by the water circling the pool she barely took notice of the others who were disappearing one by one through the misty archways.

"Yo, Lucy, are you coming?" Ben was standing in line with Tibs and Puddles. The others were already gone.

"Sorry," said Lucy, brushing a long red curl out of her face and joining Ben in line. "Banks was right; I think I need some sleep."

Puddles was standing in front of the archway. His knees were shaking under his holey shorts and his face was ghostly white.

"Go on little dude," said Tibs, putting a hand on his shoulder. "Gotta go with the flow."

Puddles looked back at Ben who gave him a reassuring nod. Drawing a deep breath, he scrunched close his eyes and stepped forward into the mist. Immediately he disappeared.

"Alright!" exclaimed Tibs, giving Lucy and Ben two thumbs up. "Catch yeh later!" And with a giant leap he was gone leaving Ben and Lucy alone in the cavernous entrance hall.

"Flip you for it," joked Ben.

"I'll go," said Lucy. Although the thought of making another topsy-turvy journey through the mist didn't thrill her, worse was the idea of being left alone in this strange new place. Holding her hands over her eyes, she bit her lip and stepped forward into the mist. To her relief there was no wind, no tumbling about, no sense of moving at all. As a matter of fact no sooner had she stepped forward than she felt her foot land on solid ground.

The delicious scent of hot chocolate spilled over her as she opened her eyes and found herself standing in a cozy lodge filled with overstuffed furniture and an array of odd looking objects. In the corner by a stone fireplace that was crackling with a warm blaze stood a tall parrot lamp that bathed the room in a golden light.

"ARGH!" Lucy stumbled to the floor. In her shock at arriving at the cottage, she had forgotten to step out of the archway before Ben appeared.

"I'll tell Puddles the score is even," he laughed as he helped Lucy up off the floor.

"Good, we're all here," said Banks, counting heads as Lucy and Ben joined the others who were gathered in front of the fire.

"This will be your home while you are in training. I trust you will find it very comfortable." Haddie gave a small huff. She was looking at the room as if it contained a foul odor.

"We will meet in this room again before heading to breakfast. And now, if there aren't any questions, I will show you to your rooms."

"Oh my goodness!" said Anna, pointing at a cluster of small crystal tables. "I do believe I just saw someone's face in that table!"

"Ah yes," said Banks, stepping up to the glowing pedestals. "Our occuscopes…each cottage has a set. Since new attendants aren't allowed to leave the station grounds we felt you would enjoy being able to keep up with what was happening in the outside world. Each scope is focused on a different area of the Kingdom. See that one there?" He pointed to the table in the middle. "That one is fixed on the Village."

Lucy peered over Puddles' shoulder. On the glassy top of the small round table she saw the familiar shops and cobbled streets of the Village. It was nighttime in the small town and the streets appeared deserted, however Lucy thought she saw a tiny figure sipping a drink in the café.

"This one here shows the Field of Awakening and that little one is focused on the zoo," said Banks, pointing to a screen that was almost pitch black. In the moonless night all that was visible in the zoo were a few large shadowy figures wandering slowly across the screen.

Lucy was beginning to feel very tired and was glad when Banks finally insisted they get some rest. Each of them had their own room off the main lodge, except for Anna and Arthur who shared a room. Lucy's room was at the end of the hall. It was rather small but very comfortable with a tall window looking out over the mountains. In the middle of the room stood a high, four poster bed with a squishy deep purple comforter. Feeling like she could sleep for an eternity, Lucy fell into bed and dropped off into a deep sleep.

A sharp wind slapped her face as Lucy stood on the edge of a lake straining to hear the cries for help whipping around her. "...get it away from me!...make the pain stop!...I didn't do it!...you're lying!...NO!...." The screams peppered the air, calling out to her then disappearing.

The lake was bubbling and churning in rhythm with the voices. Mesmerized by the swirling water, Lucy drew closer. Suddenly a burst of lightning cut through the air as a shriek erupted from the far side of the lake. Then everything went silent.

Lucy sat up in bed with a start, her heart beating frantically. It felt as though she had been asleep for only a few minutes but sunlight was pouring in through her window and the sky outside was bright blue. Lucy rubbed her eyes trying to remember her dream, but the voices were gone and the only sound was a loud tapping at her door. Climbing out of bed, Lucy scurried across the cold stone floor and opened the door.

"Morning!" chimed Ben and Puddles. They were standing in the doorway proudly displaying their new white robes.

"Nice dresses," smirked Lucy, as she rubbed the sleep from her eyes.

"Glad you like 'em. Yours is over there," said Ben, pointing to a folded white garment on top of Lucy's dresser. "Better hurry; the others are already in the lodge. Banks said we're leaving for breakfast in two minutes."

They said goodbye and hurried down the hall with Puddles' long robe dusting the floor behind him.

Lucy glanced across the room at the neatly folded robe on her dresser, trying to remember if it had been there last night. Suddenly she felt a tingle shoot up from her toes. This was it. As soon as she put on that robe, her new life would officially begin. Biting her lip, she took a deep breath and began to undress.

CHAPTER SIX

A VERY BAD DAY

The bleachers in the Meeting Hall had disappeared overnight and in their place stood five large round tables. Lucy noticed that several long wooden benches had also appeared along the edge of the room. The vacant benches faced the podium where Tobias was busying himself with paperwork.

Lucy and her new cottagemates followed Banks to the table on the far right which they found overflowing with an amazing assortment of pastries, omelets, crepes and other foods that Lucy didn't recognize. As they took their seats and began to fill their plates, a gong rang out and a group of Guardians filed into the hall. In deep discussion and seemingly unaware that there were dozens of eyes following them, the Guardians wandered over to the benches and sat down.

"I understand that the Guardians are highly respected throughout the Kingdom," said Babu in a reverent whisper. "It would be an honor to be chosen by such a distinguished group." Without taking his eyes off the row of Guardians, he stuffed a large cinnamon roll into his mouth.

"Nah, blue's not my color," Sandy said, wiping her mouth on the sleeve of her robe. "I kind of fancy those red dresses. Course anything'd be better than this ghastly white thing."

"I would hardly call that white," said Haddie as she glared at the jam stain smeared down Sandy's sleeve.

Conversations around the table bounced between discussing the food, which all agreed was the most amazing they had ever tasted, and general chatter about their previous lives. As Lucy listened to her new cottagemates calmly comparing stories of their untimely deaths and the welcoming parties waiting for them when they arrived, the sense that she didn't belong here grew. Even Puddles seemed to be settling in to this new life. He hadn't said a word since they left the cottage but there was a look of joy in his eyes as he shoveled an unending stream of food into his mouth.

Finally, after Puddles had cleared his plate for the fourth time and Tibs had begun entertaining the table by juggling strawberries, Banks stood up and cleared his throat. There was a sharp clink as Puddles' fork fell on to his plate followed by the thud of strawberries hitting the floor. The side of Banks' mouth twitched up in a smile as he reached into a bag and pulled out a number of tightly rolled scrolls.

"I have just one thought to share before you set off..." Banks' eyes carefully scanned the circle. "As Tobias mentioned last evening, the skills you learn here will prove very important in the days to come. This isn't school – this is training. You might argue they are the same but I assure you that the differences are great. I encourage each of you to give your instructors the attention they deserve."

Without further explanation Banks handed each of them two scrolls; one contained their training schedule, the other was a map of the Station. He then bid them good luck and quickly vanished, leaving them on their own to find their way around the massive grounds.

"Looks like most of our classes are in the CATS wing," said Ben, surveying his map closely.

"Cats?" said Puddles, staring at the crumpled map in his hands.

"Celestial Attendant Training Section. See..." Ben turned Puddles' map right side up and pointed to a long hallway cut in half by a circular staircase. "It's over there on the south side of the Station across from the Department of Guardian Services."

"Really!" said Haddie rolling her eyes. "You would think they could come up with something a bit more original."

Puddles glanced at Lucy but she just shrugged.

Haddie gave them an exasperated look. "Really people…the *Department of Guardian Services*…**D.O.G.S.** What will they think of next, a BIRD wing I suppose?"

According to their schedules, Rejuvenation Training was the first stop of the day but since it was to take place before breakfast they wouldn't have to worry about it until tomorrow. Next was Teleporting with Madame Mira, followed by Guide Techniques with Master Christof, Guardian Training with Colonel George and Messenger Rules and Regulations taught by Master Linus. After that was dinner and then Reflection in the South Tower with Madame Anaja.

Teleporting was held in the garden which was at the bottom of the hill just east of the Station. Lucy rolled her schedule and map together, shoved them into the white sash tied around her middle and headed outside with the others. As the group hurried down the grassy slope they were met by a wave of thick perfume wafting up from the tangled mixture of exotic vegetation stretching out in front of them. The chaotic overgrown garden was dotted with boulders the size of mini-vans and surrounding it all was an army of giant evergreens.

"Guess they're going for the natural look," said Ben with a laugh as he stepped over a large rhododendron that had taken over the path.

"OOPS! Sorry 'bout that." Lucy had pushed aside an oversized fern, smacking Puddles in the face.

"Ith alwight," choked Puddles, picking the leaf out of his mouth.

"Ladies and gentlemen…if you would please quickly gather round."

Madame Mira was standing in a small clearing in the middle of the garden. Other than the fact that she was wearing a long red robe, Lucy thought she looked amazingly like Glenda the Good Witch from the Wizard of Oz. Her crisp voice, however, made it clear that she was not to be disregarded as some fluffy fairy.

"This, as you know, is Beginning Teleportation," she said once they were all gathered in a circle. "Typically new attendants would be trained in the history of teleporting before being allowed to practice the actual art – a step in your training which I believe to be invaluable. However, against my personal recommendation, the Council has mandated that all new attendants begin immediate training in practical teleporting."

"What do you suppose that's about?" Ben whispered.

Lucy shrugged; whatever was going on – and she was becoming quite certain that there was definitely *something* going on - it sounded like Mira wasn't too happy about it.

"No use dilly dallying; we can't avoid what must be done. Everyone into groups of three…" Mira clapped her hands together sharply which everyone clearly understood meant *do it quickly*.

Without a word Lucy, Ben and Puddles quickly formed a group. Sandy, Tibs and Babu moved to the far end of the clearing, leaving Anna and Arthur stuck with Haddie. Lucy noticed she wasn't the only one feeling anxious about the lesson. Ben, who usually seemed so confident, was bouncing up and down on the balls of his feet and Puddles was nervously picking at his sleeve.

"Everyone ready?" said Professor Mira surveying the group.

The class nodded in unison.

"Good. Now, the key to teleporting is to forget the physical and *see* yourself where you want to be." Madame Mira closed her eyes, raised her arms, then in one graceful movement lowered them to her sides and promptly vanished.

"Oh my!" exclaimed Anna. "Where do you suppose she went?"

"I am right here," said Mira, stepping out from behind the trunk of a nearby oak tree to a round of applause.

"And now it is your turn."

Lucy felt her stomach flop and wished she hadn't had that extra helping of eggs at breakfast.

"You will line up in your groups with the teleporter in the middle and a spotter on either side."

Everyone scurried into place. To Lucy's great relief Ben volunteered to go first, moving to the middle spot with Lucy facing him and Puddles reluctantly covering his back.

"On the count of three the teleporter will raise their arms up, palms facing the sky, and silently repeat, 'Five feet forward'. Then you will slowly lower your arms and if all goes well by the time your hands touch your sides you will find yourself standing on the other side of the person you are now facing. If something happens to go awry, your partners will be there to catch you."

Puddles took a large step backwards.

"Remember! *Concentrate* on your goal and *see* yourself standing five feet in front of where you are now."

Ben closed his eyes and Lucy could see his lips repeating the steps.

"Everyone ready? One…two…"

"WHOA!"

All heads spun towards the voice coming from high up in the air. Lucy's mouth dropped open as she spied the gangly figure clutching the top branch of a tall evergreen.

Looking quite pleased with his accomplishment, Tibs waved to his cottagemates below.

"And that is why you must focus when teleporting," said Madame Mira, letting out a weary sigh. She held up her hands and Lucy wondered if she intended to try and catch Tibs as he fell from the sky. Instead, Mira disappeared and as the class looked around the clearing she reappeared on the branch next to Tibs. Lucy couldn't hear their conversation but moments later the two of them were safely on the ground and Tibs was hopping about pulling needles out of places they didn't belong.

"Let me repeat…" said Mira in a slow, deliberate voice that suggested her patience was ebbing, "…teleporting is a delicate art requiring concentration, imagination and a touch of finesse. Those with flighty thoughts will soon find themselves in precarious predicaments." She plucked a rather large twig from her hair.

"Yo, she so totally knows what she's talking about," said Tibs, grimacing as he yanked a long needle from his behind.

The rest of the lesson passed by uneventfully. With the exception of Tibs who appeared to have a natural knack for teleporting, no one managed to transport as much as an inch. Lucy was relieved when Mira, looking thoroughly exhausted, announced that class was over.

"Remember, you are not to attempt teleportation outside of this class," said Mira with a sweeping gaze of the class, her eyes resting on Tibs a second longer than the others. "I don't have time to be sent on wild goose chases after lost attendants!"

Lucy's spirits were dragging as they made their way back up the hill.

"I don't get it," she said, helping Puddles up after he tripped for the second time on his robes. "There's a lot of stuff I suck at but sports were always sort of my thing."

"Technically teleporting isn't a sport," said Ben very matter-of-factly. "It's more of a mental game."

"Ben's right," said Puddles, struggling to keep up as they reached the top of the hill. "That's gotta be why Tibs could do it. You have to admit, he's pretty mental."

As they reached the steps of the station Ben pulled his schedule from his waistband. "Guide Techniques is next," he said, surveying the paper.

Lucy felt her sash for her map and schedule. "Oh no…" She shook out her robes. "It's gone! I must have dropped it in the garden."

"You can share mine," said Puddles, holding out his crumpled scroll.

"Thanks, but I better get mine back. I doubt Banks would be too happy to find out I lost it on my first day."

"We'll wait for you," Ben said, as he eyed the other members of Hill Cottage entering the Station.

"Don't bother. There's no use all of us being late," said Lucy glumly. The day was quickly going from bad to worse.

Promising to save her a seat, Ben and Puddles headed off to join the others as Lucy turned and started back down the hill.

After scouring the garden with no success, Lucy gave up. Returning to the Station with a sense of despair hanging over her, Lucy scanned the deserted entry hall trying to remember where Ben had said Guide training was held. The halls of Drookshire Station snaked in every direction and it didn't take long before she was totally lost.

As she passed a familiar marble statue for the third time, Lucy slumped against the wall and let out a frustrated sigh.

"Got any ideas?" she asked, looking up into the angel's stone face.

As though answering her question, a trail of voices drifted towards her from the end of the hallway. Lucy's pulse quickened as she followed the sounds to a large silver door.

Not wanting to barge into the wrong room, Lucy put her ear to the door hoping to hear Ben or Puddles or even Haddie's annoying voice. The voices were louder now but they were toppling over one another making it impossible to clearly hear what anyone was saying. Lucy felt a sliver of hope. With all of the chaos, she might actually be able to sneak in without being heard. She reached for the door handle but as her fingers grasped the golden knob the door suddenly swung open and Lucy let out a yelp of surprise peppered with a few colorful words.

"Now that's a greeting you don't often hear around here," laughed Banks.

"I'm sorry…I didn't know…I…"

Banks held up his hand. "No apologies needed. I'm sure I gave you a bit of a scare."

"I was looking for Guide training," Lucy said, her voice still shaky. "When I heard voices I thought it might be in there."

"Voices?" Banks looked quizzically at Lucy. "I'm afraid your ears are playing tricks on you. I was quite alone in the Dream Chamber."

"The Dream Chamber?" Lucy's heart did a flip. Desperate to find her cottagemates, she had almost broken into the one room Tobias had declared off limits.

"Tell you what," said Banks, stepping into the hall and shutting the door behind him, "I don't have anywhere to be right now. Let's see if we can't get you to Master Christof before he realizes one of his flock has gone astray."

As Banks guided Lucy through the maze of hallways he pointed out different statues and tapestries that would help her find her way around the Station. Finally he stopped in front of a large portrait of a distinguished looking attendant in a billowing green robe hovering in mid-air over a man battling a lion.

"Just follow this hallway to the left," said Banks, pointing down a long corridor next to the portrait. "Fifth door on the right."

"Thanks," said Lucy, flashing Banks a sheepish smile. "You saved me."

"That's my job." Banks winked as though he had just shared a private joke with Lucy. Then with a sweep of his hand he disappeared.

Coming to the fifth door on the right, Lucy stopped and put her ear to the door. She didn't want to risk wandering into the wrong room again.

"*This is it*," she thought as she heard the unmistakable sound of a lecture in progress. Opening the door as quietly as possible, Lucy slipped into the room and quickly took a seat behind the others.

Master Christof was standing with his back to the class writing something on what looked to be a large glass chalkboard. His gray hair stuck out in all directions and it bounced as he jotted notes on the board. As he turned around, his eyes immediately fell on Lucy and his bushy white eyebrows began to twitch.

"Miss O'Sullivan, am I to assume you have a reasonable explanation for your untimely arrival? Perhaps you found a more valuable way to spend your morning?"

"No sir," Lucy said, avoiding the looks of her cottagemates. "I…I got lost."

Christof stared at Lucy in silence for several long seconds. Finally he whipped around sending his green robes flying behind him. "I suggest in the future you refrain from wandering from your group. They seem to have a more keen sense of direction than yourself."

Lucy was relieved when a short time later a gong rang out signaling time for their next lesson. Before releasing them Christof called out their first assignment.

"Complete an essay on why proper timing and promptness are important to a Guide, to be written on a nine inch scroll....front *and* back."

"Homework!" griped Sandy. "Do you know how long it's been since I had bloody homework?"

Arthur smiled. "I'm not complaining; makes me feel like a kid again." He winked at Anna as she giggled and blushed.

Next on their schedule was Guardian training. As they wound through the corridors to Colonel George's room Ben filled Lucy in on what she had missed. Apparently Professor Christof was quite brilliant, and more than a little eccentric. To prove his point about weather making techniques he had created a spectacular blizzard over Puddles.

"It was r..r..really n..n..neat," said Puddles through chattering teeth as he wrung out his sleeve.

Learning she had missed such an exciting lesson didn't improve Lucy's mood and she was starting to wonder what else could go wrong today. The answer was waiting for them, pinned to the door of Colonel George's classroom.

"Cancelled," exclaimed Babu disappointedly. He held out the note for everyone to see. Standing on her tip-toes to see over Ben's shoulder, Lucy read:

Guardian training is indefinitely postponed as Colonel George has been unavoidably detained. Until training resumes, you will use your time wisely by studying Chapters 1-10 of Guardian Victories Through the Ages.

Tobias
Chief Attendant & Drookshire Station Master

Choosing to ignore the note's suggestion that they should be studying, the group decided to take advantage of the free time by heading outside to soak up some sun. Only Haddie stayed behind.

"You're all going to be sorry when Colonel George returns and learns that *I* was the only one who bothered with lessons!"

"Ah, quit yer blabberin'," said Sandy. "If yeh ask me it's right cheeky to expect us to worry about studyin' when the instructor didn't even bother to show up. Remember what Banks said, this isn't school, this is trainin' and I don't see anyone here to train us up so I'm out o' here."

Deciding to explore the gardens, Anna, Arthur and Babu said good-bye and headed down the green slope towards the tangle of vegetation. Tibs and Sandy had other plans. Muttering something about "a bit of practice" they left for the forest on the north side of the Station.

"I have a feeling Madame Mira is going to have a busy afternoon," said Ben with a smirk as he watched their friends disappear around the corner.

Being left to themselves, Lucy, Ben and Puddles decided to take a walk around the grounds. As they wandered, Lucy recounted how she had gotten lost and when she came to the part where she had almost broken into the Dream Chamber Puddles let out a small gasp.

"You were really lucky Banks stopped you," said Ben.

"Yeah," said Lucy. She decided not to mention the voices. Despite what Banks had said, she was certain she had heard others talking in the Dream Chamber.

Ben pulled out his schedule and scanned the list. "Looks like all we have left is Messenger training before dinner. It's downstairs just off the Meeting Hall in the CATS wing so it should be pretty easy to find." He shot Lucy a wary glance. "Then at twilight we meet for

Reflection in the Meditation Chamber on top of the south tower and then back to the cottage. Pretty easy day!"

"You think today has been easy?" choked Lucy. The frustration of the day bubbled up inside of her. Shaking her head with disbelief she ticked off the day's disasters as she paced back and forth.

"Let's see, yeah it was a real smooth start – first, I totally sucked at teleporting, then I lost my schedule, then – and this is probably my FAVORITE part - I almost broke into the DREAM CHAMBER which just happens to be FORBIDDEN. To top it all off I somehow managed to become Christof's *least* favorite student before I even sat through a whole class which is probably some kind of Station record. You're right; pretty easy day!"

Lucy kicked at a small stone on the ground, missed and stubbed her toe. "Perfect!" she cried, grabbing her foot and falling back onto the grass.

"Okay, first of all, we *all* sucked in teleporting," said Ben firmly as he sunk down on the ground next to Lucy.

"Tibs was pretty good," said Puddles brightly before Ben gave him a scathing look. "I…I mean…well…he was okay. Probably just luck."

"That's right, and you're making way too big of a deal out of losing your scroll. I'm sure it will turn up somewhere. As far as the Dream Chamber is concerned, you didn't really go inside did you?"

"Yeah, and you don't need to worry about Christof," said Puddles, sitting down on Lucy's other side. "He got all over Tibs for a bunch of stuff; I think that's just the way he is."

Lucy looked at her friends and felt her anger evaporate. She plopped back on the grass feeling like a deflated balloon. In a matter of just a few hours any hope she had of fitting in at Drookshire had vanished. The gnawing feeling that had eaten at her since she first arrived was now chewing her up. She didn't belong here; it would never feel like home. But where was her home now that she couldn't go back to earth?

"Like my grandma used to say," said Puddles, lying down in the grass and looking up at the cloudless sky, "when you fall on your face, just roll over and you'll be headed in the right direction."

Lucy rolled over and stared at Puddles.

"Grandma was a little odd."

That was all it took. Ben burst out laughing and soon Lucy had joined in. Puddles stared at them curiously, obviously not sure of what they found so funny.

To Lucy's relief, the day quickly improved. Messenger training wasn't bad at all; as a matter of fact it was pretty exciting. Master Linus turned out to be an ancient man wrinkled from head to toe with a kind face and a toothless grin. He wasted no time jumping into their first lesson, a demonstration on the use of music in Walker communication. As a head-pounding rendition of Crocodile Rock blared from invisible speakers, Lucy found herself thinking of a summer's day shortly after her 12th birthday. With a flash she remembered the compass she had hidden from Digby. Lucy had gotten in horrible trouble when she couldn't remember where she had buried his favorite toy and she had spent the rest of the summer doing extra chores to pay for a new one. Suddenly she remembered the exact spot where the compass still lay hidden.

Amazed by her sudden memory, Lucy looked around the room and saw that the others seemed to be having similar experiences. She glanced up at Master Linus. He caught her eye and gave her a wink of satisfaction.

After dinner, which turned out to be as spectacular as breakfast, Lucy and the others traipsed up the long, circular stairway that led to the top of the south tower. There had been no need to check their scrolls to see what came next; Reflection was the last class of the day.

The Meditation Chamber was a cavernous circular room with a sweeping view of the grounds surrounding Drookshire Station. Scattered throughout the chamber were small brightly-colored blankets, cushy poufs and over-stuffed chairs. Unlike her other lessons, Reflection time was shared by all of the cottages making the room rather cramped.

Tibs quickly plopped upside down in a bright green bean bag chair and began chanting, his long blond hair sweeping the floor. Ben found a squishy round ottoman to lean against and the others settled into comfortable positions throughout the room.

Lucy looked around the crowded chamber. Spying an empty mat on the far side of the room, she walked carefully around the students stretched out on the floor taking care not to step on anyone. The sun was low in the sky and it painted the room in a warm golden glow. Lucy scooted her mat into the direct path of a sunbeam, then leaned against the wall and closed her eyes. The warmth flowing over her made her body feel relaxed and heavy. Lucy gave a small sigh of relief; finally a class she could handle!

"Welcome," cooed a voice from across the room. Squinting into the sun, Lucy saw the silhouette of a tall, willowy woman with short curly hair that spun out in all directions.

"I am Anaja," said the silky voice as she glided into the center of the room. "I will be guiding you through the arts of Reflection and Rejuvenation."

Madame Anaja's regal appearance reminded Lucy of an African princess doll her father had once given her.

"Our purpose here is to help you free your senses and release your spirit so you can see clearly the path you must follow. In the days to come you will learn how to retreat into your inner self, a journey of the most rewarding kind. However, this evening we will simply try to reflect quietly on the day's events without falling asleep." She gave a small grin and Babu reached over and shook Tibs who was snoring.

The sun was dipping low in the western sky as everyone closed their eyes. Having no desire to relive the day's events, Lucy propped herself against the wall and stared out over the mountains. The sky to the west was oddly dark. Large black clouds had moved in over the horizon and every now and then a streak of bright light cut through the sky suggesting a storm was raging in the distance.

"Is there a problem?" whispered Anaja.

Lucy looked up with a start.

"Huh? Oh…no, I'm fine," sputtered Lucy. Her voice echoed through the quiet room and she saw Haddie glare at her with one eye open. Dropping her voice she whispered, "I was just noticing it looks like we're going to get a storm."

Madame Anaja looked at the darkened sky and Lucy thought she saw a note of sadness in her eyes.

"There are always dark clouds over the Forgotten City. However you're not to worry, they have never wandered over Drookshire's borders. Now, I believe you will have more success if you attempt meditation with your eyes closed."

Hearing a snicker from Haddie's direction, Lucy shut her eyes determined to be better at this than the little General. She fought to focus on the day's lessons but the warmth from the last few rays of sun soaked into Lucy's exhausted body and within seconds she was sound asleep. The soft chanting in the room slowly melted away, replaced by the familiar voices of her dreams. Perhaps it was because she was so tired, or maybe it was because there was a palpable energy vibrating through the Meditation

Chamber, but whatever the reason tonight the voices were much clearer than they had ever been before.

"Lucy...*wake up.*"

Lucy groggily opened one eye and saw Puddles kneeling next to her. Throughout the room people were yawning and stretching as they stirred from their meditations.

"You fell asleep and I think you were having a nightmare," said Puddles. He was staring at Lucy as though he was afraid she might suddenly get sick. "You were mumbling and shaking and you looked really scared."

It was true; she had dreamt about the lake again. The voices had grown stronger and there had been something else; this time she hadn't been alone. Someone was there with her. Pinching her forehead Lucy tried to remember what the stranger looked like, but all she could recall was feeling terribly sad.

Ben was standing next to Puddles staring down at Lucy.

"Are you okay," he asked, sounding worried. "Should I get Madame Anaja?"

"No!" Lucy said sharply. Ben and Puddles exchanged looks and guilt washed over Lucy for snapping at them. "I'm fine...It was just a bad dream, that's all."

Madame Anaja adjourned the lesson and a stream of weary-eyed attendants made their way down the stairway to the cottage portals.

Banks had left a note on the hearth explaining that he had been called away but promising he would be back in time for breakfast. Making herself comfortable in a large wing-backed chair, Lucy sat quietly staring into the fire and listening to the others as they recounted their day. A movement from one of the occuscopes caught Lucy's eye and she watched as a pair of shadowy figures crossed the cobblestone street and entered the Village town square. The sun had long since disappeared behind the mountains, and the only light in the Village came from the fountain which was spraying up streams of crimson. Staring at the figures as they wandered in the red glow, Lucy felt her eyes begin to droop. She was ready to put this day behind her. Puddles was listening to Arthur tell stories about life back in Salisbury and Ben and Babu were locked in a heated discussion about the rumors surrounding Colonel George.

Figuring no one would miss her, Lucy slipped out of the room without saying good-night. It had been a long, exhausting day and she was anxious to put it behind her. Surely tomorrow would be better.

Lucy's room was just as she left it; the purple comforter was in a heap at the foot of her bed and the old clothes she had hastily torn off that morning were scattered on the floor. Why was she surprised that her room had not been cleaned? Had she really expected there to be maid service? Grinning at the thought of a robed housekeeper with a feather duster and wings, Lucy carefully folded her clothes to be put away forever.

There was a small *plink* as Lucy opened the dresser drawer. Looking down, she saw a scroll had toppled off the dresser onto the floor. It was her schedule! Grabbing it up, she quickly unfurled the paper and discovered the Station map tucked inside along with a note scribbled in violet ink.

Thought you might need these. I've traveled around a bit myself and know how helpful maps can be in keeping you out of the wrong places.

Forever True,

A Fellow Traveler

P.S. I know about the voices and I suggest you listen to them.

Lucy's hand quivered as she read the note over again. How could this be? No one except her mother knew about the voices. No one.

Folding the note she slid it into the back pocket of her jeans and stowed them in the top drawer of her dresser. With her mind reeling, Lucy sank on to her bed and stared up at the ceiling trying to imagine who could possibly know her secret. Any thought of sleep quickly disappeared. It was going to be a long night.

CHAPTER SEVEN

SECRETS AND STAMPEDES

"I'm fine...*really*."

Ben's brow raised as he surveyed Lucy's wrinkled robe and runaway hair. Puddles didn't say anything; he simply backed away from the door as though he suspected whatever had caused Lucy's disheveled appearance might be contagious.

"It's just you skipped out on us last night without saying anything, and then this morning you look, well, you know, kind of gross," said Ben, giving an apologetic shrug.

Lucy glanced in the mirror hanging over her dresser and understood their concern; deep, dark, circles hung under her eyes and her complexion which was always rather pale was ghostly white. She had gotten very little rest last night, and what little sleep there was had been filled with more nightmares of those awful voices. When Ben and Puddles came banging on her door before the sun was even up she was actually relieved the night was over.

Stepping over to the wash basin by the window Lucy splashed some cold water on her face. Then brushing a hand over her crumpled robe and throwing her hair back into a tangled pony tail, she turned back to her friends and said in an overly cheery voice, "See? Good as new."

She felt a slight pang of guilt for not telling her friends about the mysterious note, but that would mean having to tell them about the voices and she wasn't ready for that. After all, hearing voices in your head wasn't usually accepted as a good thing.

They caught up with their cottagemates on the long stairway leading up to the south tower. As they reached the top step a flood of blinding light poured out of the open doorway, smacking them awake.

"Who turned on the bloody lights," yelped Sandy, shielding her eyes.

The sun had broken over the horizon and was streaming into the Meditation Chamber, bouncing off the white marble floors and transforming the place that had been so soothing and peaceful for Reflection into an annoyingly bright and cheerful space.

The cushy pillows and chairs from the night before had vanished and in their place stood dozens of golden instruments scattered about the room.

"Excuse me," said a teenage boy, pushing by Lucy.

Like Reflection, all cottages attended Rejuvenation together making the room extremely cramped. As Lucy, Ben and Puddles squeezed through the crowd toward the middle of the room Puddles' head twisted from side to side gawking at the sparkling, golden instruments. Lucy's eye caught a beautiful flute with sapphires running down the side. In sixth grade she had begged her mother for flute lessons until she had finally given in. But it hadn't taken long before the flute, like other things Lucy had become bored with, had ended up under her bed.

"Ladies and gentlemen, welcome to Rejuvenation," said Madame Anaja, her silky voice bringing the room to silence. "I trust you all are well rested and ready to begin."

Lucy started to laugh but Ben caught her eye and she bit her lip.

"As you can see, there have been a few additions to our room. Music, you will learn, can infuse the soul with an energy that will carry you to your loftiest desires. Find the music in your heart, and your path will unfold before you."

Anaja paused to make sure everyone had grasped the importance of her words.

"In a moment I will have you select the instrument that will become your companion for the remainder of your stay at Drookshire. For those of you who prefer the instrument of voice, you may gather by the west window." Professor Anaja gracefully gestured towards the only area free of instruments.

"Are there any questions?"

There was silence in the room as heads craned to search for their desired instrument.

"Very well, you may begin."

There was a mad scramble as the crowd sprinted into action. Ben quickly latched on to a jewel-encrusted clarinet and was waving it in the air for Lucy to see. Puddles dodged through the crowd towards a large bass. Wrapping his arms around it in a giant bear hug, he looked nervously at anyone who appeared like they might try to take it from him.

Everywhere people were grabbing up instruments and holding them close. Tibs was caressing an electric guitar with a watery look of awe in his eyes.

"It's the spittin' image of the one Hendrix played," he said lovingly.

Professor Anaja smiled. "It was Jimmy's favorite while he was here."

"Hendrix was *here*?" Tibs eyes popped wide and he nearly dropped the guitar.

Lucy felt a jolt of panic. A teenage boy had grabbed the flute she wanted and the other instruments were being quickly scooped up. She scanned the room; there was a violin sitting on a nearby table, some cymbals lying ignored on the floor and a giant harp which everyone carefully stepped around apparently wanting to avoid the stereotype of harp playing angels. Lucy didn't have a clue how to play the violin so she reluctantly reached for the cymbals.

A large man with a round belly that barely accommodated his sash grabbed the cymbals at the same instant.

"Please," he begged under his breath, "my buddies will give me hell if I have to play that thing." He jerked his head towards the harp. Lucy looked over his shoulder and saw a group of rough looking men standing in the corner snickering and pointing their way.

"Go ahead," said Lucy, reluctantly letting go of the cymbals.

The man looked extremely relieved as he held up the cymbals for his buddies to see. "Here's a real instrument for ya! Nothing sissy about this." And just to prove his point he banged them together sending a sound like crashing trash lids echoing through the room.

Lucy sighed and looked around the room. Every instrument she could possibly play had been taken. *Great*, she thought, *stuck in choir again*. When her short-lived flute career ended, Lucy's mother had insisted that she do something musical so reluctantly Lucy had signed up for the school choir. Unfortunately Lucy's voice didn't fit into any of the usual ranges the choir director was looking for and Lucy had spent the year silently mouthing songs. As she grudgingly made her way over to the west wall, Lucy wondered if Anaja would ask her to do the same.

"I didn't know *you* could sing."

The voice hit her like a bucket of cold water. Lucy had been so busy feeling sorry for herself she hadn't noticed who else had gathered with the singers.

"Hi, Haddie," said Lucy thickly. "You can't play an instrument either, huh?"

"On the contrary. I have studied the piano, the violin and the oboe. I don't like to brag but I was quite good with all of them."

"Then why are you over here," Lucy asked, praying that Haddie would change her mind.

"There was some big oaf in my way and Anna got to the piano before I did…"

Lucy glanced across the room and saw Anna and Arthur sitting side by side on the piano bench.

"…then I tried to get the oboe but some boy stuck it in his mouth and put it back down…well, I wasn't about to touch it after that."

"What about the violin?" said Lucy, not giving up hope.

"I didn't want anyone to think I was taking it just because it was the only thing left…how would that look?" Haddie gave a flip of her braid to emphasize her point. "Besides, mother always told me I have the voice of a songbird. Why are *you* here?"

Lucy wanted to lie and tell Haddie that she too had the voice of a songbird, but the truth was she probably sounded more like a crow. Plastering a sugary smile on her face, she turned to Haddie. "The truth is I just wanted to be with you. After all, like Banks said, we're family now. What's wrong with wanting to spend some good quality time with my new little sister?" Lucy put her arm around Haddie's shoulder and gave her a squeeze.

It worked. With a mortified look, Haddie wiggled out from Lucy's grip and mumbled something about needing to talk to Madame Anaja, then quickly scurried off.

Bingo! The loving-older-sister routine had worked on Haddie exactly the same as it had always worked on Digby. Lucy smiled as she felt her spirits lift.

Madame Anaja spent the remainder of class wandering from student to student, listening to them play and dividing them into groups. Finally she came to the singers.

"As I come to you, please sing your scales. Don't be frightened," she said, noticing the look of horror on the face of a gawky teenage boy. "We are not expecting Pavarotti; I just need to know where to place you in the choir."

Lucy tried to swallow but her mouth felt like it was full of sand. She understood how the boy felt; the thought of singing in front of Anaja...or worse, in front of Haddie...made her suddenly nauseous.

Haddie was the first to sing and much to Lucy's dismay she really was good.

"Lovely dear, lovely," said Madame Anaja. Haddie beamed and shot Lucy an I-told-you-so look.

Lucy felt a little better after listening to the next few people in line. None of them could sing nearly as well as Haddie, and the gawky teenage boy actually squawked when he attempted to hit a high note.

Finally it was Lucy's turn. Anaja looked at her and smiled. "Whenever you are ready."

The lump in Lucy's throat suddenly felt like a boulder. Ben gave her a thumbs-up from across the room which only made her more nervous. Praying for a miracle, Lucy closed her eyes and opened her mouth just wide enough to let out the smallest of sounds. Taking a deep breath, her voice slowly began to climb the scales.

A hush fell over the room. From somewhere in the tower a beautiful song came floating through the air. Lucy opened her eyes. Every head was turned her way and Puddles' mouth was dangling open in surprise. Lucy looked from side to side before it hit her...that sound...that incredible, amazing sound...was coming from *her*!

Finishing on a perfect note, the room erupted in whoops and hollers and thunderous applause. Lucy looked blankly at Anaja who was staring curiously back at her.

"Well done, dear. I must say you had me fooled. Your look of concern had me expecting something slightly less stellar."

Lucy gave a nervous laugh and shrugged. "Yeah, kind of surprised me, too."

Suddenly the sun pouring into the room, which had been so annoying just moments ago, felt wonderful.

"Did you see the look on Haddie's face?" laughed Ben, as they made their way to breakfast moments later. "It was brilliant! I have never seen anyone look so shocked in all my life. That's a picture I never want to forget!"

"How come you never told us you could sing like that," said Puddles, stumbling over his robe as he hurried to catch up with them.

"It just never came up," said Lucy dismissively. She thought it would sound really stupid to say she didn't know she could sing, but the fact was that until this morning she *couldn't* sing...at least not like that. Maybe the acoustics in the tower were just really good, or maybe sounds were different here than they were on earth; whatever the reason, Lucy didn't care. She had found something she could do without looking like a fool, and as an added bonus it had totally demolished Haddie. Lucy knew that competing with someone from her own cottage wasn't right, but she had to admit it felt great.

It didn't take long for news of Lucy's newfound talent to sweep through the Station. By the next morning the south tower was packed with senior attendants who had shown up for Rejuvenation in order to hear the G.O.A.T. with the heavenly voice. To Lucy's great relief Anaja had shooed them all away. "This is a classroom, not a concert hall!"

Unfortunately Anaja's admonitions didn't stop the whispers that followed Lucy throughout the Station and she found herself growing tired of the stares and pointing fingers.

"What's the big deal if I can sing?" Lucy said crossly one day after overhearing a well-coifed elderly woman from the Mayanian Cottage mention that someone with such a lovely voice should practice better grooming.

"Have you heard yourself," asked Ben. They were headed out of the Station to enjoy another free period thanks to a still-absent Colonel George. "It's not even like you're singing, it's more like you're making some kind of weird music." He tried to imitate the sound but it came out sounding like a sick cow.

"Thanks, I feel loads better now."

"Ben's got it all wrong," said Puddles, picking up a rock and tossing it into the garden's reflecting pond. It sank with a plop. "It doesn't sound anything like that. It's more like...well, like the sound in your head when you're really happy."

"Exactly!" shouted Ben. "Well put, Puddles...that's exactly how it sounds."

Puddles grinned sheepishly and whipped another stone across the water watching in amazement as it skipped effortlessly seven times before disappearing.

Lucy watched as a small frog hopped onto a nearby lily pad and stared up at her. "Well whatever it sounds like, trust me I'm not doing it on purpose." She gave the water a splash with her toe and the frog let out a croak before slipping into the water.

The days came and went so quickly that Lucy soon lost track of how long she had been at the Station. Other than her success in Rejuvenation, training wasn't going well. Teleporting was a miserable failure and she continued to fall asleep in Reflection. Messenger training wasn't any better. Lucy kept mixing up the difference between physical and mental messages and twice sent lightning bolts across the room when she was supposed to be sending happy thoughts.

But by far the worst class was Christof's. He had started holding sessions in the forest in order to train them how to "guide Walkers through the maze of life." Lucy soon learned this meant blindfolding your partner and leading them through the tangled forest using only riddles to guide them. After Lucy accidentally led several partners into the river Christof moved training back inside the Station.

The only bright spot in her day was Guardian training. The mysterious Colonel George had yet to make an appearance giving them a glorious free hour every day.

"Yep, still gone!" said Sandy, flicking the note on the Colonel's door after another wasted trip up the stairway.

"Hmmph!" Haddie glared at the note. "This is completely unacceptable. Apparently he expects us to learn how to be Guardians by osmosis."

"Os-whats-its?" said Puddles, shooting a worried look at Lucy.

"I have a good mind to complain to Tobias," Haddie said.

Ben opened his mouth to argue but Babu raised his hand.

"I am afraid I must agree with Haddie. How can we possibly hope to be chosen for the Guardian division if we have no training?"

"Perhaps, considering the circumstances, they would allow us to study with another instructor," offered Anna optimistically.

"Won't work." A voice from behind them caused everyone to jump.

"Jumpin' joeys! Where d'ya come from?" exclaimed Sandy, as Harrison appeared beside them.

Harrison laughed and flashed the group a playful grin. "Tobias sent me. He's worried that you might be using this free time to do something radical."

"Radical?" said Ben.

"Certainly! If you're not careful you might actually have some fun. So he has sent me to put a stop to it before it can begin."

"Isn't that rather like putting the mouse in charge of the cheese?" chortled Arthur.

"My good man," said Harrison, clutching his chest with mock indignation, "I am extremely insulted by your insinuation that I would be anything other than a perfect role-model!" He smiled and gave Arthur a wink. "Thanks for the compliment."

"So are you fixin' to train us up on this Guardian thing?" asked Sandy, looking hopeful.

"Are you kidding! If George found out I was training you..." Harrison gave a shudder. "No I'll leave that to the pro."

"And we can't study with another instructor?" asked Anna.

"I'm afraid not," said Harrison, shaking his head. "You're stuck with...I mean, you have been assigned to Colonel George for a reason. Don't ask me what the reason is..." he held up his hand as Babu opened his mouth, "After a while you just learn to trust that things will fall into place."

"Well, if we're not going to have class, then what *are* we going to do," Puddles asked sounding somewhat worried of what Harrison might have in store.

Harrison gave a devilish grin. "Follow me."

Puddles was right in his suspicion; Harrison indeed had something up his sleeve. Using the same portals they had used the night of their arrival, the group soon found themselves standing in the brilliant sunshine outside the Village clock tower.

"You do realize we are going to be late for our Messenger lesson if we don't turn around right this instant," called Haddie, as she watched her cottagemates parade after Harrison toward the heart of the Village.

"Are you sure this is okay?" said Ben, looking around at the Village residents who were eyeing them suspiciously.

"I will have you know that this outing is purely for educational purposes," said Harrison, picking up his pace. "Anyone up for a cup of tea?"

"Ooooh, that would be lovely!" exclaimed Anna, grabbing her husband's hand and heading for Café Monet.

"Excuse me," panted Haddie as she caught up with the group, "but exactly what does drinking tea have to do with our training?"

Harrison stopped and turned on Haddie. For a moment it looked as though he was going to let her have it, but to Lucy's surprise when Harrison spoke he was surprisingly calm.

"Miss Whitney, you will discover that not all lessons can be learned in class. I am going to join Anna and Arthur for tea to practice the lesson of friendship. If you wish to explore more academic pursuits, may I suggest the History Pavilion? Undoubtedly there will be plenty there to quench your thirst for knowledge." His unblinking gaze was friendly but firm.

"Fine!" snapped Haddie, and she stomped off towards the Pavilion.

Harrison let out a deep sigh and scratched the back of his head. "Anyone else up for a slice of the best lemon meringue pie in the Kingdom?"

"I'm in!" said Sandy, patting her stomach.

"Not me," said Tibs. "I'm gonna hit the Hall of Review."

Babu whispered to Lucy, "Banks told him of the Past Life Exhibit. He wants to learn if his dreams about chasing cats meant he was once a dog."

Lucy, Ben and Puddles also declined Harrison's offer, deciding they would rather do a bit of sightseeing. Agreeing to meet back at the clock tower when the sun shifted directly overhead, they set off towards the large stone arch entrance to the Kingdom's zoo.

Growing up in the mountains Lucy had been surrounded by animals all her life. In the spring, about the time when the hardy blue Columbine began poking through the snow, it was common for the local family of black bears to come visit the O'Sullivan's backyard looking for the blackberries Katie O'Sullivan had planted in a short-lived attempt to make homemade jam. Lucy had spent many mornings eating her breakfast with a large black bear peering at her from the back porch.

The O'Sullivans played host to a number of other animals as well. When Digby began leaving food out for the neighborhood's army of wild cats, it didn't take long for a party of raccoons, possums and skunks to discover the buffet. However the day Lucy's mom opened the door to find a mountain lion munching on their bowl of Meow Mix the O'Sullivan's wildlife restaurant was officially closed.

As they entered the zoo Lucy was pretty sure she wouldn't find any raccoons in a place that boasted to be "The Kingdom's Only Extinct Animal Habitat", but what she found stole her breath away.

There were no cages, no fences, not even a wide moat to separate the four-footed inhabitants from their two-legged visitors. There was only a vast open field filled with the oddest creatures Lucy had ever laid eyes on. Tortoise-like creatures with sharp spines on their shells were sunning themselves by a small pond as a flock of gigantic birds with deadly-looking beaks circled overhead. A bright yellow monkey with a springy tail spotted them and slowly wandered over eyeing them with mild curiosity. Apparently deciding they were harmless, he sniffed the air, threw open his arms displaying a set of leathery wings and soared off.

"Oh my…" Lucy's mouth fell open as she watched the canary monkey fly out of sight.

"B...B...Ben..." stuttered Puddles, his voice barely above a whisper. He was tugging on Ben's robe, his eyes wide as pancakes and a look of terror on his face.

Ben and Lucy turned and together let out a scream. Standing not 100 feet away, contentedly munching on the top branch of a tree, was a beast Lucy recognized immediately. The massive body, the long slender neck, the sweeping thick tail and the small dark eyes that were watching them with disinterest...she had seen pictures of this creature in her science books.

"I think I'm feeling thirsty now," Puddles squeaked, slowly backing towards the entrance.

"You've got to be kidding," said Ben, excitedly. "This place is great!" He seemed to have gotten over the shock of standing in the shadow of a live dinosaur and was searching the horizon for more mammoth beasts.

"I'll make you a deal," Lucy said quietly to Puddles. She couldn't blame him for wanting to put some distance between them and this prehistoric eating machine. "Let's check out those trees over there. I promise that I will take you back to the café if we see anything that looks like it wants to have us for lunch."

Suddenly the ground beneath them shook as the giant beast lumbered over to a tree twenty feet away. Lucy reached for Puddles but he was already racing for the trees.

"Come on!" Lucy yelled to Ben as she took off after Puddles.

The thicket of trees was much larger and denser than Lucy expected. Stopping at the tree line to catch their breath, Lucy wondered if this was really a good idea. If flying monkeys and dinosaurs wandered around in the open, what kind of strange creatures might be hiding in here? Lucy caught Ben's eye. He seemed to be thinking the same thing. She was just about to suggest joining the others at the café when another loud rumble shook the ground.

"Inside!" commanded Ben, and he disappeared into the forest.

Lucy grabbed Puddles' hand and followed. Only a few steps in, she noticed that the temperature was much cooler under the lime green canopy.

"There's a clear spot over there," said Ben, as they caught up with him.

Keeping their eyes peeled for any sign of movement, they climbed over the massive roots snaking across their path until they reached the clearing.

Puddles quickly scrambled on to a large rock and drew up his knees to avoid any prehistoric bugs that might be crawling on the ground. As Ben investigated the clearing, Lucy sat down on a nearby log and gazed up into the curtain of leaves dancing above her. A family of bright orange primates was swinging on to the limbs high above playing a lively game of tag and giving no mind to the fact they were being watched.

"They look like some kind of a mixture between an orangutan and a chimpanzee," declared Ben, who had also noticed the activity overhead. Two of the smaller monkeys scampered down to a low branch just above their heads. Lucy, Ben and the monkeys stared at each other with equal curiosity until finally the smallest monkey gave a small blink with his warm dark eyes, nodded, and began grooming his friend.

Puddles had not noticed the monkeys; he was busy watching a large green beetle slowly scuttling across the dirt.

"This place isn't so scary," said Lucy, refocusing her attention on to the beetle. "Looks pretty much like the bugs we had back home."

Puddles took a stick and gently poked at the beetle. With a loud CRUNCH the bug opened its mouth and bit the stick in two. Puddles threw the remaining end of the stick in to the air and leapt to his feet nearly falling off his perch.

"Just like the beetles back home!" he cried, lifting his robe to his knees.

"Okay, maybe it's not *exactly* like the ones back home," said Lucy, quickly backing away from the bug.

A sudden scurry of activity in the branches overhead caught their attention. Something seemed to have spooked the monkeys. Over the loud chattering Lucy thought she heard voices. She motioned to Ben and Puddles to be quiet. Suddenly a man's voice exploded from somewhere inside the tangle of trees.

"SILENCE! Your threats are empty! Do not push me Tobias or I will be forced to reveal secrets that will make you most unhappy."

The outburst had startled the monkeys sending them flying through the trees chattering loudly and blocking out the rest of the conversation.

By the time the commotion in the trees died away the voices were gone. Lucy, Ben and Puddles stood motionless, frozen with fear. Lucy strained to listen for some sign of the visitors but the air was silent.

"I think they're gone," she said quietly, her heart still pounding.

"Was that…?" said Puddles, his eyes darting from Ben to Lucy in disbelief.

"Banks," Lucy confirmed. They had all recognized the voice, but never had it been filled with such fury.

"Do you think they saw us?"

Ben shook his head. "If Tobias knew we were here he definitely would have said something."

"Yeah, something like, 'Pack your bags'," said Lucy.

Ben forced a laugh, but the look on his face showed he knew she was probably right.

The goose bumps on Lucy's arms were tingling sharply as she tried to make sense of what had just happened.

"Banks is in trouble," she said.

"Sounded more like Tobias was the one getting yelled at," said Ben.

Lucy shook her head. "You don't understand – Banks is worried, *really* worried. Something's gone wrong."

Ben and Puddles looked confused but Lucy knew what she had heard. Behind Banks' screams a voice had slipped into her mind. She held her head trying to remember exactly what the voice had said, but it was like trying to remember the details of a dream that was quickly fading away.

"Banks has done something really bad and now he doesn't know how he's going to correct it."

"Lucy," Puddles spoke softly, "we don't know that. All he said was…"

"I know what he said, but it's what he *didn't* say."

Ben and Puddles exchanged concerned looks. Obviously they thought she was cracking up.

Lucy was about to explain about the voice when a low rumble began to shake the ground. Peering through an opening in the trees Lucy saw a cloud of dust rising in the west and heading towards them. Before she realized what was happening, the forest around them began to shake.

"STAMPEDE!" Ben yelled, as the trembling threatened to knock them off their feet.

"Quick!" yelled Lucy, holding on to a nearby tree to keep from toppling over. "We need to get to higher ground!" Her voice vibrated as she screamed. "The boulders we passed just before the forest…we need to run for it!"

The sound of hundreds of pounding feet was growing louder as they dashed from the clearing and headed for the rocks. Puddles tripped on a log that had rolled into the path. "DON'T LEAVE ME!"

Lucy and Ben raced back and grabbed Puddles under the arms, yanking him up and tearing his robes. The cloud of dust was getting closer and above the swirling mass of earth Lucy saw dozens and dozens of small gray heads bobbing up and down. Dinosaurs!

"RUN!" she screamed over the deafening roar.

Ben was the first one to scramble up the largest boulder. He fell on to his stomach and held down his hand for Lucy.

"Don't worry about me," Lucy said, pushing away his hand. "Get Puddles!"

Ben tore off his sash and lowered it down to Puddles. "Tie it around your middle...AND HURRY!" The stampede had reached the grove of trees which were quickly toppling under the force of the massive dinosaurs.

Lucy grabbed the end of Ben's sash and looped it around Puddles, tightening it with a yank. Then she hiked up her robe and quickly began scaling the rocks. Reaching the top, she took hold of the free end of the sash.

"PULL!" she cried, as the gray wall of dinosaurs trampled the last of the trees. With one giant tug they hoisted Puddles to the top. As he scrambled over the edge, the stampeding herd thundered by, their heads thrashing from side to side and their beetle-black eyes flashing wildly.

"That was close," gasped Ben, as he wiped the dirt from his face. "I wonder what caused them to stampede."

"I don't know, but it looks like we weren't the only ones who noticed." Lucy pointed towards the zoo's entrance. Dozens of robed figures were hurrying into the zoo. Some were heading off in the direction of the fading dust storm while others were standing around gawking at the path of destruction left behind. In the middle of the crowd Lucy spotted Samuel and standing next to him was Truman.

Lucy felt her stomach jolt. Even at this distance it was easy to see, Samuel was not happy.

By the time they climbed down from boulders and made their way across the field to the zoo's entrance half the Village had shown up to find out what had happened. People stared in disbelief at the flattened trees and trampled ground. Harrison and the other members of Hill Cottage rushed in; one look at Puddles' torn robes and Lucy and Ben covered in dirt and the color drained from Harrison's face.

"What in the name of St. Peter happened to you?" Harrison exclaimed loudly. His usual jovial look was gone.

"Please…" Samuel held up his hand. "We will discuss the details of what has just occurred at another time. Right now we need to make sure no creatures have been injured. Truman…" Samuel turned to Truman who had been standing silently by his side looking at Lucy with eyes that glistened with disappointment. "…I need you to find Jacques and Louisa and see if they need help calming the animals. If necessary, contact Milo and have him enlist the help of the primates; they've always had a good relationship with the dinosaurs."

Lucy wanted to ask what Samuel meant by this, but decided now was not the time for questions.

"And as for you three," Samuel's blue eyes blazed as he looked from Lucy to Ben and finally to Puddles who let out a small whimper, "I will want to speak with you to find out exactly what happened."

Ben opened his mouth but before any words could escape Samuel interrupted. "Now is not the time; I will be in touch with you later. Harrison, please escort your charges back to Drookshire."

"Yes, sir." Harrison gave a nod to Samuel and then with a weary look herded them out of the zoo.

As Lucy passed under the large stone arch she heard Samuel call out to her. Turning back she was confused to find he had disappeared.

CHAPTER EIGHT

SUMMONS TO THE BEACH

Lucy leaned over the stone basin and splashed cold water on to her face. Peering out her bedroom window she saw nothing but black. If she guessed right it would be a while before the sun was up giving her time to carry out the plan she had thought up while lying awake all night.

Harrison and the others had given them the silent treatment on their trip back to Drookshire. It was apparent they all thought Lucy, Ben and Puddles were responsible for the dinosaurs' stampede. But far worse than the silence was Haddie's smug look. Lucy hated to admit it but she had been right, going to the Village had been a bad idea.

Pushing the memory of last night out of her mind, Lucy focused on what needed to be done. Slowly opening the door so it wouldn't squeak, Lucy slipped from her room and quietly snuck down the hall to the cottage's sitting room. The room was dark except for the faint glow of the fire's fading embers. She did a quick check to make sure no one was hiding in the shadows. There were no rules forbidding wandering the Station alone, but after yesterday's disaster she thought it would be best not to be caught leaving the cottage at this hour. If everything went as planned she would be back before anyone missed her.

Inside the Station Lucy was surprised to find a bustle of activity going on in the pre-dawn hours. Ducking her head to avoid being noticed by a group of Messengers who were huddled together deep in conversation, she hurried towards the south stairway.

"Hold on!"

Lucy froze, her heart leaping to her throat.

"Are you telling me Cassiel approved that plan?"

Lucy forced herself to breathe again as the Messengers continued loudly debating something having to do with Morpheus. She had not heard anyone speak about Morpheus since her first day in the Kingdom and she was tempted to stop and listen but there was no time. Her cottagemates would be waking soon and she needed answers. Keeping her head low, she hurried past the stream of attendants and darted up the stairs.

Pushing open the door to the south tower, Lucy let out a sigh of relief. It was empty, just as she had anticipated. Shutting the door behind her, Lucy glanced around the dark chamber. By day the circular tower offered a panoramic view of Drookshire, but at the moment the world outside was bathed in inky shadows. Spying the outline of a squat chair against the far wall, Lucy felt her way through the maze of blankets, mats and ottomans that still remained left over from last night's Reflection class. Climbing into the cushy wing-backed chair, she drew up her legs and rested her chin on her knees. Hopefully here, in the stillness of the deserted tower where energy seemed to fill the chamber, she would be able to will herself to hear the voices. First her dreams, then Samuel and now Banks…she had to find out why they were calling her. Focusing her eyes towards the mountains she knew were sitting somewhere out there in the darkness, Lucy waited for the voices to come.

****

"I liked it," exclaimed Puddles cheerfully, as Lucy shot him an annoyed look. "I don't care what you say, that class is tons better than the others. Just because you're embarrassed that everyone stares at you when you sing…"

"That's not it at all," argued Lucy, feeling her face go red. Truthfully, that was a big part of why she liked Rejuvenation far less than everyone else, but today she had another reason for her grumpy behavior. When she had not shown up in the cottage that morning, Banks sent out a search party to scour the Station. To Lucy's great misfortune it had been Tobias who had found her in the south tower, curled up in the chair, sound asleep.

She didn't know which had been worse – listening to Tobias scold her for not informing Banks of her "aimless wanderings" or having to endure the taunts from Haddie when Tobias let it slip that he had found Lucy whimpering in her sleep.

To top it all off, the plan hadn't worked. Try as she might, she had not been able to summon any of the voices. Then, just as the sun had begun to tinge the horizon pink, she had fallen asleep and slipped back into her nightmare. There, in her dream, the voices came willingly.

Circling around her like a wolf circling its prey, the cries for help had bitten at her from all directions. Lucy pressed her hands to her ears but the cries managed to seep between her fingers. The air was thick with a cold, gray mist which hovered over the ominous black lake stretching out for miles in front of her. The water churned and bubbled and something deep inside told Lucy she must not touch it. She wanted to run but a pair of steely gray eyes cutting through the mist kept her frozen in her tracks. Suddenly a bony hand had grabbed her shoulder and Lucy awoke with a start to find Tobias standing over her.

If Lucy had any hope that the day would improve, it was dashed as they entered the Meeting Hall for breakfast. Sitting on the table resting neatly against her water goblet was a large golden envelope with her name boldly inscribed in loopy blue script. Glancing across the table

Lucy saw that Ben and Puddles had similar envelopes waiting for them.

"You don't suppose…" she said to Ben in a hushed voice.

"What else could it be?" said Ben, carefully turning the envelope over to examine the golden wax seal.

They cut their conversation short as the rest of their cottagemates joined them at the table. Haddie was busy lecturing Tibs on proper grooming for attendants, while the others were laughing over a joke Sandy had just finished telling – something about the difference between an elephant and an angel.

Lucy and Ben quickly pocketed their notes but before they had time to warn Puddles he caught sight of his envelope and excitedly grabbed it up.

"Hey, look!" he exclaimed, clearly thrilled that someone had sent him a letter. Waving the golden envelope in the air, he loudly announced, "Look what I got!"

The table fell silent as all eyes turned to Puddles. Lucy felt her stomach grow sick as she watched him rip open the envelope. She silently mouthed "not now" but his eyes were glued to the golden note.

As Puddles quickly scanned the page his smile melted away and was replaced by a sickly green look of terror.

"Whatcher got there?" said Sandy, leaning over to take a look.

Before Sandy could read it, Puddles hastily folded the note and jammed it back in the envelope.

Lucy didn't need to ask who the note was from. With a sinking feeling, she pulled out her own note.

"It's okay," she said, forcing half a grin. "I got one, too."

"Me, too," said Ben glumly as he held up his envelope.

Realizing there was no use delaying the inevitable Lucy cracked open the wax seal and pulled out her letter. As she read the message written in loopy blue script, it felt as though the air was slowly being sucked from the room.

Dear Miss Lucy,

Please come to my office today after dinner to discuss the situation that occurred yesterday within the premises of the Kingdom's Animal Sanctuary. Madame Anaja has been notified that you are to be excused from her class. Master Banks will direct you to my office.

Sincerely,

Samuel

Keeper of the Book of Destiny

"Well I don't know what you expected," said Haddie, reading over Ben's shoulder.

"If you don't mind! I believe mail is supposed to be private," Ben growled, quickly folding up his note and thrusting it back into the envelope.

"There's no need to get all huffy with me, *I'm* not the one who destroyed the zoo."

"It wasn't our fault!" Puddles blurted in a voice so strong it took everyone at the table by surprise. "We weren't the only ones there."

Lucy glared at Puddles in horror. The last thing they needed now was for Banks and Tobias to discover they knew about their meeting. Thankfully before Haddie could ask what he meant the gong rang out announcing the Scouts had arrived.

The first time the trumpet had sounded on their second morning at Drookshire, the room had erupted with a unified scream. But now, after two weeks of this morning ritual, they had gotten used to the disruption.

A parade of men and women in ruby-colored robes filed silently into the room, passing the senior attendant benches, circling around the cottage tables and climbing the steps onto the platform where Tobias stood solemnly waiting for them.

As a young man with spiked brown hair passed their table, Tibs waved enthusiastically.

"Jonas! Over here!"

Jonas kept his eyes straight ahead but Lucy saw him wave from under his robe.

"Whoa! You know a Scout?" said Puddles, clearly impressed by Tibs' connections.

"Oh yeah, we're buds." Tibs gave Jonas two hardy thumbs in the air. "I kind of got lost the other day…bad teleport you know…ended up somewhere way off in the mountains."

"You're kidding!" Puddles looked terrified at the mere idea.

"No foolin'. Anyway, there I was just sittin' there wondering how I was gonna get back when all of a sudden out of nowhere Jonas showed up." Tibs put his hand over his heart and sniffled. "The little dude saved me."

"LADIES AND GENTLEMEN…" Tobias's voice cut through the chatter like a knife and the room instantly fell silent. "…if you would kindly suspend your conversations we will proceed with the distribution of today's assignments. Clarence, are the Scouts ready with their daily assignments?"

With military precision a pudgy, middle aged man marched forward from the line of Scouts and handed Tobias a scroll which he had unfurled to reveal a long list of names. "Sir, the Scouts are ready." Without turning around Clarence stepped back into line.

Lucy had learned that the daily assignments, or DA's, were handed out by the Scouts to the senior attendants every morning. After conferring with their Scout, the attendant would then depart to Earth to help their Walker through whatever trouble they were having. Banks had explained to her that the tricky part was accomplishing the task without the Walker getting wise to the fact they were being helped.

Everyone quickly forgot about Puddles' outburst as they watched Tobias call forth the senior attendants one by one. As each attendant climbed the stage, they were met by a Scout who would hand them a red scroll with their assignment and then escort them to the small portal room in the back corner of the Hall.

Deciding to take advantage of the distraction, Lucy scooted her chair closer to Ben and Puddles and leaned in so she wouldn't be overheard. She had made up her mind while waiting in the dark for the voices to come. Her friends deserved to know the truth.

While in the background Tobias continued to call out names, Lucy launched into her story. She told them about the dreams, about the cries for help that haunted her and about the mysterious anonymous note. Ben and Puddles listened in wide-eyed shock, not uttering a word until Lucy came to the voices she had heard during their disastrous visit to the zoo.

"NO WAY!" said Ben, dropping his butter knife which clanged loudly against his plate.

"Do you think you could say that a little louder?" Lucy's green eyes flashed at Ben. "I don't think the folks over at the Forest Cottage heard you!"

"Sorry," he said, lowering his voice and glancing around the table to make sure no one was listening. "Now tell us again exactly what you think you heard."

"I don't *think* I heard anything; I DID hear it," said Lucy in a hushed voice.

"Does this mean you're tele-pathetic?" asked Puddles, gawking at Lucy.

"I think you mean tele*pathic*, and no, I'm not. You don't need to worry…" Lucy said, turning to Ben, "…I can't read your mind. Your thoughts are safe."

"I wasn't worried," said Ben shrugging, but Lucy thought he looked relieved as he grabbed for a plate of blueberry scones.

"And you think Samuel knows you have this tele-thingy," said Puddles in amazement.

"I think so. I mean, you didn't hear him call out when we were leaving the zoo, did you?"

Ben and Puddles both shook their heads.

"And there was another time – back on my first day – I think I heard his thoughts then, too."

Ben let out a low whistle. Suddenly his eyes grew wide. "Hey, do you think Samuel wrote the note? I mean, it makes perfect sense doesn't it? He obviously knows you can hear his thoughts…what was it you heard him say again?"

He just said, "Lucy, be careful."

"Careful of what?" asked Puddles.

Lucy shrugged. She had been wondering the same thing.

"Ith iv weely umbeweevable," Puddles declared a little too loudly through a mouthful of scrambled eggs.

"What's that?" said a familiar deep voice from behind them.

Lucy jumped, knocking over her orange juice as Banks pulled up a chair next to her.

The color drained from Puddles' face as he swallowed hard. "The, uh, food…it's unbelievable. Try some?" He held up his plate which shook slightly.

"Thank you, but I'll pass. I just came down to see how everyone was doing this morning."

He made no mention of yesterday's events but Lucy thought she sensed an odd note in his voice. Did he know they had overheard his argument with Tobias?

As the last attendant descended the steps with their assignment in hand, the morning chime rang out and a scuffling of chairs declared the end of breakfast.

"BEFORE YOU LEAVE..." Tobias's voice boomed out again and everyone stopped what they were doing. "...I am pleased to announce that Colonel George will be returning to Drookshire this evening and is anxiously looking forward to beginning training tomorrow. Therefore any extra-curricular outings you might have been planning for this previously free period..." he glared at the members of Hill Cottage, "...are hereby canceled."

"Bugger," grumbled Sandy, as they made their way down to the garden for Teleporting. "I was lookin' forward to seein' a few of them animals."

Banks cleared his throat and Sandy dropped the subject. To everyone's surprise Banks had announced he would be joining them for today's training. He claimed that he wanted to see how they were progressing but Lucy had the sneaking suspicion she was being watched. By tagging along he guaranteed that there would be no time for Lucy, Ben and Puddles to discuss what they had heard.

Teleporting was a grand failure as always. Lucy and Babu were the only two who hadn't successfully teleported and Madame Mira was losing patience.

"No, no, NO! You cannot flap your way there like a blue jay," Mira scolded, after Babu whacked Sandy in the face.

Banks said nothing as he sat on a large boulder observing them, but when Lucy fell on her face after one especially miserable attempt she caught him shaking his head.

Guide training went only slightly better but it was definitely more interesting. Entering the room Anna gave a small gasp and Sandy let out a loud curse as they came face to face with a crowd of ghosts. Puddles darted from the room and Lucy was just about to join him when she noticed the ghosts weren't moving. The group of transparent men, women and children were simply floating in mid-air as if in some kind of trance.

"Holograms!" Christof announced from the back of the room. "Since we cannot risk you practicing on actual Walkers, these holograms will be an adequate substitute."

Each person was assigned a Walker hologram in some sort of mortal danger. Ben was given an old lady cornered by a bear. Puddles – who Banks had dragged back into the room – was assigned a little boy playing with matches.

Lucy's Walker was a young woman being stalked by a masked figure. Even though she knew it wasn't real, something about the attacker seemed eerily familiar.

After Christof explained the ground rules – no direct interaction, no verbal contact and most definitely no lethal acts against attackers - Ben wasted no time launching into action. With a wave of his hand a thunderstorm erupted over his hologram. The bear shook its head against the rain but continued towards the old lady.

"Oh no you don't," exclaimed Ben, and with a snap of his fingers a bolt of lightning skidded past the bear's nose. The beast jumped back, let out a roar of anger and pelted off disappearing into thin air.

Banks nodded his head in approval and Ben beamed.

The others were not having quite as much success. Anna's Walker seemed to be sinking in a patch of quicksand and Babu's hologram was kicking frantically at the nose of a shark.

Ignoring the shriek from Puddle's hologram which had just set his pants on fire, Lucy turned back to her own assignment. The woman with long blond hair was walking down a dark street. Behind her the shadowy figure was creeping closer. As she quickened her step, the attacker reached into his coat and Lucy saw the glint of a blade. Before she could plan what to do the attacker lunged at the woman. Without thinking Lucy threw her hand forward and a flash of light shot from her fingers. Like an invisible shield, the light knocked the man backwards and the woman escaped. It was over before Lucy realized what she had done.

"Nice work," said Banks, giving her a pleased look. "But next time trying circling your Walker with the light. Better protection."

Lucy just smiled and nodded, pretending to understand. There was no way she would ruin this moment by admitting her rescue had been a fluke of good luck.

The rest of their training session passed by quickly as Lucy watched the various holograms either be rescued or die a gruesome death. The cry from Tibs' Walker had just faded away when the chime rang out announcing the end of class.

With Banks along the group had no choice but to follow Tobias's instructions and so for the first time they spent their free period studying. Haddie was quick to point out to Banks that she had already finished the assigned chapters and was well into the intermediate lessons.

"Pint-sized brown noser," muttered Sandy, as she flipped the page of her book without reading it.

After a painfully long time in which several people nodded off, the chime rang again and the group headed to Messenger training.

Although Master Linus's lesson didn't involve anything as spectacular as holograms, Lucy thought it was by far the most fun. Following up on their last lesson regarding the role of Messengers on earth, Linus demonstrated the importance of wearing proper disguises while on Walker missions.

"I think the look works for yeh," snickered Sandy, as they sat down for dinner a little while later.

From across the table Babu shot her a nasty look as he stabbed at a pork chop. Unable to get rid of his disguise, he was still sporting red braids and a mass of freckles.

"You know, you two could be sisters," said Puddles, looking from Lucy to Babu.

Babu grumbled something under his breath and went back to attacking his food.

"Yo! I so totally forgot," said Tibs, reaching into his sash and pulling out a small silver scroll tied with a red ribbon. "One of the Scouts asked me to give this to you."

He held out the scroll to Lucy. One glance at the purple ink and she knew who it was from.

"Thanks," she said, hastily taking the scroll and shoving it into her sash.

"Why…" Haddie began, giving Lucy a suspicious look. But just then the gong rang out signaling the end of dinner and the shuffling of chairs drowned out the rest of Haddie's question.

"Great!" exclaimed Lucy, relieved that she had been saved by the bell. "Time for Reflection."

"Uh, Lucy, haven't you forgotten something?" said Ben, pulling Samuel's note from his sash.

Lucy's stomach gave a queasy turn. Between the excitement of the holograms and the anxiety of receiving another mysterious note, Lucy had completely forgotten about their appointment.

As the others waved good-bye and headed up the stairs, Lucy, Ben and Puddles followed Banks out into the warm night air.

"This way," Banks said solemnly, as he led them down the sloping hill towards the library.

Lucy and Ben exchanged looks wondering if perhaps Samuel's office was in the large marble library, but when they reached the bottom of the hill Banks changed directions and began heading towards the mountains. For several minutes they walked in silence through the growing darkness until finally Banks stopped in front of an old gnarled tree that stood alone in the middle of the meadow. The ancient tree appeared dead and seemed oddly out of place in a field so alive with flowers. Its twisted, bare branches and tattered bark reminded Lucy of a very old man misshapen by a long, hard life.

"Here you are," said Banks, finally breaking the silence.

Ben gave a nervous laugh. "Good one, Banks!"

Banks raised his brow causing his forehead to crinkle. "I'm glad to see you're in such high spirits. Most people who had been called before a Keeper would show a little more concern."

Ben's laugh dissolved into a strained cough as the smile faded from his face.

"I was told to bring you to Samuel's office and that's what I've done. You are on your own from here."

Puddles looked from side to side and finally up into the bare branches overhead. Lucy could tell they were all thinking the same thing: *where was Samuel?* Before anyone could ask what was going on Banks stepped up to the tree and gave the twisted trunk three hard raps.

"Enter," said a voice from within the tree, causing Lucy, Ben and Puddles to jump.

Suddenly a rough archway appeared in the gnarled trunk and a familiar greenish mist began spilling out.

"Step on up...our Keeper's a busy man," said Banks, waving them forward. "Samuel will show you how to get back to the cottage when he is through with you."

"You aren't coming with us," said Lucy, her voice sounding unnaturally high.

The corner of Banks' mouth twitched upwards.

"Our honorable Keeper has not eaten an attendant yet and I seriously doubt you will be the first. Of course most would not make him wait so long after being bid to enter."

Lucy glanced over at Puddles who had turned as green as the mist pouring out of the portal. Ben gave her a nod which she understood to mean '*go ahead*'.

Looking back at the green fog, Lucy tried not to think about what was waiting on the other side. With her legs trembling as though they had no bones, Lucy stepped forward into the mist; in a flash of light she left the meadow behind.

A spray of salt water stung Lucy's face as she blinked against the bright light. With a sudden crash a splash of cold water washed over her feet and Lucy felt her toes sink into the wet sand. Before she could fully register where she was there was a loud THUD and Puddles toppled on to the sand by her side.

"Where are we?" he asked, scrambling to his feet.

Before Lucy could answer there was another crash and Puddles' feet were swept out from underneath him leaving him in a pile of seaweed.

"Tahiti, I think."

Ben's voice made Lucy jump. With all the confusion she hadn't seen him arrive.

He reached down and lifted Puddles' soggy figure out of the seaweed. Surveying their surroundings, Ben wiped the perspiration from his forehead and declared with certainty, "My gram took me to Tahiti for my 14th birthday and it looked just like this."

Lucy was just about to point out that Tahiti was on earth which must be a million miles away when a familiar voice called from up the beach.

"Welcome!"

Samuel was strolling towards them, his long robe leaving a trail in the sand.

"I'm glad you are here...I just received an urgent message that I am needed elsewhere, so our time is limited. Please," he gestured towards a small grass hut that rested at the edge of the beach beneath a crooked palm tree, "follow me."

Lucy, Ben and Puddles mutely followed Samuel up the sandy incline to the primitive hut that sat on a small patch of thin grass. Overhead Lucy could hear the squawking of a pair of brightly colored birds that were watching them with interest. The hut, which appeared to be made out of old palm leaves, was swaying in the breeze. Taking a deep breath, Lucy caught the sweet smell of island flowers.

"This is your office?" said Puddles, gawking at the tiny hut.

"For today," said Samuel matter-of-factly. "I felt the need for a bit of sun and I've found I rather like the waves." He grinned as there was another crash on the beach below.

Stepping through the lopsided doorway of the hut, Lucy was caught by surprise at the sight of the humble decor. She had half expected the shack to be another portal leading into an elaborate office filled with mahogany bookshelves and elegant furniture, a symbol of the importance of Samuel's position. But the hut was not a portal and inside all she found were a few colorful, woven mats spread out on the sand and a long golden staff propped up in the corner. Lucy recognized the staff at once as the one Truman had used to save her from the dream passage.

"Please sit." Samuel waved a hand toward the mats. "You will have to excuse me, but I must gather some things together while we talk."

Lucy looked curiously around the room. As far as she could tell there was nothing there to gather.

"Who would like to start?"

Ben opened his mouth but before he could speak Puddles let out a surprised gasp. A small stone table had appeared out of nowhere cluttered with books and papers.

As Samuel began shuffling through the papers he glanced over at Ben who was staring at him with his mouth hanging open. "Please proceed; I assure you I can listen and work at the same time."

Giving a shaky nod, Ben began to explain what had happened before, during and after the dinosaurs' stampede. To Lucy's relief he left out the part about Banks and Tobias; she doubted Samuel would approve of eavesdropping on their Cottage Master's private conversation.

Samuel continued to sort through his papers, arranging them into stacks and filing them into a leather satchel which had appeared at his feet. He listened without interrupting, offering only an occasional, "*I see*" or "*Hmmm*".

When Ben finally came to the end of his story he let out a deep breath and gave Lucy a shaky smile. Lucy glanced up at Samuel expecting him to hand down their punishment but he continued to sort through his papers, seemingly unaware that Ben had stopped speaking. For several long minutes the only sound in the hut was the ruffling of papers and the crinkling of Puddles' mat as he squirmed nervously waiting for Samuel to speak. Lucy was beginning to wonder if she should say something when one of the brightly colored birds waddled into the hut and let out a loud squawk. Samuel nodded to the bird, then picking up the last stack of papers and tucking them into his satchel he looked up and said, "Thank you. Now I must be off."

"That's it?" The words poured out of Lucy's mouth before she could stop them.

Samuel's crystal blue eyes fell on her. "Is there something else you feel I ought to know?"

Lucy gulped as she had the familiar sensation Samuel was reading her thoughts. She tried to wipe her mind clear but it was like trying not to imagine a pink elephant. The harder she tried not to think of the voices, the more stubbornly they stood out in her mind.

Finally Lucy shook her head. "No, Ben pretty much covered it all."

Samuel said nothing for a moment. Finally he reached down and picked up the bulging satchel. "Well then, I must be off. You will find that when you leave this hut you will be returned to your cottage." He started for the opening that led out to the beach.

"Sir!" said Lucy suddenly.

Samuel stopped and turned around. "Yes?"

"Sorry, it's nothing really…it's just that I was wondering…what would have happened if we hadn't made it to the boulders? I mean they couldn't have hurt us, could they? The dinosaurs? After all, we're already…well, you know."

The smallest of smiles crossed Samuel's face but Lucy thought in some odd way it made him look sad. "You will learn that there are other deaths besides those of the body; deaths that are far worse."

"Worse?" said Ben. "I don't understand."

Samuel let out a small sigh that seemed to carry the weight of the world. "*Fear* of death – even for those who no longer have a body to harm – can paralyze the soul and demolish hope. The Forgotten City is filled with those who have suffered death by fear. Refusing to believe that their bodies are gone, they exist in a nightmare where they are forced to relive their greatest fears over and over."

Lucy felt an awful tingle run through her body.

"Does that mean that if we had really believed the dinosaurs were going to harm us then we would have fallen into some kind of dream where we would keep being trampled to death?"

Lucy hoped she had misunderstood, but Samuel's silence confirmed it.

"That's awful," whispered Puddles.

"But why can't you just go in to the Forgotten City and wake them up?" asked Ben.

"We all must learn our own lessons in our own time; no one else can do that for us. When they are ready, they will awaken. It's a slow process, but we can wait."

The parrot who had been standing in the doorway gave another squawk.

"Unfortunately some things can't wait. Thank you for sharing your time with me this evening." With a nod good-bye, Samuel stepped out of the hut and in a blink was gone.

As Samuel had promised, when they stepped out of the hut Lucy, Ben and Puddles found themselves back in the cottage. To Lucy's relief, the lodge was deserted. Thoughts of being trampled by prehistoric beasts in an eternal nightmare had left her shaken and feeling less than sociable. Tomorrow their cottagemates would want to know all about their meeting with the Kingdom's most famous inhabitant, but tonight all Lucy wanted to do was go to bed.

Ben and Puddles seemed anxious to put the night behind them as well, so without any further discussion of the night's events they said goodnight and headed for their rooms.

Lucy's room was dark except for a warm light flickering from the lantern hanging by her bedside. Feeling like she could sleep for days, she flung herself on to her pillow. As she rolled over something slipped from under her sash and slid onto the bed. The note! Her meeting with Samuel had completely driven it out of her mind. Sitting up, Lucy moved closer to the light and hastily untied the ribbon. As the parchment unfurled Lucy squinted at the fine purple script. Holding the paper closer to the flickering lantern Lucy saw that this note was considerably longer than the first. With her heart racing, she scanned the page.

Dear Ms. O'Sullivan,

I was pleased, albeit surprised, to learn that you have already begun receiving voices outside of your sleep. This is quite impressive for a new attendant and suggests that you have been placed here for reasons outside our understanding.

However, and this is a very important point, until you learn how to control your power it will prove to be useless…and possibly dangerous. Therefore, I am offering my services to help you hone your skills. For reasons I am not at liberty to explain, our lessons must be conducted via written communication. I must also ask that you not mention our arrangement to anyone other than your closest and most trusted friends. Masters Ben and Puddles should be safe, but please impress upon them the importance of keeping your secret.

I will be in touch again soon. In the meantime, listen closely to what the voices are saying but do not forget…the only voice you can completely trust is your own.

Forever True,
A Fellow Traveler

Lucy read the note several times before rolling it back up and tucking it inside her old jeans alongside the first note.

Her mind was swimming as she wandered over to the window and looked out at the starlit night. The moon was full, illuminating the forest in the distance.

"Who are you?" Lucy whispered, peering into the shadows. Someone out there was watching her very closely.

CHAPTER NINE

THE MIGHTY COLONEL GEORGE

The next morning Lucy pulled Ben and Puddles aside after Rejuvenation and showed them the note. Ben read it several times, his eyes growing wider with each reading.

"You know what this means don't you?" said Ben, lowering his voice.

"That someone creepy is watching us?" said Puddles, nervously glancing over his shoulder.

"No, it means that all these voices Lucy hears aren't just some dream. They're real, and more importantly they *mean* something." He looked back down at the note. "'...*you've been placed here for reasons outside our understanding*.' Lucy, this is big. This is destiny stuff."

"Destiny?" Lucy had no idea what that meant, but she didn't like the sound of it.

Thankfully today was their first lesson with Colonel George and the note was soon forgotten. The rumors surrounding the Colonel were impressive but a bit frightening and Lucy was hoping they weren't all true.

"I heard he fought beside Cassiel in the last dark war," said Ben, as they made their way up the south stairway to George's room.

"A guy from Island Cottage told me the dark forces are really scared of George," said Puddles, the color draining from his face. "You don't suppose he'd try anything, you know, *scary* in class do you?"

"No way," said Lucy, trying to sound braver than she felt. "We may not be angels, but we're hardly dark forces."

"Unless you count Haddie," said Ben, sending Puddles into a fit of giggles.

By the time they reached the fifth floor their cottagemates were already gathered around the classroom door.

"Go on dear, you were the first one here," said Anna, gently pushing Babu forward.

"I do not see why I should be punished for promptness," said Babu, backing away from the door.

"Blimey, what a bunch of namby-pambies" grumbled Sandy. "I'll open the bloody door. How bad can this guy be?"

With a look that could have withered a crocodile, Sandy reached for the door knob. As her fingers touched the handle the door suddenly swung open and the group let out a gasp taking a giant step backwards and nearly knocking Puddles down the stairs.

"I have tried holding class on the landing, but I find it far more comfortable inside."

No one moved. Lucy looked from Ben to Puddles and then back at the figure in the doorway. This must be a joke, she thought.

Standing before them, with arms folded and casting a steely glare that would put Sandy to shame, was a small girl with round pink cheeks and bouncy golden curls streaming down her back.

"Who are *you*?" asked Lucy, wondering if this was some kind of practical joke.

The girl, who Lucy guessed couldn't be more than eight, raised her eyebrows in an oddly mature manner for someone so young. "I am Colonel George – Georgina to be quite correct – and if I am not mistaken, you are my class."

The group exchanged skeptical looks.

"But...you're a *child*," Haddie finally announced in a tone of disgust.

"And a girl!" blurted Tibs.

"A very astute observation, I must say. You have a keen sense for the obvious, Master Tibs. Now if you would all be so kind as to step inside."

Colonel George turned and entered the room as the class reluctantly filed in behind her still in shock.

"*She* scared out the forces of darkness?" Ben whispered to Lucy, as they found a couple of empty seats towards the back of the classroom. "She doesn't look like she could even scare Puddles."

Indeed, Puddles was looking unusually happy. He didn't seem at all disappointed with Colonel George's appearance and was the only one to choose a seat in the front row.

"I see the rumors of my escapades are still flourishing," said Colonel George, surveying the empty seats up front. "However, you should not believe all that you hear."

"Then the stories about you aren't true?" asked Puddles, sounding extremely relieved.

"Oh no, they are all perfectly true. But as a general rule rumors are not trustworthy."

Puddles' smile faded.

Pulling out an empty chair, Colonel George delicately hoisted herself on to the seat and looked around the room. "There, that is much better. Being four feet tall has distinct advantages in certain situations, but it can be rather a nuisance when addressing a class."

The professor's eyes swept the room. "Now, who can tell me why you are in this class?"

The room was silent. Lucy gazed at Ben who was sitting with his mouth hanging open; he was obviously still trying to figure out what was going on.

"My, you are a quiet bunch. Master Tibs, perhaps you can help us. Why are you here?"

"Because I died?"

Sandy snickered.

"Ah, yes," said Colonel George, smiling down at Tibs. "Thank you for yet another insightful observation. We really must make sure to put that talent to use."

Tibs' face broke into a wide grin as he glanced around the room to make sure everyone had heard that the Colonel thought he had talent.

"I was, however, looking for something a bit more specific. Can anyone tell me why you are in this *particular* class?"

No one spoke.

"I see," said George, glancing around the room. "It appears that Master Tibs speaks for you all?"

Ben's hand slowly rose into the air. "Excuse me, sir...I mean, ma'am...I mean, Colonel George."

"Yes, Master Benjamin, do you have something to add to the 'we died' theory?"

"Well..." Ben looked as if the words were sticking in his throat, "...aren't we here so you can teach us how to protect Walkers...you know, Guardian stuff?" Ben lowered his hand, his face glowing red.

"Brilliant," whispered Haddie under her breath, rolling her eyes.

"Exactly!" exclaimed George, and Lucy heard Haddie give a loud huff. "Teleporting, materialization, telepathy...these are merely fancy tricks unless put to proper use. My task is to train you on how to use these tools and many others so that you might protect your charges and, yes, battle when necessary the forces that attempt to get in your way. In other words to, as Master Benjamin so eloquently put it, do 'Guardian stuff'."

Everyone but Haddie seemed excited by this news. Babu was practically bouncing in his chair; finally they were going to learn something worthwhile. Haddie sat with her arms crossed, her eyes boring into Colonel George.

Now that, thought Lucy, *is a look that could scare the dark forces.*

"Before you can proceed, it is crucial that you understand the first rule of Guardianship." Colonel George gave a casual flick of her hand and to everyone's amazement a large blackboard suddenly appeared. As she spoke, a piece of yellow chalk transcribed her words on to the board.

"Rule # 1: A Guardian's job is not to determine the path taken but to protect the traveler once the journey has begun."

She snapped her fingers and the words floated off the board and hung in mid-air. "In other classes you will discuss how to guide poor, clueless souls in the right direction. That is not our purpose; a Guardian's job is far more precarious. We must intimately understand the world of darkness and the way it weaves through the fabric of life; we must use instinct to determine which strands must be delicately plucked and which must be left in place. For a life without danger is a life without lessons." She looked each student in the eye to make sure the importance of this message was not missed.

Hopping off her chair, Colonel George began pacing between the rows of chairs. Lucy couldn't help but notice that standing on flat ground she was only as tall as the rest of them were seated.

"So who can tell me how we might accomplish this impossible feat of determining which threads of danger are to be removed and which should be left alone?"

Out of the corner of her eye Lucy saw her friends shifting in their seats, looking down, hoping not to be called on.

"You...." Lucy's heart sank as she raised her eyes and discovered Colonel George staring directly at her. "...any ideas?"

"Well," said Lucy, feeling suddenly like someone had turned up the furnace, "…I guess I would have to say…that probably…you know, most of the time… under the right circumstances…" She wondered how much longer she could drag this out before Colonel George would demand an actual answer.

Someone suddenly spoke out. Lucy looked around the room to see who it was but all she saw were nine pairs of eyes staring back at her.

"What I was saying…," she continued.

There it was again! But this time Lucy knew exactly where it was coming from. Closing her eyes she listened to the voice in her head that had begun rapidly firing off information.

"Miss Lucy…"

"We don't!" Lucy blurted before she could stop herself.

"Excuse me?" said Colonel George, with a chill in her voice.

"What I mean," said Lucy, trying to ignore the look of horror Puddles was giving her, "…is that it's not really the Guardian who makes the decision; the decision is made, well, higher up."

There was a numbing silence throughout the room as her cottagemates stared at her in disbelief.

"So," said Colonel George, her dark eyes drilling into Lucy, "are you suggesting that a Guardian is some kind of puppet waiting to have their strings pulled so they will know which direction to turn?"

Lucy closed her eyes again and listened for help but the voice had disappeared; she was on her own. Swallowing hard, she tried to remember what it had said. Looking up she met the Colonel's unblinking gaze.

"Not a puppet," she said, picking her words carefully. "More like…well, like a detective."

"Go on."

Lucy now understood how Colonel George had scared away the forces of evil; although only half Lucy's size, she suddenly seemed ten feet tall and utterly terrifying. Mustering all the strength she had to keep her voice from shaking, Lucy straightened up in her chair and looked Colonel George dead in the eye. If she was going down, she would do it with dignity.

"Like you said," Lucy said, in a falsely confident voice, "a Guardian doesn't determine the path someone takes, so it would make sense that they don't choose the risks either. That's already been decided by their destiny." There was that word again. "So in order to figure out which obstacles to remove and which ones to leave alone, a Guardian needs to be really good at reading the signs – like a detective."

Complete silence hovered over the room as Colonel George glared at Lucy with an expression of stone. The confidence she had felt just moments ago was quickly evaporating as everyone sat speechless waiting for Colonel George to unleash her legendary temper. Lucy could feel her heart pounding in her ears. Why had she listened to the voice? She didn't even know where it came from. It could very likely belong to some deranged spirit with a warped sense of humor who thought it would be a great laugh to see Lucy make a fool of herself and she had been stupid enough to take the bait.

After what seemed like an eternity, Colonel George turned and walked briskly to the front of the room. "What are you waiting for?" she called over her shoulder. "You heard her; write it down!" Colonel George hopped back on to her chair and when she turned around Lucy was relieved to see she was smiling.

"Miss Lucy, that was a brilliant guess. If I didn't know better, I would think someone had told you the answer."

Lucy choked but quickly hid it with a cough. For the briefest of moments she thought she caught a knowing glance from Colonel George before she launched into her lesson.

After reiterating Lucy's description of Guardian responsibilities and answering numerous questions – mostly from Haddie who was exceedingly irate that Lucy had stumbled upon a correct answer - the Colonel spent the rest of the class regaling them with stories of how she had helped some of the world's greatest figures navigate their destiny.

"...and that is how I saved Ben Franklin from being toasted by his little kite-flying trick." Colonel George took a small bow and the class erupted in applause.

"Brilliant!" exclaimed Ben, who was staring awestruck at the Colonel. "She's amazing."

"She's beyond amazing," said Puddles in a reverent whisper. "She's incredible." The Colonel's stories were so exciting that he had temporarily forgotten to be scared of her.

"Really you two, get a grip on yourselves," said Haddie. "You would think she was Joan of Arc the way you're carrying on."

"No way," said Ben, waving off Haddie's comments. "She's way cooler than Joan of Arc."

The chime announcing the end of class was met with a groan of disappointment by everyone but Haddie.

"Before we adjourn," called Colonel George over the shuffling of chairs, "I must hand out your assignments."

She opened the drawer of her ornate mahogany desk and pulled out a bright green folder. "Each of you will receive a Walker case study for training purposes. It will be your task to unravel the hidden meaning of your Walker's destiny, evaluate the obstacles presented and design a course of action to guard them against all unnecessary - and possibly dangerous - situations."

"Blimey," muttered Sandy, who suddenly looked like she would rather be wrestling a crocodile than trying to work out someone's destiny.

"What if we screw up?" said Puddles. "I can barely manage my own life without getting in trouble."

"Not to worry," said Colonel George, ignoring the snickering coming from Haddie's direction. "Each Walker has already been assigned to a senior attendant who is overseeing their case. Your job is to merely develop a plan of action; not to actually execute it. Direct Walker contact is expressly forbidden at this stage of your training."

Colonel George opened the folder and pulled out a small, glistening sheet of green paper.

"Master Arthur, I think you will find your Walker quite interesting. He is a lion trainer in Paris. Fascinating story."

Arthur took the small green slip of paper from Colonel George.

"Oh my, a lion tamer!" he said excitedly. "Not hard to imagine what kind of piddly-wickets he might get in to."

Colonel George continued down the rows of students commenting on each Walker as she handed out the glimmering forms. Lucy was the last to receive a green slip of paper.

"Quite unusual," said George, eyeing the form suspiciously before handing it to Lucy.

The smooth green paper was made of an odd jelly-like substance that felt cool in Lucy's fingers. She flipped the paper over and saw the name of her case study was written in distinct golden script:

Please allow the bearer of this receipt to withdraw the Life Map of <u>Agatha Louise O'Sullivan.</u>

Lucy's eyes flew over the name again. This couldn't be right.

"Uh…Professor, I think there's been some kind of mistake." As much as Lucy wanted to believe this was true, surely she wouldn't be assigned a member of her own family.

"There's been no mistake," said George. And then with a look that clearly meant this was serious business, she added, "I trust you will give this assignment the attention it deserves."

Before Lucy could say anything, Colonel George briskly turned away sending her blond curls flying and marched back to the front of the class.

"You will begin your assignments by gathering information on your Walker. Unlike attendant Life Maps which are kept in the Dream Chamber and are off limits, Walker Life Maps may be obtained in the library. Tomorrow we will discuss your findings."

Colonel George took her seat behind the giant desk, her tiny frame nearly disappearing. She lowered her head over a stack of papers and began scribbling notes. Apparently class was over.

Everyone exchanged anxious glances wondering if it was okay to leave. When Colonel George continued to ignore them Ben gave a shrug and started towards the door. Lucy had just begun to follow him when Colonel George's voice made her stop in her tracks.

"One last thing before you go," said Colonel George, not bothering to look up from her work. "Life Maps can only be checked out with the official Life Analysis Map Procurement – or *LAMP* - forms you are holding in your hands. A few *creative* students have attempted to forge these forms in order to check out unauthorized Life Maps. I assure you all attempts have failed."

She looked up and Lucy thought her face looked much older than it had before.

"Knowledge of a person's destiny can be highly useful, but it can also be extremely dangerous if not handled properly."

For a split second the professor's eyes rested on Lucy and Lucy felt a strange connection. There was no inner voice confirming her suspicion, but somehow she knew the warning was meant for her.

****

Despite her rough beginning at Drookshire, Lucy eventually settled into a routine and the days began to speed by. As their skills grew so did their mountain of homework. Besides George's Life Map assignment, they were also expected to learn 100 different ways to send messages through dreams for Messenger class, construct a Walker ancestral chart complete with past life information for Christof and prepare for a concert that would demonstrate the importance of music in the evolution of the soul. The only class that was homework-free was Reflection and Lucy guessed it was only because Anaja hadn't figured out a way to make them study while meditating. On top of everything else Lucy was still the only one unable to teleport so Mira had added extra practices for her every evening.

Lucy also had to contend with the mysterious notes which now arrived almost daily. Her secret correspondent, whom Ben had nicknamed The Traveler because of the way the letters were signed, had taken to sending Lucy odd trinkets of advice which she dismissed as completely useless.

"*When voices speak to you, engage them in conversation. Unfriendly spirits want to command, not to converse.*" or, "*To increase your energy, upon waking face the east and breathe in the rising sun.*"

"Breathe in the sun?" said Lucy, crumpling up the latest note. "I mean really, how exactly how am I supposed to do that?"

Lucy, Ben and Puddles were huddled together at their usual table in the library. In the weeks since Colonel George's return they had spent every free moment tucked away in the glimmering, white marble, five-story complex that housed the Life Maps of every human on earth. Besides the maps – which were carefully guarded on the third floor by Chester, the Master Librarian – the brightly lit library was filled with row upon row of glass shelves filled with thousands of books covering subjects Lucy had never known existed.

The members of Hill Cottage had taken over a large round table near an immense circular window that looked out over the field leading up to the station. Across the table Tibs, Babu and Sandy were in a heated discussion about whether or not it would be okay for Tibs to *accidentally* drop a boulder on his Walker's boss.

"The guy's like a total creep…we'd be doin' the world a favor."

Anna and Arthur were reading a book together, taking turns flipping the pages, and Haddie had buried herself behind a fortress of books and was trying to act as if she didn't know them.

Heaving a heavy sigh, Lucy shoved the crumpled note into her sash and hoisted a large book off the stack Ben had collected for their studies.

They had quickly learned that Life Maps were more of a complex riddle than a clear outline of a person's future and deciphering them was proving to be a difficult task.

"This is hopeless," said Lucy, flipping open the massive book to a chapter labeled *Why Walkers Love Chaos*.

Ben and Puddles were buried in their own studies and didn't bother to look up.

"Why can't they just come out and say, 'Agatha O'Sullivan will grow up to be a good person, although slightly eccentric; she'll be obsessed with board games, have a weird attraction to really bad décor and will eventually die from an overdose of banana cream pie.' I mean, would that be so tough? But *noooo*, they have to write some confusing, esoteric crap that makes absolutely no sense."

"Listen to this…" Lucy reached over and nudged Ben to get his attention. He put down the paper he was studying and gave Lucy a look that suggested she better make this quick. Ignoring his glare, Lucy unrolled the green scroll that was Aunt Aggie's Life Map and began reading out loud.

"You will be born to the family of O'Sullivan in the earthly year of 1946 on the date of December 24 and you will be called blessed by the angels for you will nurture the light that has been sent to break the darkness. Your life will be played with joy and you will be an example to all who see the beauty of the garden is found in each flower.

"On the day that has been destined by the Power of Life, darkness will overcome your spirit as the light is extinguished and day is thrown into endless night. It will be your journey's task to find the key that will unlock the spirit of one who has forgotten how to fly and in doing so set the stage for the light to return."

"Honestly," Lucy exclaimed, throwing the Life Map on to the table, "does any of that make sense? How am I supposed to figure out how to help Aunt Aggie if I can't even decipher this…this *thing*!"

"SSSHHHH!" Haddie shot Lucy a nasty look from across the table.

"You wanna trade," said Puddles glumly. He was slumped in his chair staring at the Life Map in front of him.

"My guy is supposed to do something with 'curing the evils that vex men's souls'. I'd take your aunt's garden of flowers over vexing evils any day."

"Look," said Ben, ignoring Haddie's drilling gaze, "I've told you, you just need to read between the lines. All that stuff about being thrown into endless night and finding a key is just a metaphor for something else. What you need to do is just relax and forget about it for a while. You need a diversion and I've got just the thing." Ben held up a book titled *Angelic Forces at Work*.

Lucy groaned and shook her head. After their meeting with Samuel, Ben had given up his idea that Samuel was behind Lucy's notes; instead he was now convinced that The Traveler was an angel. Determined to prove his new theory, he had begun ignoring his Walker studies and had thrown himself into learning all he could about their mysterious winged counterparts.

"Look," he said, dropping his voice to a whisper and opening the book to an earmarked page, "it says right here…'*Angels are sentient beings, accomplished in the art of tele-sensory communication. This rare skill makes them valuable allies in matters requiring non-standard communication.*'"

Lucy was sure The Traveler was no angel – after all, written notes could hardly be considered "non-standard communication" - but she was too tired to argue. As Ben went on about the mystical power of angels, Lucy leaned back in her chair and gazed out the window at the sun drenched grounds. She had been amazed to discover when she woke up that morning that the world outside had transformed overnight. Gone were the translucent green leaves that glittered across Drookshire's wide valley. Instead she found that the hillside was painted in brilliant colors of red, orange, gold and purple as though someone had snuck in overnight and painted every leaf in the valley. Apparently fall had arrived in Drookshire.

"Lucy…*LUCY*! Are you even listening to me," said Ben, waiving a hand in front of Lucy's glazed eyes.

"Huh? Oh, sorry, I must have drifted off for a second."

"Hey!" cried Puddles excitedly. "Here's one on disembodied voices! OW!"

Lucy had kicked him hard under the table.

"Do you mind?" snapped Haddie, glaring at them over the top of a monstrous book titled *Celestial Warriors, Tricks and Tactics*. "Some of us are trying to study."

"Oh, get off it," said Ben. "You haven't studied anything on your Walker in two weeks."

It was true; in the time since Colonel George had given them their assignments, Haddie had spent most of their library time with her head buried in books about the history of celestial battles.

"Can I help it if I found that ridiculous assignment laughably easy? Honestly, I had the whole thing finished in three days. Surely she could have thought of something a little more challenging for us to do; we aren't children after all."

Haddie always referred to Colonel George as "she" or "that girl".

"Anyway," said Haddie, gathering up her papers, "I'm working on something much more important than some silly assignment we can't even put to use."

"And what exactly is this big, important project? A forty foot wall to put around the Kingdom?" said Ben, leaning across the table to get a better look at Haddie's notes.

"Hardly," said Haddie, snapping shut her notebook. "Putting up a wall would be useless in a world where people can teleport. Even *you* should realize that."

"Well if we're so dimwitted why don't you just tell us what you're doing?" said Lucy.

"In time," said Haddie, standing up to leave. "But not before I've explained it all to the Council. I've asked Banks to set up a meeting. Samuel and the other Keepers will be very interested to see what I've got in here." She patted the notebook, giving them an annoyingly smug grin. Then turning sharply, she marched out of the library.

"She's nuts if she thinks Samuel gives a hoot about her *big plan*," said Ben, picking up one of the books Haddie had left behind. "Look at this…*The Forgotten City – Are They Really Sleeping?* I mean, who's interested in this stuff?"

"Quite a few people actually," said a familiar, deep voice.

"Banks!" said Lucy, slipping Puddle's book on disembodied voices under the table. "I didn't know you were back."

Although Banks still occasionally attended their training sessions, he frequently disappeared for stretches of time claiming to be working on something for Samuel. It had been six days since they last saw him.

"Let me guess," he said, picking a book up off the table, "Walker research for George's class?"

"Yes, sir," said Puddles.

"How well I remember," Banks sighed. "That woman gave me nightmares when I was a new attendant."

Lucy looked at Banks in surprise. Staring up at his massive frame it was hard to imagine him as a freshman attendant, but it was even harder to believe he had ever been scared by tiny Colonel George.

"Don't be so surprised," Banks laughed, seeing the look on Lucy's face. "The little Colonel has toppled men mightier than me, I assure you."

Lucy gave a nervous laugh but this information didn't make her feel any better about her unfinished assignment.

"Well, I won't keep you from your studies," he said, and he placed the book back on the table. "I just stopped by to give you this."

Banks reached into his sash and pulled out a small, ancient-looking leather bound book.

"I understand that you've been having some difficulties with bad dreams," he said, handing the battered book to Lucy. "This should help."

Lucy looked at the book's worn cover. *Just Say No to Nightmares*.

"Uh, thank you, sir. But how did you know…"

"It's my job to know everything about my attendants. I've found things run much smoother if there are no secrets."

Goose bumps sprang to life on Lucy's arms as she remembered Banks' threat, "Do not push me Tobias or I will be forced to reveal secrets that will make you most unhappy."

What did he know about Lucy's secret dreams and who had told him? For someone who didn't like secrets, Banks seemed to have quite a few of his own.

After Banks left the library, Lucy, Ben and Puddles gathered up their things and headed up the hill for dinner.

"So," Ben whispered, checking over his shoulder to make sure they were alone, "did you hear anything?"

It took a moment for Lucy to realize what he was asking. She shook her head. "Nothing," she replied.

"But last time you picked up his thoughts and he wasn't even near you," said Ben. "It has to be easier when he's standing right in front of you."

"I told you, it doesn't work that way; I can't just summon people's thoughts," Lucy said, annoyed that Ben seemed to be suggesting she hadn't tried hard enough.

They walked the rest of the way in silence and when they reached the Station Lucy claimed she had lost her appetite and was going to bed.

"What about Reflection?" said Puddles, looking shocked at the thought of deliberately skipping class.

"Tell Anaja I'm not feeling well," Lucy said. This wasn't a lie. Their meeting with Banks had left her feeling unsettled. Before Ben could argue, she said good-night and started for the cottage portals.

Plopping on to her bed, Lucy pulled out the book Banks had given her and studied the worn cover. It had definitely seen better days. Flipping it open she turned to the index and began scanning the chapter titles.

Chapter I: *Why Dreams Matter*
Chapter II: *Bad Dream or Nightmare? How to Decide*
Chapter III: *Dream Walkers: Can They Help?*
Chapter IV: *What to do When Your Nightmare Comes True*

Lucy felt the air go out of the room as her eyes fell on the next chapter. With her heart beginning to race she shuffled through the pages until she came to the right spot.

Chapter V: *Voices in Your Dreams: Why You Should Be Worried*

At some point in your life you will undoubtedly experience voices in your sleep which seem to be coming from an outside source. In most instances these voices are actually a type of internal monologue – or more simply put, your own thoughts making themselves known. These auditory thoughts are harmless and can even be useful if dealt with properly.

However, on rare occasions outside voices can infiltrate dreams and this must be taken very seriously. (Note:

Remember, there is an important difference between hearing thoughts and hearing voices. Since all living things are interconnected by a stream of energy, it is reasonable to expect that from time to time thoughts might inadvertently cross over from one person to another – rather like taking the wrong off-ramp on the Super Thought Highway. For more on this subject, see Chapter XII: I'm Having My Sister's Nightmares.)

Voices, on the other hand, are comprised of a lower frequency and do not randomly fall into dreams; they must be sought out by the dreamer. Seeking outside voices via dreams requires the dreamer to enter into another's consciousness which is expressly forbidden by the Universal Code for Privacy as set forth by the Celestial Council. Individuals found guilty will...

Lucy turned the page and found the rest of the chapter had been torn out.

"Will what?" she said, frantically rereading the passage. What did it mean that voices were sought out by the dreamer? She had never gone looking for the voices; she didn't want the voices!

Quickly searching the rest of the book for more information, Lucy's mind began to spin. She had convinced herself that the voices were just part of her bizarre dream, but now she had to wonder if those terrible cries for help were real. And if the voices were real did that mean that the horrid place of her nightmares was real, too?

Finding no more mention of voices, Lucy slammed the book shut and fell back on her pillow. Contrary to what Banks had said, this was not going to help her sleep.

CHAPTER TEN

AN UNLIKELY PARTNERSHIP

Lucy shuffled into the Meeting Hall and dropped into her chair. She had overslept, missing Rejuvenation and barely getting to breakfast before it ended.

"Don't take this the wrong way," said Ben, eyeing Lucy with concern, "but you look awful."

"No she doesn't," said Puddles defensively, pouring Lucy a large glass of orange juice.

Lucy gave Puddles a weak smile of appreciation, took a sip of juice and managed to spill a large portion down her front.

"Okay, that was pretty gross," he said.

Glancing around the table, Lucy saw that Banks was missing again. This boosted her spirits; as much as she liked Banks, she didn't think she could look him in the eye this morning. She couldn't help but wonder if he had been the one to rip out those pages and if so, why?

Arriving late, Lucy didn't have time to tell Ben and Puddles about what she had learned from the book before the chime rang out for the beginning of lessons. Gulping down the rest of her juice she tucked a piece of toast in her sash for later and prepared to join the queue leaving the hall.

"Ladies and gentleman of Hill Cottage…" Tobias's voice carried over the scraping of chairs. "Madame Mira has been sent to rescue a member of the Island Cottage from a bad teleport, therefore today's lesson is cancelled."

Lucy saw several of the Island Cottage attendants snickering at their cottagemate's misfortune. Her own cottagemates also seemed quite pleased by Tobias's announcement. Unlike her, they had mastered teleporting and weren't worried about missing a lesson. Each having their own idea on the best way to spend a free period, they said their good-byes and took off in different directions. Only Ben and Puddles stayed behind with Lucy.

"So, what do you think?" said Ben. "Anyone up for hike in the forest?"

"You go ahead," said Lucy. "I'm going down to the garden to practice. Maybe Mira will get back early; I could use the help."

"I'll help you!" said Puddles enthusiastically.

Lucy thought he looked relieved for an excuse not to go into the forest.

Ben shrugged. "Fine, we'll all go. I could use a good laugh."

Lucy pretended to be offended, smacking him on the shoulder and sending Puddles into a fit of giggles.

The air was crisp and filled with the scent of pumpkin pie as they headed down the hill towards the garden.

Picking up where he had left off the day before, Ben started in once more about the obvious similarities between The Traveler and the mysterious beings known as angels.

"You've got to admit it's a possibility," he said, as they ducked under the ivy-draped arch leading into the garden.

"Ben, exactly how many angels have you seen hanging around Drookshire?" asked Lucy, dodging the low hanging branch of an apple tree.

"Well, none, but…"

"My point exactly. Whoever this Traveler person is they are close enough to know exactly what I'm doing; they're not hovering out there in angel land." Lucy waved her hand towards the sky.

"The place is called Nayopi and I've told you, they don't need to be standing next to you to know what you're up to," Ben said, helping Puddles over a fallen tree trunk.

Lucy rolled her eyes and pushed through the overgrown lilac bush that led into the clearing where they held teleporting class. Puddles dropped onto a moss covered bench and wiped his forehead with the sleeve of his robe.

"I think it would be kind of cool if you had an angel watching you," he said, squinting up into the sea of blue overhead. "Dad used to say mom was my angel and that she was up here watching over me. Guess he was wrong." He gave a shrug and pretended to become interested in a caterpillar crawling along the bench.

"Your mom wasn't here when you arrived?" asked Ben, sounding surprised.

Puddles shook his head and tried to disguise a sniffle.

Lucy shot Ben a look. She couldn't believe how insensitive boys could be at times.

Realizing it was up to her to do something, Lucy stuck out her finger and let the caterpillar crawl onto her hand. Puddles kept his eyes on the long green worm as it inched its way up Lucy's arm.

"You know," she said softly, "I expected my dad would be here too. We were really close and I thought for sure he'd be the first person I'd see when I died."

Puddles sniffled and Lucy saw his eyes were glistening. Pretending she hadn't noticed, she continued, "But Truman explained to me that my work isn't done yet; that's why I'm here. And somewhere my dad…and your mom…are finishing up their work. But he promised me that one day when the time is right we'll be together again."

Puddles wiped his eyes with his sleeve as Lucy gently lifted the fat caterpillar off her arm and placed it in the grass. "Now," she said more cheerfully than she felt, "since I can teleport about as well as that caterpillar can fly, I think we should start practicing."

"GREAT IDEA!"

Lucy, Ben and Puddles all jumped letting out a unified scream as Harrison and Riley suddenly appeared out of thin air.

"Don't do that!" Lucy chastised, clasping her chest.

"Ah don't get so ruffled," said Riley, still chuckling. "We just thought we'd pop in to see if yeh might need a bit of help."

"How did you know we were here?" said Puddles, nervously glancing around as though he expected someone else to pop up.

"We were enjoying watching Tobias get an earful from Haddie after breakfast when we saw you three leave," said Harrison. "We knew Lucy was having trouble with her teleporting so we thought you might sneak down here for a bit of practice."

Lucy felt her face go red. Apparently her failure at teleporting was a well-known secret.

"What was Haddie talking to Tobias about?" asked Ben suspiciously.

"Some rubbish about beefin' up border patrol," said Riley with a smirk. "Said she'd come up with a way to make sure the Sleepers don't mosey on over into Drookshire." He laughed and shook his head.

"Sleepers?" said Lucy.

"Yeah, the poor buggers in the Forgotten City," said Riley, giving a nod towards the western mountain.

Harrison nodded in agreement. "Souls that end up in Morpheus usually have a nasty bit of business to work out, so they stay asleep until they learn to get over whatever's bothering them."

"How do they do that while they're asleep?" said Puddles.

"You've heard the saying, 'Time heals all wounds'? Well, we've got a lot of time around here." Harrison chuckled and sat down on the grass. Leaning against an old tree stump he put his hands behind his head and closed his eyes. "Eventually a Sleeper will start to feel the energy being sent into Morpheus by the attendants assigned to the border. Of course, the folks up in Nayopi do their part, too."

Ben gave Lucy a satisfied grin at Harrison's confirmation that Nayopi existed.

"And Haddie thinks these Sleepers could get into Drookshire?" said Lucy.

"It's a bunch o' dinosaur dung if you ask me," said Riley. "As long as they keep sleepin' they're not goin' nowhere."

Puddles flinched at the mention of dinosaurs, but the talk of Sleepers had given Lucy other concerns.

"What would happen if a Sleeper woke up?" she asked. Ben shot her a suspicious look which she ignored.

"It happens," said Harrison, his eyes still closed.

"It does?" Lucy said, trying not to sound shocked by this information.

"Sure, but not as often as we'd like. If a Sleeper wakes up it means they've overcome their fears and they're ready to join us. When that happens we have someone waiting at the border to bring them over."

"But what if they don't want to leave?"

Riley barked out a laugh. Harrison opened his eyes and surveyed Lucy carefully; he didn't seem to find the question funny.

"Let's put it this way," he said, his words slow and deliberate, "anyone who would choose to live in the Forgotten City would be someone I wouldn't want to meet."

"Harrison's got a point," said Riley. "I've heard stories from blokes who've come out o' there and it's not pretty. They say that big ol' lake is a dumpin' ground for every bad dream that's ever been. Gives me the willies just thinkin' about it."

"There's a lake in the Forgotten City?" said Lucy, panic starting to rise up her body. Suddenly the puzzle pieces all began to slide into place.

"Sure," Harrison said, "but you don't need to worry…"

Lucy didn't wait for him to finish. Without offering an explanation, she took off for the Station hollering over her shoulder, "Tell Christof I might be late!"

Ben and Puddles called after her but she didn't have time for explanations. She had to get to Tobias and tell him Haddie was right, Drookshire was in danger. Why hadn't she figured it out earlier? Cursing at all the time she had wasted she raced up the steps and into the entrance hall. It was deserted except for an elderly Guardian shuffling by with his head buried in a book.

"Excuse me," Lucy said, seizing the sleeve of the man's robe, "do you know where I can find Tobias?"

The Guardian raised his bushy gray eyebrows with suspicion before pointing up the stairs that led to the D.O.G.S. wing.

"Third floor, end of the hall – he should be in his office," he said in a wheezy voice.

"Thanks."

Lucy let go of his arm and gave him a weak smile which was not returned. As he shuffled away she heard him mutter something about "bothersome GOATs".

Tobias's office was hidden at the end of a long, twisting corridor that was devoid of any tapestries or artwork. Dozens of doors lined the vacant hall and if it had not been for the small, barely noticeable, plaque on the wall that bore his name Lucy would never have suspected this unimpressive door led into the office of the Station's highest ranking official.

Standing in front of the closed door, Lucy suddenly felt her insides tumbling about. She hadn't given any thought to exactly what she would say to Tobias when she found him. How could she tell him that she knew one of the Sleepers was awake and causing trouble without telling him about the voices in her dreams? The book had clearly stated seeking out voices was against some kind of celestial law and even though she hadn't done it on purpose Lucy doubted that Tobias would bend the rules for her. He wasn't the rule-bending type.

Deciding she would just have to make something up, Lucy took a deep breath and knocked on the door. She waited but there was no response. Putting her ear to the door Lucy swore she heard voices. She knocked again, but still no one answered. Her courage was quickly disappearing. If she didn't talk to him now, she might never build up the nerve again. With a sinking feeling that she was making a huge mistake, Lucy reached down and turned the brass knob.

The tiny room was a perfect match for Tobias's personality. Fastidiously clean and devoid of any clutter, it looked more like it was for show than for actual use. There was a delicate Queen Ann writing desk against the far wall with a single straight backed chair. Lucy looked around but saw no other places to sit. Obviously Tobias didn't receive many visitors.

Out of the corner of her eye, Lucy thought she saw something move. Expecting it was Tobias, she spun around but the room was empty. Instead she found hundreds of tiny portraits covering the wall. Stepping up to get a better look at the miniature portrait nearest her, Lucy choked back a scream. It wasn't a picture at all. Inside the small golden frame was a young woman dressed in a white attendant's robe. As Lucy watched, the woman stood up from the dinner table, waved good-bye to her friends and left the Meeting Hall. The picture followed her like some type of hidden camera.

Lucy quickly glanced at the next photo. It too was focused on an attendant – this one wearing a red Messenger's robe – leaning over an occuscope, completely oblivious to the fact he was being watched. Lucy's stomach became nauseous as she scanned the other pictures. It was the same in every frame; tiny figures going about their business unaware that their every action was being monitored.

"I suppose there is a reason for this uninvited intrusion," spat a voice from the doorway.

Lucy jumped and spun around so quickly that she knocked one of the photos off the wall. The tiny picture fell to the floor, shattering into a thousand pieces.

A curse flew from her lips before she could stop herself. Feeling her face turn crimson, she dropped to her knees and tried to scoop up the slivers of glass strewn across the floor.

"It is futile to try and repair the damage you have wreaked," said Tobias coldly. "Nayopian Mirrors are forged by far more skillful hands than your own."

With a sickening realization that her meeting with Tobias was off to a disastrous start, Lucy let the shards of glass fall from her hands as she got to her feet.

"I'm very sorry," she said softly. "I came looking for you, and when you didn't answer the door…"

"You thought you would break into my private office?"

Lucy didn't know what to say. She couldn't possibly tell Tobias about her suspicions now. He would demand to know how she knew a Sleeper had awakened and was causing trouble and that would mean admitting she had been visiting the Forgotten City in her dreams. Tobias was livid to find she had intruded into his office; Lucy couldn't imagine his fury at learning she had broken into Morpheus – even if it was by accident.

"I…uh…I was just wondering if Madame Mira ever found the missing attendant," she stuttered unconvincingly.

Tobias glared at Lucy through narrowed eyes. He obviously wasn't buying her weak attempt at an explanation.

"Your concern is heartwarming, I'm sure. However, perhaps instead of worrying about others you ought to focus on your own teleporting problems. I understand from Madame Mira that you are woefully behind every other new attendant." A small, ugly smile curled the corners of his mouth.

"Yes, sir," said Lucy, trying to keep her voice steady. Now was not the time for a fight.

A loud crash from one of the photos on the wall drew Tobias's attention away from Lucy. A portly woman in one of the frames had tripped, toppling over a table laden with platters of food. Taking advantage of the diversion, Lucy ducked out of the room and hurried down the hall in an attempt to put as much distance as possible between her and Tobias.

Stopping in the entrance hall to catch her breath, Lucy's mind started racing through her options.

Option number one: Forget about the voices. After all, she had no proof that the eyes that had been watching her in her dreams belonged to a Sleeper who was no longer asleep; and even if someone did believe her it would be admitting she had broken the Universal Code for Privacy. Not knowing the consequences, it would definitely be safer just to keep her mouth shut.

Lucy began to pace around the empty entrance hall. But what if she wasn't crazy, she thought as she listened to her footsteps echoing through the hall. If a Sleeper really was awake and causing trouble in the Forgotten City, then she had to warn someone.

That led her to option number two: Tell someone. But who? The first person Lucy thought of was Banks. She had a sneaking suspicion he knew about the voices already. Perhaps he had given her that book so she would figure out what the voices were and go to him for help. But if that was true, then why would he have torn out the pages that warned her about the danger of seeking out the voices? Lucy's mind flashed back to Banks' words in the zoo. She shook her head as she continued pacing; until she knew Banks' secret, it would be best not to tell him her own. There had to be someone else she could tell.

Briefly Lucy thought about telling Samuel, but quickly dismissed the idea. He had made it clear that the inhabitants in the Forgotten City were not to be disturbed.

A sickening feeling in the pit of her stomach told Lucy who she had to tell. The very thought of it made her cringe but she had no other choice. Knowing the day was about to get a whole lot worse, Lucy set out to find Haddie.

Her search didn't take long. Haddie and the others were gathered outside Christof's door waiting for him to arrive. As Lucy joined them Ben cut short his conversation with Tibs and hurried over to her.

"There you are," he said, sounding half aggravated and half relieved. "Where did you go running off to?"

"I don't have time to explain right now," she whispered. "I need to talk to Haddie."

At the sound of her name, Haddie turned around.

"What do you want to talk to her for," Ben asked irritably. Lucy could tell he didn't appreciate being pushed aside for Haddie.

"Well?" said Haddie, crossing her arms and giving Lucy a smug look of impatience.

Lucy had a sudden urge to abandon this whole idea. Surely whatever was lurking in the Forgotten City couldn't be worse than Haddie.

"Not here," she said under her breath, noticing all eyes were now on the two of them.

"Fine, you can speak to me after dinner."

"No, I need to talk to you *now*," Lucy said through gritted teeth.

For a moment Haddie said nothing. Lucy could tell she was weighing her desire to refuse against her curiosity to know why Lucy so desperately needed her.

"You have five minutes," she said finally, and Lucy knew that curiosity had won. "But if we're late for Guide training you need to tell Christof it's all your fault."

Lucy agreed. Being in hot water with Christof was the least of her worries. They found an empty room just up the hallway and slipped inside. Lucy closed the door and herded Haddie to the far side of the room where they wouldn't be overheard by anyone walking by.

Now that they were alone, Lucy realized she had no idea how to begin. Deciding the best tactic would be to play to Haddie's ego, Lucy launched into her story.

"I'm not going to beat around the bush," she said, trying her best to sound humble. "You were right; you've been right all along."

This piqued Haddie's interest and her glare softened. "Go on," she said, giving Lucy a nod to continue.

"Drookshire is in danger. I can't explain how I know –" Lucy had decided it wouldn't be wise to tell Haddie about the voices. " – but I have proof that one of the Sleepers in the Forgotten City has woken up and it's not good. I believe he might try to escape from Morpheus."

In saying this, Lucy realized she had called the Sleeper "he" and her mind flashed to the gray eyes hidden beneath the hood. Somehow she knew they belonged to a man.

"Why are you telling me instead of Samuel?" Haddie asked, studying Lucy with narrowed eyes. "I thought the two of you were friends." She couldn't hide the jealousy in her voice.

Lucy thought about making up a lie but decided on the truth instead.

"Samuel thinks the Sleepers are best left alone."

"And you disagree?" said Haddie. She was smiling now and Lucy could tell she loved hearing that Lucy wasn't Samuel's obedient little angel.

"In this particular case, yes," said Lucy, fighting not to let Haddie get under her skin. "This thing, this *person*, is trouble and we need to make sure he doesn't cross over the border to Drookshire. That's where you come in."

Haddie's face beamed with triumph. Lucy knew this was the moment she had been waiting for.

"Alright," Haddie said, barely able to contain her glee, "I'm in – on one condition. When we win this battle, and we *will* win, you must tell Samuel that it way *my* plan. I won't have you taking credit for my hard work."

"Fine," agreed Lucy, wondering if she had just made a huge mistake. But it was too late to turn back; the dice had been tossed and the goose bumps racing up her arms told Lucy the game had just begun.

Agreeing that it would look suspicious if the two of them were seen together, Lucy and Haddie decided not to meet again until Haddie's plan was complete and then they would rendezvous in the forest. Haddie would let Lucy know she was ready by sliding her brooch under Lucy's door. Lucy remembered the gaudy gold pin that had been stuck to Haddie's school uniform. She agreed this would work better than a note which risked being discovered.

Unfortunately Master Christof had returned in their absence and was not pleased when Lucy and Haddie walked in half-way through class. Keeping her word, Lucy took full blame and had to stay behind as the others left for Guide training. By the time Christof was done lecturing her she was late for George's class and didn't have time to speak to Ben and Puddles. It wasn't until Reflection that she had the chance to fill them in on what had happened.

Pretending to meditate, Lucy turned her back to Anaja and quietly recounted the entire story. As she explained her suspicions about the dark figure in her dreams Puddles' eyes grew wide and when she told them about the Nayopian Mirrors he gasped. Apparently the idea that they were being watched was even worse than the possibility a Sleeper was wandering loose. Ben gave an annoyed grunt when Lucy got to the part involving Haddie.

"I don't get why she has to be involved," he whispered under his breath, as Anaja looked their way.

"Unless you've been secretly working on border control plans, I don't think we have much of a choice," Lucy argued.

Anaja cleared her throat and Lucy looked up to find her standing over her shoulder.

"Sorry," Lucy silently mouthed.

Anaja gave her a small nod and Lucy understood the conversation was over. Realizing she had no choice but to join the others in meditation, Lucy closed her eyes and waited for what she knew would come.

Like the slash of a knife, the cold air cut across Lucy's face as she opened her eyes into the stinging wind. She strained to see through starless night. Over the howling of the wind cries came bubbling up from the water. It felt like the calls for help were seeping into her skin and Lucy had to fight the sadness from overtaking her.

From somewhere over the middle of the lake two specks of light appeared. Barely visible at first, the dots of cold gray light grew brighter as they drew closer. He was flying over the lake towards her. Lucy tried to wake herself up, tried to convince herself it was only a dream, but it was useless. The screams for help and the cold gray eyes were real and they were about to consume her.

Like a puppet under someone else's control, Lucy started walking towards the lake. Her arms and legs were trembling as she realized what was about to happen. He was commanding her into the water. She strained against the invisible power knowing somehow that she must not touch the water but the more she resisted the harder he pulled her forward. Her toes sank into the wet sand as a wave raced up the shore and wrapped around her ankle. As the water began to carry her into the lake a streak of lightening lit up the sky followed by a deafening scream.

Thrown from the dream, Lucy cried out and fell to the floor. There were gasps and a scurrying of footsteps as the room came to life.

CHAPTER ELEVEN

A DOG, A CAT AND A SONG

News of Lucy's collapse during Reflection spread throughout the Station and once again she was the object of side-way glances and whispered rumors. No matter how strongly she insisted that it had just been a bad dream, rumors grew that Lucy had been overcome by a terrifying vision. She wouldn't admit how close they were to the truth.

"Yeah, that's right, it was a ghost…a huge, three-headed ghost with fangs," replied Lucy, rolling her eyes. She had just been cornered after breakfast by a young girl wanting to know if her vision had shown her the "dark force" mentioned by the Book of Destiny.

The girl gave Lucy a nasty look and marched away.

"What's her problem?" said Ben, joining Lucy just in time to hear the girl mutter something rude under her breath.

"Same as everyone else; no one wants to believe it was just a bad dream."

Lucy could tell by the look on Ben's face that he didn't believe it either. She hadn't told Ben and Puddles about what really happened knowing they would insist she tell Banks. But she couldn't tell Banks, or Tobias, or Samuel; she couldn't tell anyone. All she could do was wait for Haddie's plan.

Luckily there wasn't much time to dwell on what might, or might not, be happening in Morpheus. As Madame Anaja had promised, a concert was scheduled to open the Festival of Wonder, an event held every year on the first day of winter. Lucy was mortified to learn that she was to have a solo but at least the additional practices seemed to have people talking about her singing again and whispers about her collapse began to fade away.

Unfortunately none of Lucy's other instructors seemed to care that she had rehearsals twice a day so she spent her evenings tucked away in a corner of the lodge trying to dig out from under her mountain of assignments.

Guardian Training was by far the most draining. Colonel George had been growing increasingly snippy and when Tibs suggested that his Walker should just chuck work and become a professional surfer, George let loose with a tirade that sent her blonde curls flying and left Tibs glowing red. As punishment for what she claimed was "abysmal work with the insight of a tree frog" she had sent everyone back to the library to start from scratch. So when it was announced at the beginning of class one day that the following week they would be joining Harrison on a fieldtrip to earth, a cheer went up throughout the room.

Trips to earth required tremendous preparation – site selection, special portal arrangements, signed forms declaring the attendants were aware of all rules and regulations regarding the interaction with earthly bound spirits (aka Walkers), and most importantly approval by the Council – therefore it was decided that all cottages would attend the fieldtrip together rather than attempt five separate outings.

The morning of the fieldtrip broke clear and crisp. Drookshire was now firmly entrenched in fall and brightly colored leaves covered the hillside leading down to the garden where they were all to meet.

"Do you think we'll go someplace exotic…like Tijuana?" said Puddles excitedly, as they marched down the hill.

"I certainly hope not," said Babu. "Exotic places typically have very large bugs."

Sandy gave Babu a shove sending him flying into a pile of leaves. "Ah, yeh big baby. Let *me* pick the place and I'll show yeh some *real* bugs!"

The conversation about where Harrison would be taking them continued, but Lucy wasn't listening. That morning The Traveler had left another note and although she was getting used to the daily messages they still managed to unravel her a bit.

To top it off, this morning's note had foregone its typical bizarre riddle-like lesson, choosing instead a very clear warning.

Beware! The wall between worlds is thin and must not be broken. Do not, UNDER ANY CIRCUMSTANCES, act on anything you hear today.
Forever True,
A Fellow Traveler

Like she had done with every other note, Lucy showed it to Ben and Puddles as soon as they had a moment alone. As Lucy predicted, Puddles panicked and made her promise to do exactly what the note instructed. Ben, however, wasn't worried.

"He probably just doesn't want you to get in trouble again," he said, after Lucy made him read the note for the third time. "Face it, we were lucky to get off easy after what happened at the zoo."

Lucy pretended to agree but secretly she knew there was something more behind the message. She had never acted on any of the voices before so why did The Traveler think she would choose today to start? A creeping worry swirled in the pit of her stomach and settled there like a sleeping cat.

Harrison arrived as the bell in the south tower rang to signal the beginning of lessons and to Lucy's delight Riley was with him.

"Alright you motley crew," Riley shouted playfully to the crowd that had gathered in the garden. "Time to get this show on the road…or in the water as the case may be."

Everyone exchanged curious looks and one of the old men from the Island Cottage asked what was going on, but Riley ignored him.

"This way – and don't lag behind. I don't need George on my back for losin' one of yeh."

Without any further explanation of where they were going, Harrison and Riley started off across the garden with Riley waving a long stick like a baton. They led the group out of the garden, around the station, down through the forest along the river, past a large tangle of prickly giant roses that sat against a dense tree line and finally out into a clearing.

As the students tumbled from the forest into the clearing they froze at the sight spreading out in front of them. Glistening in the early morning sun, still and perfect looking, was a magnificent, turquoise blue lake. Lucy slowly turned her head from side to side to take in the full view. To the north and east the water melted into the horizon, a seemingly endless ribbon of water; but to the west the lake seemed to stop abruptly at the cliffs separating Drookshire from Morpheus.

A tiny shiver ran up Lucy's spine. Something about the lake felt oddly magical. The others must have felt it too because they had all gathered around the grassy bank and were staring into the turquoise water that sparkled as if the surface was blanketed with a million tiny lights. The only one who didn't seem hypnotized by the lake was Puddles; he remained at the edge of the clearing, keeping as far from the water's edge as possible.

"Step back! Step back!" Harrison called, as he pushed through the crowd with Riley until they stood between the attendants and the lake. Holding up a hand for quiet he added, "There are a few things we need to cover before anyone enters the water."

A boy from the Island Cottage laughed, obviously believing this was a joke.

"You can't be serious," said Haddie. Standing with her hands on her hips glaring at Harrison, Lucy was reminded of the look her mother had given her when she caught Lucy filling Digby's tennis shoes with pudding.

"We're not dressed for swimming," Haddie declared in a voice that clearly indicated she had just put an end to the ridiculous idea.

"Good thing yeh won't be swimmin' then," said Riley, looking Haddie dead in the eye. "Course if yeh don't wanna be goin' to earth then yeh best be haulin' yourself back to the Station."

For a few tense moments Haddie returned Riley's glare, but finally her desire to get back to earth won out and she folded her arms and looked away.

"Fine then," continued Harrison, "before we leave there are a few rules you need to know. First," he said holding up a red velvet bag, "the energy on earth has a tendency to make you feel like a giant bag of rocks; that's why it's important that you hold on to one of these."

He opened the bag and held up a glistening walnut-sized stone. A gasp went up from an aristocratic looking woman from the Mayanian Cottage who excitedly cried out, "Diamonds!"

"Ahhh, these puppies are far more valuable than diamonds," said Riley, taking one of the glittering stones from Harrison before passing the bag around to the attendants. "This li'l beauty is a talis stone and it will help yeh keep yer energy up. Without this little guy," he shook the crystal in the air, "you'll have a bugger of a time getting home."

The sleeping cat in Lucy's stomach shifted positions as Ben handed her the velvet bag. Feeling around inside, she pulled out the largest stone she could find hoping it would have enough power to make up for her abysmal teleporting skills.

"Secondly," Harrison continued, over the excited whispers, "no one is to leave the group. Anyone wandering off will be grounded from any future fieldtrips."

Lucy heard Tibs let out a disgruntled moan. She knew he was aching to visit his old haunts and she hoped Harrison had been wise enough to choose an inland location far away from any beaches.

"And finally," said Harrison, in an unusually stern voice, "this is an observation mission only. NO ONE is to attempt to make contact with the subject. I doubt any of you are strong enough yet to actually get through to a Walker, but we're not going to take any chances." His eyes landed for a moment on Lucy. "Therefore no one is to speak when in the presence of a Walker. Anyone who thinks I'm joking should talk to the last attendant who tried to speak to a Walker during a fieldtrip. You can find him in the Forgotten City."

This was too much for Puddles. Taking a giant step backwards he tripped and tumbled into the middle of an especially thorny rosebush letting out a cry of pain. Lucy and Ben rushed to his aid but he had become so thoroughly tangled in the snarled branches that it took them several minutes to pry him loose. When they finally managed to pull off the last of the prickly vines binding him, Puddles looked down and let out a deep moan. The rip in his robes from their narrow escape at the zoo had grown into a giant tear giving a clear view of Puddles' skinny, scratched, white legs.

"My dear boy," said Anna soothingly as she gingerly wiped away the thorns from his hair, "we really must do something with that robe."

"By jiminy I've got just the ticket!" exclaimed Arthur, clapping his hands. "If my years of sailing taught me anything it was how to do a dandy job of mending a tattered sail."

Puddles started to say that he was fine and didn't need any help, but Arthur had already disappeared into the bushes reappearing seconds later with a handful of thin twigs. Tearing the twigs apart with surprisingly nimble fingers, he proceeded to poke them through Puddles' tattered robe and "lace up" the rip. The result was a roughly sewn primitive looking garment that had leaves sticking out at odd angles.

Puddles muttered his thanks and the attendants who had been watching his mishap turned their attention back to Harrison who gave Puddles a wink and a hearty thumbs-up approval of his new robe.

"Okay, everyone ready?" said Harrison, unable to hide his excitement.

The group nodded in unison and Harrison waved them forward towards the water's edge. Ben and Lucy each took one of Puddles' arms and gently dragged him forward.

"Riley will demonstrate use of the portal," said Harrison, as Riley gave a deep bow and several people applauded.

Stepping up to the water's edge, Riley turned, gave a wave to the crowd, then turned back and with his head held high and his chest puffed out he stepped into the pond and proceeded to walk towards the middle until the water crept up to his head and finally, with a watery gulp, consumed him. As the water closed over his head Lucy could swear she caught a faint whiff of peanut butter and jelly in the air.

A minute later Riley was back clutching a purple pansy in his fist. He climbed out of the water looking perfectly dry and waved the flower in the air to prove he had made the journey. Lucy noticed the pansy seemed terribly dull in comparison to the strikingly bright flowers in the Kingdom.

The attendants excitedly formed a line on the shore and Harrison began to lead them one by one into the watery portal. As Lucy and Ben joined Puddles at the end of the line, Lucy elbowed Ben and pointed to Haddie who was next to go in. Haddie looked terrified and had turned an unflattering shade of green as she flicked the water with her toe.

After Harrison impatiently reminded her that they were on a tight schedule, Haddie reluctantly stepped into the lake, took a few cautious steps and immediately sank down to her chin. As her long braid began to bob on the water's surface, Haddie opened her mouth to say something but at that moment her head fell beneath the water and all that came out was a loud gurgle.

A wide smile spread across Lucy's face. Her unavoidable partnership with Haddie didn't keep her from thoroughly loving the sight of the little general sinking like a stone. Wanting to firmly imprint the picture on her brain, Lucy closed her eyes and replayed it several times.

"NEXT!"

Lucy opened her eyes to find Riley waving them forward. Only she, Ben and Puddles were left on the shore.

"So who's the next victim?" said Riley, rubbing his hands together with a look of glee.

This was the wrong thing to say. Puddles' face turned ghostly white. Lucy was pretty sure she knew what the problem was; Puddles had died in a freak swimming accident so the thought of submerging into a bottomless pond was probably not high on the list of things he wanted to do. This was perfectly understandable; after all if going back to earth meant stepping in front of a speeding truck, she would most likely feel the same way.

"Tell yeh what," said Riley, eyeing Puddles. "You two go on. Me and my mate here will be right behind yeh."

"Are you sure you're going to be okay?" Ben asked Puddles. "I'll stay with you if you like."

"It's okay," said Puddles, looking nervously up at Riley.

"Go on," said Riley, shooing them away. "Harrison's waitin' for yeh. We'll be there soon enough."

Promising Puddles that they would wait for him on the other side, Lucy reluctantly waved good-bye, took hold of Ben's hand and followed him into the water. To Lucy's surprise the water didn't feel cold; as a matter of fact it didn't feel like water at all. Instead it felt like she had stuck her foot in a bowl of warm, swirling air. She tightened her grip on Ben's hand and they slowly sunk down into the lake. As the water lapped at her chin, Lucy once again caught the sweet smell of peanut butter in the air. Before she could ask Ben if he smelled it too, her head was under water and she felt the familiar tumbling as streaks of color twirled around her.

Lucy's feet hit the ground with a jarring thud. Letting go of Ben, she threw out her arms to catch her balance. She felt uncomfortably heavy and awkward as though she was wearing a thick winter coat several sizes too small. Opening her eyes Lucy felt her mood plummet at the sight of the dreary, bland world surrounding her.

They had landed in some sort of park but it had none of the life of the garden back in Drookshire. The trees which were dressed in their fall colors were uninspired and spiritless and the few flowers that dotted the ground were dull imitations of their cousins in the Kingdom. Lucy tried to move her feet but they resisted as though gravity had taken hold and glued her to the ground.

In the middle of the park, standing around a rusty old red swing set, Harrison had gathered the attendants together. Seeing Lucy and Ben he waved them over.

"Use your talis stone!" he shouted.

Ben pulled his crystal from his sash and rubbed it between his hands. Immediately Lucy noticed his shape grow brighter and there seemed to be a faint blue glow surrounding him.

"That's loads better," said Ben, shaking out his arms and legs. "Better hurry; it looks like they're getting started."

Fumbling in her sash, Lucy's fingers found the stone. Grasping it tightly she clutched it to her chest. A warm trickle ran down Lucy's fingers and through her arms, spreading quickly through the rest of her body. At once the cold ache melted away and Lucy suddenly felt like laughing. Shaking out her arms as though she was casting off the last remnants of the lake, Lucy instantly felt lighter. With their feet no longer bolted to the ground, Lucy and Ben sprinted across the park to join the others.

"Now that we're all here we can begin," said Harrison, as Lucy and Ben worked their way into the circle of attendants huddled around the swing set.

"But we're not all here," Lucy said, looking back to the spot where she and Ben had landed. "Puddles and Riley aren't here yet."

"What d'yeh mean?" Riley's red head popped out from behind a group of surprised attendants. "We've been here for ages waitin' on the two of yeh."

"How did you…" said Ben, looking bewildered as he stared at Puddles who was standing beside Riley with a dizzy, but happy, look on his face.

"Young Master Puddles here is quite the teleporter," said Riley, slapping Puddles on the back and sending him stumbling forward.

The crowd exchanged surprised looks and a few attendants whispered to each other as Puddles gave a small grin, his ears turning pink.

"Alright people, time to get to work," said Harrison, doing his best impersonation of a teacher. "If you will turn your attention to that tree over there, you will find the subject of this little outing."

Lucy looked in the direction Harrison was pointing and saw a young boy and a dog relaxing under a large walnut tree. The small boy looked to be around six years old but that could have been because of the peanut butter that was smeared across his face and the mop of uncombed blonde hair that hung in his eyes. Although Lucy felt perfectly warm, she guessed it must be cold because the boy was wearing a heavy denim jacket that was buttoned up to his chin. He was sitting on top of a pile of shriveled leaves that had collected under the tree and in his lap was the drooling yellow head of a fat golden retriever. The boy calmly petted his companion's head completely oblivious to the fact that there were fifty pairs of eyes staring at him.

As the group approached the boy, the dog raised his head and his floppy ears pricked up. His wet, black nose sniffed the air in their direction and he cocked his head as though listening for intruders he couldn't see. After a few moments he must have decided that his boy was safe, and he laid his head back in the boy's lap and closed his eyes.

"Dewey has been going through a bit of a rough time," Harrison whispered in a voice so low that Lucy could barely hear him. "Six months ago his mom died and his dad's not handling it very well. Dewey has pretty much been left on his own with only Barney here to take care of him." Harrison reached down and petted the retriever making the dog sneeze. "If anything were to happen to old Barney I'm afraid it would be too much for Dewey to handle. That's where we come in."

Harrison waved to the group to follow him. They crossed the park to a busy four lane street that was filled with cars racing in both directions. Lucy couldn't help but wonder what all those people in their cars would think if they knew there was a group of dead people standing by the side of the road watching them.

Harrison raised his voice to be heard over the cars flying by. "In three minutes earth time Barney is going to see a cat and take out after it. The cat will lead him right to where we are standing then out into the street."

A gasp went up from the group. There was no doubt in anyone's mind what would happen if Barney followed the cat.

"Our job," said Harrison, holding up a hand to silence the group, "is to keep Barney safe therefore saving Dewey from another unbearable loss. Any ideas?"

For several seconds everyone stood blankly staring at one another and Lucy began to panic that they weren't going to come up with a solution in time. Surely Harrison wouldn't let Barney die just because they didn't know what to do.

"Best be thinkin' quick," said Riley, glancing up towards the sky. "Only got a couple o' minutes left."

"Oh really people," said a huffy voice hidden in the middle of the group. Haddie pushed her way out from the crowd. "Everyone knows the best defense is a good offense."

"Meanin' exactly what," said Riley.

"Meaning," said Haddie in her usual superior tone, "that we simply need to stop the cat before the dog sees it. No cat, no chase, no dead dog. Problem solved."

"Interesting idea, but how do you plan on diverting the cat," said Harrison.

"Follow me." Haddie whipped around and the crowd parted to let her through.

"I hope she knows what she's doing," said Puddles, as Haddie marched towards the tree where Dewey and Barney were still sitting unaware of the work going on to save them.

"That poor dog's done for if you ask me," muttered Sandy.

Lucy had a sinking feeling that whatever Haddie had in mind could only lead to disaster. As she anxiously followed the group parading behind Haddie she realized the goose bumps on her arms were tingling. Not a good sign.

"There it is!" a young girl from the Mayanian Cottage whispered loudly. She was pointing to a thick branch just above the boy and his dog. Sure enough, reclining on a thick branch just above Dewey's head was a fat, calico cat. Its tail was flicking wildly as it watched the dog, but neither Dewey nor Barney had spied the cat whose brown and orange fur blended amazingly well into the tree decked out in its fall colors.

Lucy hoped desperately that Haddie wouldn't do something stupid just to show off but it looked like Haddie was determined to save the day. Before Harrison could stop her, Haddie waved her arms and in the blink of an eye was straddling the branch facing the cat.

"Get down from there," Harrison commanded in a quiet, but no-nonsense, voice.

Haddie ignored him as she scooted nearer the cat.

Riley muttered something rude under his breath and started for the tree but Harrison stopped him.

"We'll only make it worse if we go after her," he said, and he motioned to everyone to move back giving Haddie more room to work.

"Does she know what she's doing," asked a short, stout woman from the Forest Cottage.

"She's a bloomin' nut case," said Sandy, shaking her head.

Up above Haddie was leaning forward whispering something to the cat that seemed completely unaware he was nose to nose with a little girl. Raising his haunches, the cat's nose began to twitch and his tail flicked sharply as his eyes fixed on Barney with increasing interest.

Haddie reached inside her sash and pulled out her crystal.

"NO!" shouted Harrison, giving up all concern of being heard.

But it was too late. Haddie took the crystal and rubbed it between her hands and then just as the cat reared back ready to pounce, she reached out and grabbed its tail. To everyone's astonishment the cat let out a screeching howl, hissed and swung a paw at its invisible attacker. As Harrison and Riley leapt forward to stop what everyone knew was about to happen, the cat dove from the branch landing flatly on Barney's back.

Barney let out a yelp of pain as the cat's claws dug into his fur. Bolting to his feet he threw off the cat which took off running across the park with Barney in close pursuit. The chase was on with Dewey following far behind, his short legs no match for a wild cat and his crazed dog.

Harrison and Riley didn't wait to see what would happen next. With a quick jerk of their arms both arrived at the street an instant before the animals. The cat, closely pursued by Barney, tore into the street directly in the path of oncoming traffic. In a flash it leapt into the air trying to avoid the four lanes of cars speeding his way. Then something very peculiar happened. Everything seemed to go into slow motion. Stretching his arms high over his head, Riley's feet left the ground and he soared over the cars, his body turning into a kind of liquid red blur. As the cars below swept by in slow motion, the red stream of air swirled around the cat, encircling it like some kind of large bubble. Lucy and the others stared in amazement as the red bubble lifted the cat above the chaos and flew it to the opposite side of the street, depositing it safely on the ground.

And then, as though a switch had been flipped, everything sped back into action. With a furious bark Barney bolted out into the street after his prey.

"NO!" Dewey screamed, as the sound of screeching brakes and blaring horns broke the air.

Lucy watched in horror as Dewey ran straight for street oblivious to the mass of cars hurdling towards him. Tears were spilling down his face as Lucy heard him shout, "DON'T LET HIM BE DEAD! NOT HIM TOO!"

She looked frantically around at Ben and Puddles who seemed paralyzed by the horrible scene unfolding in front of them. Dewey screamed out again but no one else seemed to hear him. They were watching helplessly as he darted into the street after his runaway dog.

Suddenly a teenage girl appeared out of nowhere. She was dressed in torn black jeans and a sleeveless black t-shirt that had a glaring white skull printed on the front. She wore a spiked collar around her throat and her face was decorated with a mixture of piercings.

Without hesitation the girl stepped calmly into the street and held up her hand to the oncoming traffic. There was another deafening screech of slamming breaks as a large red truck stopped inches away from Dewey. The shaken driver jumped out of the truck, gave the girl an apprehensive look and ran to Dewey who was pointing to the middle of the road and crying.

"Are you okay," asked the man, his voice shaking.

"M...m...my dog," Dewey's voice broke as he tried to speak though his sobs.

Lying lifeless in the middle of the street was Barney and kneeling next to him, invisible to the onlookers, was Harrison.

Dewey dropped down in the street next to Barney and buried his head in the blonde fur.

Again Lucy heard Dewey as he sobbed clutching tightly to his friend, "No! You can't have him too; you've got momma…you can't have Barney!" But this time Lucy realized, Dewey wasn't speaking. She was hearing his thoughts.

Lucy would never know what caused her to do what happened next. She didn't mean to do it, she certainly didn't know why she did it, but without thinking Lucy opened her mouth and began to sing. There were no words to her song, just a simple, perfect melody that floated on the air.

For a moment it seemed like time stood still as Lucy's song drowned out the chaos around them. Then slowly Dewey lifted his head and looked around. His tears had stopped and he had a curious look on his face as his eyes searched the sky. Then he cocked his head to the side and quietly said, "Momma…is that you?"

Horrified with the realization of what she had done, Lucy slapped her hand to her mouth and the music stopped. Harrison was staring at her with an unreadable expression and Lucy could hear the muffled whispers of the other attendants who were backing away from her as though she had somehow become poisonous.

Before Lucy could explain what had happened there was a shout from the street that drew everyone's attention back to Dewey.

"Stand back for God's sake! Give them air!" said the gothic-looking girl as she pushed her way through the crowd that had gathered around Dewey and Barney.

The girl knelt down next to Barney and put her hand on his still chest.

"Is he…" Dewey looked at the girl with dying hope.

"Have faith," she said quietly, and Lucy noticed for the first time that buried beneath a crust of black makeup were a pair of soft steel-blue eyes that right now were focused intensely on Dewey.

After several long seconds that seemed to stretch on for an eternity, the girl leaned over and gently kissed Barney on the head. For a moment nothing happened, and then with a sudden jerk Barney let out a loud sneeze spraying Dewey with a healthy dose of dog snot. A cheer went up from the crowd that had gathered as Barney scrambled to his feet and began barking happily at all the people there to see him. Dewey threw his arms around Barney's neck, tears of relief pouring down his face as he scolded his dog.

"You scared me! No more cats for you!"

The crowd laughed and patted each other on the back, obviously relieved by the miraculous turn of events. As the girl helped Dewey and Barney back to the sidewalk the people waved good-bye and returned to their cars.

When the crowd had disbursed, Riley waved to the attendants to follow him and they all quietly headed back across the park. Harrison stayed behind with Dewey, Barney and the girl apparently checking to make sure everyone was okay. Lucy lagged behind the others as they crossed the park towards the rusted old swing set. Now that Dewey and Barney were safe she felt a sense of dread wash over her as the realization of what had just happened sunk in…she had made contact with a Walker. It hadn't been intentional – she didn't even really know how it happened – but there was no denying the fact that Dewey had heard her. Harrison's warning echoed in her ears: "NO ONE is to attempt to make contact with the subject." At the very least Lucy was certain she would be forbidden to attend any more fieldtrips. But what if it was worse than that; what if she had to leave Drookshire? Harrison said the last attendant to make contact with a Walker had been sent to the Forgotten City. Had she just bought herself a one-way ticket to Morpheus? The thought sent a shiver down her back.

The silence of the group as they gathered back at the deserted swing set made Lucy's spirits sink even lower. No one would look at her, not even Ben and Puddles. They all hung their heads as though they were gathered at a funeral.

"*Yeah*," thought Lucy, "my *funeral*."

"Blimey! Why the long faces?" crowed Riley, straddling the top bar of the swing set and looking down on the solemn group. "Didn't any of you sad-sacks notice…THE DOG LIVED!"

No one said anything but several of the attendants shifted their eyes to Lucy before quickly looking away again.

"It's me," said Lucy, not able to stand the silence any longer. "They're all wondering what's going to happen to me since I…you know."

"Oooooh….that," said Riley, scratching the back of his head. "That was pretty weird. Ever done that before?"

"No!" said Lucy quickly. "Never! I didn't mean to do it this time, it just…happened."

"What do yeh think, Harrison? Should we send her off to the Sleepers?"

Lucy turned around and saw Harrison had joined the group. To her surprise he was smiling.

"I wouldn't do that to the Sleepers. They've got enough problems."

Harrison gave Lucy a wry smile and the air around them suddenly felt lighter. Lucy wasn't sure how, but it looked like she had escaped being kicked out of Drookshire for a second time.

"Hey," said Puddles, looking around. "Where's Haddie?"

"I believe our cat wrangler is rethinking her plan," said Harrison, nodding towards the tree.

Still sitting on the branch with her chin in her hand and an extremely foul look on her face was Haddie; and seated by her side curled up and looking extremely contented was the cat.

Lucy couldn't hold it any longer. She burst out laughing and soon everyone had joined her. Barney was safe, Dewey had his best friend and Haddie had been put in her place in front of the whole class. Life was good.

"Be wary of happiness gained from another's misfortune," Aunt Aggie had often warned. "The universe has a wonderful way of balancing life and soon you may find the laugh is on you." As usual, Aunt Aggie was right.

The trip back to Drookshire was fairly uneventful. Given that there weren't any portals on earth, Harrison had instructed them on how to use their talis stones to return to the Station. With the help of Ben and Puddles and the energy boost from her crystal, Lucy soon found herself popping out of the pond and back into the brilliant colors of Drookshire.

Feeling much lighter now that they were back in the Kingdom, Lucy practically flew out of the pond and ran smack into a skinny tree stump. The stump stumbled and fell backwards letting out a squawk. To Lucy's horror she saw Tobias splayed out on the grass.

"Let me help you up, sir," said Ben, rushing forward.

Shooing Ben away, Tobias clambered to his feet and fixed Lucy with an icy stare.

"You," he said pointing a boney finger, "follow me."

CHAPTER TWELVE

THE LOOK BACK

"Wait here."

Tobias had marched Lucy back up to the Station without saying a word. He had led her through the DOGS wing of the Station, up several flights of stairs and through a maze of hallways. Several times Lucy had thought about asking where they were going, but Tobias did not look in the mood for chit-chat. Finally he came to a stop outside a door at the end of a long hallway.

Directing Lucy to wait outside, Tobias entered the room and quickly closed the door behind him. Glancing up the hallway Lucy suddenly felt her world go from bad to worse as her eyes fell on the familiar stone statue of an angel holding a man in the palm of her hand. Why had Tobias brought her here of all places?

A loud pop erupted by her side as Riley suddenly appeared.

"So what's the sentence," he said brightly, looking around at the empty hallway. "Gotta polish ol' Toby's collection of mirrors?"

"I don't know yet. Tobias told me to wait here and then he went in there." Lucy nodded towards the door.

"Odd place for a meetin'," said Riley, staring curiously at the closed door. "Course I don't suppose you know what's behind that door bein' that this place is off limits to newbies." Riley shifted his gaze to Lucy and she suspected he knew the answer.

"It's just a classroom, isn't it?" said Lucy, her voice sounding unnaturally high.

Before Riley could answer there was another loud pop and Harrison appeared looking like he had just run a marathon.

"Am I in time?"

"They're all in there," said Riley, giving a nod towards the room at the end of the hall.

"The Dream Chamber?" said Harrison, sounding surprised. "That's odd."

"That's what I said! Isn't that what I said?" Riley nudged Lucy but she wasn't paying attention.

What did Riley mean '*They're* all in there'? How many people did he think were waiting for her? Lucy had a sudden horrible image of bleachers filled with senior attendants all looking down on her, shaking their heads as Tobias banged a gavel and declared her guilty of Unauthorized and Inappropriate Communication with a Walker punishable by 100 years in the Forgotten City!

The door creaked open and Lucy shook the thought from her mind. Tobias stepped into the hallway with his thin lips turned up in a menacing grin. Lucy's spirits sank. Anything that made Tobias happy was not likely to be good for her.

Tobias's look of satisfaction disappeared as he spied Harrison and Riley.

"This is not an open hearing," he said coldly, his eye twitching slightly as he spoke.

"We're here to support Lucy," said Harrison, using his most official voice.

"Yeah, that's right," said Riley, puffing out his chest. "After all, unlike some people in this hallway *we* were actually there and saw what happened."

Tobias's eyes narrowed as he glared up at Riley. "I warn you…"

"It's alright, Tobias," said a deep voice from inside the room. "We have no secrets to hide and I'm quite sure our visitors will be on their best behavior."

"See there," said Riley, his face breaking into a wide grin as he slapped Tobias on the shoulder, "we're all just one big happy family! Come on, sis." Riley waved to Lucy to follow him into the forbidden room.

Lucy looked up at Harrison not sure whether or not to move. He gave a small nod and Lucy was relieved to see a sparkle of confidence in his eyes. "After you," he said, gesturing for her to follow Riley.

Lucy squeezed by Tobias who was still standing like a skinny pillar in the middle of the doorway. "Excuse me," she said trying to flatten her body against the doorframe. As their eyes locked a strange uneasiness poured over her. There were no voices, but Lucy could read Tobias's thoughts and the feeling was perfectly clear…he wanted her gone.

Lucy hastily pushed past Tobias into the room, anxious to put some distance between them.

The Dream Chamber was nothing like Lucy had imagined it would be. She had envisioned that it would be dark and filled with whirling dream passages like a miniature version of the Land of Dreams; but the Dream Chamber couldn't have been more different.

Pouring in from the glass dome overhead a flood of light rained down over the sparsely furnished room and reflected off of the highly polished marble floor making the room extremely bright. Scattered across the room were a dozen odd looking thin, silver pedestals, each with a small cup on the end. The pedestals, which looked like something you would more likely find in an art museum, were sparkling in the light adding to the chamber's already brilliant appearance.

Encircling the room were seven large stained-glass windows each depicting a dramatic scene of Walkers in various perilous situations being saved by confident-looking attendants. As Lucy stared at the picture of a muscular Guardian pulling a poor young man from the jaws of a shark she felt her stomach tighten. Was this what was expected of them?

Riley leaned over and whispered in Lucy's ear, "As yeh can see, they went for the warm, cozy look. Downright homey don't yeh think?"

Lucy smiled up at Riley, glad he was here. Although the room was hardly what she would call "homey", and the pictures of attendants performing heroic acts made her somewhat queasy, she had to admit that there was something oddly pleasing about this place.

"Welcome," said a rich, deep voice from across the room.

Lucy jumped. For a split second she had forgotten why she was here. Looking up she saw a tall, dark man standing behind a long golden table at the far end of the circular chamber; he was pointing to a chair in front of him.

"Please make yourself comfortable."

Lucy had never seen this man before but his golden robe and emerald sash told her this had to be Gadwick, Keeper of the Book of Creation. Seated to Gadwick's right, looking less jovial than the last time they had met, was Cassiel. She was sitting with her hands folded across her plump lap and she was examining Lucy very closely as she took her seat.

To Gadwick's left sat Samuel. Although he said nothing, his silent, crystal blue gaze somehow made Lucy feel worse than any lecture ever could. Samuel believed her when she told him they hadn't caused the stampede in the zoo but here she was again sitting in front of him, this time for something far more serious.

Lucy fought back the lump growing in her throat. Looking up at the three members of the Celestial Council it was perfectly clear why she was here. She had been called before the Council because she had made unauthorized contact with a Walker. No wonder Tobias looked so smug; Lucy had broken the unbreakable rule and now she was on trial for her actions. She was going to be exiled from Drookshire.

"Please, before you begin I would like to make a statement on Lucy's behalf," said Harrison, stepping up and putting a hand on the back of Lucy's chair.

Tobias glared at Harrison. "I don't remember the honored members of the Council asking for personal references."

"Aw git off yer high horse," said Riley, crossing over to Lucy's other side. "Last I heard it was the Council that ran these meetings, not you."

"GENTLEMEN!" Gadwick's eyes flashed as he silenced the room. "This is neither the time nor the place to hash out old grievances. We are here for one reason only…to learn what happened today. And I have full confidence that if we would allow Miss O'Sullivan to speak she would be able to provide us with precisely the information we need."

Riley and Tobias exchanged glares before each waving an arm in the air to produce a chair. Tobias took a seat in the straight backed wooden chair he had conjured while Riley plopped down in the red squishy arm chair that had appeared on Lucy's other side.

"Now that we are all settled," said Gadwick, taking his seat, "would you please tell us what occurred today?" Gadwick's voice was official, but his eyes twinkled as he smiled and nodded to Lucy to begin.

.

"Well," said Lucy, trying desperately to keep her voice steady, "I guess it started shortly after we arrived in the park."

Drawing all the courage she could muster, Lucy retold the story of how Haddie had spooked the cat which caused it to run off towards the street with Barney chasing behind and how Dewey had run after them. She paused for a moment not sure whether or not it would be wise to tell the Council that she had been able to hear Dewey's thoughts.

Samuel seemed to sense Lucy's dilemma and quietly offered, "Would it be fair to say that at that moment you understood the young boy feared the loss of his beloved pet?"

The look in Samuel's eye told Lucy not to explain further.

"That's right," said Lucy cautiously.

"Dear, was that when you decided to sing to the young boy?" asked Cassiel.

"No!" blurted Lucy a little too loudly. Cassiel's brow raised and Lucy quickly added, "Sorry…what I meant to say is that I didn't decide to sing, it just kind of happened. One second I was watching Dewey and the next second, well, I just opened my mouth and this song came out. I wasn't trying to talk to him, you have to believe me."

Tobias gave a small snort which he poorly disguised as a cough. Lucy waited for the Council to speak, but they said nothing. For several eternally long moments they sat silently staring at Lucy as though they were trying to determine if her story was true. Lucy looked up at Harrison, wondering if she should say anything else. He must have known what she was thinking because he gave a very slight shake of his head.

Lucy' palms began to sweat as the Council continued to stare at her like some kind of bug under a microscope.

Trying not to think about what was about to happen, Lucy's eyes began to wander around the room.

Two large chests sat to the right of the Council's table. The first was made of silver with a golden chain binding the lid shut. Lucy imagined it must hold some type of very valuable treasure. The second chest was not nearly as impressive. It had a roughly carved wooden casing that looked old and worn and it was sealed with a tarnished lock that appeared not to have been opened in a very long time. The old wooden chest seemed oddly out of place in this room of marble and crystal and Lucy couldn't help but wonder why a chest like that would be tucked away in the Dream Chamber.

A chair scraped against the floor and Lucy's attention was brought back to the situation at hand. Gadwick stood up, his large frame looking regal in his golden robes. Without consulting Cassiel or Samuel he declared, "This Council has come to a decision. Lucille Margaret O'Sullivan, please rise."

Tobias gave a thin-lipped grin as though he knew what was about to happen.

Lucy looked nervously up at Harrison. He tried to force a smile but Lucy saw the worry in his eyes. Reaching down, Harrison helped Lucy to her feet. Her legs suddenly felt as though they had forgotten how to stand and Lucy prayed she wouldn't faint in front of the Council. If she was going to be banished, she wanted to receive her sentence upright.

"Miss O'Sullivan, as you know unauthorized contact with a Walker can carry grave consequences. We have listened to your story and the Council is in agreement. On the charge of intentional and dangerous communication with an earthly spirit, we believe you to be…"

"NOT GUITLY?" Ben's eyes nearly popped from his head. "You're kidding! That's great!"

Lucy shoved another piece of toast into her mouth. Luckily Ben and Puddles guessed she would be hungry having missed dinner so they had snuck food into the cottage where they waited for her to return.

"Luce, I was really worried," said Puddles, handing Lucy a mug of hot chocolate. "Tobias looked like he was out for blood."

Lucy took a long drag off the mug of thick, warm chocolate. The gooey liquid felt wonderful as it slipped down her throat and into her growling stomach.

"You should have seen his face when Gadwick said my punishment was that I'm not allowed to sing again until they can figure out what went wrong. Tobias turned so red I thought he was going to explode."

Ben and Puddles wouldn't let Lucy go to bed until she had told the story several more times. Ben was anxious to hear all about the Council... "They never talked to each other? Outstanding! They must use some type of really sophisticated telepathy."

Puddles kept asking Lucy to retell the part where Gadwick told Tobias to behave. Each time she mimicked the look of indignation on Tobias's face Puddles rolled on the ground clutching his sides in laughter.

As Lucy sat watching her friends reenact their own version of the trial in which Tobias got sacked, she felt her troubles slowly melt away. Finally the excitement of the day began to take its toll and Lucy longed for the comfort of her bed. Draining the last of her hot chocolate she gave a wide yawn and announced she was calling it a night. Ben and Puddles congratulated her again before reluctantly heading off for their rooms. As Lucy shuffled up the deserted hall to bed she could hear Puddles' laughter as it faded into the night.

Ben and Puddles weren't the only ones excited by Lucy's news. When Haddie learned that Lucy had been forbidden from singing it was like Christmas had come early. With Lucy demoted to playing the triangle, Haddie could take center stage as soloist for the upcoming concert and she accepted the spotlight like a queen accepting the throne.

As the story of Barney and the cat spread throughout the Station, attendants Lucy had never spoken to clapped her on the shoulder with words of congratulations. Rumor was that her little song had some kind of mystical power and those same attendants who had avoided her in the park now wanted to be her friend. But not everyone was standing in line to join Lucy's new fan club. Since their meeting in the Dream Chamber Tobias had been noticeably absent from meals and whenever their paths crossed he acted as though Lucy was nothing more than a foul odor in the air.

Lucy was being ignored by someone else as well; in the days following their fieldtrip Lucy did not receive a single note from The Traveler. She had done exactly what The Traveler had warned her against and now her punishment was silence. Oddly, even though she had no idea of who The Traveler was, the thought of disappointing him bothered her. But since getting a message to him was impossible, Lucy decided it was useless to worry about it and decided to just enjoy the note-free days.

The morning of the concert Lucy awoke to a feathery frost painted across her windowpane. Running to the window she placed her hand against the glass. A cold chill licked her fingers. Wiping a circle in the frost, Lucy peered out on to a sea of white. Snow!

The arrival of winter made the Station glisten like an enormous ice sculpture sitting in a blanket of white. Joining the others for Rejuvenation, Lucy stared out the windows of the south tower at the snow banks reflecting the morning sun. It made it seem as though they were hovering above rolling hills of sparkling diamonds.

"A glorious sight, I agree," cooed Anaja.

Turning away from the window, Lucy's breath caught in her chest as she gazed at the beautiful woman in front of her. In honor of the Festival, Anaja had exchanged her usual red robe for a glittering white gown that draped regally over her willowy figure. Standing tall in a beam of sunlight pouring in from above, their Rejuvenation instructor looked like a snow queen. Even her black hair that spun in every direction glistened with frost.

"You look…wow," Ben said, looking awestricken.

Anaja smiled and Ben's face glowed red.

The Festival of Wonder took place in the Village and since the clock tower was being used as an arrival point for visitors coming from outside the Kingdom, attendants from Drookshire were forced to use a portal that dropped them off on the hillside just outside the Village.

The stories they had heard about the Festival didn't come close to the grandeur of the actual event. Standing on the hill looking over the Village, Lucy marveled at how the entire town glittered like some magical, fairytale kingdom. Snow blanketed the ground giving the Village the appearance of floating on a cloud and the boughs of the Mayanian trees sparkled frosty white except when someone wandered under their branches causing them to flutter in various colors. Lucy watched as crowds of attendants filed into the Village creating a kaleidoscope of colors in the treetops.

"Where should we go first?" asked Puddles, as they joined the throng of attendants crowding into the streets.

Lucy glanced around at the shops adorned with gold and white decorations. The quaint little Village had been transformed into a spectacular, sparkling city. Even the most ominous shop in the Village, *Inventions Through the Ages*, glistened pristinely in the bright sunshine.

"We're not going anywhere until after the performance," said Ben, grabbing Puddles' arm and guiding him towards the bandstand that had been set up in the Village Center.

Lucy's stomach grumbled as the delicious smells from Café Monet wafted through the air reminding her that they had left before breakfast.

"We have time for just one mango muffin," she said, taking hold of Puddles' other arm and pulling him in the opposite direction.

"No way," argued Ben in his deep, I'm-older-than-you-so-I'm-in-charge voice. "Just for today let's try actually doing what we're supposed to do."

"Fine." Lucy let go of Puddles who appeared glad to no longer be in the middle of a tug-of-war. "But don't go getting all mature on us; one Haddie in the group is enough."

The concert turned out to be a great success even without the voice of their star performer. The only glitch came when Haddie hit a sour note and Ben laughed so hard into his clarinet that it gave a loud squeak. But all in all Lucy thought they sounded surprisingly good.

"Magnificent!"

A smile leapt to Lucy's face as she recognized the familiar voice. Truman was fighting his way through the crowd, his plump frame being bounced about by the horde of attendants.

"Truly remarkable! I must admit that in all my days I've never heard such a performance," he panted, finally reaching Lucy and drawing her into a bear hug.

To Lucy's relief Truman was beaming at her with pride. She had not seen him since the incident in the zoo and the look he had given her then was far different.

"Thanks," Lucy said, her face growing hot. "I didn't really do much." She suddenly wished she was holding a flute or a violin or even that horrible harp…anything besides the pathetic little triangle she was hiding behind her back.

"Hogwash! You were brilliant. I could hear the sweet chime of your triangle all the way in the back row."

Lucy gave Truman a weak smile. She strongly suspected he was lying, but appreciated his attempt to make her feel good.

"There you are!" called a cheery voice. Harrison appeared out of the sea of people followed closely by Riley who was waving a large stick of pink cotton candy above his head.

"Comin' through," Riley cried. "Step aside…we've got important business!"

Lucy laughed at the sight of Riley waving his sticky pink baton to part the crowd.

"YOU!" Harrison and Riley exclaimed in unison, pointing at Lucy. "You're coming with us."

Before she knew what was happening, Riley and Harrison had hooked Lucy by the arms and were leading her away as Riley swung his cotton candy sword in front of them to clear a path.

"Pardon me, but where do you think you're going with our star triangle player," Truman called after them with mock concern.

"We'll never tell!" Harrison yelled back over his shoulder.

"Don't wait up!" said Riley, as they melted into the crowd and the confused faces of Ben, Puddles and Truman disappeared from view.

"We've got a surprise for you," said Harrison mysteriously, and he shot Lucy a wicked smile.

She tried to ask where they were going but Harrison and Riley had suddenly broken out in song and were paying no attention to her pleas for information. Every time Lucy opened her mouth, the song got louder until finally she gave up. Resigning herself to the fact that she wouldn't get any information until they were done with their little ditty, Lucy stopped fighting and let them march her up the street to the bemused stares of attendants out enjoying the Festival.

"Ring the bells and toot your horns,
Wake the dead and those not born,
Clap your hands and stomp your feet,
It's your past we're off to meet.
No use delaying; don't try to stall,
We're only helping after all,
Just take a look and then you'll see
The past's not passed; it's history!"

Finally, just as Lucy was about to protest that this had gone on long enough, Harrison and Riley came to a screeching halt. Hitting the final sour note of their song they flung out their arms in unison, pointing proudly towards a flight of long, stone steps that led up to an intimidating gray marble building.

"So what do you think?" said Harrison, looking at Lucy with a gleam in his eyes.

"Uh…." Lucy looked up at the gray wall looming in front of her, not sure of exactly what she was supposed to say. "It's quite a surprise alright."

"Don't be daft," Riley said, pushing Lucy up the steps. "Your surprise is *inside*."

The lobby was cold and cavernous like an immense bank lobby with windowless stone walls rising up several stories to a carved ceiling. The only light came from an odd looking 10 foot crystal obelisk that stood in the middle of the room giving off a pale green glow. Completely empty of furniture, the only other object in the room was a heavy iron stand planted near the entrance that held a large sign reading:

WARNING!
AUTHORIZED ATTENDANTS ONLY
Viewing permits may be obtained at the
Village Central Office

"Guys, I don't think we're supposed to be here," said Lucy, her voice reverberating off the walls. Goose bumps had sprouted on her arms and she doubted it had anything to do with the cold.

"Sure we are," Riley cooed, pushing Lucy further into the room. "That ol' sign's just a technicality. Here, if it makes yeh feel better we'll play by the rules."

Riley turned to Harrison and, standing at attention, declared, "Master Harrison, I hereby authorize yeh to be here."

"Why thank you," said Harrison, giving an overly dramatic bow. "Master Riley, I am honored to bestow upon you the same authority."

"Outstanding! And now that just leaves…"

"No, guys….really…I don't think…"

But before Lucy could finish Harrison and Riley bellowed in unison, "LUCILLE MARGARET O'SULLIVAN, WE AUTHORIZE YOU…"

"No," said Riley holding up his hand, "we *COMMAND YOU…*"

"…TO ENTER WITHIN!"

At this command there was a loud crack and Lucy gasped as a glimmering golden door appeared on the wall to her right. No taller than four feet, the tiny door was dwarfed by the mammoth lobby surrounding it making it appear as though it led into some kind of beautiful dollhouse.

Too surprised to fight, Lucy didn't resist as Harrison and Riley guided her silently towards the door. As they drew nearer Lucy's mouth dropped open. In the middle of the door was a small plaque engraved *Lucille Margaret O'Sullivan*.

"What..." Lucy looked from Harrison to Riley but couldn't find the words she was searching for.

"Perhaps a quick explanation is called for," said Riley. "This here place is the Hall of Review, otherwise known to the residents around here as the Look Back. Yeh see sometimes when yer having a hard time figurin' out where yer supposed to be goin' it can be helpful to see where yeh've been."

Something clicked in Lucy's brain. She remembered hearing some of the senior attendants talk about this place. Glaring at the door, she felt a sudden surge of excitement. "Are you telling me that behind that door is my...my past?"

Riley smiled. Lucy didn't need to hear any more. Barely able to control her excitement at the thought of seeing her family again Lucy lunged for the door.

"Hold on," said Harrison, throwing his arm in front of Lucy and blocking her way. "There is something you need to understand before we go in."

Lucy couldn't believe it. She was inches away from seeing her family and *now* Harrison wanted to chat. "Harrison, *please!*"

Harrison didn't budge. "What you need to know is that there is a reason this place is off limits to new attendants. The Council seems to think most newbies can't handle the shock of seeing their families so soon after getting here. They think you need time to get used to this place before you go getting all sentimental about what you left behind."

"Bullpucky!" cried Riley, his voice echoing through the room. "When Harrison told me they hadn't even given yeh a proper welcoming party I couldn't believe it. Everyone gets a welcoming party. The whole reason is so yeh can see yer family who are already here…kinda makes up for the lot yeh left behind."

Lucy was tired of listening to their explanations; she didn't care about any stupid concerns of the Council. She just wanted to see her family.

"Look guys, I appreciate the warning and all, but I'm a big girl. I promise I won't go to pieces. Now can I go inside?"

"That's my girl," Riley said, slapping Lucy on the back.

Harrison looked for a moment like he was having second thoughts, but then his eyes lightened.

"Go on," he said, and he stepped aside.

Lucy felt a surge of excitement as she stepped up to the door. Trembling slightly she reached out and grabbed the polished silver handle. With her heart pounding so fiercely that she was afraid it might explode, Lucy turned the handle and pushed open the door.

As she ducked through the tiny opening Lucy was surprised to find the room was much larger than she expected. A short, squat crystal pedestal sat in the center of the room emitting an eerie green glow that cast tall shadows against the walls. The shadows danced as the trio moved towards the middle of the room.

"It's okay," Harrison said in a hushed voice, ushering Lucy to the pedestal. "Just put your right hand on the screen."

"Yeah, it's all set," Riley whispered, "we snuck up here while everyone was at the concert and made sure it was programmed just right. Hope yeh like the memory we picked for yeh."

Riley and Harrison stepped back to give her some privacy as Lucy reached out a trembling hand and placed it on the face of the pedestal. A green light scanned the palm of her hand sending a warm tingle to her fingertips. For a moment the top of the pedestal flickered and then, as Lucy held her breath, a group of blurred figures in the occuscope began to take shape.

CHAPTER THIRTEEN

THE CHRISTMAS KEY

Never had Lucy felt such a longing for her home.

As though someone had adjusted the lens of a microscope, Katie O'Sullivan's features came into sharp focus as she looked up towards Lucy. The room suddenly felt devoid of air as Lucy felt a grabbing in her chest and tears sprang to her eyes.

The scene was instantly familiar; it was Christmas four years earlier. Lucy knew exactly which Christmas it was because in the corner, peeking out from behind the Christmas tree, were the cherry red handle bars of the bike her father had given her that year.

A rustling from under the tree drew Lucy's attention away from the bike. As the boughs of the tree shook and an ornament dropped to the ground, Digby's pajama-clad butt wiggled out from between the presents. Lucy clasped her hand to her mouth laughing through her tears as her pudgy little brother with his thick mop of blond hair emerged from beneath the tree clutching a large package topped with several real pinecones. The gift was from Aunt Aggie who was standing nearby in her pink, fuzzy, footy pajamas beaming at Digby as he tore into the package. A moment later there was a loud squeal of delight as Digby pulled out the sleek, silver remote-controlled Chevy Corvette with lightning bolts down the side. Lucy knew that a month later the car would be crushed when her mother backed over it in the driveway.

As Digby played with his new toy unaware of its impending doom, the invisible camera drew back showing the rest of the room. Lucy felt her heart jump to her throat.

There, sitting in his favorite old worn recliner and laughing in a way that made Lucy ache with homesickness, was her father. Hot tears began to trickle down her cheeks as Lucy stared transfixed at the man who had been her hero and who had been ripped from her life much too soon. Leaning closer to the screen Lucy swore she could smell the after shave Jack O'Sullivan had always worn. Lord, she missed him so much.

Lucy watched, unable to breathe, as her mother sat on her father's knee, rustling his orange hair and giving him a playful kiss on the cheek. They were all so happy; none of them could have guessed at that moment that in just a few months their entire world would be torn apart.

Suddenly Oscar came bounding into the room barking madly at the ceiling. The O'Sullivans had always thought Oscar was a bit deranged due to his peculiar habit of breaking into fits of barking for no apparent reason. But as Oscar continued to bark at the empty air above, Lucy noticed something; bits of light were floating about the room, hovering over each member of the family. As she stared in disbelief the wisps of light slowly took shape.

Lucy turned to Riley who was wearing a wide, knowing grin.

"Yeh didn't think yeh was alone down there, did yeh?" he said, laughing at Lucy's look of surprise. "I think if yeh take a closer look yeh might just recognize a few faces."

Lucy looked back at the screen. Sitting on an invisible perch just over the shoulder of her younger self was Truman! He had that familiar twinkle in his eyes as he watched the ten year-old Lucy rip off the paper from the computer game she had desperately wanted. And there, to Truman's side hanging just above Lucy's father, was another familiar face.

"Harrison…" Lucy felt dazed as she gazed up at her friend. "It's you. You were my dad's Guardian?"

"One of several. I did have a bit of help."

Lucy's mind began spinning with questions but before she could say anything a bright spark of light on the screen caught her eye. The light spun for a moment over Aunt Aggie's head and then burst into a brilliant white specter. Squinting at the light, Lucy saw it was a woman cloaked in a gleaming white gown.

Bending so close that her nose nearly touched the screen, Lucy whispered, "Are those...wings?"

"Aw, she's somethin' isn't she?" cooed Riley, peering over Lucy's shoulder. "That's Calista, back when she was a guardian angel."

A guardian angel? Ben had tried to tell her that angels were all around them, but she had never really given them much thought. Now, staring at the image in front of her, Lucy wondered how she ever could have missed anything so unbelievably magnificent. Just then Riley's comment fully registered.

"What do you mean, 'back when she was a guardian angel'?" said Lucy. "Isn't she an angel anymore?"

"Oh she's still an angel," said Harrison, staring at the beautiful creature hovering over Aunt Aggie. "She's just been reassigned; she's an earth angel now." Then he added, "But you should know that; after all, you've seen her in person."

"No way," said Lucy. She would certainly remember if she had ever run into this amazing woman – or any other earth angel for that matter.

"Yeh got to admit Harrison, she looked a bit different last time we saw her," said Riley. "Traded in those wings for a black spiked collar if I recall correctly."

"GET OUT OF HERE!" shouted Lucy, her words echoing through the room. "You're trying to tell me that this...*THIS* is the same person as that creepy girl back in the park?"

"Careful," warned Riley. "Angels are right powerful and I don't imagine she'd like bein' called creepy. Though I must admit it was a rather interestin' costume choice."

Lucy felt numb. She couldn't believe it. That girl back in the park had seemed so weird, and definitely not heavenly, not like the woman on the screen who looked exactly like Lucy had always imagined an angel would look. She watched as Calista bent down and whispered something in Aunt Aggie's ear. With a look as though she had just come up with a great idea, Aunt Aggie went to her purse and pulled out a small package.

"The box!" Lucy exclaimed, remembering the gift.

A chill of anticipation swept over her as she watched Aunt Aggie cross the room and hand a small brown box to the young Lucy who excitedly opened it. With a poorly hidden look of disappointment the ten year-old Lucy pulled out a rusty old key. Little did she know back then that this seemingly insignificant key would one day save her life. Ironically, that same key would also lead Lucy to her death.

"Not exactly what you were hopin' for huh?" said Riley, watching the young Lucy thank her aunt for the key with a pained smile.

Lucy felt her throat tighten as her mind flashed back four years.

She remembered how Aunt Aggie had waited for the others to become caught up in a game of Sorry before quietly pulling Lucy aside out of earshot. In a soft, but excited voice she told Lucy to quickly bundle up in her warmest coat and then, with a quick glance over her shoulder to make sure they weren't being watched, Aunt Aggie had led Lucy out into the middle of a blizzard.

They walked for more than a mile in the storm, going deeper and deeper into the forest until Lucy had complained that her toes were going to freeze off. Aunt Aggie just brushed the snow off Lucy's head and said,

"Dear, the truly wonderful things in life never come without a bit of strife."

Just when Lucy was sure she couldn't walk another step in the deep snow they turned the corner of a large boulder and there, sitting like some fairytale cottage tucked away from the storm, was the most amazing little house Lucy had ever seen. With a gentle push, her aunt prodded her towards the door.

Somehow Lucy knew what she was supposed to do. Taking the small box from her pocket, she brushed the snow from the lock and inserted the key. Giving it a quarter turn, the lock clicked and the door swung open.

A rush of warm air poured out of the cottage as Lucy stepped inside feeling as though she was in some kind of dream. There was only one room but Lucy thought she had never seen anything more wonderful in her life. A small settee sat in front of the stone fireplace which crackled with a blaze that licked at the two large logs in its grate; a reading lamp stood by the side of the sofa casting a golden light throughout the cottage and on the opposite side of the small room was a round, wooden table covered with a lace cloth. On top of the table, unfolded and ready for play, was a game board. The empty LIFE box sat on the floor.

The memory of the cottage and the countless hours of comfort it had given her caused Lucy's eyes to burn and she blinked fast to keep back the tears.

"That was the most wonderful key in the world," whispered Lucy. "It kept me alive after dad died. That's why I wanted Bird to have it; I thought maybe it would help him deal with his mom being gone."

Lucy cleared her throat and wiped her eyes forcing herself to smile.

"So much for that plan. The note I left him didn't say anything about what the key was for; he'll have no idea…" Lucy's voice faded away as she caught sight again of

Calista whispering something into Aunt Aggie's ear. Aggie beamed and gave a slight nod of understanding.

Suddenly Lucy felt her heart skip a beat. *Of course*, she thought as a rush of excitement exploded inside of her. She had been stupid for not thinking of it sooner!

"You're brilliant!" said Lucy, throwing her arms around Harrison and then around Riley.

"Thanks for noticin'," said Riley, turning slightly pink.

"You knew that if I saw this it would help me figure out the riddle!"

Harrison and Riley exchanged clueless looks before shrugging and shamelessly accepting her praise. Lucy didn't care; planned or not, they had just shown her the answer to Aunt Aggie's Life Map!

****

"There you are!" exclaimed Ben, looking up from his breakfast plate with a piece of bacon still dangling from his mouth. "Where have you been? Puddles and I stayed up half the night waiting for you."

Lucy pulled up a chair, squeezing between her friends and reached for a large plate of pancakes. Even though she had been up all night formulating her plan, she was still reeling from the excitement of last night and didn't feel the least bit tired.

"Yeah," yawned Puddles. "We tried to stay up but Banks showed up and told us we had to go to bed."

"Banks is back?" asked Lucy, temporarily forgetting about the news she had for them. "Did he say where he had been?"

"No, but he looked really tired," said Puddles, stabbing a sausage link and shoving it in his mouth. "W'ever he wuv, didn't look like it wuv muff of a vacathun."

Lucy stared across the table at Banks' empty seat. She had not seen him at the Festival yesterday. Where was he disappearing to that made him so tired?

"Lucy!" Ben waved his hand in Lucy's face bringing her out of her daydream. "Are you going to tell us where you were last night or do we have to find Harrison and Riley and drag it out of them?"

Forgetting about Banks, Lucy took a quick glance around the table to make sure the others weren't listening and then quietly launched into her story. Ben and Puddles stared at her with rapt attention as Lucy recounted the evening's events between mouthfuls of pancakes. When she got to the part about Calista, Ben slapped the table.

"I told you!" he said, beaming with satisfaction.

"Told us what, dear?" said Anna, looking up from her conversation with Babu.

Ben stuttered trying to quickly come up with a lie but before he could say anything he was saved by the morning chime. With a loud shuffling of chairs, the hall began to empty and the members of Hill Cottage prepared to set off for teleporting. Lucy hung behind as they reached the doors leading out onto the grounds. Grabbing Ben and Puddles, she pulled them back inside.

"What's going on?" said Ben, yanking his sleeve from Lucy's grasp.

"I need you guys to tell Madame Mira that I had to run an errand for Banks so I won't be in class today."

"What are you doing for Banks?" asked Puddles, looking confused.

"She's not doing anything for Banks," Ben said. "She's skipping out on teleporting."

"Look, I'll explain later. Just tell her, okay?"

Lucy felt a pang of guilt as she turned away from her friends. Telling herself that she would make it up to them later, Lucy bolted up the stairway that led to the south tower.

When she reached the fifth floor landing, Lucy stopped to catch her breath. Retrieving the crumpled Life Map from her sash, she tried unsuccessfully to smooth out the wrinkled, green paper. Hopefully George wouldn't care about its slightly damaged condition once she learned about Lucy's discovery.

Stepping up to the door Lucy gave three loud raps then stepped back to wait for Colonel George to answer. There were no footsteps, no bid to enter. Lucy was starting to wonder if perhaps George was not in her office when the door slowly creaked open apparently on its own. She began to step forward when a terrible thought sprang to her mind…what would George say when she learned that Harrison and Riley had taken Lucy into the Hall of Review without permission? She had been so excited to tell the Colonel she had solved her Life Map that she hadn't even thought about how she would explain her revelation.

I've got to get out of here, thought Lucy with a rush of panic. Knowing her only escape was back down the stairs, she spun around to leave but it was too late. Before her foot could hit the first step Colonel George's small voice floated out of the open doorway.

"Please come in, Miss O'Sullivan."

"Crap," Lucy cursed under her breath. Realizing she had to come up with something fast, Lucy turned back around and slowly entered the brightly lit room. Colonel George was seated behind her desk, her head barely visible above the large stack of papers in front of her.

"Good morning," Lucy said, trying to keep her voice casual. "How are you today?"

George looked up from the paper she was grading. With her bouncy blond curls pulled back into a knot and a pencil stuck behind her ear Lucy thought she looked like an extremely young librarian.

"Is that why you missed your teleporting class this morning? To inquire about my health?" said George, piercing Lucy with an icy stare.

Lucy felt her face grow hot as her smile slid out of place. "Yes…well not entirely…but mostly…" Lucy's voice wilted under Colonel George's unblinking gaze.

"Funny," said Colonel George, although Lucy thought she did not look the least bit amused. "I thought you were here to tell me about your visit to the Hall of Review."

Lucy's heart skipped a beat. "You know about the Hall of Review?"

"Masters Harrison and Riley are not known for keeping secrets. They were both quite eager to share the story of your little outing upon their return. Apparently they are under the impression that the result of your visit overshadows the small detail that freshman attendants are forbidden to use those particular facilities."

"I…I don't think they meant any harm," Lucy said, forcing a smile. "It's just I didn't get a welcoming party…"

"I'm fully aware of the circumstances of your arrival; however I'm afraid that still does not give them the right…"

"But it worked," interrupted Lucy before she could stop herself.

Colonel George leaned back in her chair, her pale blue eyes locked on to Lucy.

Taking George's silence as permission to continue, Lucy kept going. "The memory they showed me – it made me realize what Aunt Aggie's Map was talking about. Look…" Lucy held out the worn Life Map that was still clutched in her hand. "The last line, it says, '*It will be your journey's task to find the key that will unlock the spirit of one who has forgotten how to fly and in doing so set the stage for the light to return.'"*

"I've been trying to figure out what the key was, like it was some kind of a symbol or something. But it's not – it's a real key! Don't you see, my friend Bailey he's the one who has forgotten how to fly! His nickname's *BIRD*…how much clearer can it be?"

Colonel George did not answer; she simply continued to silently stare at Lucy as though she was waiting for the climax to the story. Lucy's brief moment of bravery began to falter and she could feel tiny beads of sweat forming on her forehead. But there was no turning back.

"Don't you see?" said Lucy, sounding more desperate than she intended. "Once Aggie finds out that Bird has the key, she can tell him about the cottage and he can start to use it to do whatever he's supposed to do and then…well, I'm not sure what that stuff about the light returning means, but obviously it's really important that he discovers the cottage. It's all part of Aunt Aggie's destiny…*she's* the one who is supposed to give him the key, not me."

For a brief moment Lucy thought she saw a flicker of compassion on Colonel George's face but it quickly disappeared. Standing up, George moved around the desk and held out her hand for the Life Map. Confused, Lucy handed it to her.

Colonel George gazed down at the paper for several moments before folding the crumpled paper in half and placing it on her desk.

"Taking into consideration that you were not responsible for instigating the unauthorized visitation, and trusting that you will be more cautious the next time Masters Riley and Harrison suggest an outing, there will be no retribution at this time."

"Uh…," Lucy muttered, feeling confused by those big words coming out of that small body.

"It means you're free to go," said the professor, with the smallest hint of a smile.

"But what about the map? How are we going to let Aunt Aggie know that Bird has the key?"

"*We* are not going to do anything," replied Colonel George, the smile erased from her face. "I must remind you that this was only an assignment; there will be no practical application."

Lucy couldn't believe what Colonel George was saying. *They weren't going to do anything?*

"If you write up your findings I will accept it as completion of your assignment."

"I don't care about my assignment!" blurted Lucy, feeling outraged by George's lack of concern. "What about Bird? He has to find out about the cottage or…"

"Or what?" said Colonel George, her voice rising above Lucy's. Lucy could tell she had crossed the line.

"Look," said Lucy, steadying her voice and trying to remain calm, "I know these people and I could help."

"This discussion is over," said Colonel George sharply. She returned to her seat and disappeared again behind the pile of papers. "I'll expect your paper by the end of the week."

With that final note she plucked the pencil from her hair and went back to work. Lucy knew there was no use arguing. Feeling completely deflated, she shut the door behind her and slunk back down the stairs.

****

Life at Drookshire Station took on an air of quiet desperation as winter melted into spring and the end of their first year loomed just around the corner. It seemed as though every instructor was determined to cram as much knowledge as possible into their heads and despite Banks' claim that this was training not school Lucy couldn't help but feel like they were being prepped for final exams.

With the date for their Life Map assignments drawing nearer, the library felt like a morgue as blurry-eyed attendants barricaded themselves behind fortresses of books.

"Hey, Luce, could you hand me that book?" said Ben, rubbing his eyes.

Lucy picked up *How to Know When Your Walker Should Run* and slid it across the table. Ben set down his copy of *Fun Facts About Fear*, and yawned.

"If I don't find it in here I'm giving up."

"You'll find it soon; you're getting really close."

Per George's instructions Lucy had completed her paper on Aggie's destiny and now was reduced to being a cheerleader for her friends.

As the late afternoon sun streamed into the library Lucy began to feel her head nod. Despite the warning to forget about the key, Lucy had remained determined to find a way to get word to Aunt Aggie and for weeks had spent her nights pouring over Messenger books on how to send secret clues to Walkers. Although she no longer needed regular sleep, the warmth of the sun spilling over her was too much to resist. Before she realized what was happening, Lucy's head drooped and she was back at the lake.

The sun was gone, as were the library and her friends. In the darkness she could hear the cries for help that were muffled by the wind and the sound of water as it hit the shore. After months of returning to the lake every time she closed her eyes, Lucy had learned what needed to be done. Quickly scanning the horizon for the eyes that would emerge from the darkness she scrambled up the bank to the gravel road circling the lake.

Ignoring the calls for help that were coming at her from all directions, Lucy closed her eyes and forced her breathing to slow. If she panicked she would fail. Her lips parted as she felt the air around her turn to ice. Forcing herself not to think about the eyes she knew were closing in on her, Lucy pushed out one trembling note.

"AHHH!" A scream of pain pierced her ears at the same moment the dinner bell rang out and ripped Lucy from her dream. Startled to find herself back in the library, Lucy toppled out of her chair sending a stack of books flying into the air.

"REALLY!" exclaimed Haddie, ducking to avoid being hit. "Can't you ever wake up like a normal person?"

If Lucy had thought that her secret partnership with Haddie might somehow improve their relationship she was sorely mistaken. It had been months since Lucy had asked Haddie for help and still they had no plan. To make things worse, Haddie's mood seemed to grow more sour with every failed idea.

"Luce, are you okay?" Ben asked, picking up the scattered books. From look on his face she suspected he knew where she had been.

"Yeah, the bell just startled me," she said, wiping away the drool that had drizzled down the side of her mouth. "They need to give us some kind of warning before they set that thing off."

Throughout the library there was a shuffling of chairs as throngs of exhausted attendants staggered off to dinner.

"You guys go on," said Ben, opening a huge, leather bound book and stretching. "I'm just going to check a few more facts."

"Forget it," Lucy said, grabbing the paper he was scribbling on. "Your brain is fried; you need a break."

"I'm fine, just a little ti…tired," said Ben, trying to stifle another yawn.

"Oh really? Well let's just take a look at what you have so far."

Holding the paper out of Ben's reach, Lucy began to read out loud, "In conclusion, I suggest my Walker should eat his challenger's head and not steer away from obstetricians playing before him."

"That's not what it says," said Ben, snatching the paper back from Lucy. "It clearly says...oh, well, I might have made a few spelling mistakes." He took out his pen and quickly scribbled over the text. "There, that's better. 'I suggest my Walker should meet his challenges head on and not steer away from obstacles placed before him.'"

"I think I liked the first one better," giggled Puddles, but he quickly folded up his own paper and put it away before Lucy could get her hands on it.

"Look, either you pack up those books and take a break, or I'm going to tell that blonde girl from the Mayanian Cottage that you can't keep your eyes off of her in Reflection," said Lucy.

"You're bluffing."

"Try me."

Apparently not want to take the chance that Lucy might go through with her threat, Ben began shoving papers into his bag.

As they emerged from the Library a burst of warm air greeted them. Lucy gazed up at the sky glad to be away from the dark chill of the lake. The sweet smell of Calla Lilies was drifting up from the garden and overhead the sun was beginning to lean towards the west creating long, dancing shadows as they walked toward the Station.

Ben and Puddles decided to get in a little teleporting practice and began popping in and out as they made their way up the hill.

"You know," said Ben, as he reappeared next to Lucy, "you never told us what your folks said when you told them about that house your aunt gave you."

"I bet they went nuts," said Puddles, suddenly materializing on Lucy's other side.

"I never told them," Lucy said matter-of-factly, flapping her arms in a pathetic attempt to teleport. Still planted in the same spot, having failed yet again to move as much as an inch, she gave up and plopped down in the grass.

Ben and Puddles both stared at her with their mouths hanging open.

"You never told them?" Puddles said, his eyes wide with disbelief.

"Don't look at me like that," said Lucy, plucking up a blade of grass and twirling it mindlessly between her fingers. "I was going to tell them, but then my dad died and…well, it's hard to explain."

"But Lucy, this was a *house*," Ben said. "How could you keep that secret from your mom?"

"You don't understand, that cottage saved my life," she said, focusing on the blade of grass. "After dad was killed I didn't want to talk to anyone so I used to sneak off to the cottage and just throw things or stomp on the floor or just lie on the sofa and scream into the pillows. The adults were all trying to say things they thought would make me feel better, but the cottage just listened."

Ben and Puddles didn't say anything.

"It's okay," said Lucy, breaking the awkward silence. "Look, I'm not saying I'm glad that my dad died, but after it happened I learned a lot of things about myself. All that time alone in the cottage helped me realize that I'm a lot stronger than I thought I was. It also helped me realize that even though dad was gone my life kept going and that's when I knew that there was still stuff I had to do. That's when I came up with the idea of giving Bird the key."

"Man, you're a lot nicer than I am," said Puddles, shaking his head. "If I had a secret house all to myself I don't think I could give it away."

Lucy stood up and brushed the grass from her robe.

"I'm not that nice; I kept the cottage to myself for almost four years without telling anyone…not even Bird who probably needed it more than I did. And then one day it dawned on me that maybe one of the reasons I survived the car accident was so I could be there to help Bird and…"

Lucy's voice faded as a thought suddenly popped into her mind. Staring off into the distance she could feel the puzzle pieces fall into place.

"That's it!" she blurted, turning abruptly to face Ben and Puddles.

"What?" said Ben, looking confused.

"The key! Originally I thought I was the one who was supposed to give it to him, but I was wrong; Aunt Aggie's map is clear that she's the one who is supposed to do that. But what if I wasn't *totally* wrong? What if I am supposed to help…but from this side? Maybe that's why I was sent here instead of wherever most people go when they die."

Lucy began pacing; her mind was racing as the realization of what this meant began to gel.

"Think about it…I was given a relative to research when everyone else was assigned a total stranger. Why? And how come I can hear voices when people need help? Maybe it's because I'm supposed to be able to help them. Wouldn't that explain why Dewey was able to hear me when I sang? It all makes sense. That's why I'm here…so I can help Aunt Aggie complete her task!"

Puddles, who had resumed his teleporting practice, stopped with his arms in mid-air.

"I thought Colonel George told you not to do anything."

"Yeah, Luce, don't you think that you ought to leave this up to the senior attendants?" said Ben. "Don't take this the wrong way, but you could really screw things up for your friend."

"But I won't! Don't you see? It's my destiny." Lucy's heart was pounding. For the first time she felt as though being sent to Drookshire was not a mistake.

Speaking softly as though he was trying to soften bad news, Ben pointed out what he obviously thought was painfully clear.

"Lucy, you don't know that. You want to believe it's true, but there is no way of proving it's your destiny."

"Yes, there is," said Lucy, rounding on him. She had known the moment the idea came to her that it was the only way. "My Life Map…if I could just see it I would know…"

"WHAT? Are you serious?" Ben was staring at Lucy as though she had gone completely mad. "The only way you could get hold of your Life Map is if George gave you a LAMP form for it and you're crazy if you think that's going to happen. She seems to think that knowing your own destiny is a bad idea – and she's right!"

"Actually," said Lucy, waving off Ben's ranting, "I've been thinking about it and, well, there might be another way."

"Forget it!" said Ben harshly, and he fixed Lucy with a stern glare. "I know what you're thinking and it won't work."

"What won't work?" asked Puddles, looking from Ben to Lucy in confusion.

"Lucy – she's planning on stealing a LAMP form," said Ben, his voice daring her to deny it.

Puddles looked at Lucy. "Really?" he exclaimed, sounding both impressed than shocked.

"No! I am not going to steal a LAMP form. I'm not going to steal anything."

"So I suppose you're just going to walk up to Chester and say, 'Excuse me, would you mind if I borrow my Life Map for a while?'"

"Chester doesn't have anything to do with it. Don't you remember; George said that attendant maps are kept in the Dream Chamber. And I think I know where they are; I saw them, or at least I think I did, that day I got called in front of the Council."

"You *think* you saw them?" said Ben, barking out a harsh laugh. "And now you *think* you're going to just waltz into the Dream Chamber which, oh by the way, just happens to be off limits, and steal your Life Map?"

"I told you, I'm not going to steal anything. I just want to take a look at it."

Ben threw his hands up in the air and walked away shaking his head and muttering something about Lucy being totally nuts.

"I suppose you think I'm nuts, too," Lucy said, glaring at Puddles.

Puddles fiddled with the sleeves of his robe but didn't answer.

"Fine," Lucy griped, turning towards the Station. "I don't care if anyone believes me."

"Do you really know where they keep our maps?" Puddles called out suddenly.

Lucy stopped. Puddles was staring at her wide-eyed and pale but he was no longer fidgeting. Lucy's mind flashed back to the large silver chest she had seen in the Dream Chamber. At the time she had wondered what kind of treasures it held, but now she was certain she knew the answer.

"Yeah, I think so."

"Okay, then," Puddles said, looking as though he had just come to a very difficult decision. "I'm in. But do you think we could find my map too?"

"Puddles, I can't ask you…"

"You didn't ask me," he said, cutting her off. "I'm volunteering. You need to know why you're here and,

[235]

well, I've kind of been wondering the same thing about myself."

Lucy shook her head; she wouldn't risk Puddles getting in trouble because of her.

"No," she said firmly. "It's too dangerous. Do you have any idea what Tobias will do if he catches us?"

"Kill us?" said Puddles flatly.

Lucy laughed despite herself.

"Look," said Puddles, sounding surprisingly determined, "the worst thing they could do is kick us out of here and I'm not sure that would be so bad. Like I said, I don't really even know why I'm here."

Lucy glanced back up at the sky. The sun was starting to sink behind the mountains which meant that Reflection would be starting soon. The lights of the Station made it glisten in the twilight and Lucy knew that inside her friends were enjoying dinner and laughing at another of Tibs' stories. A shiver ran down her back as she wondered what life outside of Drookshire would be like.

"Are you okay?" asked Puddles.

"We'll do it tonight after everyone's in bed," Lucy said, and she felt the strange calm of someone who had just sealed her fate. Stealing one more glance at the sunset she might never see again, Lucy turned and marched up the path towards the Station.

CHAPTER FOURTEEN

MORPHEUS

Ben made an excuse to go to bed as soon as they returned to Hill Cottage that evening. He claimed that all the Walker research had drained him, but Lucy had a suspicion that he just wanted to get as far away from them and their plan as possible. She and Puddles had spent their time in Reflection quietly plotting how they would sneak into the Dream Chamber and by the time the chime rang signaling the end of the day they knew what they would do.

As one by one their cottagemates slowly wandered off to bed, Lucy could feel her heart beat faster. Finally only Banks was left in the main lodge.

"That does it for me," he said, pocketing the small crystal orb he had been surveying. He glanced suspiciously at Lucy and Puddles sitting by the fire. "What are you two up to?"

Puddles choked on the hot chocolate he was drinking and Lucy jabbed him with her elbow.

"We're just finishing up an assignment," said Lucy. She shot Banks a wide grin which had guilt written all over it.

Banks' eyes narrowed as he studied Puddles who was wiping the chocolate from his face and trying hard not to meet Banks' gaze.

"Perhaps I could help…"

"NO!" Lucy and Puddles blurted at the same time.

Banks' eyebrows rose so high that his bald head crinkled.

"It's just that Colonel George told us we had to do it ourselves," said Lucy hastily. "And you know how she is."

She tried to laugh but it came out as a strained gurgle. "Thanks anyway."

Banks' eyes moved from Lucy to Puddles and then down to the hand drawn map of the Station they had been poring over. Lucy quickly set her own mug of hot chocolate on the map to hide it from view.

"Well then, I will leave you to your studies," he said, giving a slight nod. "But I suggest you get to bed soon. People have a tendency to make foolish mistakes when they're tired."

Lucy got the distinct feeling Banks wasn't talking about their homework.

Once they were certain everyone was in bed, Lucy and Puddles grabbed the map and slipped into the portal that would take them to the Station. To her great relief Lucy found the entrance hall was deserted. Waving for Puddles to follow, Lucy quickly padded across the marble floor to the circular stairway that led to the DOGS wing. From her two previous visits to the Dream Chamber she knew that it was located at the top of the north tower.

They encountered no one on the way up, but it wasn't until they reached the top floor and found the room guarded by the marble angel that Lucy felt herself breathe again.

"What now?" whispered Puddles, nervously eyeing the closed door.

Lucy put a finger to her lips and placed her ear to the door. Silence. Nodding that the coast was clear, she stretched out a trembling hand and slowly turned the golden handle. As the lock clicked and the door swung open Lucy felt a cool stream of air pour out from the dark chamber.

Puddles said nothing but Lucy could hear his heavy breathing as they slowly crept into the room shutting the door behind them. Unlike her last visit, there was no sun coming into the chamber this evening; instead the only light came from the blanket of stars hovering just above the domed ceiling. Looking up at the flickering lights Lucy got the eerie feeling they were being watched.

"Where is it?" whispered Puddles, his voice echoing through the chamber.

"Over there," Lucy said, pointing towards an area hidden in shadow on the far side of the room.

Straining to see through the murky darkness, Lucy led the way across the chamber being careful not to run into any of the long silver pedestals scattered in her path. A creak from the hall outside halted Lucy in her tracks but Puddles, who had been following closely at her heel, didn't have time to stop. With a loud grunt he smacked into Lucy sending her flying into the nearest pedestal. A thunderous crash echoed through the room as Lucy and the pedestal landed hard on the cold marble floor. The ringing from metal meeting marble seemed to go on forever as Lucy remained frozen in place, certain that the entire station must have heard the commotion. Listening for footsteps hurrying up the hall, all she could hear was the quick shallow breathing coming from Puddles' paralyzed form standing over her.

"Maybe we ought to get out of here," suggested Lucy.

But before Puddles could answer, Lucy heard a click and the door to the chamber swung open. Puddles stumbled backwards as a tall figure appeared in the doorway silhouetted by the light flooding in from the hall. Lucy felt her heart pounding in her throat as the dark figure slowly lifted the lantern it was carrying. The light cast a ghostly shadow across the intruder's face.

"Ben!" cried Lucy, with a rush of relief as the feeling returned to her body. "You scared the life out of us. What are you doing here?"

Smiling broadly at the shocked look on his friends' faces, Ben cranked up the light in the lantern as he entered the room and shut the door behind him.

"I thought you two might need some help, and apparently I was right. What were you trying to do anyway? Wake up the entire station?"

He reached down and helped Lucy to her feet.

"But you said you weren't coming," said Puddles, finally finding his voice again. "What made you change your mind?"

"This." Ben held out a small white envelope with Lucy's name scrawled on the front in purple ink. "Harrison stopped by to deliver it after you left; said it had been sent to him with directions to deliver it immediately. When he couldn't find you he knocked on my door. Don't worry," Ben said, as Lucy let out a curse. "I told him you were doing some late night research on your Methods of Persuasion paper for Christof."

"Thanks," said Lucy, realizing that Ben had lied to save her.

"Yeah, well I recognized the handwriting and figured you would want to see it right away."

Lucy took the envelope from Ben and without looking at it, shoved the unopened note into her sash.

"You're not going to read it?" said Ben, and Lucy could tell he was upset that his delivery was being ignored.

"Puddles and I are kind of busy right now," she said coldly. The relief she had felt at seeing Ben had turned to resentment now that she realized he had only shown up to play delivery boy for the Traveler.

"Besides," she said, reaching down to pick up the fallen pedestal, "the Traveler hasn't bothered to send me anything in months…I don't see what the rush is now."

Ben opened his mouth as though he was going to protest, but shut it again.

"Well you've done your duty, so you're free to go," said Lucy. She realized she sounded ungrateful for his efforts, but Ben had hardly been supportive of their plan and now was not the time for another reminder from the Traveler that Lucy should keep her nose clean and stay out of trouble.

Ben didn't budge. Lifting the lantern he glanced around the chamber.

"I...uh, well I thought as long as I was here I might as well stick around...that is if you want me to."

"We do!" said Puddles, before Lucy could answer. He looked at Lucy pleadingly. "Tell him we want him to stay."

Lucy looked up at Ben and felt her anger melt away. He had a way of making her feel a lot braver than she really was and right now she needed all the bravery she could get. "Fine," she said, giving a small shrug. "He can stay if he wants to."

"Great," said Ben, flashing a wide smile. That was all it took; everything was forgiven.

Taking the lantern from Ben, Lucy held it high to get a better look at the room.

"Bingo!"

On the far side of the chamber a shimmer of silver reflected in the lantern light. Careful not to run into any more pedestals, Lucy quickly navigated her way across the room with Ben and Puddles following closely behind.

"Which one is it?" asked Puddles, as they approached the two large chests.

"It's gotta be this one," said Ben, gently stroking the polished surface of the silver chest. "Of course," he added quickly, "it's Lucy's call. Which one do you think?"

Lucy carefully surveyed the two trunks. On the right was the roughly carved wooden chest. Its faded brown casing looked weathered and stained and the tarnished iron lock hung open. Surely no one would keep anything valuable in there.

To the left was the shining silver chest engraved with decorative symbols that Lucy didn't recognize but felt certain stood for something important. A thick, braided golden chain looped through two silver rings tying the lid shut. Not the most foolproof lock, thought Lucy, but certainly more impressive than the other.

With one final glance towards the old wooden chest, Lucy reached out and placed a hand on the lid of the silver trunk. This was it.

Taking a long, deep breath Lucy bit her lip and forced a smile. "Kind of like Christmas isn't it?"

Ben laughed. "I don't know about Christmas at your house, but my presents never looked like that."

With her fingers trembling from both fear and excitement, Lucy slowly untied the heavy golden chain. The instant the chain slipped from the loops the chest gave a quiver and then, as though it had been waiting for someone to unlock its treasure, the lid sprang open.

Puddles gasped and Lucy clapped a hand to her mouth as they stared in wonder at the contents of the box.

"Uh, Luce, I don't think this is the right chest," said Ben warily.

Sparkling as though it was some kind of strange luminescent bubble bath, inside the chest were thousands of small crystal orbs.

"Get of load of these things," said Puddles, plucking one of the glass balls from the chest and holding it up to the lantern for a better look. "What do you suppose they are?"

Lucy looked curiously at the small globe in Puddles' hand. A murky brown ribbon of mist was swirling through a white fog filling the orb.

"What are you doing?" exclaimed Ben, staring wide-eyed at the glass ball in Puddles' hand as though he expected it to explode. "Put that thing down!"

A sour look washed over Puddles' face. "Don't get your panties in a bunch," he said in a harsh voice. "I was just looking at it."

Lucy shot a stunned glance at Ben. Something was wrong with Puddles.

"Just put it down and let's get out of here," said Ben slowly, trying to remain calm.

Puddles' expression hardened as he wrapped his skinny fingers tighter around the glass ball.

"Puddles," said Lucy, realizing that their plan was taking a very dangerous detour, "if you put that thing down we can try to find your Life Map."

With a glassy stare Puddles slowly held out the orb, but rather than putting the ball back into the chest he turned and dropped it onto the top of the nearest silver pedestal.

The effect was instantaneous. With a whoosh the lantern light was extinguished and a tornado of wild, whirling color shot up in front of them.

"Oh crap!" cried Lucy, as she yanked Puddles away from the dream passage.

"Let's get out of here!" yelled Ben over the roar of the tornado.

Grabbing Puddles, they turned heel and darted for the door knocking over more pedestals in the darkness. With the howl of the passage and the clanging of the fallen pedestals reverberating around her, Lucy reached for the door handle. But before she could reach it Ben threw out his arm blocking her way.

"Wait! Listen," he panted, in a voice so low that Lucy could barely hear him over the commotion.

Quick footsteps were echoing up the hallway. Out of breath from their dash to escape, Lucy fought to regain control of her senses as she listened to the steps drawing nearer; she needed a plan and she needed it fast. Quickly pulling Ben and Puddles back into the shadowy center of the chamber away from the door Lucy drew them into a huddle.

"You two have to teleport out of here," she said, just loud enough to be heard over the gyrating dream passage.

Ben started to protest but Lucy clasped her hand over his mouth. "Listen to me…this is the only way. Ben, you need to get Puddles out of here and make sure he's okay." She glanced over at Puddles who looked shaken but coherent.

"We're not leaving you," Ben said, pulling Lucy's hand from his mouth but not letting go.

"You have to. I'm a mess when it comes to teleporting – it's true," she said, stopping Ben before he could argue. "Don't worry about me, I'll be fine. I have a plan but I don't have time to explain it. Now go!" Lucy yanked her hand from Ben's grip.

With a look that clearly showed he thought he would never see his friend again, Ben grasped Puddles tightly to his side and with a wave of his arm they were gone.

Lucy looked frantically around the darkened room for another exit but it was useless, she was locked in. She had lied to Ben about having a plan, but it had worked. No matter what happened to her, at least Lucy knew her friends were safe.

Before she could think of what to do next there was a loud click and light from the hallway spilled into the Dream Chamber. The world seemed to be thrown into slow motion as over the din of the dream passage Lucy heard someone calling her name. But it was too late.

Startled by the intruder Lucy had tripped backwards sinking her foot into the swirling mist of the tornado hovering behind her. Grabbing for support Lucy reached out for the silver pedestal and felt her hand wrap around the small crystal ball. As her body was yanked from the floor Lucy caught a fleeting glance of a blue robe entering the room, and then the world went dark.

An ice cold wind slapped at Lucy as she fell through the dream passage. Tumbling end over end she caught glimpses of horrible, grotesque figures flying past her, their faces distorted with pain. High, piercing screams sliced through her brain. She tried to cover her ears but she was falling too fast. And then suddenly, with an earth-shattering crash, Lucy landed face down on a mound of hard barren ground. As the world around her slowly spun to a halt, Lucy felt a cold chill wash over her broken body and she knew...this was the end. With no energy left to fight, Lucy gave in to the darkness.

****

The dull thumping of hooves shook Lucy back to life. She had no idea how long she had been asleep but her head was pounding and her arms and legs felt as though they had been filled with cement.

She struggled to get to her feet, but her energy was gone and she tripped and fell back to the ground. A sharp pain tore through her leg as something splintered beneath her knee.

Curse words that Lucy had never used before tumbled out of her mouth as she yanked out a large shard of glass. The remaining pieces of the glass orb were scattered on the ground.

Rubbing her knee, Lucy strained to see through the thick brown haze that choked the air. The sky was a sickly burnt orange and the stench of sewage stung her throat. Covering her nose and mouth Lucy looked around for some sign of where she was.

Across the dusty dirt road a row of dilapidated structures sagged with the weight of age and neglect. A sign dangled off the eave of the largest building. Lucy cocked her head and tried to make out the faded writing. SNAKE CANYON BANK. The hairs stood up on her neck; she hated snakes.

With both her head and knee still pounding, Lucy slowly got to her feet. After taking a few deep breaths of putrid air she set off across the street to see if possibly there might be someone who could tell her how to get out of here – wherever *here* was.

The windows of the bank were crusted with layers of grime. Lucy wiped her sleeve across the glass which did nothing but smear the dirt making it even harder to see inside. A sign on the door warned:

Leave Your Gun at the Door
By order of the Sheriff

A rather obvious request for a bank, she thought.

Pushing the door open so the sign swung loudly against the splintered wood, Lucy cautiously stepped into the bank. Unlike the decaying exterior, the inside of the bank was clean and brightly lit by two large oil lamps hanging from the ceiling. She was so spellbound by the contrast that Lucy failed to notice the thin, sallow man scurrying behind the counter until he dropped a deposit box on the floor, let out a loud curse and bent to retrieve the spilled contents.

Too stunned to scream, Lucy watched in silence as the man swept up fistfuls of coins and threw them back into the tin box all the while grumbling under his breath. He appeared very nervous and kept glancing up at the door as though expecting – or possibly fearing - a visitor. Although Lucy was standing in plain sight, he showed no sign of seeing her.

As though he had willed his worst fear to occur, the door of the bank banged open and a large, burly man strode in.

The man was filthy and unshaven with greasy dark hair brushed down over his eyes. He let out a low, rumbling growl as he scanned the room passing over Lucy as though she wasn't there. Finally his eyes fell on the spindly man crouched on his hands and knees. His growl rolled into a deep, hoarse laugh. The banker dropped the deposit box he had just refilled and looked up at the intruder, his eyes wide with panic.

"W...w...what d...d...do you want?" stuttered the banker, as he clambered to his feet. "Y...y...you don't have any b...b...business here."

The large man didn't answer. Without taking his eyes off the trembling banker he strode over and grabbed him by the collar hoisting him into the air.

The banker began pleading for his life, stuttering for forgiveness and sobbing uncontrollably. Lucy watched in horror as the intruder twitched the fingers of his free hand before reaching into his belt and withdrawing a large knife. With a cold sneer he drew his arm back and prepared to plunge the blade into the banker's belly.

Lucy covered her eyes and turned away as an agonizing scream pierced the air. The cry seemed to hang in the room for an unbearable length of time until finally with a sharp gasp it faded into silence.

Seconds ticked by with no sound of movement. Fearing the worst, Lucy slowly turned and opened her eyes expecting to find the banker's bloody body stretched out on the ground. But there was no blood and no body. The intruder was gone, and for a moment Lucy thought the Banker had disappeared as well. Then the clang of a coin being dropped into a box hit her ears and Lucy turned towards the counter.

Standing there, with the deposit box open in front of him, was the banker quietly counting his money.

Lucy's mind began to swim as she watched the banker pick up a coin, examine it, then toss it into the box. He made a quick note in the ledger book spread out in front of him and reached for another coin. A sense of déjà vu washed over Lucy as she watched the man's elbow knock the tin box off of the counter sending coins scattering across the floor. Cursing, he bent down to retrieve the coins.

It's happening again, thought Lucy. Panicking, she raced over to the banker and knelt down next to him as he scooped the coins off the floor.

"You have to get out of here!"

She was close enough to see the beads of sweat gathering on his forehead, but he was deaf to her warning.

Not knowing what else to do, Lucy grabbed for the man's bony shoulders but her hand swept through him as though he was nothing more than a dream.

Just then the door of the bank swung open and the killer strode into the room. Lucy yelled again at the banker to leave, but the scene was already set in motion.

Realizing there was nothing she could do, and not wanting to witness a repeat of the man's death, Lucy dashed past the killer and out into the hazy brown afternoon. With no idea of where she was going, she turned and ran up the deserted street as the banker's faint scream chased after her.

Lucy didn't stop running until she nearly collided with a large marble statue fixed in the middle of a stone paved courtyard. Out of breath from running, she leaned against the wishing pool that surrounded the statue and tried to calm her racing heart. The world around her had somehow changed. The orange sky had been replaced by steely gray clouds and there were puddles on the ground suggesting she had just missed a rain storm. A drop of water hit Lucy's head and trickled down her face. Looking up she saw the statue of a man seated on a horse, brandishing a sword; it was glistening with moisture and Lucy had to duck out of the way as a large drop fell from the tip of his weapon.

The weather wasn't the only thing that had changed. Around the courtyard grand stone buildings blended into the gray, misty backdrop making it hard to tell where the buildings stopped and the sky began. Lucy felt like she had seen this place somewhere before, perhaps in a text book or a movie. Suddenly a large, ornate carriage appeared in the distance. It was coming towards the statue at a quick trot, followed closely by a band of raggedy looking children. The carriage driver gave a hard pull on the reins and the horses reared up bringing the carriage to a halt no more than ten feet from Lucy. The children swarmed the carriage. They were dressed in rags that hung from their tiny bodies and their faces looked as though they had never seen soap. By the look of it, none of them had eaten a decent meal in weeks.

The carriage driver descended from his perch, tugging on the tails of his waistcoat and holding himself with an official air. Shooing back the children he reached up and unlatched the carriage door. A round man with an immense belly stepped from the carriage. His red velvet vest strained against the bulk of his stomach and numerous chins rippled over his ascot. The portly man ran a pudgy hand through his thick gray hair and sneered at the children who were crowding around him holding out their grimy hands.

"Please, sir, a farthing to spare?"

"Me baby sister is nearly starved to death…"

"Mum's right sick and we don't have no money for a doctor…"

The pleas buzzed around the fat man like nothing more than an annoying fly that he dismissed with a swat of his hand. Pushing his way through the young beggars, he waddled up to the pool of water surrounding the statue and pulled a large gold coin from his pocket. The children's eyes grew wide at the sight of the treasure. Without hesitating, the fat man flipped the coin into the water, smirking smugly as it splashed and then sank to the bottom of the basin.

He then turned to the children who were staring in disbelief at the point where the water had swallowed the precious golden coin.

"If I catch one of you filthy little buggers going into that water after my coin I promise I will throttle you to within an inch of your life!"

Lucy felt an intense dislike bubble up inside her for this foul human being. How dare he dismiss these children as though they were nothing more than a pack of hungry dogs? Not even dogs should be treated so cruelly!

Not sure why she was doing it, Lucy followed the man as he climbed back into his carriage, slammed the door and bellowed out to the driver, "Be off, and if any of those urchins dares get in our way you have my permission to run them over!"

Once the carriage was under way, the man heaved a large trunk from the floor and placed it on the seat beside him. His eyes gleamed with excitement as he pulled a large green cloth from his pocket, tied it around his neck and smacked his lips.

"Now for a bit of nosh," he said, rubbing his hands together. He lifted the lid to the trunk and Lucy saw that it was filled to the brim with enough food to feed a large family: roasted turkey legs, meat pies, tarts, baguettes of bread and an exceptionally large wheel of cheese.

Letting out an obscene sigh of pleasure, he reached in and pulled out a large, golden-brown turkey leg. The man raised the meat to his lips but before he could sink his teeth into the crisp brown skin his eyes flew wide with fright and he let out a howl of disgust.

Throwing the leg on the floor, the man cowered in the corner of the carriage. "What kind of devilish work is this," he cried, staring at the food in horror.

Lucy looked down at the roasted turkey leg and began to gag. Lying on the floor, covered in maggots, was a moldy old bone wrapped in putrid, green flesh. Feeling as though she was going to be sick, Lucy covered her mouth and looked away. But there was no escaping the foul odor that had filled the carriage. The entire trunk of food had transformed into a gooey mass of rotting food.

Out of nowhere flies suddenly filled the carriage, buzzing in the man's eyes and mouth as he squirmed wildly trying to get away from the stench and chaos. As Lucy watched unable to tear her eyes off the grotesque scene, the man suddenly threw open the carriage door. They were hurtling across a bridge high over rushing river. With a wild look of madness the man flung himself out of the open door. A curdling scream told Lucy the man had plunged to his death. Lucy sat frozen in her seat. If her guess was right, she knew what was about to happen. As she predicted, before the man's scream had died away, the carriage had been restored to its pristine state; the flies had vanished and the trunk was once again sitting on the floor emitting wonderful smells. The carriage door opened and the fat man stepped in and growled to the driver, "Get me to Sir Calloway's fountain. I need a bit of luck before my meeting with Lord Brantley."

This was enough for Lucy. Before the carriage driver shut the door she darted out, relieved to be away from the pompous aristocrat. She watched as the carriage sped away, leaving her by the side of a gravel road.

The sky was crimson now and an icy wind had kicked up bringing with it a damp mist. Lucy hugged herself trying to chase off the cold as she glanced around for some sign of where to go from here. On one side of the road there was a dense thicket of trees; on the other, a vast lake that spread into the horizon until it joined with a distant mountain range. Realizing she had no choice but to follow the road, Lucy lowered her head against the wind and started up the path.

As she walked Lucy listened for some sign of life, but the only sound audible over the wind was the crunching of gravel under her feet and the splash of whitecaps as they lapped against the shore.

She stopped for a moment to rub away the goose bumps that were blossoming over her arms and neck, and then she heard it. From somewhere on the other side of the lake there was a faint cry of voices. Lucy strained to hear what they were saying, but the storm was too strong. Maybe if she got closer…

Climbing down the narrow embankment towards the black water Lucy inched forward until she felt the stinging cold waves burning her feet. The voices were louder now; they seemed angry and Lucy felt herself growing sadder and more helpless the longer she listened.

With a jolt of panic Lucy suddenly recognized where she was. This was no random dream; she had stepped out of the carriage into her own nightmare. Fearing what she knew would come next, her eyes darted towards the sky.

Overhead a churning, black mass of clouds had begun to spread out over the horizon threatening to extinguish what little light was left. Lucy knew she had to get away from the lake. Digging her foot into the side of the embankment she tried to climb back up to the road, but the rocky earth simply crumbled beneath her feet sending her tumbling back down to the water's edge. A large wave rolled up on to the shore and wrapped around her ankles like an icy chain. Lucy kicked frantically to get free from the watery grip but it was too strong. She stretched out her arm and grasped for a small shrub that lay just beyond her fingertips; as she strained to grab hold Lucy looked up and caught sight of something that made her blood turn cold.

Standing above her with a face hidden in shadow was a black cloaked figure, cold gray eyes gleaming from underneath the hood. He gave a silent nod to the lake and Lucy felt the water yank her from the shore. The crushing cold pressed in on all sides as Lucy struggled to keep her head above water but the force was too great. Just before she sank into the watery grave Lucy shot a final look at her executioner. With a chilling laugh that cut through the wind the shadowy figure slid back his hood.

BANKS!

CHAPTER FIFTEEN

THE OTHER BROTHER

Lucy would never remember what occurred while she was held prisoner in the bowels of Morpheus; as a matter of fact the only memory she would ever really recall would be the flashing glimpses of a large white bird hovering over her and the music – the haunting, strange music that seemed to wrap itself around her. The words were indecipherable and foreign but the tune seemed deeply familiar.

It was this music that kept Lucy company during her long sleep. Its magical tone was like balm on a deep wound. From time to time Lucy's eyes would flicker open as she would struggle to wake up and she would catch glimpses of horrible dark shapes or hear piercing cries for help; and then her eyes would close again and she would drift back to sleep, back into the arms of the music.

Time lost all meaning for Lucy while she slept, so she had no idea of whether it had been a day or a week or a year when a familiar, deep voice finally managed to cut through the fog of her dreams.

"Lucy –" the sound of her name felt strange to her ears. "It's time to wake up."

Something touched her forehead and Lucy felt a jolt of electricity shoot through her body. She gasped and the sting of frigid air filled her chest. Coughing as her lungs seized up from the cold, Lucy rolled over on to her hands and knees and felt the hard rocky ground beneath her. Fighting for breath, Lucy slowly opened her eyes. Dim light seeped under her lids burning her eyes as though she had just emerged from a dark cave into the blinding sun.

Blinking against the misty glow Lucy looked up and saw the blurry outline of four figures hovering over her.

As she fought the uncontrollable shivering that had gripped her body someone said, "She's going to be okay, you can go."

There was a scuffling of feet followed by a loud whoosh and a flash of light as three of the figures disappeared. Lucy struggled to get to her feet but her body felt as though it was made of lead and she fell back to the ground.

"Don't struggle," said a man's deep voice.

Lucy's blood turned cold at the familiar sound; the memory of where she was suddenly raced back to her.

Trembling but unable to move, Lucy was helpless to do anything but watch as the man bent nearer and his blurry outline came into focus. She felt a scream explode from deep inside but it never made it past her lips. In the misty glow of the fog that blanketed Morpheus, Lucy took in the face of her Cottage Master.

"Welcome back," said Banks, as he reached for Lucy.

Lucy recoiled. She struggled to get away but her arms and legs refused obey.

Banks drew closer. Kneeling over her, he reached out and placed his large, powerful hands above her heart.

"AHHHH!" Lucy screamed out in pain as a sharp current of fire cut through her body burning her from the inside out. It felt as though every molecule in her body was engulfed in flame; and then it was gone.

A rush of energy filled Lucy like a balloon that had been instantly inflated. The pain had vanished and its place there was feeling of tingling weightlessness. She tried to sit up but Banks put a hand on her shoulder.

"Not yet. Your body needs to adjust to the energy."

"You…" said Lucy, struggling to find words that would make sense of the situation, "…you sent me into the lake."

"It wasn't me," Banks said, but Lucy cut him off with a biting laugh.

"I saw you! Just before you told whatever lives in that lake to drag me under. You dropped your hood and I saw you!"

Lucy was feeling stronger now and the memory of the cold, heartless laugh that had followed her into the water rang in her ears.

"Lucy, you need to listen to me…"

"Listen to you? I've been listening to you every night when you've invaded my dreams! All year you've been pretending to help me but all you really wanted to do was get into my head. But it's over! As soon as I get out of here I'm going straight to Samuel and I'm going to tell him everything."

Banks sat down on the rocky shore and stared out over the lake. He swept a hand over his face and Lucy thought he looked much older than she remembered.

"He knows," said Banks wearily.

Lucy couldn't believe this. Samuel knew that Banks had been haunting her sleep and he hadn't done anything to stop him? She felt her anger melt into confusion.

"That's impossible," she said, more to herself than to Banks. "Samuel never would have let you stay at Drookshire if he knew - "

But Lucy didn't get a chance to finish. From behind her a gravelly voice growled with laughter.

"She's rather dim, isn't she?"

Lucy swung around and at once felt the air sucked from her chest. Towering over her, holding Samuel's golden Keeper's Staff, was the cloaked figure from her dreams.

"Stay away from her, Tiberon," said Banks, in a voice that was low but deadly serious.

"Stay away from her?" barked the raspy voice hidden beneath the hood. "Why it's *she* who has trespassed into my world. For months she has followed me where your kind is forbidden to go and yet I did nothing. But that ends now."

He raised the Keeper's Staff and pointed it towards Lucy.

With a roar that sounded like a wounded beast, Banks leapt to his feet throwing Lucy to the ground and lunging at the dark figure. Before Lucy could scream out a warning the shadowy figure raised his hand and bellowed out words that Lucy didn't recognize. In a flash Banks dropped to ground and began writhing in pain.

"STOP IT!" cried Lucy, staring in horror at Banks' contorted body. "You're hurting him!"

With a hoarse laugh the cloaked figure lowered his hand and Banks' lifeless body fell still.

"Little girls should not make such nasty accusations. I have not done anything to your precious Cottage Master. No, I am pleased to say that my dear brother has done this quite all by himself."

"What are you talking about?" demanded Lucy. Her mind was swimming as she tried to make sense of what was happening.

"Of course," hissed the voice from under the hood, "he has deceived you like he has deceived all the others. Your beloved Banks didn't tell you that he had a brother locked in the Forgotten City; not a surprise really – considering he is the one who put me here."

"You're lying. I don't know who – or what – you are, but I don't believe that Banks is your brother, and I don't believe he sent you here. He wouldn't do that." As she said it, Lucy realized it was true; Banks wouldn't send someone to Morpheus. She looked down at his crumpled body which had stopped twitching and was now lying lifeless on the ground and she knew it couldn't have been him that sent her into the lake.

"Then you are as naive as you are foolish," growled the man Banks called Tiberon. "Perhaps this will help convince you that I am not the one who has been lying."

Tiberon pulled back his hood and Lucy felt herself slammed into an invisible wall. It was Banks. Every feature was identical: the large, broad nose, the small ears, the smooth, bald scalp - only the eyes were different. These eyes, these lifeless gray eyes, could not be more different.

Tiberon's face broke into a joyless, evil grin. "Spooky, isn't it?"

"I...I don't understand," Lucy stuttered, looking from Banks to Tiberon in disbelief. "This doesn't make sense."

"Exactly which part of the story confuses you?" said Tiberon, as he began slowly pacing around Lucy and Banks like a vulture circling its prey. "Is it the fact that my worm of a brother was able to deny his own flesh and blood, or is it simply that you are having a hard time believing that two brothers who appear so similar could be so seemingly different?"

Lucy didn't answer; she was watching Tiberon as he moved around them holding the golden staff firmly in his grip.

"Can't decide? Let me help you..." Tiberon stopped over Banks' body. With a swift kick of his foot he shoved Banks on to his back. A scream of agony split the air as Tiberon's bare foot touched Banks' flesh.

"You see, we're not so different after all. Only someone who harbored true darkness in their soul could show so much fear."

"Get away from him!" Lucy yelled, an eruption of fury exploding inside her. She rushed to Banks' side but in his pain he didn't seem to notice she was there.

"Hard to learn that your brave Cottage Master is actually a lying, quivering worm, isn't it?"

"He isn't a worm," spat Lucy. "I don't know what's going on, but I do know that Banks is nothing like you."

"Tut, tut…," said Tiberon condescendingly. "I expected so much more from you."

Lucy had no idea what Tiberon was talking about, but she wasn't going to play his game. "You're wrong about him," she said, forcing her voice to remain calm.

Tiberon stared down at her, his gray eyes unblinking. "Am I? Unconditional love…isn't that what your kind likes to preach? Apparently my dear brother decided I wasn't worth the effort, so when they gave him the choice to either accompany me to the Land Beyond and teach me the quaint ways of the so-called righteous or to throw me in to this dark hole he chose to abandon me so he could return to his comfortable little life in that insipid village."

"I don't believe you," said Lucy coldly.

"But my dear, ignorant girl, the proof lies before you. Only someone who had done something so low and despicable could descend into a nightmare of that power."

Lucy looked down at Banks. His hands were pressed hard over his eyes as though he was trying with all his might to erase the vision he was seeing.

A dark shadow passed over them and Lucy heard the rumble of angry voices rolling overhead. Peeling her eyes away from Banks, Lucy looked up and found that the sky had been transformed into a thick wave of muddy purple fog.

Tiberon's ghostly gray eyes followed the bubbling dark mist with excitement.

"Beautiful, isn't it," he said, a note of thrill in his voice as he watched the vapor begin to circle overhead. "Someday my companions will make their way into every corner of the Kingdom that has been withheld from us for so long; and then that pious group who, like my brother, has insisted on treating us like second-class citizens will know what it is like to be thrown into hell."

Lucy's skin crawled and she felt her stomach grow sick. The putrid smell of rotting garbage hit her nostrils and she clapped a hand to her mouth to keep from gagging.

"Ah, the sweet smell of fear," Tiberon laughed, drawing a deep breath. "Not to worry; you'll get used to it after a century or two." He gave a deep, throaty laugh and lifted the Keeper's Staff; a roar of thunder shook the air.

Over the rumbling Lucy heard a moan and looked down to see Banks, weak and trembling, roll over and struggle to get to his feet. Something in the thunder had shaken him from his nightmare.

Quickly grabbing him around the waist, Lucy threw his arm over her shoulder and hoisted him to his feet, her knees buckling under Banks' considerable weight.

"So sweet," growled Tiberon. "The master and his protégé. Too bad my dear bother is in no position to save you."

Banks lifted his head and Lucy saw fire in his eyes.

"Tiberon, I can't let you do this. Your battle is with me…using Lucy to get revenge will only guarantee you an eternity locked in this hell."

Tiberon's eyes flashed at Banks. "Revenge? You think this is about some kind of pitiful need to even the score?"

The nightmarish fog overhead seemed to react to Tiberon's anger and another crash of thunder vibrated the air.

"Really brother, you think far too highly of yourself. However soon you will realize that I am the one with the true power."

Lucy saw Tiberon's grip tighten around the Keeper's Staff.

As though he had read her thoughts, Tiberon peered into the staff's crystal globe and an oily smile spread across his face.

"Ah yes, I forgot to thank you for bringing me this little gift."

"I didn't bring that thing in here," said Lucy, still struggling to hold Banks steady.

"Stupid girl, I wasn't talking to you," snarled Tiberon, and his gaze shifted to Banks.

"The Keeper's Staff was meant for Lucy," Banks said, his voice still weak.

"And yet it has found its way into my possession. Funny how fate works – I had been pondering how I was going to rid myself of this place, and voila! You appeared with just the thing I needed. Surprising, however, that you would bring the Keeper's most cherished belonging into Morpheus when you are undoubtedly aware that there are many here who would do anything to control its power."

Tiberon ran a hand over the small crystal globe that sat on top of the staff. A storm of lightning strikes flashed inside the orb at the points where he touched its surface.

"Really, for one so revered you have made some very foolish decisions," said Tiberon. "And for that I am in your debt." He gave Banks a thin, evil smile.

Before Banks could respond, Tiberon aimed the staff at Banks' heart and cried out, "MORS MORTIS!"

Lucy reacted without thinking. With a wave of her hand a cage of light surrounded them. The lightning that flew from the tip of the Keeper's Staff ricocheted off the cage and shot back towards Tiberon who ducked just in time.

"Impressive," said Tiberon, straightening up. His voice was calm but his smile was gone. "I see not all the stories about you were exaggerated. But let's see how you handle a different kind of pain."

Tiberon thrust the Keeper's Staff towards the sky and a chorus of a thousand voices began screaming in agony. Lucy felt a cutting sorrow penetrate her very core with a sadness that felt like it would destroy her. The pain of her death, the loss of her family; it all hit her with a tyrannical force. The cage of light began to flicker as Lucy felt her body crumble under the grief.

Banks' arm tightened around her shoulder. Now it was him keeping her standing. He leaned over and whispered in her ear, "Remember your dreams. You know what you need to do."

The screams were filling Lucy's head making it impossible to think. What did Banks mean she knew what to do? She hadn't done any fighting in her dream, all she had done was open her mouth and…could it really be that simple?

Pushing the cries for help out of her mind Lucy closed her eyes and opened her mouth to sing but nothing happened. Tiberon began to laugh as Lucy opened and closed her mouth several more times with no success.

"THIS is what I've been worried about? All those nights I kept my distance, certain this child must have some great power and all she can do is act like a fish thrown out of water? Perhaps her friends will offer more of a challenge."

Lucy's eyes flew open. "NEVER!"

"The cod speaks," said Tiberon, tightening his grip on the staff.

"The cod can do more than that," said Lucy, feeling her energy rise. The thought of her friends had given her the power she needed. She didn't need to sing to get out of this mess; she had never needed to sing. What she needed was the power behind the music.

Lucy loosened herself from Banks' grip and looked Tiberon dead in the eye. Visions of Puddles and Ben came into her mind. She thought about Babu in his red braids and Tibs hanging from the top of a tree. She heard Anna's voice and saw Arthur's smile and remembered Sandy's stories and Lucy began to laugh.

At first Tiberon smiled obviously thinking Lucy had gone mad, but as her laughter grew his smile faded. Banks figured out what Lucy was doing and joined in. Together their laughter filled the air until there was a sudden flash and the cage of light burst into flames sending a blast of light into the sky. The dark clouds vanished along with the screams.

"SILENCE!" cried Tiberon, his eyes dark with fury. "This little reunion has gone on long enough."

With a sudden wave of his hand the sky split open and Lucy heard a crackle of electricity. As though the world had suddenly been set in slow motion, Lucy saw a flash of light head straight for the golden staff. Without stopping to think, Lucy lunged for the staff but Tiberon twisted and her hand flew past the staff wrapping instead around Tiberon's leathery wrist. The flash of light hit the staff's crystal globe with a blinding explosion and Lucy felt a current of electricity surge through her body locking Tiberon in her grip.

A cold, high pitched laugh of triumph filled Lucy's ears, and then, as though a powerful force had grabbed her around the middle, Lucy was ripped from Tiberon and thrown to the ground. When the light faded, Tiberon was gone.

"Lucy, are you okay?" said Banks, rushing over to her side.

"I'm fine," said Lucy, wincing as her brain pulsated from the sound of her own voice. She reached up to massage her aching head and her fingers sank into a tangled mass of snarled wire.

"Oh crap," she moaned. She tried to smooth down her hair but it kept bouncing out at all angles.

"There's no time to worry about that now," said Banks, averting his gaze from Lucy and staring up at the sky.

Lucy looked up and understood immediately what Banks meant. The sky had turned a sickly shade of green and in the distance a thin line of black clouds was beginning to bubble up on the horizon. The storm began crossing the lake, growing larger by the second. Lucy knew it would soon be on top of them.

"We've got to get out of here," Banks said, raising his voice to be heard over the mounting wind.

"But I can't teleport!" Lucy cried, unsure if Banks could hear her as the roar of the wind swallowed up all other sound.

Banks grabbed Lucy by the shoulders and pressed his face close to hers. Shouting so he could be heard over the turbulence he yelled, "ON THE COUNT OF THREE, HOLD ON TO MY HAND AND *DON'T LET GO*."

Although he was screaming inches from Lucy's face, his words were carried away by the wind the moment they left his mouth and all Lucy heard were faint whispers. Hoping she had understood what he wanted her to do, Lucy nodded her head.

Banks held up three fingers and Lucy grabbed his free hand tightly. Mouthing the countdown he lowered his fingers one by one. As the last finger dropped, Banks flung his arm in an arc over his head and shouted something Lucy couldn't hear.

For a moment Lucy thought it hadn't worked. Feeling a jolt of panic she watched in horror as the massive black cloud closed in on them. And then it happened; a blast of wind unlike anything Lucy had ever felt picked her up and tossed her into the air like a rag doll in a hurricane. Over and over she tumbled, the wind so fierce that, try as she might, she could not open her eyes. She squeezed her hand and felt something warm and strong in her grasp; Banks was still with her.

Lucy tightened her grip on Banks' hand but as the squall whipped her about she wondered how much longer she could hold on. Then, just as she felt her fingers begin to slip, the wind abruptly stopped and Lucy found herself tumbling to the ground. With a crunching thud Lucy landed on a mound of what felt like hot cement and felt a wave of oppressive, scorching heat press in on her from all sides.

Somewhere near her side Banks coughed. "Not exactly a joy ride," he said in a worn voice.

Opening her eyes, Lucy found herself looking out through a sickly orange haze on to a parched, barren desert that stretched out endlessly in every direction. The dry, cracked earth looked like it had never seen rain and the air was heavy with the stench of sulfur.

This, Lucy thought, *has got to be hell.*

"We haven't got much time," said Banks, getting to his feet and peering off at the distant horizon. "This was just a temporary solution; it won't take them long to figure out where we are."

"Them?" said Lucy, getting to her feet and shaking the orange dirt from her robe.

"That wasn't just any storm back there," said Banks. "That was Tiberon's army of Sleepers. I believe that once he left there was no one to keep them at bay so they attacked. Sleepers are drawn to light; they have none of their own so they seek out other's and devour it – a kind of energy feeding frenzy."

Lucy felt a chill run down her arms. "I don't understand. If they wanted to attack us why didn't Tiberon let them do it right away?"

Banks gazed at Lucy for several seconds before answering. "It's only a guess, but I think Tiberon wanted to meet you face to face."

Lucy thought Banks was finally going to tell her what was going on, but a loud crack of thunder stopped him.

"We'll have to continue this later," said Banks. "The time has come for us to part company."

"WHAT?" Lucy stared at Banks not believing what she was hearing.

"I can't go back to Drookshire, not yet at least. I have a job to do – something I should have done long ago."

"So you're just going to leave me here?"

"Think, Lucy!" Banks said impatiently. "You know the answer. You are no more captive here than Tiberon was imprisoned against his will. Leaving is a choice. It's important that you understand that."

Another crash of thunder caused Lucy to jump.

"We're running out of time," said Banks, stealing a glance towards the sky. "But before I go I need to request a favor."

Reaching into his pocket Banks pulled out a golf ball sized glass ball filled with swirling black smoke. Lucy recognized it as the same globe he had been studying the night she and Puddles had snuck into the Dream Chamber.

"I need you to take this to Samuel," said Banks, placing the orb in Lucy's hand. It is Tiberon's marker. Samuel will know what to do with it."

"His marker?" said Lucy, staring at the inky black glass ball.

"I don't have time to explain, just promise me you will take it to Samuel."

Lucy stared at the dark mist storming inside the glass orb. For a second she thought she saw a small spark of light but when she blinked it was gone. She looked up at

Banks and nodded. "Okay," she said, and she pocketed the ball in her sash.

"Thank you," said Banks, and Lucy saw a sad look of relief cross his face. "And now it's time for me to go."

"But how are you going to find him?" Lucy hastily asked, not wanting to be left alone in this awful place.

She was surprised to see Banks smile. "The Keeper's Staff holds a few secrets of its own. Nonetheless," he said, the weariness returning to his face, "there are still plenty of places Tiberon can hide which means I might not return for a while."

"Where are you going to start?" Lucy asked, hoping to stall Banks departure a little longer.

"I thought I would start in the lake."

"No! You can't!" Lucy said, shocked that Banks would willingly throw himself into that nightmare. "It swallows you up and traps you in this trance."

"Not a trance," said Banks, "…a dream. That lake – The Lake of Dreams – lulls you into a world of endless sleep. Of course for most people being trapped in a world of sleep is no different than being trapped behind iron bars; however, for those of us who know a thing or two about dream walking, it's more of an adventure than a prison sentence."

In the distance Lucy could hear the howl of the approaching storm.

"I can't delay any longer," Banks said. He shook back the sleeves of his robe and lifted his arms to the sky. "Remember," he called over the rumbling, "get out of here as soon as I'm gone." Then, as a wind gust blew his robe tight against his massive frame, Banks dropped his arms and in a flash of light he disappeared.

Lucy stared at the empty patch of cracked earth where Banks had just stood. Her stomach churned from the stifling heat and the realization that she was alone.

"Don't think about it," she lectured herself. The bubbling black clouds were almost on top of her now and the hot, putrid wind felt as though it was eating away at her skin.

Drawing in a deep breath Lucy fought off the impulse to gag on the thick air. Banks was right; she knew what she needed to do. When you enter a dark room you don't strike at the darkness, you just turn on a light. It was time to turn on the light.

Focusing again on her friends, Lucy waited until she felt the familiar sense of happiness inside of her and then, reaching her hands high into the air, she stared at the sickly orange sky and said, "I want to go home!"

As the words left her mouth they seemed to stick for a moment in the heavy air and then, to Lucy's amazement the words melted into song and floated away.

Overhead black spiraling clouds were beginning to devour the burnt orange haze. Lucy waited for the sound of someone racing to save her, but all she could hear were angry cries cutting through the wind.

Then, as she began to panic that it hadn't worked, a brilliant flash of light tore through the sky and encircled her like a cool, gentle pool of water. The light tumbled over and under her until she was no longer sure if she was standing still or flying.

Stretching out her arms Lucy felt weightless as though her body were a mere feather floating on a puff of air. Through the light a chorus of beautiful music rained down and as the song lifted her into the air Lucy felt happier than she had ever felt before in her life. Pure joy, pure love; she was going home.

CHAPTER SIXTEEN

HOME AND BACK

No sooner had the thought of home crossed Lucy's mind than the breeze faded, the light softened and Lucy caught first sight of a world she had only imagined in her dreams.

Perfection. That was the only word that came to mind. And yet it was entirely inadequate to describe what surrounded her. Music – but no, it wasn't music, at least not like music Lucy had ever known before – vibrated in the air, transforming into colors Lucy had never imagined, swirling, dancing, and then melting back into song. It was as though happiness had been given shape and sound and life and it was everywhere. The feeling inside of Lucy was so enormous she knew she could not contain it all and she felt it – no, she *saw* it - spilling out of her in waves of sound and color. She had become part of the world around her and it had become part of her; she was everything and she was nothing.

Lucy had no idea how long she drifted in this world; it could have been a century, it could have been a few seconds. Time ceased to exist. But she didn't care; she could imagine nothing better than to spend eternity in this very spot.

As Lucy listened to the song that permeated the air she sensed a change in the energy. The notes of the music shifted and Lucy saw three figures materialize out of thin air. Although they were standing no more than ten feet in front of her, their outlines were blurred as though they were formed of some ethereal vapor.

"It has been a very long time, but not as long as we believed it would be."

The notes of a woman's song transformed into words as the figure in the middle stepped forward and her face came into clearer focus.

Lucy felt her breath catch in her chest at the sight of the woman's unearthly beauty. Ebony curls framed her perfectly chiseled features and her eyes glistened with what appeared to be tiny stars.

"I am Sanyu," she said, as she leaned forward and kissed Lucy on the cheek leaving a warm tingle on the spot where her lips had touched Lucy's skin. As Sanyu stepped back Lucy swore she saw something feathery white flutter behind her.

The figure left of Sanyu spoke next. It was the voice of a man but it was gentle and rich and flowed like smoke as it encircled Lucy like a warm blanket.

"It is I, Amon," said the man. As he drew closer Lucy saw that his face was lined with age and he wore a short, snow-white beard, however his voice sounded like it belonged to a much younger man.

"We have been sent to guide you back to the Kingdom. Although you have come here as directed by the Great Plan, your journey is not yet over. The fates of many souls rest in your hands."

"I don't know what you mean," Lucy said, and she was surprised at the lyrical tone of her own voice. "I'm not here because of any plan; I was just trying to get out of Morpheus."

Amon simply smiled and held out his hand. In his palm rested a small star-shaped pendant on a fine silver chain.

"That looks like a talis stone," Lucy said, unable to take her eyes off the glimmering pendant.

Amon slipped the chain around her neck and she felt a warm tingling where the star rested on her skin.

"Ah, but this is not just any talis stone," he said. "The star stone will help you find the answers you are searching for."

"It's magic?" Lucy asked, touching the stone lightly and feeling a slight vibration.

Amon let out a soft chuckle. "There is no such thing as magic; there is only truth. However truth is far stronger than any magic and it is always present, whether you are aware of it or not. When you doubt your strength, the star will help remind you of the truth."

Lucy wanted to ask how it worked but before she could find the words the figure on the right stepped forward and Lucy gasped.

"Calista!"

The woman smiled and gave a slight nod of acknowledgement.

"But you…I mean, I saw you with Aunt Aggie, and then…" Lucy looked at the beautiful woman with long golden hair and couldn't believe what Riley had told her, "…you saved that boy in the park."

"Apparently I need to work on my disguise," said Calista, and she gave a laugh that didn't match her regal appearance.

"No, it was brilliant," said Lucy. "My friends Riley and Harrison told me it was you; otherwise I never would have guessed it."

"They have never been good at keeping secrets," said Calista, her crystal blue eyes sparkling.

Lucy felt an odd twinge of recognition as the ghost of a memory flickered deep inside her mind.

"It's time for us to go," said Calista, abruptly turning away from Lucy.

"Wait!" cried Lucy. She couldn't believe she was about to be left alone for the second time in one day. "I….I don't know how to get back." Lucy's face grew flush. The truth was she wasn't at all anxious to go back; this place – whatever it was – felt more like home than Drookshire ever had.

"Don't worry," said Sanyu. "We have someone to escort you back to the Kingdom's border."

Amon and Sanyu stepped aside and Lucy saw the indistinct figure of a man approaching in the distance. As he came closer Lucy felt her chest tighten until she could no longer breathe. Was she dreaming? The man stopped at Calista's side and Lucy looked up into those familiar green eyes.

"Lucy," he said gently, as he held out his arms, "…it's good to see you baby girl."

The world seemed to vanish as Lucy ran into her father's arms. If this was a dream she never wanted to wake up.

"Daddy," Lucy said, burying her head into her father's neck, "I've missed you so much." She wanted to say more but her words were lost as the tears that had been building since the day her father left were all set free.

"I know," said Jack O'Sullivan, kissing the top of Lucy's head. "I've heard every word. I told you I would never leave you, and I never did. Just because you haven't been able to see me, it doesn't mean I haven't been with you." He gave Lucy a squeeze, gently stroking her head. "Have you done something new with your hair?" he said curiously.

Lucy laughed as she pulled away from her father and wiped her eyes on the sleeve of her robe. In all the excitement she had completely forgotten about the red porcupine quills on top of her head. "Do you like it? I think it's the new me."

"Hmmm…" Jack O'Sullivan stroked his chin and surveyed his daughter. "I've never seen you look better."

Lucy beamed at the gleam in his eye.

Calista cleared her throat and Lucy suddenly remembered they were not alone.

"Before we go," Calista said, approaching Lucy and her father, "there is something I must request of you."

"Anything," said Lucy, and she meant it. Considering Calista and the others had rescued her from Morpheus and then given her back her father there was nothing she wouldn't do for them.

"I need you to take this to the Council."

Calista held out a small, thin scroll made of shimmering green parchment. Tied around the scroll was a red silk ribbon inscribed in fine golden script – *Lucille Margaret O'Sullivan.*

Lucy stared at the scroll in Calista's hand, her mouth hanging open in surprise.

"I believe it belongs in the Kingdom," Calista said, as she placed the scroll in Lucy's hand. "I trust you to deliver the map without opening it; after all, knowledge of one's destiny can be quite dangerous if not handled properly."

Lucy looked quizzically at Calista. Those were the exact words Colonel George had used. Then something occurred to her. "Why was my Life Map here? Aren't they supposed to be kept in the Dream Chamber?"

Amon spoke up, "Even here things get misplaced from time to time, but that is quite another matter. What is important now is that you return to the Kingdom as quickly as possible. Your friends are quite worried about what has happened to you. Jack," he said, turning to Lucy's father, "would you please escort your daughter back to the border? I believe there will be someone waiting there for her."

Jack O'Sullivan nodded. "It would be my pleasure."

"Then it is time for us to part ways," said Sanyu softly. "Lucy, we will see you again when destiny declares it prudent."

Before Lucy could thank them for saving her, a breeze swept in and Sanyu, Amon and Calista melted away into a swirl of music that vanished on the wind.

The journey back to the edge of the Kingdom was the happiest time Lucy could ever remember. For what seemed like hours, or possibly days, Lucy basked in the company of her father as they followed a stream that meandered through a field where colors whirled into the shapes of trees and flowers before evaporating and reforming into something new.

One by one she asked the questions that had bothered her since the day her dad had been torn from their family. Jack O'Sullivan patiently answered all her questions – "Yes, I was there for your 8th grade graduation. Beautiful dress by the way….No, I never helped you pass your exams; you did that all by yourself kiddo…No, I'm not an angel. I'm what they call a herald. Since angels aren't allowed to enter the Kingdom of Attendants and attendants can't cross the border into Nayopi, I act as a kind of courier between the two."

"Why can't angels and attendants cross the border?" asked Lucy. "Aren't we all supposed to be on the same side?"

"There aren't really sides, just a direction…forward; and we're all moving that way. But angels and attendants play different roles in getting us there. Keeping them apart helps prevent confusion over the jobs they have to do. Think of it this way," said Jack, obviously seeing the confusion on Lucy's face, "attendants are the worker bees. They help the folks on earth deal with their day to day troubles, keep them out of mischief and help them stay on track. Angels are more interested in the big picture. They rarely get involved with individual cases unless, of course, that individual has an important role to play in the master plan."

Lucy watched the water gently flowing in the stream as she thought about what her father had just said. The colors of the landscape had steadily grown bolder as they followed the water east and vibrant green foliage now spotted the banks of the river. Staring at a particularly bright fern, a new thought came into Lucy's mind.

"Does that mean that the boy Calista helped back at the park has something important he's supposed to do?"

Her father shrugged. "I don't know for sure, but if Calista got involved with this boy's destiny then it would be my guess that something's up with his life."

Lucy pondered what Dewey's role might be as she and her father continued on, stopping only occasionally to admire the scenery or reminisce about a long lost memory. Before she was ready for their journey to end, Lucy found herself standing in front of a glistening sheet of opaque mist that formed an endless wall stretching out of sight to the north and south.

"Well, kiddo, we made it. The Kingdom is just on the other side of this wall."

Jack O'Sullivan drew his daughter into his arms and hugged her tightly. "You have great things ahead of you," he whispered in her ear. "Be safe."

"It's not fair," Lucy said, feeling her throat growing tight. "I just found you again…you weren't even there to meet me after I died." There, she had said it. The thing that had been haunting her since the day she arrived had finally been let out. If her father truly loved her – if he had always been with her like he claimed – then why hadn't he been waiting for her when she came here?

There was a long, heavy pause as her father stared silently into Lucy's eyes. He had a sad, but resolute, look on his face that reminded Lucy of the look he used to give her back on earth whenever he had something to say that was "for her own good" but that she didn't want to hear.

Finally he drew a deep breath and when he spoke his voice was firm. "You have a right to be angry, but I have to ask you to trust me when I tell you that everything happened just the way it was meant to happen. Sometimes what seems brutally unfair is actually a blessing in disguise."

A blessing, thought Lucy. Was it a blessing that she had been thrown all alone into a world she had no idea even existed? How was it even remotely fair that she had been denied what every other new arrival got – a chance to see someone, *anyone*, from their family? But there had been no one there to meet her…not her dad, or her grandparents, or even some long-forgotten dead aunt. There had only been Harrison and, entertaining as he was, he wasn't family.

Lucy's father seemed to read her thoughts. "What is necessary isn't always fair," he said in the fatherly tone that signaled she should drop the topic. His face softened and he cupped a hand on Lucy's cheek. "I promise it will all make sense someday. Do you trust that I'm telling you the truth?"

It seemed impossible to Lucy that she would ever make sense out of the things that had happened since the day she arrived in this strange place, but she trusted her father. Reluctantly she nodded.

"Good," said Jack, kissing Lucy's forehead. "Now, it's time for you to go. I believe there are more than a few folks anxious to see you again and don't forget, you need to get that Life Map to the Council."

Lucy remembered her promise to Banks. "I'll give it to Samuel," she said, figuring she could give him both Tiberon's marker and the Life Map. "But first I want to see my friends."

"Your friends will understand that you have business to take care of. They are quite an amazing group; don't underestimate them."

"How do you about my cottagemates?" said Lucy, eyeing her father suspiciously.

Jack O'Sullivan smiled and there was a glint in his eye. "I told you I've been with you all along."

With one long, final hug good-bye Lucy drew a deep breath and stepped up to the curtain of mist. She glanced back at her dad, unable to take the step that would take her away from her father again.

"Go on," said Jack. "I'll be right here waiting for you."

Feeling her heart tear in two, Lucy closed her eyes against the tears and stepped into the mist and out of Nayopi.

She braced herself for the tumbling that had come the last time she stepped into a curtain of mist, but her foot landed on solid ground. Opening her eyes Lucy found the mist was gone and in its place stood a forest of towering evergreens. Before she could register where she was there was a sound of footsteps pounding towards her and a voice calling out, "There you are!"

Lucy couldn't have imagined a sweeter sound. Whirling around, she saw Ben and Puddles racing towards her.

Bolting across the forest floor she threw her arms around her friends and drew them into a tight squeeze.

"Luce…can't breathe…" gasped Puddles, prying Lucy's arm from around his neck.

Lucy loosened her grip and stepped back to take in the sight of the two people she had missed most while she was trapped in Morpheus.

"How did you know I'd be here," she asked, unable to wipe the grin from her face.

"It was really weird," said Ben, who was staring at Lucy as though he was seeing a ghost. "Just a few minutes ago

Puddles and I were on our way to guard duty when this hologram appeared."

"Yeah, we knew it was a hologram because of the ones we worked with in Christof's class," said Puddles excitedly. "But this one wasn't a Walker."

"Lucy, I know you're not going to believe me, but I think it was an angel," Ben said.

"It was an angel, I'm sure of it," Lucy said, and she had to laugh at the look of surprise on Ben's face. "Angels can't cross over into the Kingdom; I guess a hologram was the only way they could get a message to you."

"But how do you know..." Ben started, but Lucy interrupted.

"Long story. I'll explain later."

"Anyway," Ben continued, "the hologram said that you would be arriving in the forest by the lake and that we needed to hurry to meet you."

"Then the thing just disappeared and we teleported right away," said Puddles, his eyes wide with excitement. "We didn't even get the chance to ask where you'd been or how you were getting home."

Lucy was about to launch into the story of how she got there when something Ben said suddenly registered.

"What did you mean you were on your way to guard duty?"

Ben and Puddles exchanged looks.

"A lot has happened around here since you left," said Puddles, and his eyes flitted up towards the western sky.

Lucy felt a surge of panic. "The Sleepers broke through?"

"No, luckily we were ready for them," said Ben, giving Puddles a nod which he returned with a weak smile.

"But how did you know..."

"Actually it was Haddie who figured it out," said Ben, and Lucy was surprised to see he actually sounded impressed. "When you didn't show up back at the cottage we went to tell Banks what had happened but we couldn't find him anywhere. We were on our way to find Samuel when we ran into Haddie. She said she had been waiting for you in the forest but you hadn't shown up."

"She was waiting for me? But that means that she must have come up with a plan," said Lucy.

"I didn't want to believe it, but she was right," said Ben, giving a grimaced smile. "There really is a break in the border. Haddie found a cave where the water from this lake…" he gestured toward the water behind them, "…flows into Morpheus. No one guards it because the water feeds some lake in the Forgotten City that the Council thinks is some kind of impassable barrier."

"They're right," said Lucy, remembering how she had been imprisoned in the Lake of Dreams.

"No, they're not," said Puddles. "Haddie discovered that the flow of water into Morpheus has been growing weaker and the night you disappeared it actually changed. The water has started flowing out of the Forgotten City!"

"But that means those nightmares are all headed this way," Lucy exclaimed. She turned towards the lake half expecting to see ghosts of the banker and the aristocrat floating out of the water.

"Don't worry," said Ben. "Thanks to Haddie we got there before anyone could escape. Tobias showed us how…"

"Hold on a second! Tobias? Why did Haddie have to get him involved?" Lucy's voice echoed across the forest sending birds flying from the trees.

Ben held up his hand. "Luce, I know you're not real fond of the guy, but he's a pretty powerful attendant. We needed all the help we could get."

"And he agreed? That doesn't sound like Tobias."

"Well, Haddie kind of persuaded him," said Puddles, a mischievous grin blooming across his face.

Lucy looked over at Ben who was grinning too.

"What's up?" she asked, wanting in on the joke.

"Apparently Tobias was using those mirrors of his to do more than just keep an eye on the attendants," said Ben, barely able to contain his delight. "In typical Haddie fashion, she barged into his office without knocking and caught him monitoring Samuel, Cassiel and Gadwick having a private meeting."

"He was spying on the Council?" Lucy exclaimed, half in shock, half in sheer joy at the thought of Tobias doing something so forbidden.

Ben and Puddles both beamed.

"Beautiful isn't it?" said Ben, laughing at the look on Lucy's face. "Haddie promised it would be their little secret if Tobias would agree to help us out. Obviously he didn't have any choice, so he agreed. It was his idea to set-up guard duty at the entrance to the cave and he showed us how to send light into the water to create a kind of energy filter. So far it's kept the Sleepers on their side of the mountain."

Puddles was nodding his head so fiercely he resembled a bobble-head doll. "And when I told him about the glass ball we had found in the Dream Chamber and how it had turned into a Dream Passage, he figured out what had happened to you."

The thought of Tobias knowing that she had broken into the Dream Chamber and, once again, fallen into trouble caused Lucy's face to burn red.

"I'm sure he got a big laugh out it," she said dully.

"Actually he was pretty upset," said Puddles. "He muttered something about warning Banks this would happen and then he disappeared for a while. When he got back we asked what was going on but he got all snippy and said it was being taken care of."

Lucy began to pace across the forest floor as she tried to figure out what this all meant. What had Tobias warned Banks about and where had he gone when he disappeared? As she traced her steps back and forth trying to make sense of everything she felt something slip from beneath her sash.

"Hey Luce, you dropped something," said Ben, bending to pick up the scroll lying on the ground. Before Lucy could stop him Ben's eyes fell on the name written on the red ribbon.

"Lucy! Where did you get this?"

Lucy reached out a grabbed the Life Map from his hand. "It's nothing…and it's not important. I haven't read it. I'm just delivering it to Samuel."

Suddenly Lucy remembered that she was supposed to go to Samuel the moment she got back to Drookshire. "Crap," she cursed, shoving the scroll back into her sash. "I've got to go."

"But you just got . back," said Puddles, sounding alarmed.

"I didn't mean back there," Lucy said, motioning over her shoulder although the curtain of mist was gone. "I have to see Samuel. I promised some friends…" She stopped, knowing the story was too long to go into right now. "I just need to go. I'll explain later, I promise."

Lucy could tell by the look in Ben's eyes he wasn't happy that she was running off again without him but there was nothing she could do. Judging by the warm breeze and the flowers lining the lake, Lucy knew she had been gone much longer than she thought. While she had been asleep in the bowels of Morpheus summer had come to Drookshire. Tiberon could have been on the run for weeks by now. There was no more time to waste.

She stepped up to Ben and took his hand and then reached out her other hand to Puddles who timidly accepted it.

"I never stopped thinking about you guys while I was gone, and if I had my way we'd never be separated again," she said, giving their hands a squeeze and feeling a squeeze in return. "But I can't think of myself right now. Banks needs my help – "

"You know where Banks is?" Ben asked.

"No, but I know what he's doing and he can't do it alone. Banks wanted me to find Samuel and tell him what's going on and that's what I'm going to do." Lucy stopped herself from adding *it's the least I can do since he saved my life.*

Releasing their hands Lucy took a step back and looked around. "I don't suppose you know where I might find Samuel?" she said, realizing she had no idea where he might be.

"I'd try his office," suggested Ben. "But the portal is pretty far from here; can you teleport?"

Lucy was just about to shake her head when a hot prickle burned her neck.

"Ow!" she yelled, grabbing the star pendant. A shot of electricity ran through her fingers.

"What is that thing," said Puddles, pointing at Lucy's neck. His eyes were fixed on the pendant glowing between Lucy's fingers.

"It was a gift from a friend," she said, rubbing the spot where the talis stone still burned against her chest. The shock from the star stone had reminded Lucy of Amon's words.

"I think I'll be able to teleport as long as I have this to help," she said, grasping the pendant tighter and feeling the energy surge through her hand.

"We'll come to," said Ben, and Puddles agreed.

Lucy looked from Ben to Puddles feeling a rush of warmth bring a smile to her face. Her dad was right, her friends were amazing.

"Thanks," she said, resisting the urge to hug them again, "but I need to do this alone. Go find the others and tell them I'm back and that I'll see them at the cottage as soon as I'm finished with Samuel."

Ben and Puddles looked unwilling to leave.

"I'll be fine," Lucy said, in a falsely brave voice. "Go on, you don't want to keep Haddie waiting."

The thought of an angry Haddie seemed to do the trick. Promising to meet back at the cottage as soon as they were done with guard duty, Ben and Puddles gave one last reluctant good-bye then raised their arms and in a flash were gone.

Alone in the forest, Lucy looked up at the tree spires bending in the breeze. Closing her eyes she felt the sun warm against her face and caught the faint scent of cinnamon rolls in the air. It must be breakfast time at the Station, she thought. Suddenly she shivered as goose bumps shot up her arms and Lucy had a strange feeling life in Drookshire was about to change.

Shaking off the feeling of approaching trouble Lucy raised her arms into the air. She had work to do. Whatever was coming would be dealt with when it got here. Concentrating on the talis stone pulsating against her skin, Lucy dropped her arms and felt the uncomfortable sensation of twisting about inside her own skin. When her eyes opened she found herself under the bare, gnarled branches of a familiar tree.

Lucy's heart began to race. She reached out and gave the trunk two solid knocks.

Just as it had on the night that she, Puddles and Ben had been summoned to Samuel's office, the rotted tree trunk slowly twisted into an archway and a belch of swirling green mist tumbled into the air.

Through the mist a rather tired voice poured out.

"Please come in."

CHAPTER SEVENTEEN

WHY?

"Welcome back," said Samuel, giving Lucy a small smile. He had been waiting for her on the beach as though he knew she was coming.

Lucy stared blankly at the Keeper. Samuel seemed to have aged while she was gone; the sparkle was gone from his eyes and there was a weariness about him. Lucy opened her mouth to speak but realized she had no idea what to say. Samuel seemed to read her mind.

"I have received a full report on everything that happened since the night you disappeared from the Dream Chamber. There is no need to rehash what is now in the past."

Lucy felt a wave of shame wash over her. Samuel knew she had broken into the Dream Chamber in search of her Life Map, he knew that she had entered the forbidden territory of the Forgotten City, and that Banks had gone after her and soon he would learn that Banks was gone – possibly forever – all because of her.

"I believe you have something for me," Samuel said, and Lucy suddenly remembered the map and marker.

Fumbling with her sash Lucy withdrew the two items and held them out to Samuel.

A lump seemed to have formed in her throat. "The marker is from Banks," she said, her voice sounding hoarse. "He said you would know what to do with it. And Calista asked me to bring you the Life Map…I didn't look at it, I promise."

Samuel didn't seem to hear Lucy's remarks about the Life Map. His eyes were fixed on the dark fog swirling inside Tiberon's marker.

"We have work to do," he said, suddenly appearing energized. And without further explanation Samuel turned and quickly headed up the beach towards the thatched hut he used as an office.

Lucy hurried after him wondering what was going on. What kind of work did Samuel have in mind? An image of them building a stone fortress around Morpheus popped into her head.

"Take a seat," Samuel said, pointing to a straight-backed wicker chair as they entered the hut.

As Lucy sat down her eyes swept the room; it appeared very much like it had on her last visit except for the noticeable absence of the golden staff. There was also the addition of a squat glass table that Lucy recognized at once to be an occuscope and a carved stone lectern which was holding a large, ancient-looking book.

"A lie has been told," Samuel said somberly, his eyes still focused on the marker "…a very serious lie; and one that quite possibly will affect the entire Kingdom."

Lucy felt her insides freeze.

"Sir, I swear I haven't…," she said in a weak voice that made her sound very guilty.

Samuel looked up at Lucy. "You misunderstood," he said, holding up the marker for her to see. "The lie was not told *by* you, it was told *to* you…to all of us."

A heavy silence descended upon the room as Samuel's words sunk in. Someone had lied to her? *But who*, thought Lucy.

Once again Samuel seemed to read her thoughts and before she could ask the question he answered, "Banks."

"You're wrong," Lucy blurted before she could stop herself. "No disrespect intended, sir, but Banks wouldn't lie to me. I mean, it's true that I thought he had been the one haunting my dreams but it wasn't him, it was Tiberon. He *saved* me from Tiberon."

Samuel didn't appear to be listening. He had stepped over to the lectern and was thumbing through the pages of the large black book as though searching for a particular passage. Without looking up from the book, Samuel asked, "Did your Cottage Master happen to tell you how Tiberon came to live in the Forgotten City?"

It was as though someone had kicked Lucy in the stomach. In a flash Tiberon's wheezing voice seethed back into her memory hissing, "...when they gave him the choice to either accompany me to the Land Beyond and teach me the quaint ways of the so-called righteous or to throw me in to this dark hole he chose to abandon me so he could return to his comfortable little life in that insipid village."

Lucy tried to speak but her words came out barely above a whisper, "Tiberon said Banks left him in Morpheus so he could return to the Kingdom."

Samuel looked up from the book and Lucy was relieved to see he looked neither angry nor surprised by this information.

"Tiberon has a knack for molding the truth to fit his needs. In this case the only particle of truth is that yes, Banks did choose to leave him in the Forgotten City; however it had nothing to do with Banks' desire to rid himself of the burden of caring for his brother."

"You know Tiberon is Banks' brother?"

"Banks is more than Tiberon's brother; he is also his Guardian," Samuel said, and Lucy thought she detected a sadness in his voice. "Tiberon believes Banks deserted him in the Forgotten City, but the truth is that Banks has been keeping a very watchful eye on his brother."

"That must have been how Banks knew that I was in Morpheus," said Lucy, as she suddenly felt the pieces of the puzzle begin to slip into place. "He must have seen me when I ran into Tiberon at the lake."

"That was only one of many times Banks saw the two of you together," said Samuel fixing Lucy with a piercing stare. "I believe you know what I am referring to?"

Lucy stared blankly back at Samuel not at all sure what he meant, and then it hit her. "My dreams," she said excitedly. "He saw Tiberon in my dreams."

Samuel nodded. "Precisely. As you are aware, our friend Banks is a gifted Dream Walker and as such it is his responsibility to check on our new attendants from time to time to ensure they are adjusting to their new life. You might find this hard to believe, but some of the freshman attendants find this lifestyle a tad stressful."

Lucy laughed. Calling this place "a tad stressful" was like calling Haddie "a little annoying"; both were extreme understatements.

Samuel continued, ignoring Lucy's laughter, "It was during one of these routine outings that Banks came across your dream and discovered that Tiberon was infiltrating your sleep. As you have undoubtedly figured out Tiberon, too, is an accomplished Dream Walker."

"Banks said you knew about Tiberon," Lucy said, trying hard not to sound like she was accusing Samuel of any wrongdoing. "Wasn't there something you could do to stop him?"

"If Banks had been completely honest with me I might have been able to help. Unfortunately he led me to believe that Tiberon had simply awakened before he was ready, and as such I assumed he would most likely fall back to sleep without causing any real damage. As we now know, I was wrong."

There was an awkward silence in the room as Lucy sat motionless not knowing what to say. After several painfully long seconds Samuel held out the small glass ball and nodded for Lucy to take it.

"Do you notice anything strange about this marker?"

Lucy held the dark orb in her hand watching as the black mist swirled and bubbled inside. Other than the feeling of sadness it seemed to produce, there was nothing particularly unusual about it. She was just about to hand it back to Samuel when a small flash of light cut across the dark fog.

"That light," she said, not taking her eyes off the globe, "...I remember seeing it back in the Forgotten City. It's like some sort of lightning bolt bouncing around inside."

"Exactly," said Samuel, reclaiming the marker and holding it up for both of them to see. "Markers are highly useful objects. They can tell us many things, but primarily they show us the current state of their owner's enlightenment."

Lucy's face must have shown that she didn't have a clue what Samuel was saying because he quickly added, "Let me put it this way, a Sleeper's marker will always be dark because they have chosen to deny the existence of love. On the other hand an angel's marker will always shine white because they understand that love is all that truly exists. The rest of us typically fall somewhere in between with varying shades of gray. However, if you were to examine the marker of someone still living on earth you would see a virtual storm of electrical activity as their energy sails between the realms of spirit and earth."

"Then why..." but Lucy stopped as the realization of what Samuel was saying hit her. Her eyes widened as she stared at Samuel not wanting to believe what she knew was the horrible truth. He nodded his confirmation.

"Now you understand our problem," he said, gazing at the orb as another flash of lightening split through the black fog. "Tiberon never truly died."

"But…I don't understand…how can that be," stammered Lucy.

"It appears that Banks pulled Tiberon's soul just before the actual moment of death occurred," said Samuel heavily. "On occasion this is allowed to prevent someone from suffering what is sure to be a painful death; however in this case it seems that Banks misjudged the situation. After the spirit was pulled Banks must have discovered that Tiberon was not destined to die that day, but by then it was too late; his body had been destroyed."

Lucy grimaced. "That's horrible," she whispered, feeling nauseous at the thought of a soul being ripped from a living body.

"I believe Banks acted out of compassion," said Samuel. "He knew he couldn't send Tiberon back to earth, nor could he enter the Land Beyond while he still had a breath of life, so Banks undoubtedly felt his only choice was to cast his brother into a deep sleep and place him in the Forgotten City where he could keep an eye on him, albeit from a distance. Unfortunately it appears that Tiberon's last spark of life has allowed him to shake off the blanket of sleep and unless I am mistaken, I believe he is going to try and find his way back to earth."

The gruesome image of Tiberon half dead, half alive returning to earth sent a shiver down Lucy's back. Thankfully the vision was driven from her brain as she recalled what Samuel had said back on the beach.

"Sir, you mentioned that we have work to do."

"You're right," said Samuel, and with one last glance he pocketed the marker in his sash. "It's time we got down to business."

Crossing back to the lectern, Samuel began flipping quickly through the pages of the old book until he found what he was looking for.

"Here we go," he said, as he swiped a hand over the page. There was a soft jingling of chimes as a flurry of silvery symbols floated up off the page and into the air. Lucy felt her mouth drop open in amazement as the glittering characters dangled magically in front of her.

"This," said Samuel solemnly, "is why you are here."

Lucy stared bewildered at the fluttering characters hovering before her eyes. If Samuel thought this would make things clearer he was seriously mistaken.

"Perhaps this will help," Samuel said, and he waved his hand once again over the page. To her astonishment the bizarre symbols quivered and then slowly transformed into letters creating a message that hung in mid-air.

"The day before the summer sun makes its maiden journey through the sky the Kingdom will welcome a lamb who shall become the shepherd.

You will recognize this courier of light for she will hear those who are silent and walk among those who dream. Her powers will awaken the light in the darkened city and she shall cast the living from the dead.

Before the shepherd completes her journey she will usher a new day into the world of night, she will fight the battle of the dead among the living and she will make the angels weep with joy and sorrow.

When her task is completed a new order will reign and the Kingdom as it is known shall be no more."

Lucy stared at the words dangling in front of her. There was a buzzing in her brain as her eyes hung on the last line, "*the Kingdom as it is known shall be no more*".

"Samuel," she said, her voice quivering slightly, "what does this mean?"

"The Council received this information the night before you arrived. At first Gadwick and Cassiel were skeptical, and I have to admit that there were times when even I doubted the possibility, but now there is little doubt."

"Little doubt of what?" asked Lucy, knowing she did not want to hear the answer.

"That you are the one who will fulfill this prophecy," said Samuel, and his piercing blue eyes locked on to Lucy.

As she met Samuel's gaze Lucy felt her body go numb.

"It's true then," she whispered, barely able to push out the words. "It's all my fault. I cast the living from the dead. I'm the one who set Tiberon free."

"The Book of Destiny does not assign blame," Samuel said calmly. "Like any prophecy it simply tells a story."

"If it's just a story, then all that stuff it says might not actually happen," said Lucy, desperately hoping there was some way to reverse what was written.

Samuel remained silent, but the corners of his mouth turned up into a sympathetic smile.

Lucy slumped in her seat, burying her face in her hands. She wanted to rub away the vision of those words. But she had learned in Morpheus that wishing away your problems didn't work.

"Fine," she sighed, feeling anything but fine, "let's assume this prophecy is about me. I still don't get it. All that stuff about ushering in a new day and fighting the dead and making angels cry…what does it mean?"

"I believe it means you still have some interesting times ahead," said Samuel, as he closed the Book of Destiny and the prophecy disappeared.

Lucy stared into the empty air, the words still lingering in her mind. Finally she decided to ask the question which seemed blatantly obvious.

"Samuel, if I don't know what all this means how am I supposed to get started?"

"Ah, I was hoping you would ask that particular question," said Samuel, a note of excitement in his voice. Reaching into his sash he pulled out the scroll Lucy had given him on the beach.

"Perhaps the answer you are looking for is in here," he said, holding out the Life Map.

Lucy looked from the scroll to Samuel, not sure what to do. No one was supposed to see their own Life Map; Colonel George and Calista had both made that perfectly clear.

"It's okay," said Samuel, obviously sensing her reluctance. "What they don't know won't hurt them." He gave her a small knowing wink.

Lucy slowly reached out and took the scroll but didn't open it.

After several long seconds of silence Samuel asked, "Lucy, do you understand the purpose of a Life Map?"

"I think so," said Lucy, wondering if this was a trick question. "We worked on Life Maps in Colonel George's class and they all seemed to talk about what the person was supposed to do with their life."

"Very good," said Samuel. "Life Maps are very much like the prophecy you have just read; they tell a story – nothing more, nothing less."

Lucy looked at the scroll in her hand. Something about all of this wasn't right.

"I don't get it," she said, looking up at Samuel, "if a person's life is already laid out for them, well, it doesn't seem quite fair, does it? I mean, what if I wanted to be a teacher but my Life Map said I should be a...a...banker?" Lucy's mind flashed back to the banker she had seen in the Forgotten City. "It just seems that if the whole reason we go to earth is to learn how to be better people then shouldn't we be given the chance to succeed or fail on our own? If we just blindly follow the path that someone else thought would be good for us, well, what does that teach us?"

"Here..." said Lucy, holding out the unopened Life Map. "...I don't want to see what someone else thinks I should be doing with my life. I'd rather choose for myself."

Samuel didn't take the Life Map; his eyes met Lucy's and she was happy to see the familiar twinkle had returned.

"Well done," he said. "Most people would not have the courage to walk away from such information; after all it is much easier to follow a preset path than to cut your way through unknown territory. However, in this case I don't believe it would hurt to take a peek."

Lucy shook her head. "I told you, I don't want to follow someone else's plan for my life," she said firmly. "Besides, haven't I already seen what's going to happen to me?" Lucy's eyes flitted towards the large black book.

"Ah," said Samuel, holding up a finger to make a point, "two different stories, two different authors. The prophecy was written by a Power that knows what is ultimately best for the progress of all souls, however your Life Map was written by someone who knows what is infinitely best for *you*. You see," he said, reaching out and untying the ribbon around the scroll, "we all write our own Life Maps before our journey begins. That scroll you are holding in your hand…it was written by you."

For a moment Lucy could do nothing but stare speechlessly at the paper in her hand. How could she possibly have written this Life Map when she had absolutely no recollection of ever seeing it before?

Samuel's voice broke through the silence, "What Colonel George never told you is that before starting out every soul determines what they need most from their journey and they put it down in writing. Think of it as a journal in reverse; instead of describing what has already happened you are writing what you *want* to occur…what you most need to learn from the trip you are about to undertake. When the lesson you prescribed for yourself is achieved your map is given back to you and you start again. It's like a school where you are both the teacher and the student."

Lucy let Samuel's words soak in. The idea made sense in some bizarre kind of way. "If you're giving this back to me," she said slowly, "does that mean I've completed whatever I set out to learn?"

"Only you can know that for sure. Why don't you open it and find out?"

Lucy bit her lip. Somehow, knowing that what was written had been placed there by her earlier self – a self she did not remember – made reading it even more frightening. Straining to keep her hand steady, Lucy unrolled the scroll.

"I…I don't understand," she said, staring with confusion at the paper. She flipped the parchment over expecting something to be written on the back but it was blank.

Turning the scroll back around she stared bewildered at the handwriting she recognized as her own. Written in golden ink was a single word – "**Why?**"

"It would seem to me that you wanted to know the meaning of something," said Samuel, peering curiously at the paper. To Lucy's annoyance he looked almost amused by the riddle.

"The meaning of WHAT? This doesn't make any sense!"

"My guess is that once you understand the question you will be close to having the answer."

Lucy fought the urge to scream. If anything, she was more confused now than she had been before.

"This," she said, waving the Life Map in the air, "doesn't help me at all with the prophecy. I still have no idea what I'm supposed to be doing."

"Are you sure about that?" Samuel said, and he turned to face the occuscope sitting quietly in the middle of the floor. Before Lucy could respond he ran a hand over the screen and the occuscope flickered to life. At first it was impossible to make out the fuzzy shape on the screen, but as the picture came into focus the outline of a house began to appear.

Samuel looked up and caught Lucy's eye. "I think you know exactly what you are supposed to be doing."

As Lucy watched the cottage take shape, something clicked and she knew Samuel was right. The night she snuck into the Dream Chamber she had been in search of confirmation that she was supposed to be helping Aunt Aggie find the key to the cottage. Then she had fallen into Morpheus and had forgotten about everyone's problems but her own. But now she was back and Lucy knew that before she could do anything else she needed to find a way to lead Aggie to that key.

"But what about Banks? Aren't we going to help him find Tiberon?" Lucy asked, feeling a pang of guilt for deserting her Cottage Master.

"Every chapter of our lives is a continuation of the story that came before and a foreshadowing of what is to come.

Before you can understand what is coming, you must understand what has been."

Samuel gazed at the occuscope. It was summer on the mountain and the cottage was surrounded by wildflowers. From somewhere out of sight they could hear the rushing of a nearby river.

"I believe once you have closed the chapter of the cottage you will better understand how to help our friend. Don't be in a rush to reach the end of your story."

Suddenly a bell chimed from somewhere in the distance and Lucy and Samuel looked up to see a large, white piece of paper float in through the open doorway. Casually plucking the paper from the air, Samuel glanced briefly at the note then with a flick of his wrist he sent the paper back out of the opening and Lucy saw it vanish into the sky.

"I have to go," he said, and Lucy sensed he was avoiding her gaze. Without further explanation Samuel reached down and picked up a red velvet bag that had suddenly appeared next to the occuscope then scooped up the large black book under his other arm.

"Wait!" cried Lucy. She was tired of people leaving her on her own. "I still don't know how I'm supposed to help Aunt Aggie find the key."

Samuel set down the bag and reached into his sash. "Here," he said, pulling out the crystal orb and handing it to Lucy. "This might give you some ideas."

Lucy looked blankly at the small glass ball wondering how Tiberon's marker could possibly help her get a message to Aunt Aggie. A spark of lightning cut through the swirling black mist and at the same moment the star stone pendant burned against her chest. Looking up to see if Samuel had noticed the flash of light, Lucy saw that he was gone.

Reluctantly Lucy pocketed the marker. Something about the glass ball made her feel uneasy and she wished she could leave it behind but if Samuel thought it would help her she was willing to hold on to it…at least for now.

Glancing over at the occuscope, Lucy noticed that the sky above the cottage had turned stormy and rain had started to fall. Trying not to think that this was an omen of things to come, she turned away from the cottage and placed her Life Map on the empty lectern. She wouldn't be needing it. That word – *Why* – was permanently etched in her mind, its meaning hanging just outside of her memory like the shadow of a dream she couldn't quite remember.

Lucy stood in the doorway looking out at the perfect summer day. Waves were rolling onto the beach and overhead a cloudless blue sky showed no signs of trouble. Lucy wondered how long the peace would last.

Feeling the same mixed emotions of fear and excitement she used to feel on the first day of school, Lucy stepped out of the hut and returned to Hill Cottage.

CHAPTER EIGHTEEN

THE TRAVELER UNMASKED

Hill Cottage had changed while she was gone. The lodge which had been filled with an assortment of squishy arm chairs and overstuffed sofas had been transformed into an army command post. The only furniture was a large, round table in the middle of the room and a parrot lamp standing nearby illuminating the piles of papers scattered across the table. Maps of the Kingdom were tacked up on the walls like cheap wallpaper and a single Nayopian Mirror was perched on top of the fireplace. Lucy stepped closer to the mirror and saw it was focused on the entrance to a cave.

"They're gone – for now."

The harsh voice made Lucy jump. Stumbling backwards she knocked the mirror from the mantle, barely catching it before it hit the floor.

"A habit of yours?" scoffed Tobias.

"You scared me," Lucy said, wishing she had been found by anyone else. "What are you doing here?"

The words had slipped from her lips before she could stop herself.

"I was about to ask you the same thing," Tobias said, his small eyes scanning Lucy's uncombed hair and disheveled robe. "I thought you had grown tired of this place and had taken up chasing Sleepers."

Lucy felt her face burn. She didn't care what Ben and Puddles said; Tobias hadn't changed.

"I'm back now, that's all that matters," she said, determined not to tell Tobias more than she had to.

Lucy glanced down at the mirror in her hands and saw a beam of light reflecting off the water coming from the cave. "I see you've discovered these things are useful for more than just spying on people," she said, placing the Nayopian Mirror back on the mantle.

This time it was Tobias's face that turned red. Lucy braced herself for his attack but Tobias remained calm.

"It's a shame the other mirrors were all destroyed," he said, his voice cool and steady. "If I still had your mirror I would have known that you had returned and I could have told them to hold up the ceremony." He shook his head and gave an unconvincing sigh of regret. "Unfortunately it's too late now. Perhaps your timing will be better next year."

"Ceremony?" said Lucy.

"Surely you know what today is?" said Tobias in mock surprise. "I would have thought our illustrious Keeper would have told you."

"Told me what?" asked Lucy, immediately regretting that she had fallen into Tobias's trap.

His thin lips curled up in a triumphant grin. "That this is the Day of Declaration of course. As we speak your friends are receiving their division assignments ...an honor I'm afraid you *will not* be receiving."

Lucy felt as though she had just been punched in the stomach. *D Day?* How was that possible? The Day of Declaration was held the week before the summer solstice and she had fallen into the Forgotten City in early spring.

"But Ben and Puddles didn't say anything about D Day when they met me in the forest," said Lucy, talking more to herself than Tobias.

"It appears that no one wanted to break the unfortunate news," said Tobias, sounding perfectly happy to be the one to tell Lucy she would be stuck in Drookshire for another year.

A dull ache filled Lucy as the reality of the news sunk in. Her cottagemates would be returning soon excited about their new assignments and then they would be leaving for their new homes. Lucy wondered where Ben and Puddles would be assigned. All she knew for sure was that they wouldn't be with her...wherever she would be. The thought sent goose bumps up her arms. Where would she be? What if they wouldn't allow her to stay at Drookshire? Her thoughts flashed to the Village and she imagined herself serving pumpkin scones at Café Monet.

"I have to go," Lucy said suddenly, crossing the room to the portal.

"I understand," said Tobias, his tone was sympathetic but there was joy in his eyes. "What should I tell your cottagemates?"

Lucy stopped but did not look back at him. "Nothing," she said quietly. Then, stepping into the portal, she disappeared into the mist.

In a hurry to get out of the cottage, Lucy hadn't paid attention to which portal she was taking. Stepping out into the Meeting Hall she was surprised to find it filled with a mass of blue, green and red streamers. A fountain sat in the middle of the hall spitting out large bubbles that floated up to the ceiling making it look like a sea of luminescent clouds and over the platform hung a giant banner declaring CONGRATULATIONS APPRENTICES!

Wanting to get out before the partiers arrived, Lucy quickly headed for the door.

"You're going to miss quite a celebration if you leave now," said a familiar voice, as Truman stepped out from behind a curtain of streamers.

Lucy wanted to race over and throw her arms around his neck but she couldn't. It wasn't Truman's job to save her anymore.

"I'm back," she said, not sure what else to say.

"I see that," Truman said, smiling warmly. "However it looks like you weren't planning on staying long."

Lucy glanced at the door and shook her head. "This party's not for me."

"No, it's not," said Truman, surveying the decorations as he approached Lucy. "But didn't I ever teach you Rule # 3? You can't wait for life to send you an invitation. You must begin the celebration and the party will come to you."

As though they had been waiting for Truman's signal, the doors to the Meeting Hall banged open and a mass of cheering attendants piled into the room. People were hugging and shouting and gathering together in groups of red, blue and green to excitedly congratulate their new division members.

In the middle of the chaos Lucy spotted Tibs; he was standing with his arm draped over Sandy's shoulders and they were singing at the top of their lungs, quite out of tune, as Babu directed them with dramatic flare. Nearby Anna, Arthur and Haddie had huddled around Puddles and were patting him on the back as they examined the sash clutched in his hands. Lucy stared in disbelief at the royal blue sash they were admiring. Little Puddles, who was scared of his own shadow, was going to be a Guardian! Lucy started to laugh as she watched Puddles proudly hold up the sash with a goofy grin plastered on his face.

From somewhere in the room Lucy heard someone call her name. Craning her neck to see above the mass of attendants she saw Ben waving at her as he pushed his way through the crowd.

"LUCE!" he yelled, squeezing past a portly attendant. "Where were you? We waited as long as we could."

Ben threw his arms around Lucy giving her a tight squeeze. When he pulled away she noticed that he had a green sash draped around his neck.

"You're a Guide!"

Ben beamed. "Yeah, I'm really excited. But did you see Puddles? A Guardian! Can you believe it?"

She shook her head as they both began to laugh.

Suddenly Lucy felt herself hoisted off the ground as a pair of arms grabbed her from behind.

"Dudette! Where've you been? Like, you missed the most righteous party."

Tibs dropped her back on the ground and Lucy whirled around to face her friends. They were all wearing their new sashes; Tibs, Sandy and Haddie had been assigned as Messengers and Anna, Arthur and Babu would be joining Ben with the Guides. Puddles alone was wearing the coveted blue Guardian's sash. Before Lucy could say anything, Sandy let out a whoop of delight and she found herself buried under a tangle of arms in a giant group hug.

"Let her breathe!" chuckled Truman, as he gently disentangled Lucy from the enthusiastic group and they began firing questions at her so fast she could barely make out what they were saying.

"Okay, OKAY!" she said, waving her hands in the air and laughing at the familiar chaos she had missed while she was gone.

As the celebration went on around them, Lucy quickly recounted what had happened from the moment she had fallen into the Sleeper's dream until she returned to the forest. They listened intently, spellbound by her description of Tiberon, his fight with Banks and her amazing rescue by Calista, Amon and Sanyu. When it came to the part where Jack O'Sullivan appeared, Anna burst into tears. "Oh my, it is all so truly lovely." Arthur handed her a handkerchief which he had produced out of thin air and she dabbed her eyes still muttering, "Remarkable, simply remarkable."

Lucy thought it was best not to bring up the prophecy and the troubles it foretold. If the things it predicted actual came true, they would deal with it; until then there was no use worrying. As for her Life Map, well there was no need to mention it either. Lucy had no idea what the mysterious inscription meant but something inside told her she needed to figure it out alone. Besides, Life Maps dealt with the future and tonight all Lucy wanted to think about was this very moment – here, with her friends, celebrating the end of a most incredible year.

When she finished her story, Sandy let out a long whistle. "Blimey! That Tiberon fella sounds like a real illywacker. Yer bloody lucky to have gotten outa there."

Everyone agreed as they shook their heads and patted her on the back, although Lucy was pretty sure none of them knew what an *illywacker* was. Even Haddie gave her a nod of approval which Lucy returned.

"And won't it be lovely that tomorrow you will get to see the rest of your family?" said Anna, still dabbing her eyes.

"The rest of my family?" Lucy said, clueless to what Anna meant.

"I forgot!" said Ben, excitedly. "You didn't hear the announcement they made at the assignment ceremony – our end of the year trip back to earth is tomorrow!"

"Tomorrow?"

"Yeah," said Puddles, stumbling forward as he tripped over his new sash. "Can you believe it? We're going home!" His face beamed with excitement.

Home, thought Lucy and she felt her stomach do a flip.

"And that's not all," said Ben, smiling slyly. He reached into his sash and pulled out a sapphire blue envelope. "When Samuel gave me my sash he also handed me this card and asked me to give it to you. He said it might help answer some questions." He handed Lucy the card.

"Samuel gave it to you?" said Lucy, wondering why Samuel hadn't just given it to her himself.

Ben nodded. "He must have forgotten he had it when you saw him. Aren't you going to open it?"

Lucy stared down at her name on the front of the envelope. It took a moment for the realization of what she was seeing to hit her and then her mouth dropped open. She looked up at Ben and Puddles who were both grinning broadly.

"We flipped when we saw the handwriting," said Ben, looking at Puddles who nodded in agreement. "Of course we recognized it right away."

For a moment Lucy stared at her name scribbled in the familiar purple script and then her eyes grew wide as she suddenly remembered the note that Ben had given her the night she had disappeared from the Dream Chamber.

Feverishly searching the folds of her sash with her free hand, Lucy's heart gave a flip as her fingers found the small crinkled note. She hadn't lost it! Pulling the note from her sash she quickly glanced from the Traveler's note to the envelope Ben had just given her. The writing was identical.

"Which one should I open first," she said, her hands trembling slightly as she held out the two letters.

"That one," said Ben and Puddles together, each pointing at a different note.

"You two are loads of help."

Closing her eyes, Lucy shuffled the two notes between her hands finally holding up the card in her right hand. "This one!" she said, opening her eyes.

She had chosen the Traveler's note Ben had given her that night in the Dream Chamber.

As her friends watched with excitement, Lucy opened the envelope and pulled out the small folded paper.

Quickly unfolding the note, she felt her knees go weak as she began to read the message out loud:

"Miss O'Sullivan,
Recent developments lead me to believe you are in danger. Although I greatly regret being forced to make this decision, I believe the time has come for us meet face to face. Come to the dream chamber this evening after your cottagemates have gone to bed.
Forever True,
A Fellow Traveler"

"Great," said Lucy with a groan, as she handed the note to Ben who read it and passed it around the circle. "If I had just read this when you gave it to me..." But she couldn't finish the sentence. She had messed up everything. Because of her stubbornness she had ignored the letter, ended up in the Forgotten City and had been the reason Banks went to Morpheus and was now missing.

"It's okay," said Puddles, patting Lucy on the shoulder. "We all screw up. Besides, maybe you were supposed to fall into that dream. I'm starting to realize that things happen for strange reasons around this place."

"Our newest Guardian is right," said Truman, causing Puddles to turn red. "Accidents are merely plans we don't yet understand."

"Rule #4?" said Lucy, forcing a small laugh.

"You're catching on," Truman said, with a wink.

Lucy looked down at the second note wondering what questions Samuel thought it would answer. Was she about to find out who had secretly been watching over her all year? The thought sent goose bumps racing over her entire body. Turning over the envelope she carefully broke the blue wax seal. Her heart was pounding in her ears as she slowly pulled the card from the envelope and began to read.

Dear Miss O'Sullivan,

This note is to inform you that for your apprenticeship I will serve as your Chief Attendant and mentor. Since you have not been assigned into one of the Kingdom's divisions you will remain at Drookshire Station. Special quarters have been arranged.

You will report promptly to your new assignment immediately following your fieldtrip to earth, so please make all final preparations before leaving Hill Cottage.

I look forward to continuing our journey together.

Forever True,

Colonel Georgina, Chief Attendant

Lucy scanned the note several more times as the puzzle pieces all fell into place.

"Well?" said Ben anxiously. "Who's it from?"

Lucy numbly held out the card.

"GEORGE?" cried Puddles, glaring at the signature. "*She's* the Traveler?"

"Unbelievable," said Ben, shaking his head.

"Well, well, it looks like you've got quite an interesting year ahead of you," chuckled Truman. "The stories I could tell you about our little Colonel…" He laughed and shook his head. "Come to think of it, perhaps they're better left untold."

As everyone took turns expressing their surprise at this turn of events, Lucy felt the weight of the last few months start to lift. Samuel was right; the next chapter of her life was certainly going to be an adventure. Soon she would leave Hill Cottage for the last time and she would travel to earth to see her family. After that, no one could tell her what would happen next. Lucy looked at Ben who was still staring at the note, shaking his head in shock. She felt an ache of emptiness churn inside her. She hated the thought of moving on without him but she knew their friendship wouldn't end just because he was going to be a Guide and she would be left at Drookshire. No, something told her their journey together was just beginning.

"Well, I guess we ought to head back to the cottage and get packed," said Lucy, and she blinked to keep back the tears.

"It's okay, Lucy," said Puddles. "You'll still have me around. The Department of Guardian Services is stationed here, remember? I'll make sure George takes care of you."

Lucy laughed at the vision of tiny Puddles protecting her from Colonel George. She wrapped her arms around him in a bear hug.

"Hey, what about me," said Ben, holding open his arms. "I've got Christof for a mentor – I'm the one who needs the hug!"

Lucy let go of Puddles and threw her arms around Ben's neck giving him a tight squeeze which he returned.

"I'm going to miss you," she whispered in his ear.

"Bugger! Catch a load of that sunrise!" said Sandy, pointing out of the window towards a brilliant orange and pink sky that was breaking over the trees to the east.

Everyone stopped to gaze at the incredible sight.

"Looks like it's going to be a pretty amazing day," said Lucy, wiping away a tear that had snuck down her cheek.

"Really, people," huffed Haddie. "You would think you had never seen the sun come up before." Without a word of good-bye she gave a fling of her long braid and marched out of the room.

"It's nice to know some things will never change," said Ben brightly, as they all burst out laughing.

Lucy looked around at her friends hugging and saying their good-byes. She knew she should feel sad, but she didn't. There was a sense of excitement in the air as though they were standing on the brink of a great adventure. Banks was gone, but Lucy knew in her heart he would be back. Tiberon was also gone for now but Lucy felt that he, too, would return someday. But it was okay, they had become part of her story – a story she knew was far from over.

Made in the USA
Lexington, KY
12 October 2010